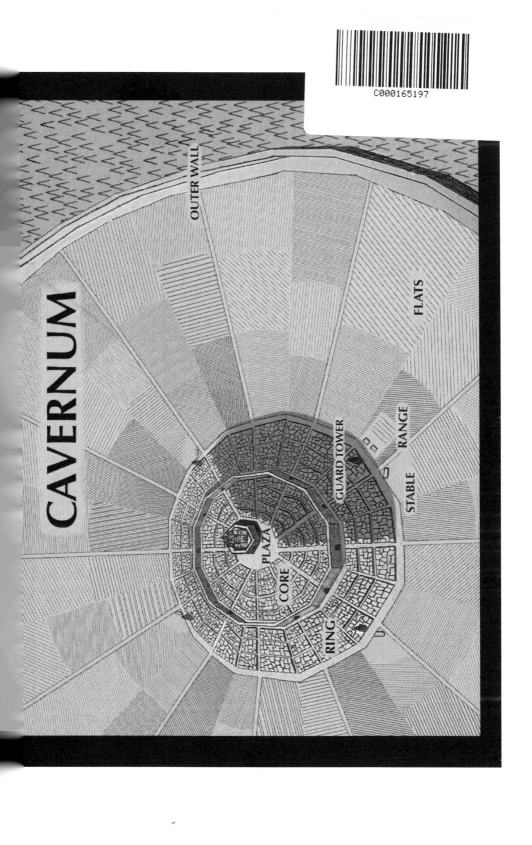

CAVERNUM

OUTER WALL

FLATS

RANGE

STABLE

GUARD TOWER

PLAZA

CORE

RING

This book is dedicated to all of my unborn children. When you guys read this thing, you better think your dad is freakin cool.

THE DIVIDING

The Adamic Trilogy Book 1

Devin Downing

Published by Devil Down Books, 2020

THE DIVIDING

First edition. May 29, 2020.

First edition

Cover design by Ricardo Montaño Castro

Library of Congress Control Number: 2020902509

Acknowledgements

Wow, if you guys are reading this, you must be dreadfully bored. Who wants to read a thank-you letter addressed to a bunch of strangers. Alas, feel free to experience my thanksgiving firsthand.

First off, I'd like to thank my wife, Melissa, for listening to me blab on and on about Adamic for years. Mel, thanks for believing this book could be great and for convincing me that someday I might have fans crazy enough to get Adamic tattoos.

To my brother, Derek. Thanks for all those hours we spent talking plot. I've bounced so many ideas off of you, I'm surprised you're not permanently bruised.

To my parents, thanks for conceiving me. Your sperm and egg gave birth to a great story.

Prologue

Screams filled the cold night air. Screams for help. Screams to run. Screams of pain. Screams of mourning.

Each scream was a map to Jenevrah, guiding her through the alleyways. She weaved through the dark cobblestone streets, avoiding the screams as much as possible. A scream to the right. *Turn left.* A scream up ahead. *U-turn.*

Feeders were everywhere. She couldn't count how many, but the plenitude of prey increased her chances of escape. She just needed to make it to the fields unnoticed, and everything would be okay. She was close now. Just a few more streets.

A scream to the right, a quiet alley to the left. Jenevrah turned left and froze. A woman lay dead in the street, blood still oozing from the teeth marks on her neck. Jenevrah searched the shadows for any feeders, and finding herself alone, she tiptoed over the body and ran. Another scream, another alley, this time empty.

An explosion rocked the night, almost knocking her off her feet —this one more distant than the last. For several moments, the thunderous roar ricocheted off the surrounding mountains. Jenevrah looked back. On the horizon, fire and smoke billowed from the palace wall. It was over. The last great wall had fallen. The sanctuary was no more.

Jenevrah focused on the street, concentrating only on placing her feet. She was running as fast as she could without falling. She couldn't risk tripping, not with the baby in her arms. Ezra howled his disapproval, his cries muffled by Jenevrah's shoulder. She tried to hold his head steady, but it bounced violently with each stride; she couldn't afford to slow down. Better this than dead.

So many had died already.

Finally, Jenevrah broke free from the buildings. The fields were quiet. The dead usually were. Their bodies littered the long dirt road, each with bite marks of their own. Two guards. A little boy. A tiny toddler. All dead. All victims of the feeders.

In the distance, a field of corn crops huddled together in the dark. Beyond that, the outer wall towered over the flatlands. It was presumed impenetrable… until tonight. That's where Kildron would be waiting.

Just a little further.

A feeble cry pricked Jenevrah's ears. Off to her left, a lanky figure hunched on its hands and knees, its bloody mouth buried in a young girl's neck. A long black cloak, like devil's wings, wrapped around the feeder. Beneath it, the poor girl was still alive. She writhed under its jaws and clawed helplessly at its back. Then, she fell still.

The feeder itself was nothing out of the ordinary, an average human face with a slender human body. At one point, it had been a man. But that was long ago, before it fed on human blood.

Jenevrah tried to walk quietly, but the sandy road crunched beneath her feet. At the sound of her footsteps, the feeder's head snapped up. She wasted no time. Jenevrah hugged her baby tight and sprinted for the camouflage of the corn foliage. She plunged into the corn stalks and, after several strides, dove to the soil. She huddled as still as possible, trying to silence her breathing. She hugged her son close and stroked his head to keep him quiet.

A subtle noise scratched at her eardrum: the scraping of leaves on skin. Peering through the corn rows, she saw the outline of the feeder against the starlight. It walked slowly through the stalks, waiting to pounce at the slightest movement. It took a step closer. Then, another. It stopped a few feet shy of Jenevrah and craned its neck to listen. A few moments passed… and then a few more.

"It's alright. You can come out now," the feeder called, its voice sweetly, deceivingly innocent. "Those monsters are gone. You're safe to come out. I'll protect you."

Chills raced down Jenevrah's spine. The voice was so gentle, so convincing. But Jenevrah knew better. She saw the bodies. She saw the blood dripping from its chin. *How could something so intelligent be consumed by such evil?*

The feeder paused a moment longer. "Fine! Have it your way!" it hissed, innocence replaced with rage. "Lucky for me, I like my blood boiled."

As easy as flipping a switch, the feeder's hands ignited in a swirling mass of flame. As it extended its hands, the flames leapt to the nearest stalks. The burning leaves crackled as the heat drew nearer to Jenevrah. If she ran from the flames, the feeder would see her. If she didn't, it would hear her dying screams.

I'm sorry, Ezra. I've failed you. I've failed everyone.

As quietly as she could, she wrapped Ezra within her cloak, shielding him from the smoke that already choked her. The flames were only inches away. She grit her teeth as the heat seared her nerves.

God help me!

Shlink!

A knife buried itself in the feeder's throat. The creature screeched and clawed at the blade before slinking to the ground. It thrashed amid the burning stalks for several seconds before submitting to its inevitable death. A moment later, the flames shrunk until they disap- peared completely, snuffed out by an invisible blanket. Only the smoking skeletons of corn remained.

Jenevrah rose to her feet and spotted him instantly. He raced through the corn, his silhouette tall and lean. His features were hidden in the shadows of his cloak. Without thinking, Jenevrah ran to him, embracing her husband. She wrapped her arms around his neck while trying not to squish her infant. He was alive! Kildron was alive!

Kildron grabbed her by the face and kissed her mouth with a passion only desperation could inspire. His long blonde curls tickled her cheek. She squeezed her husband tight, laying her face on his damp chest, whether with sweat or blood, she couldn't tell. Her hair tangled around his fingers as he stroked her head. His rapid breathing hissed in her ear. It was the most beautiful sound she had ever heard. It meant he was alive.

Jenevrah pulled away first, breaking the short moment of bliss. "Where's Iris?" She asked, frantically searching for her in the dark. "Is she not with you?"

His voice whispered in short, gasping breaths. "Iris is fine. I sent her with Zane. They're on their way to Kentville."

Jenevrah breathed a sigh of relief. For now, her family was safe.

"Jen, there's no time," Kildron gasped. "The feeders have already breached the palace. You need to get out of here. Take Ezra and go to Kentville."

Jenevrah opened her mouth to protest, but Kildron didn't give her a chance. He shook her softly. "There's no time; listen carefully. Zane will wait for you at the gas station. He'll take Ezra to Cavernum. You'll both be safe there." His next words stung. "Don't wait for me. I'll find you again. I promise."

Jenevrah clung to him. "You can't face him alone, Kildron," she pled. "He's too strong. You'll die!"

"I don't have a choice. If he gets his hands on the library…" Kildron didn't finish the sentence; he didn't need to. Jenevrah couldn't speak; only nod her head, tears dripping with each bounce.

Kildron's head snapped up just as two feeders emerged from the city. They raced toward the embracing family with heart-stopping speed. Kildron kissed her one last time, so quick she wondered if it really happened. "Now, go!" He turned Jenevrah toward the outer wall and shoved her hard. "Go!!!"

Her instincts took over, and she stammered through the corn stalks. She only took a dozen steps before a blinding flash of lightning lit the field. The thunder rocked her almost instantly, a tortured scream buried within. Jenevrah didn't look back. Twice more, lightning illuminated the flatland, the shockwave rustling the leaves around her. Her eyes blurred with tears as she ran. She didn't even have time to say *I love you.* Her last words had been *You'll die.*

Jenevrah hugged Ezra close, smearing his cheek with her tears. He was all that mattered now. More than her own life, more than her husband's, Ezra had to live.

Chapter 1

Matt

18 years later…

I lift the rifle to my eye and peer through the scope. I have a clear view of them now across the lush meadow. They're half-hidden in the shadows, just inside the edge of the tree line. I'm mirroring their movements from across the meadow—two hundred yards away. Just far enough that the ATV engine won't spook them.

The elk calf is heading north, trotting and leaping playfully through the brush. Daddy elk watches from a few yards behind. Mommy elk is nowhere to be seen—likely a cougar's lunch.

I lower the rifle. At this distance, I can't hit a moving target with much accuracy. I have to be patient, but the elk are making me nervous. About 50 yards behind them, I can see the wall: a ten-foot-tall chain-link fence topped with barbed wire. A yellow sign hangs like Swiss cheese, spotted with bullet holes. In black, bold letters, the sign reads: **high radiation zone, do not enter**. The circular hazard symbol is almost entirely erased by the bullet holes. Last year, I made it the bulls-eye of my target practice.

As the elk approach the wall, I bite my lip. The fence is no better at keeping out animals than it is at keeping in the radiation. More than once, I've lost prey under that fence, cursed to die a slower death from a microscopic poison.

I crawl my ATV forward, keeping pace with them from across the meadow. Every minute or two, I peep through my rifle scope like a pirate seeking treasure. Finally, they stop to munch on some sprouting grass. The baby elk eats slowly, utterly oblivious to the lurking danger. I'm almost jealous. *If only life could be that simple.*

I squint through the scope and set the crosshairs center mass on daddy elk; I have a shot.

I roll off my ATV and kneel at its side, resting Remmy on the leather seat—Remmy is my favorite rifle, a Remington 700. I have no time to adjust the scope. Instead, I mentally calculated for distance, lifting the crosshairs slightly above the elk's shoulders. Luckily, the breeze has died down. The crosshairs now hover a foot above the elk's shoulder, almost touching the tip of his antlers. But I trust that the bullet will drop. It always does.

I try to stay as still as possible and slow my breathing. Even with the ATV seat to stabilize my rifle, the crosshairs still quiver ever so slightly. Now, it just takes the squeeze of a finger.

I hate my job. Pulling the trigger isn't so bad; it's more the idea of it: of killing. Having to face the consequences of each shot. I know it's dumb, but I worry about the baby elk. Will it be alright without its dad? Will another family take it in?

Will it miss its parents as much as I do?

I know poaching is wrong, but I have no choice. I desperately need the money. I know a butcher who will buy the meat for three dollars a pound. The antlers will get me another few hundred. In the end, it comes down to one question: who do I love more? The elk, or Judy?

I pull the trigger.

The stock slams into my shoulder, and I lose sight of the glorified deer. A thunderous crack rings out through the meadow. I don't bother reloading. Either the elk is dead or far fled. I scan the trees with my scope, searching for a lump of brown among leaves. Finally, I spot him lying face down in the brush. Motionless. Dead. The young calf is gone. It disappeared like a ghost, fleeing with the spirit of its father.

I mount the rusty four-wheeler and ride to redeem my prize. The pile of dead elk is worth 100 hours of minimum wage. But success is bitter, satisfaction swallowed up in guilt. Now that the elk can't run, I rev the engine loud. Mud sprays behind me as I tear into the openness of the sun-drenched meadow. This part I enjoy: the nature, the beauty, the serenity. Colorado really is a beautiful place, especially in the summer. I can't help but appreciate the life I'm paid to kill. I'm a parasite, admiring the beauty of my host.

I veer to the left and head for a patch of blue among the pale green grass. Dozens of sky-blue Columbine flowers dot the leafy bushes. I hop off the ATV and quickly pluck the closest flower. It has two layers of petals, one white and one blue. They twinkle in the breeze like a sky full of stars. I pick the flowers until I have a fistful. After wrapping twine around the stems to make a bouquet, I lower the flowers softly in the trunk of the ATV. I stop for flowers every single day. It's the one gift I can give Judy for free.

Satisfied with my work, I remount the ATV and speed towards the forest full throttle. The meadow is my favorite place to hunt. It has a wide, shallow river running through it and stretches a quarter-mile between two forests. Most importantly, it has an access road connecting it directly to Kentville. At the other end of the meadow, the road is blocked by the chain-link fence. By the looks of the rusty metal gate, it hasn't been opened in ages. I assume the path leads all the way to the power plant, but I'll never know for sure. A massive padlock seals the gate shut.

I could break the lock, but I promised Judy I wouldn't. If she knew I was this close to the power plant, she'd be furious. But I hunt here for a reason. The power plant works as a human repellent. I've never seen anyone on this side of the mountain, especially not so close to the wall. No rangers patrol. No hunters come. Nothing. Just peace and quiet and big game. 18 years without hunting has left these parts flourishing like weeds in a garden. Most days, I sit under a tree and read for hours, secretly hoping no animals wander into the meadow, knowing if they do, they'll die. I'll make sure of it. It's a lonely life, but it's my reality. It's the least I can do for Judy after all she's done for me.

As I approach the stream, I release the throttle. I aim for the shallowest neck of the river and lift my feet as the water level crawls up the tires. A few moments later, the ATV is climbing up the bank on the other side. It only takes a minute to reach the tree line. I slowly approached the lifeless corpse, coasting to a stop.

The elk is lying flat, its legs crushed beneath its torso in a painful yoga pose. A bloody, black stain is spray-painted on its neck. The wet paint still runs in black streams. He's dead alright. The points of his antlers are buried in the soil. His lifeless eyes are glazed like big brown marbles. I know the pay will be generous, but I can't bring myself to smile.

I glance at my watch. *Shoot!* I'm late. I'll have to come back later to gut and dress the body. Visiting hours end in just an hour, and I can't miss them. Not today of all days. I look back at the elk and sigh. I'll have to leave him here as he is: an open casket. Maybe the baby elk will come back and pay its respects—a courtesy I was never able to enjoy.

If I hurry, the service road can get me back to town in 15 minutes. From there, a bus will get me to Oakridge Hospital just in time. I flick my wrist, and the ATV leaps forward. I follow the fence line all the way until my tires connect with the old dirt road. I take one last glance at the wall and speed home, dust billowing behind me like radioactive smog.

I pushed through the door, choking down the smell of hand sanitizer and bleach. I turn down the hall to the oncology wing of the hospital. Rachel smiles at me as I pass the front desk. I wave back, heading to room 105. Visiting hours are almost over; family and friends are crammed in tiny glass rooms like white lab mice in a tank.

I slowly twist the stainless-steel handle, hoping she might be asleep. A brittle, weak voice sings from the hospital bed. "Happy Birthday, Matthew! I can't believe you made me wait so long."

I smile at Judy. She's the first to wish me a happy birthday today. "Sorry, Mom. I uh… lost track of time." At least it isn't a lie this time.

Judy clicks the remote to incline her bed. She pushes against the mattress with her wiry frame, sitting up as tall as she can without lifting her head from the pillow. Each time I see her, she looks a little older. The wrinkles layer her face like cracking paint. A hammock of skin hangs from her neck. The only light in her zombie complexion comes from her emerald green eyes. They shine defiantly against the doom of the hospital room. She seems cheerful. The morphine is doing its job.

Judy snakes her eyes over me as I pull up a cold plastic chair and sit down. The corner of her mouth curls into a smile. "Oh no, Matt. Did you do some gardening today? You got some mud on your jeans." she mocks. No one has touched the garden since her diagnosis. It used to be Judy's favorite pastime. But now, weeds plague the empty patch of dirt behind the house.

I smile back, holding up the flowers I've picked. "I thought I'd do some birthday hedging," I joke. "It was supposed to be a surprise."

Judy laughs a beautiful laugh that transforms into a hoarse fit of coughing—a subtle reminder that the cancer has spread to her lungs. The doctors say she could only have weeks left. When she goes, I'll have no one.

I reach for the water bottle next to the bed and hold it in front of her. She takes it gratefully and sips the antidote to her cough. Neither of us speaks for a moment as reality settles in. Reaching across the bed, I set the flowers in a vase next to yesterday's daisies.

Judy's eyes soften with the fondness of her memories. "You know?" She speaks slower now. "I could never keep Dave out of the forest either. You remind me more and more of him every day. I can't believe you're already turning 18."

Actually, I'm not. Today isn't my birthday; it's my found-day. Nobody knows how many weeks old I was the night Judy found me on her doorstep—the night the power plant exploded. Judy just pretends it was my birthday so that we have a day to celebrate.

"How was your birthday so far?" Judy asks. "Anything fun or exciting?"

"Not really," I lie, leaning back in my chair. "Just work." I want to tell her about my day, but I just don't know what to say. *Mom, I had a great day. I orphaned a baby elk in one shot.* Or *hey, mom, I spent all day around a high radiation zone, exactly where I promised you I wouldn't go.*

Judy frowns. "You didn't do anything exciting? Hang out with friends? Kiss a girl? Anything?"

I shrug. I don't know what to say. On a normal day, having no friends isn't such a big deal. Judy and I chat and make fun of the doctors or maybe watch a movie together. But on my birthday, it's suddenly a crisis to spend the day alone.

Before the cancer I had lots of friends, but ever since we almost lost the house, I've spent most of my time making money. At first, it was odd jobs around town, but I quickly learned I could make much more hunting and selling my forest friends.

I know Judy blames herself for all this. She doesn't want me spending my found-day hunting because of her. And I don't want her feeling guilty about it. "Eh, friends are overrated. Who needs friends when I have you, mom?"

Judy smiles a mischievous smile. "Yeah, but you can't kiss me," She teases, raising her eyebrows up and down.

I can't suppress the laughter. It seems so ridiculous coming from the tiny woman in the hospital bed. She always has a way of making me laugh when the world doesn't give me a reason to.

"C'mon," Judy begs. "There has to be some cute girl you have your eye on." She always asks about girls. Always.

I fiddle with the IV wire as I think. "I don't know… they're just all the same."

"What?" Judy exclaims defensively. "How can they all possibly be the same?"

"It's just so hard to relate. They all live in the same little bubble, and all they want to talk about is Netflix and movies and homework," I say, counting my fingers with each one. "They care so much about such meaningless stuff. I don't watch shows, I don't care about Netflix. It's so hard to relate to any of it." I stop. I didn't realize how loud I'd been talking, how frustrated I really am.

Judy holds out her hand, and I reluctantly take it. Her eyes are pained. "I'm sorry, honey. I know this can't be easy for you. I guess we're the different ones for now." She squeezes my hand until I look at her. "Someday, the perfect girl will come around who understands you perfectly. Trust me."

But I don't care about a girl right now, I just want a rest. I want it all to be over. No more cancer, no more hunting. Even if I find a girl, Judy won't be around for the wedding, for the kids, for any of it.

I fake another smile for Judy and squeeze back. "What about you, mom? There are tons of single doctors here. Just because you have cancer doesn't mean you're off the hook."

Judy holds up her hands in front of her. "Whoa there, cowboy. This old mule is retired. I'll gladly wait to see Dave again. Besides, we were talking about you." She sits forward, lifting her head off the pillow. "Any news about the scholarship?"

I sigh and look at the floor. The scholarship is my dream. I've been preparing for years. Colorado State University has a new cancer research lab, and with my grades, I have a shot at getting a scholarship. It's my dream to save Judy somehow. Or at least to help others like her.

I told Judy I applied, but I lied. The application is still sitting on the table at home. I wanted to apply, but it was useless. We have no money. Even if I got the scholarship, I wouldn't be able to pay the medical bills without poaching. And I can't leave Judy here alone. She doesn't have anyone else. Worst of all, I can't tell her the truth. She would die if she knew I was giving it up for her.

I stared at my shoelaces. "Nothing yet; I'm starting to think I didn't get in."

Judy snaps her fingers. "Hey, Debbie Downer. Don't say that. I bet it'll come any day now. You just have to stay positive."

I don't want to talk about it. "Mom? Do you think you could tell me about my birthday again? You know... the first one." It used to be our tradition when I was little. She would tell me about my found-day on each anniversary, but I haven't heard it since the cancer. I miss our old tradition.

Judy raises an eyebrow, a bit surprised. "Oh, of course." She puts her hands in her lap and collects her thoughts. "Where do you want me to start? You know it as well as me by now."

I shrug and snuggle into my plastic chair. "Just at the beginning, I want to hear it all."

Judy clasps her hands together and clears her throat. "Well, I guess I'll start with that night. Dave had only been gone for a few weeks, and I was still getting used to the empty house. It scared me a little at night. Normally, I was fine, but this night was different. At first, I thought they were firecrackers, but then they got louder and louder. I realized they were a lot, lot bigger." The more she speaks, the more animated she becomes. Her hands dance with each word as she re-lives it in her mind.

"I watched the mountains out my window for half an hour. I could see the explosions. Oh, Matt, it was terrifying. First, I would see a fireball above the mountain, and then a few seconds later the explosion would shake the house. I thought it was terrorism, so I loaded Dave's gun and locked all the doors. I was ready to shoot someone."

I smiled at the thought of Judy bolstering a shotgun. The woman won't even kill bugs in the house. She makes me catch them in a cup and release them outside.

She pauses, knowing I love this part. "Then came the lightning, but there were no clouds." The first time I heard it, I didn't believe her. The government labeled it as nuclear lightning. A rare phenomenon caused by radiation ionizing the air.

Judy takes a sip of water. The simple task of narrating is taking its toll. "I remember at least a dozen flashes. They weren't small either. The thunder was the loudest I've ever heard. And then they just stopped. The explosions too. Everything was quiet for a long time. Fires were burning all over the mountain. I was so tired, but I was too afraid to go to sleep. And then... a knock on the door. Hard though, like when they came to tell me about Dave. I honestly wasn't going to answer it, Matt, but then I heard you crying."

She clasps her knobby fingers in front of her. "Oh, Matt, you were the cutest baby. You were wrapped so tight in a wool blanket, crying so softly. The necklace was so big around your neck." Judy chuckled to herself. "I wish I could've seen the look on my face. I was so confused."

I still am. I've grilled Judy about every detail over the years, but I only have theories. Were my parents workers at the power plant? Did they get contaminated? Are they dead? I have so many questions.

Judy carries on, absorbed in her own memories. "You were the cutest toddler. You would always run…"

I'm no longer listening. I'm still thinking about my parents. I fiddle with the necklace under my shirt. It's the only remnant I have of my parents. The pendant is round, with a gaping hole in the center. The middle is thicker than the edges, like a smashed donut coated in gold. Rather than sprinkles, the golden donut is decorated with intricate ridges and interwoven gold strands. A thin gold chain loops around my neck and through the center of the pendant. Engraved around the center are what intrigue me most of all: strange symbols.

On the back of the amulet is a pair of symbols that match the tattoo on my shoulder perfectly.

I have a few more symbols tattooed between my shoulder blades. I've had them ever since Judy found me. *Who tattoos a baby? And why?* Was it so that my parents could claim me years down the road? Was it part of some crazy religion my parents believed in?

A small bell chimes; visiting hours are over.

Judy points to her purse on the counter. "Quick, I've got a surprise for you, pass me my purse."

I pick up the small purse. It's slightly heavier than normal. I would know. I carry it for her everywhere. "Mom, you really shouldn't have."

Judy furrows her brow. "Don't you tell me what I should do. I can get my son a present on his birthday." She understands my hesitation. "Besides, I've had this for a long time. I think you're going to like it. I should've given it to you long ago. Now, close your eyes and hold out your hands."

I obey, holding out my hands like a sidewalk beggar. I'm suddenly much more curious. A long, dense object plops into my hands. Wrapped in… I open my eyes. Yep, paper towels from the dispenser by the sink. I look up at Judy, who encourages me with a nod, not the least bit embarrassed by her makeshift wrapping paper. I fold back the white sheets and gasp. *Where did she find it?*

The small dagger glistens in the fluorescent hospital light. It's roughly a foot long with a spiraling black handle—maybe obsidian or jade. But what interests me most are the symbols. They carve along the flat side of the blade.

⚡🏔️🐌🌀

I untuck my necklace from my shirt. The second and fourth symbols are a perfect match. The other two symbols I've never seen. "But… how?" My eyes are wide with wonder. The dagger quivers in my hand as I run my finger over the engravings. I finally peel my eyes off the blade and stick them onto Judy. "Where'd you find it?"

She beams with satisfaction. My reaction is the best gift I could've given her. "It was yours from the beginning. I found it with you on the doorstep, just like the necklace."

"On the doorstep?" I echo to myself. Who would leave a baby with a dagger? My parents must have been lunatics.

Judy nods. "There's a leather case that goes with it, but I couldn't fit it in my purse. It's still in the storage closet."

"And you never told me?" I accuse.

"I saw how you were with the necklace. You never took it off once. How was I supposed to give you a knife? You'd take it to school and get expelled."

I understand. My frustration dissipates. I'll have to ask her more about it tomorrow. Her treatments are about to resume. I stand up and give Judy a hug. Her body feels like loosely wrapped bones. "Thanks mom, really. I love it." I kiss her leathery cheek and head for the door before the nurse kicks me out.

"Just don't sleep with it please," Judy calls after me. "If I found out you stabbed yourself…"

"Don't worry, mom. I'll see you tomorrow. I love you." I stride out the door and twist my wrist. **5:02.** I have at least three hours before the sun sets. Just enough time to harvest an elk.

I open the fridge. Some milk. A few eggs. Nothing to snack on. I really need to go shopping… and clean. Dirty dishes are jammed in the sink like a game of Tetris. Coupon-ads and unpaid bills lie strewn on the kitchen table.

I walk over to the table and picked up my application from among the pile of bills. I've read it so many times I have it memorized. But the deadline was weeks ago. Letting out a defeated sigh, I crumple the paper in my fist and toss it in the trash can. Keeping it will only make me feel worse. It's time to accept reality. I slip on my boots and head for the garage. If I want to make it back before dark, I need to hurry.

As much as I hate hunting, I really enjoy the guns, and Dave had quite the collection. Rifles are displayed on the garage wall like artwork. I already sold most of them, but a select few still hang on the wall. Each has its own strip of tape labeling the proper ammunition. That was my doing, but now I don't even need my ammo cheat-sheet.

I sling Remmy over my shoulder and grab a box of Remmy's favorite food—.308 ammunition. Then, I pick up a Browning .22 off the table. It's a small pistol I like to wear on my hip. I use it for small game. I tried the rifle once and ripped a poor fox in half.

Once everything is loaded in the ATV trunk, I walk over to the storage closet and open it up. Sure enough, a black leather harness is on the middle shelf. I can tell right away: it's not made for my waist. It's some kind of tactical knife harness. After fiddling with it a bit, I manage to fit the sheathe over my shoulder and secure it around my chest. The dagger slides effortlessly into the leather. The handle is suspended along my ribs for easy access. I pull on my sweatshirt over the sheathe and climb onto my ATV. Finally, I turn off the world with my sound-blocking headphones.

I bounce to the music as I ride up the service road. The dirt trail cuts a path straight up and over the mountain. I speed up the path like an amateur motocross track, enjoying the cheap thrill. Something catches my eye. Two tire tracks are imprinted in the dirt ahead of me, but they aren't from an ATV. The tracks are flat and spread far apart, most likely an SUV of some kind. They must be recent, not that I can really tell.

Paranoid, I veer off the trail to the right and speed through the trees, taking the road less traveled. In all my time hunting—a measly two years—I've never seen a single soul in this neck of the woods. It makes me anxious. Technically it's illegal what I'm doing; I don't have a hunting license. I'm not even sure if Dave's guns are registered. The last thing I want is to get arrested. It would break Judy's heart.

A few minutes pass as I run through possible scenarios in my head. I reach the chain-link wall and turn left, following the fence line to the meadow. I reach the crest of a hill at the edge of the tree line and stop. I'm not too far from the elk now, but the visitor takes priority.

I kill the engine and peek through Remmy's all-seeing eye. From my position on the ridge, I have a complete view of the meadow and the service road that snakes through it. I don't see any new tracks. Maybe the car already turned back? Maybe it was just a lost family out to camp?

I peer through the chain-links to my right. My mind wanders far beyond the wall. So many mysteries are behind this fence. I would give anything for answers. The necklace, the knife, the tattoo? Part of me wants to climb the fence and go searching for my parents in the power plant. I know they're not there, but something has to be— perhaps an abandoned work desk with a picture of my family.

My thought bubble bursts as a Ford truck clunks up the road. I peek through the scope. The chamber is empty, but I still feel guilty for aiming at a person. It's a lone man. From my skyward view, I can't see much other than his hands on the steering wheel.

The truck continues all the way up the road, heading directly toward the chain-link fence. On the other side of the steel links, the dirt road continues up the mountain as far as I can see.

A few feet from the gate, the vehicle stops. I wait for the man to turn the truck around, but instead, the engine goes silent. The driver door opens, and a large man steps out. I aim at his head. His face is hidden under a brown mossy beard and dark caterpillar eyebrows. He's wearing leather boots and jeans and a tan coat. But most impressive is his massive build—basically, your average lumberjack.

But what is he doing here? *Maybe the best pine is by the power-plant?*

Lumberjack walks up to the fence and bends over. Without pausing, he pulls out a bundle of keys and unlocks the padlock. I gape at the scene. Who is this guy, and why does he have a key to the powerplant?

Lumberjack leaves the open lock hanging on the fence as he drags each half of the gate out of the way. He creates a gap just wide enough for his car to fit through. Then, he climbs back into his truck and drives through the fence.

I gawk after him. *Where is his hazmat suit? What about the radiation?*

I watch his car until it disappears behind the trees at a bend in the road. It must lead to the plant. I count to ten just to be sure he's gone. Then, I start up my ATV and coast over to the fence where he entered. The two halves of the gate protrude like a gaping mouth. *Sorry, Judy, I'll make it up to you.*

I take a deep breath and feed myself to the wall.

Chapter 2

Rose

I despise today. It's my least favorite day of the year. Today is Remembrance Day: the anniversary of my parents' death.

I know I must get up, but the warm sheets seduce me. It's cold. My breath floats above me in the air as evidence. Two white charcoal logs lay in the fireplace—the cold remains of a once lively fire. Normally, Nevela would have replaced them by now. It's still dark out, but the growing glow of dawn seeps through my cotton drapes. I must hurry if I want to be the first at the shooting range. I fold the blankets off me and roll out of my massive bed. The Dividing is only a week away. The range will be packed with students trying to squeeze in some last-minute practice. Everyone wants to join the guard, and the competition is fierce.

I pull on a worn cotton hoodie and drag my long brown hair into a ponytail. My jeans are torn at the knee but fit me well. To top it off, I slip on my old Nike sneakers. I stand in front of my wardrobe mirror and give a quick spin. I look good, but most importantly, I look average. No elite would be caught dead in clothes this rugged. As far as any onlookers are concerned, I'm a commoner—a middle-class citizen of Cavernum. No one will ever suspect I'm the princess.

The only flaw in my disguise is the gold amulet around my neck. It was a gift from my father—a spiraling cylindrical necklace that ends in a dull point, resembling a seashell. Delicate Adamic symbols are carved along the curves. The gold symbols glitter in the light of dawn.

My father made it for me before he died. He was an adalit—someone literate in Adamic. He couldn't speak the language, but he could write the spells. Now, my grandfather is the last adalit in the sanctuary, except for me of course. Grandpa is giving me lessons, and it won't be long until I can make amulets of my own.

I tuck it into my shirt and bury my neck in a charcoal black scarf. I'm confident no one will recognize me without my royal attire. No one outside the palace knows my face by heart. I almost never go out in public, and when I do, I go out as princess, complete with fitted gown and blood-red lipstick. In my street clothes, I'm a different person. I doubt that even the elites would recognize me like this.

I slip out of my chambers and jog down the spiral staircase, dragging my fingers along the stone wall. The hallway is unusually noisy. Several servants are up preparing for the day's celebration—the Remembrance Day Parade.

When I arrive at the central corridor, I stare at a large portrait on the wall. It's my own. It's only two years old, yet I've already outgrown the image in the frame. It was painted by the best portraitist in the sanctuary, but still, I don't love it. He makes my chocolate brown hair look flat and plain. My neck looks too long for my head, and my shoulders look scrawny. Worst of all, he painted my smile crooked on my face.

I must admit, he captured some of my features well. My nose is petite and level. I have full lips, a tapered face, and my almond brown skin is smooth and clear. I like the way I look, but I'm not nearly as gorgeous as my mother. Her portrait hangs next to my own. She was elegant and tall with copper skin and curly brown hair. Her eyes were a beautiful, bright hazel. Fortunately, I inherited her eyes; they're my most stunning feature.

The painting of my father is that of a king. His eyes are dark and commanding. His shoulders, broad and robust. His face has a certain somberness that comes with grave responsibility.

Is this what they really looked like? Grandpa says so, but I'm not satisfied. A painting doesn't tell me how they laughed or the tone of their voice. I linger by their paintings, my mind teeming with questions. Were they kind? Merciful? Wise? What music did Mother like most? What was her favorite song? *If only a portrait could talk.*

I push the thought out of my head and hurry down the central tower. My two favorite rooms are in this hallway. I stride past the grand theater. The stage is crowded with perfectly placed instruments. My favorites are the piano and the violin. I've been playing since I was five, and for the past three years, I've been training with the lead violinist of the royal orchestra. I haven't been divided yet, but I already have a spot in the orchestra if I so desire. I even have a brand-new violin coming with the next import.

The next room I pass is the central library, complete with vaulted ceiling and ladders for the out of reach books. Every day, I spend hours in there, stuffing my head with stories of the beyond. Cars and cell phones. Unimaginable civilizations. The world is so much bigger than I can imagine. Yet I've never stepped foot beyond the sanctuary. Those books are my only glimpse of the outside world. My only escape. Hopefully, Grandpa brings me back a new novel from his trip.

I turn the corner and nearly knock the firewood out of Nevela's arms, who carries the pile up to her chin. "Oh, princess, you're up. I'm sorry I'm late with the wood. I hope you weren't cold."

I backpedal down the hall as I respond. "Not even a little bit. Don't worry about the fire. You can put my breakfast in the study. Thanks, Nevela!"

"But, princess, the parades in a few hours. I have to get you ready."

In just a few hours, I'll be riding on the royal float in remembrance of my parents. It's my big yearly display as princess. Sensing Nevela's urgency, I begin to jog. "I'll be back by eight. I promise." I don't wait for permission. I'm around the bend before Nevela can think up a reason to stop me.

It only takes me a few minutes to reach the palace wall. It's thirty feet tall and several yards thick. Giant symbols are engraved in the stone. They continue in an endless stream in both directions.

△♱♆👁◇◇⚠✹≫‡◉⛢

I recognize a few of them from my studies with Grandpa: God's all seeing eye, the tent-shaped symbol for protection, the looping symbol of eternity. Together, they form the powerful spell that protects the sanctuary. Several royal guards stand perched on top of the palace wall. Several more stand in the archway, regulating the visitors. Each wears a traditional white uniform with a red circle on each shoulder —the symbol of the guard. Ordinary guards wear black, but the royal guard is distinguished by their white uniforms. They symbolize purity and excellence.

I approach the royal guardsman I know best. He stands with an automatic rifle cradled in his thick black arms. His already massive shoulders and chest are enlarged by the armor he wears underneath his uniform. It's a synthetic material imported from the beyond. They call it Kevlar.

I know I should play the part of a commoner, but today I lack the patience. "Hello, Octavian."

"Hello, Lynn."

Lynn is short for Roselyn. It's part of my agreement with Grandpa. If I want to leave the palace, I must go in disguise. And only with Grandpa's permission. Whenever I wear my street clothes, the royal guards know to call me Lynn.

I smile at Octavian. "I'll just be going out for a quick training session. I'll be back before eight." I have all the tutors I could possibly need in the palace, but fortunately for me, the only shooting range is outside the palace wall. It's my one excuse to leave.

Octavian furrows his brow. "And King Dralton said it's alright?" I can tell he's thinking the same as Nevela. The parade starts in just a few hours.

"As long as I'm back by eight, he said it's fine," I lie.

Octavian looks doubtful, but he nods his head anyways.

"Thanks, Octavian. See you soon." I run before he changes his mind. Unlike Nevela, Octavian has the power to stop me.

It's a short carriage ride to the inner wall. Normally, I would run to the shooting range as part of my training, but today I don't have time. I hand the carriage driver a bronze coin and climb aboard.

I stare out of the carriage as it creaks down the cobblestone road. The sanctuary is built on a mountain—a dormant volcano. The palace is placed on the very peak, while the rest of the city slopes down toward the fields. Dawn is just breaking, and the city is already bustling. Bakers sell Remembrance Day pies as children play in the street. Already a line of men is stretching out of the bar. That is why I hate Remembrance Day. Nobody uses it to remember; they use it to forget.

As the palace grows smaller behind me, I watch the city transform; more people in the street, fewer guards, more trash. A strange liquid fills the gutters. As the carriage passes under the inner wall, the smell hits me. The stench is the same every time: Rotting meat and urine. I'm tempted to cover my nose, but a commoner wouldn't do that. I must act the part.

I cringe as several children run barefoot through the street, leaving ripples in the mystery liquid. Most wear tattered clothes. Others wear nothing at all. I wonder when they last bathed, last ate. The thought makes my stomach twist in knots, but ignoring it is no solution. It's typical for the ring—that's what they call the outskirts of the city beyond the inner wall. That's where the laborers are sent.

Most laborers are field workers, others are sanitation workers. All are unskilled laborers of one form or another. And they all struggle to get by. In the ring, life is tough. The sewer system is dysfunctional, illness runs rampant, and children starve. Much of it stems from the lack of electricity—a side effect of the sanctuary. But it's amplified by overpopulation. The sanctuary is only so big, and more refugees come every month.

I can already hear the pitter-patter of gunfire on the horizon. The distant clatter is infrequent but grows steadily louder. I won't be the first to arrive at the range, but it doesn't sound too crowded. Finally, the road levels and the carriage breaks free of the city. The flats stretch out before me like a carpet for the gods. The mountainous terrain flattens into an endless sea of green and gold cornfields. The wind sends waves cascading through the crops. I've never seen the ocean, but I imagine it looking like this.

The carriage pulls up next to the armory. It's a small brick building with two guardsmen posted outside, each sporting his own machine gun. Another guardsman stands on the roof with a sniper.

"It'll be 100 bars," the guard at the service desk grunts. I have the money ready. I set a stack of five silver coins on the counter and pick up my practice gear: a small box of ammunition and a rental pistol. Each student is only allowed 1 box per day. It's hard to train with such meager rations, but I know it's justified. The guard barely has enough ammunition for its own soldiers. All the ammunition in the sanctuary is imported, and shipments only come once a month.

I take my supplies and go to an open table. Steel planks are staggered in the field every 20 yards. Around me, a handful of other students are training. I watch as they hit some targets and miss others. If I choose the guard, they will be my competition. I only have a week to decide: music or the guard. The range always gives me confidence. When I'm shooting, I feel like maybe, just maybe, I can pull it off.

I point the pistol at the 40-meter plank and squeeze one eye shut. With a flick of my finger, I click off the safety. I imagine an army of feeders charging me, blood dripping from their mouths. My finger tightens on the trigger.

Ting. Ting. Ting.

I switch from one target to another, from close to far to close again. The steel sings like a metallic symphony. Finally, a hollow click replaces the gunfire. The clip is empty. I reach for the ammo box when two hands clasp around my waist. I shriek and swing my elbow, just missing my assailant's nose. Familiar laughter fills my ears.

"Antai, have you gone mad? I'm holding a gun!" I fake a glare, but I can't stay angry as I watch him smile. I drop the pistol onto the table.

Antai's smile lights up his whole face. His teeth are big and white, and most importantly, straight—a rare sight in the sanctuary. His black hair is short and trimmed in a perfect line. Most of all, I love his big brown eyes—so big I could get lost in them for days and never find my way out. Around his neck, he wears a silver amulet. A simple Adamic spell is written in the center of the amulet.

I know both symbols well. *Magnify* and *soul*. In short, the spell amplifies the wearer's ability to command the elements. Using dominion would be impossible without it. This type of amulet is standard-issue for the guard, but it's not nearly as powerful as my own—a perk of being princess.

Just to prove I'm still upset, I punch Antai on the shoulder, which hurts my hand more than it hurts him. He's not terribly tall, but what he lacks in height, he makes up for in muscle. They bulge beneath his black uniform.

"Hey." Antai fakes like the punch hurts. "Easy, ringling. At least I waited until you were reloading." Ringling is a nickname for the lower class. Some would take offense, but I know it's only a joke. Antai loves to tease me every chance he gets.

Antai grins. "Besides, you couldn't hit a feeder if it was standing right in front of you."

"Haha, so funny," I mock. "You were watching, right? I didn't miss once."

"Well, what can I say?" Antai smiles proudly. "You must have had a truly exceptional instructor."

It's true, Antai spent every morning for the past month teaching me firearms. I worried it might attract unwanted attention, but no one seemed to mind. I wonder if he instructs lots of commoner girls how to shoot. The thought makes me angry, not that I have any reason to be.

I hit him again to keep him humble. "Just because you're a Guardian's apprentice doesn't mean you can be cocky."

"That's it. You're going in the pit." Antai grabs my wrist and drags me behind him. "Commoners like yourself need to learn respect."

I don't resist. I like the attention. Antai is several years older and grew up with me in the palace. He and I are among the only survivors from Hogrum. He lost his parents too. That alone makes us close.

Grandpa practically adopted Antai, and we grew up like siblings... sort of. We were always best friends, but in recent years there's been something more... something special.

Unfortunately, Cavernic law says no one can court before they reach the age of 18. Marriage is forbidden before an individual is divided. The law is designed to keep the birth rate low and prevent pregnancy before a family is sustainable. Any children born out of wedlock are confiscated for their own benefit. They grow up as palace servants, given the food and clothes a child deserves.

Antai lets go of my wrist. His hand brushes mine, and for a brief second, I think he might hold my hand. Instead, our hands drift apart, and he hides his hands in his pockets. He stares straight ahead as we walk.

"Where are we headed?" I ask. "Are we coming back to the range later?

He doesn't respond, the stress visible on his face. It's not an uncommon sight. The weight of Antai's responsibilities would be crushing for most. He's the commander of the eastern quadrant—a quarter of the entire sanctuary. Not to mention he's my grandfather's apprentice, training to be one of the four guardians of the sanctuary —the most powerful men alive. But today, he seems extra worried. *Something's wrong.*

When he finally takes his hand out of his pocket, I grab it with my own. "Is everything alright, Antai? You can tell me."

Antai squeezes my hand. "I'll tell you in the carriage. We're heading back to the palace." He seems on edge. If I'm not mistaken, he's scanning our surroundings as we walk. He trains his eyes on the other guards as we pass the armory. His hand lingers over his holster. Something awful has happened; I'm sure of it. By the time we're alone in the carriage, I've imagined every worst-case scenario. I hold my tongue, knowing I can't force it out of him. Antai is much too stubborn.

He waits until the carriage is moving before he speaks. "Rose, there was another attack last night in the ring."

I sigh my relief. "Goodness, Antai, I thought Grandpa died or something." Grandpa has been gone on a business errand with two of the other guardians. He often leaves without explanation, placing the high council in charge.

"Rose, this wasn't a normal attack," Antai insists. "They killed eleven guardsmen."

"Eleven?" I gasp. "But… how is that possible?" Guardsmen are supposed to be the toughest fighters in the sanctuary. They are the only ones allowed to carry firearms and amulets. "It couldn't have been the equalists, could it?" Typically, their methods include strikes and the occasional demonstration. On one occasion, they set fire to a guard tower, but they don't seem capable of murdering an entire team of guardsmen.

Antai shrugs. "Whoever it was, they knew what they were doing. They stole their guns and amulets too." Without amulets, the guard can't exercise dominion over the elements. Each one stolen is a victory for the equalists.

Antai shifts in his seat. "That's not all. We found the soldiers in their underclothes. Whoever killed them stole their uniforms, almost a dozen of them."

Understanding dawns on me. My stomach twists. Antai isn't worried about himself; he's worried about me.

"Rose, I think they're going to target the parade… I think they plan to kill you."

I hate it when we argue. Typically, our arguments are meaningless and short-lived, but I know this one isn't going to disappear. And I don't plan on backing down either. We've been arguing for nearly an hour about the parade. I tried to escape to my room, but Antai followed me. He's persistent to a fault.

"Does my Grandpa know?" I ask.

Antai shrugs. "I sent a messenger hawk last night. No response yet."

I don't know what to do. I know it's risky, but this is my one chance to speak to the sanctuary, to show them who I really am. I'm thinking of anything to rationalize my decision. "What if you ride on the float with me?" I say. "Then, even if they try something, you'll be right there."

Antai drums his fingers on his holster like he always does when he's thinking. "I just don't feel good about it, Rose. King Dralton is gone with the guardians. General Zane is out with the convoy. They obviously tried to time this when the guard is at its weakest. And that's not even the worst part. They could be anyone with those uniforms. We'll have no way of knowing if it's a guardsman or an equalist."

"What about the royal guard?" I ask. "They'll be there the entire time, and we know we can trust them." The royal guard wears a distinct white uniform, none of which have been stolen.

I can see Antai thinking, trying to find a gap in my logic. Trying to find some explanation to convince me. Nothing will work. My mind is made up.

Antai shakes his head in frustration. "I just don't understand why it's so important to you?"

"This isn't about me, Antai. It's about the sanctuary. I shouldn't have to explain it to you. Half the city wants me dead, and the other half thinks I'm a helpless girl. If I can't show my face in the Remembrance Day Parade, how am I supposed to do it at the crowning... or ever?"

I didn't choose this. I don't even want to be queen. I'm the last surviving heir, and to put it simply, Grandpa is getting old. Everyone knows that when he dies, I'll be next in line. Unfortunately, not everyone likes that idea. There are a lot of factions in the sanctuary. Lots of people want their shot at power, equalists and elite alike.

Antai stares back with sad eyes. I can tell he wants to say something, but he stands silent instead.

I exhale my frustration. "If Grandpa were here, he wouldn't be worried about the equalists. They'd be afraid of him." I rethink my words. "They'd respect him. How will I ever earn their trust if they think I'm hiding from my own people?"

Antai meets my eyes. He's thinking again, tapping his foot on the ground. "They respected your mother, didn't they? She wasn't a Guardian. Just a musician, but they loved her."

"Yes, but she always had my father to protect her. He was a guardian before he even became king."

"Exactly!" Antai says. "And you could have a guardian to protect you too. You don't have to do it all alone."

I'm speechless. Is he really suggesting what I think he is? I play dumb. "I know. I'm not doing it alone. I'm trusting you to keep me safe at the parade."

"There are other ways to please the people, Rose. It's not worth getting yourself killed to prove a point. The last thing we want is a dead princess and a war over the throne. That wouldn't help anyone."

I push as much sincerity as I can muster into my voice. "Antai, I won't get myself killed. Please stop talking like it's suicide. Besides, my decision is final. Can you please let me finish getting ready?" I turn to the mirror and tease my half-finished bun. I'm only trying to look busy until Antai leaves.

"Fine, then at least wear this." His shirt is already off by the time I turn around. I've seen him shirtless before, but it feels different in my bedroom. More intimate. His muscles flex as he pulls off his black and white undershirt. It's Adamic armor. An intricate pattern is sewn across every inch of the shirt.

I recognize it from last week's lesson with Grandpa. The armor is made by overlapping the same simple symbol over and over.

Impenetrable, I read. Grandpa says the symbol is merely a fragment of a once larger spell lost to the centuries. Its protective qualities only extend along the surface of the symbol. Alone, the spell doesn't defend much; however, the individual symbols can be overlapped like the links of chain mail armor. When combined, they form an impenetrable layer of Adamic armor. Only the guardians and highly ranked guardsmen wear this kind of armor. It's much safer than Kevlar. Not even I have access to one.

After laying the shirt on the bed, Antai slips his black uniform back over his head and strides for the door.

"Hey, won't you need this?" I ask.

Antai smiles unconvincingly. "Hopefully, neither of us will."

The door shuts behind him with a soft click. As soon as it closes, I regret everything. I got what I wanted, but I feel utterly selfish. I know he's only worried about my safety.

I study the thin white cloth on my bed. The armor seems so fragile, yet I know it can stop a bullet with ease. If anything happens to Antai while I'm wearing his armor, I'll never forgive myself. His words echo in my ear. *You can have a guardian too. You don't have to do it all alone.* What did he mean by that?

A timid knock interrupts my thoughts. I've heard that knock a thousand times. "Come in, Nevela."

Nevela scurries in like a scared mouse, struggling to keep a maroon dress from dragging on the floor. A big bundle of satin spills over her arms. "Excuse me, princess, but we really must hurry. I've got the dress, and we just need to take care of your hair." She's a small girl, no more than 5 feet. Her golden hair falls to her rear. Nevela is three years younger than me, but she's my closest friend besides Antai.

I start to pull off my hoodie as Nevela dives for my shoes. "Are you excited for the parade?" she asks. Her eyes blossom wide with excitement. "Oh, everyone's going to love you."

I smile, relishing Nevela's energy. "Yeah, I suppose. It won't be the same without Grandpa." Nevela is the one thing that makes all my royal duties bearable. She's been my personal maidservant ever since she was five, but she's more than that. She's the younger sister I never had. Her mother, being underage and unable to care for a child, was relieved of Nevela at birth. Perhaps that's why she seeks my approval so desperately. In a sense, I've been both her sister and her mother.

Nevela leans in closer and whispers. "How was the shooting range? Are you getting better?"

I've told Nevela all about my crazy ideas. She's the only one besides Antai who knows about my training. Not even Grandpa knows what I'm planning.

"I'm definitely getting better. I'm not as quick as Antai, but I'll be as good as the other competitors."

Nevela squeals and shakes my arm as she helps me squeeze into the fitted dress. "Are you really going to join the guard? Aren't you frightened? You'll have to punch people and shoot people."

I laugh. "I already told you. It's just a possibility. But imagine if it works. If I became a Guardian, everyone will sustain me. There won't be any talk about rebellion or uprisings. I can unite the sanctuary like Grandpa did."

Nevela leans closer and lowers her voice. "Do you think you could kill a feeder?"

I push her back as she giggles. "Come on. No feeders are getting in the sanctuary. And besides, I'm not even sure I'll do it yet. I just want to have some options."

"I think it's cool. You'll be the first Princess Guardian. And I can do your hair, so you look hot when you shoot people." Nevela's excitement is contagious. I laugh and accidentally jerk the bun out of Nevela's hands. She restarts without complaint.

If I choose the guard, I'll really miss Nevela. I'll be demoted to a commoner and train with the other first-year recruits. I have so many things to worry about today, I can barely keep them all straight.

Nevela catches me staring at the wall. "Are you worried about the speech?"

"Yes. Petrified, to be honest." In my Grandfather's absence, he asked me to deliver the royal speech at the Remembrance Day Ceremony. It will be my first chance to address my people and give them an idea of the type of queen I'll be. Grandpa utterly refused to help me write it. I stressed about it all week, and I'm stressing about it now.

"You don't need to worry." Nevela chimes as she dusts some brown powder on my cheeks. "Once I'm done with you, they'll be too busy staring to hear a word you say."

"I might as well just dance for them."

We both laugh as Nevela puts the final touches on my makeup. She finishes by picking out a pair of sleek black flats with a thin gold strap. I stand in front of the mirror as Nevela does the final check. "I'm so jealous, you look so pretty." She beams, obviously satisfied with her work. "Are you sure you want to wear the armor?"

Nevela has folded back the armor sleeves so they won't peek out of the dress straps. The shirt, like a serpent shedding its skin, is much too loose on me. In hopes of fitting my form, a portion is scrunched underneath the zipper in the back. Hopefully, it won't be too notice-able from a distance.

"Antai suggested it. I'm sure it's just an extra precaution," I cas-ually reply. I don't want my favorite maid to worry.

"Okay," Nevela agrees. "I'm just confused why anyone would want to hurt you?"

I can list a dozen reasons.

Another knock echoes in the room. I nod my head, and Nevela opens the door. Two royal guardsmen stand in the doorway. They barely fit in the stairwell with their broad shoulders and body armor.

My escort is here; the parade is about to begin.

Before I leave, I layer my gold amulet over my dress. The gold glimmers beautifully above the maroon lace. Nevela says it makes my eyes sparkle. It's a beautiful piece of jewelry, but it's also a powerful weapon.

I take one last look in the mirror and follow the soldiers down the stairs. With everything going on, one thought lingers in the back of my mind.

What if Antai is right? What if they try to kill me?

Chapter 3

Matt

I veer off the road to avoid a fallen tree trunk. As expected, the service road looks like it hasn't been used in years. Weeds and small shrubs sprout from crevices in the pathway. I drive the ATV slowly to avoid catching up with Lumberjack. As far as I know, his car could be just around the next bend.

The road twists around the mountain, steadily gaining altitude. The trees around me are thick, blocking out most of the evening light. One glance at my watch confirms it: I've only been riding for 5 minutes, but it feels much longer.

If I want any hope of retrieving the elk, I need to turn back now, but something pulls me forward. Curiosity? Stupidity? Perhaps a mix of both. This is my one chance to see the power plant. This is my kind of birthday present.

I glance up from the road; there's another bend up ahead. The trees grow thinner and the road looks like it peeks over a small crest of the mountain. I follow it, watching the road in front of me. I dodge rocks and duck under overgrown branches. I coast to a stop as the ground flattens before me.

I look up, and my jaw drops open. It takes a few seconds to register what I see. Up ahead, the road collides with a stone archway. It's the opening of a wall that stretches as far as I can see in both directions. It's not a chain-link fence, but a real wall. A 50-foot-tall stone wall like in medieval times. On the other side of the arch, the road continues, but the forest is replaced with an enormous field of grass and small bushes. The road, barely visible under the overgrown grass, cuts a straight line through the center of the field.

But most impressive is what lies beyond the field. Off in the distance, clinging to the mountain, are rows and rows of square buildings. They layer the mountainside like the dull-colored scales of a sleeping dragon.

I tilt my head back to take it all in. A whole city has been hidden in the mountains. All the buildings cling to one central mountain peak. Even with all its growth in the last 15 years, Kentville doesn't compare to this place.

I pull back the throttle and start a slow pace toward the opening in the wall. As I approach the archway, I coast to a stop to get a better look. There are huge symbols carved into the side of the stone wall. Some are several feet tall. Most importantly, they match the style of my necklace.

△◉⚓⚚☠◁◇⛰⚘⇉⚕

Whoever my parents were, they definitely lived here. Answers are just around the corner.

Once I'm inside the wall, an eerie silence envelops me. I reach back into the trunk and sling my rifle over my shoulder. I prefer to keep it close. Shrub branches crunch under the tires as I accelerate through the field. Off to my right, deep cement ditches run parallel to the road—irrigation canals if I had to guess. This place looks like it used to be some kind of farm.

I scan the field from my seat on the ATV. No sign of life. No sign of Lumberjack. He must already be in the city somewhere. I don't mind the solitude.

Finally, I approach the city. Grey stone buildings sprout from the earth like tightly packed trees. The urban jungle blocks out most of the light. From my viewpoint in the field, I scan the city with my rifle scope. The main road stretches endlessly forward through the labyrinth of buildings. I see only empty windows and empty streets. I hear nothing but silence. I load a round in the rifle chamber and ease the ATV forward.

The dirt road gives way to a sloppy stone street. It's pieced together with rock shards arranged in a jumbled mess. Branching off the main road are tiny alleys. Dozens of them. On each side of me tower stone buildings. They all reach about the same height—two or three stories tall. They're too big to be homes. They look like apartments of some kind, but I'm too creeped out to check. Either the city is abandoned, or everyone is playing a giant game of hide and seek. I doubt the latter, but I keep my rifle close just in case.

It doesn't take long before I notice. The damage is everywhere. The exterior of one apartment building is charred black. The wall of another building has completely collapsed. Tiny brick shards litter the street. It looks like someone ran through the city tossing grenades. Almost every window is broken or cracked.

But that isn't the only thing strange about the city. Finally, it dawns on me what seems out of place: there are no lights in the street. No streetlamps, no power lines. No cars parked. It looks like a scene from medieval Europe.

What was this place?

I ride for what feels like miles, passing apartment after apartment. Thousands of people must have lived here. Probably tens of thousands. The incline of the road is constant and steep. The ground slants at a continuous 15-degree angle. If I turn around, I can see the road falling away behind me all the way to the fields.

Up ahead, surrounded by buildings, is another stone wall. This one is completely identical to the first with a wide, stone archway as an entrance. Those same familiar symbols stare back at me, daring me to find answers. Could the symbols be their language? Maybe a military code?

Above my head, little bridges connect the second wall to the surrounding rooftops. As I continue up the road, I notice more of them. All of the rooftops are interconnected by small stone bridges. I wonder what the view is like from the rooftops. If only I could've seen this place in its glory days. *If only I could've lived here with my parents.*

I hit the breaks, and my ATV jerks to a stop. Lumberjack's Ford truck is parked in the middle of the street. I stay stone still as I listen… silence. I don't see Lumberjack, but he can't be far.

I ease the ATV next to the truck as quietly as I can. I peek through the window: a few papers, an empty coffee cup, some sunglasses. No guns. No Geiger counter. Nothing out of the ordinary.

There's only one way to go: forward. I ease the throttle and accelerate up the road. The deeper into the city I ride, the more uneasy I become, and the more confused. Except for a thick layer of dust, the homes look as though they were abandoned yesterday.

Finally, my curiosity gets the best of me. I park outside the nearest apartment and push the door open. I try the first door on my right. It's unlocked. Children's toys are scattered on the floor. There's a rusty iron furnace in the corner. Old logs lay stacked on the side, still waiting to be burned. I push open the next door. It's a bedroom. Leather boots rest by the door. Blankets lay strewn across an unmade bed. A dark feeling creeps into the back of my mind. Why would someone leave their shoes? They must have left in a real hurry.

A red oval stains the stone floor by the kitchen. Another cherry-colored stain is by the stairs. I don't want to guess what it might be. I decide I've done enough exploring. I'm not very superstitious, but the city feels haunted. Something made all these people leave in a hurry, and something tells me it wasn't radiation. I haven't seen any sign of a power plant.

What is this place?

I climb back into the ATV and ride onward up the main road. I don't take any turns. I'm afraid if I do, I won't be able to find my way back. The last thing I want to do is spend the night in a ghost town. Ghosts don't make good company. The thought gives me chills.

The sinking sun catches my attention. I pick up my pace. I have less than an hour until sundown. I know it would be smart to turn around, but I'm so close to the peak. I ride a little faster.

In the distance, a third stone wall arches it's way over the road like a colorless rainbow. The ground is leveling out, almost flat. An enormous castle looms over the third wall. The grey stone towers are oddly extravagant compared to the bland, boxy nature of the rest of the city. Curiosity urges me onward. The castle is just up ahead.

The street opens up into a giant circular courtyard big enough to host the Superbowl. The far end is bordered by the castle wall, the closest three sides are boxed in by more rectangular buildings. Dozens of roads all seem to diverge in this one courtyard.

At the far end of the courtyard, a heaping section of the stone wall has collapsed. Car-sized chunks of concrete are strewn around the crumpled wall. When I get close, I notice the hole in the ground. It stretches 50 feet across where the toppled wall used to stand. This isn't any ordinary hole, I realize. It's a bomb crater. Someone blew their way into the castle. *No wonder the people left in such a hurry.*

The thought leaves me baffled. I'd expect a battering ram, but not a bomb. New possibilities swirl in the abyss of my mind. Could this place be a weapons testing facility? So much remains unanswered. The castle looms before me, reminding me of unsolved mysteries. The toppled wall is an open invitation. I park the ATV and traverse the bomb crater on foot.

A battered garden stretches between the castle wall and the castle. Broken fountains and overgrown walkways encircle the castle on all sides. A stone path guides me to what appears to be a front entrance. The closer I get, the bigger the castle appears.

I think twice as I stand before the castle door—or what's left of it. Broken hinges hang from the stone archway. The door is nowhere to be found. *So much for knocking.*

I stare past the entrance but see only an endless black. I slide my phone out of my pocket and tap on the flashlight app. It lights up the floor in front of me, but when I aim it down the center of the entryway, the darkness quickly swallows up the tiny beam. Something tells me I won't find a light switch on the wall either.

I would be an idiot to go inside. It looks like a scene from a horror movie. Everyone always dies in those movies. Indecision gnaws at me. Whenever I can't decide something, I ask myself two questions:

Will I regret going in?... no, probably not. Worst case scenario: it's creepy. Besides, I have a gun. What's the worst that can happen?

Will I regret not going in?... yes, I'd think about it all night. I need to know. I need answers!

I untuck my pistol from its holster bed. I clench it in my right hand and the phone in my left. Before I change my mind, I step into the dark. The hallway is broad, with a red rug rolled down the center. The luxury leaps out at me in the darkness. I shine the light on an elegant canvas. Beady painted eyes glare back unblinking. I'm careful not to lose myself in the maze of hallways. Left. Right. Left. I make a mental note of every turn. I move down the hallway, shining my phone like a weapon, fighting off an army of darkness. Nothing is creepier than the pale white light on the marble floor.

It doesn't take long to regret my decision, but I press onward anyway. Each corner calls me forward, promising answers. Chairs burst into view, and I tiptoe around broken vases and statues. The hallway leads me to a giant staircase that spirals downward into nothingness. I shiver. It looks like the entrance to hell.

I inhale and take the first step. As I descend, the air grows colder. My footsteps clap excruciatingly loud on each step like slow applause. The dust is a swarm of tiny gnats clouding the air. They follow the beam of light wherever it goes. Darkness and claustrophobia press on me. I feel the constant need to check behind me in the dark.

Another hallway, this one is lined with doors. Each door lets out a rusty wail as it swings open, screaming for me to leave. Every room holds a secret of its own. I find a small library, mostly burned to the ground. A long room filled with beds. I don't know what it is. A nursery, maybe? An infirmary? I stop. A tiny wooden crib sits alone in the corner. Something aches inside of me. *What if that was my crib?*

At the end of the hall, another staircase spirals downward into oblivion. My heart begins racing. Symbols mark the stones of the first step. I trace them with my phone light, searching for a meaning in the symbols. The darkness calls to me. I know it's almost night, but I'm so close to something—I don't even know what.

I sigh my disappointment. There are hundreds of rooms to explore. It could take weeks. And for the entire city, maybe years. If I wait any longer, I'll have to find my way home in the dark.

I'll be back first thing in the morning.

I'm about to turn around when I hear it. In the ominous silence, it comes from both in front and behind, echoing off of solid stone.

Creeaaaak.

Chills run down my spine. I freeze. I stare down into the stairwell, almost certain it hides the source of the sound. My heart pounds in my ears. The phone light reveals only empty steps. At first, I'm not sure if it's footsteps or my heartbeat.

Thump... thump... thump…

Now, there's no doubt; something is climbing the staircase.

Is it an animal? The ghost of some poor tortured soul? Should I run? Should I stay and fight? I'm holding a gun after all. Only one thing is certain.

I'm not alone in the castle.

My instincts decide for me. I turn around and dash the way I came at full speed. When I reach the first staircase, I climb the steps three at a time. Right. Left. Right. My feet pound like hammers on the floor. I can't tell if someone is chasing me or if it's the echo of my own footfall. I weave through the halls, running full speed. I twist my neck behind me, half expecting to see some creature in pursuit, but all I get is a snapshot of darkness. I turn back around just in time. Horrified, I skid to a stop, almost running into a wooden door. I don't remember this from my way in.

I'm lost.

I'm praying now in my head, pleading with God to guide me. I pause and listen. I don't hear any footsteps. I retrace my steps and gamble my life on a different hallway. Left. Right. Left. A vase that looks familiar. A painting. I know my way now.

Down the corridor, I see my salvation. Red sunlight spills into the hallway from the setting sun. The front entrance is at the end of the hall. I tuck my phone back into my pocket as I head swiftly for the door. Relief floods over me. The nightmare is over. I'm only a few yards from the sunlight now.

Suddenly, a hand shoots from the darkness. It grabs me by the sweatshirt and lifts me into the air. Before I even have time to shout, electricity courses through my body. Pain erupts everywhere at once. My body contracts and convulses, legs and arms seizing and shaking. My fingers curl involuntarily around the trigger of my pistol; a deafening gunshot rings out. I can't think as pain floods my mind.

1 second… 2 seconds, the volts continue. My lungs convulse. *I can't breathe! I can't breathe!*

Finally, the taser stops, and I collapse face-first on the floor. Silence echoes as I lay sprawled next to my rifle. The only audible sound is my own panting and my pounding heart. The cold stone floor kisses my cheek. My body aches and burns.

I open my eyes. I'm facing back into the hallway, the way I just came. All I see is a black abyss. Freedom is just a few feet behind me, but I can't move. My arms lay tangled in the rifle strap. I try to reach for the gun, but my limbs don't obey, somehow freed from my mind's command. I try to find my attacker in the darkness, but my face stays plastered to the floor.

Ever so slowly, a figure creeps into view. His outline is blurred by the backdrop of the hallway. He's wearing a cloak as dark as his surroundings. A black hood hides his face in shadow. The figure is dressed like some kind of catholic monk. But in the current circumstances, he seems much more sinister. Like the leader of a satanic cult come to sacrifice me to their God of blood. I'm terrified. I lay there gasping, waiting for the handcuffs to click on my wrists. But something tells me this isn't a policeman. I won't just get a fine for trespassing and be on my merry way. Something tells me I'm in real danger.

Hood man stands over me and reaches down, curling his fingers into my wavy blonde hair. With a jerk, he hoists me to my knees. I hang by the roots of hair, afraid they'll soon rip from my scalp. Hood disappears behind my back. His hand still holds my head in place.

Silence.

His breath brushes my ear as he leans in behind me. The scent is suffocating—the bitter smell of aged blood. He hovers there, inhaling my odor like a hot bowl of soup. He's inspecting me, admiring me... desiring me. Then, with the delicate hands of a surgeon, he tilts my head to the side and bites down.

His teeth sink in with sickening ease. A searing pain erupts above my collarbone, which only grows worse as his mouth suctions over the incision.

I thrash and scream. I try to reach back and claw at his eyes, but my muscles are filled with sand. I have no strength to lash out. I'm helpless. Almost immediately, I feel an unbearable pressure in my head. It feels like my brain is getting pulled in two separate directions. My skull is about to shatter. Darkness scratches at the edge of my vision.

Then, it stops. The jaws release me, and I suck in a deep breath. Before I have the chance to exhale, the silence is replaced once again with searing volts. This time, the taser is stronger. A sea of pain engulfs me. I hear a scream coming from somewhere. It sounds like my own. The pain turns into warmth. I'm floating.

Finally, the world turns black, and I escape into the safety of my mind, leaving my body to fend for itself.

A single raindrop strikes my eye. I squeeze my eyelids together to push the drop away. Another drop hits the corner of my mouth, causing my lips to purse.

Crunch, crunch. Crunch, crunch.

The sound echoes inside my head without meaning. A strange scraping. Like sandpaper. Something pokes me in the back. Something sharp.

I open my eyes. Blackness. I'm looking at the sky. But it's dark. Nighttime? Almost. There are clouds. Big black storm clouds.

Crunch, crunch.

It's footsteps in the dirt. A man is dragging me along a dirt road by the collar of my sweatshirt. The fabric cuts into the flesh of my armpits. Dirt rushes beneath my body, clawing at my jeans. A pile of sand already sits in my pants. Steps echo like a hammer in my head. I can't see the face of the man dragging me, just up the back of his cloak. He's wearing a hood.

Hood! Memories and panic rush into clarity at the same time. As reality settles in, so does the pain. My mind spins. I feel as though nails have been driven into my temples. Each bump in the path is another hammer blow to the nail.

I try to move my arms, but my veins feel pumped full of lead. I can hardly wiggle my fingers. Not that it matters. My pistol is missing. I can feel the absence of its weight on my hip. *Did Hood take it?*

No! I dropped it in the castle. My rifle as well. The memory is murky, like a distant dream. Fortunately for me, I'm not entirely defenseless. Something dense is pressed against my ribs. It's my birthday present. The dagger is still strapped to my chest underneath my sweatshirt. Either Hood didn't search me, or he did a terrible job.

Another bump jolts my head. I've never felt pain like this. It makes it hard to concentrate on anything. I try to make sense of my surroundings, but the pain fights for my attention. I just want to slip back into the comfort of unconsciousness. My neck is oozing blood, and if I don't get to a hospital soon, I'm pretty sure my wish will come true.

Will Hood kill me quick and get it over with? If he's going to murder me, why wait? Nothing makes sense. What possibly could motivate a man to do this? Drugs? Mental illness? Both scare me much more than the law. Does he want money? To harvest and sell my orga—

An exceptionally large rock grinds its way under my back. I bite my tongue and squeeze my hands in agony.

My hands! I can wiggle my fingers. Some sensation is starting to return. Just a little more mobility in my arms, and I'll be able to reach for the knife under my sweatshirt. But I'll have to wait for the right moment. I'll only get one chance.

As I stare at the sky, I can see storm clouds forming overhead. Dark clouds pull over the sky like blackout curtains. I can see trees in my peripheral vision. We're not in the city anymore.

How long was I out?

Heavy raindrops pelt my face and blind my eyes. The sky cries for me. Or maybe it bleeds. I don't know which. I feel like I'm going crazy. Will I ever see Judy again? I try not to think about it. I focus all of my energy on the knife strapped to my chest. It's my lifeline.

Hood stops, and I crack my eyes open. A car door swings open above my face. Hood lifts me by my coat and flings me into the back seat with ease. He's strong. Unnaturally strong.

I hear my door slam shut, followed by another door opening and closing. A moment later, the engine roars to life. I lay across the seats with my eyes closed, trying to keep my body limp. I can feel the paralysis slowly melting away like an arctic thaw. Yet, I don't dare move. I don't want another electric chair session. I'll play possum like a good abductee.

Eventually, curiosity gets the best of me. I slowly crack open my eyelids and choke back a silent gasp. I squeeze my eyes shut, but the image remains imprinted in my mind: Hood is no longer wearing his hood. From my view from behind the passenger seat, I can see the right half of his face. I sneak another peek.

His head is shaved bald, and his skin is black—but not naturally. It's hard to see in the dim light, but tiny black lines zigzag across his face. They stripe everything: cheek, neck, inside his ear, everything.

I squint. His tattoos are way different than mine—repetitive and angular—but they're tattoos after all. That can't be a coincidence.

I reach under my sweatshirt and grasp the knife against my chest. I can stab him right now if I act fast, but if I kill the man, his knowledge dies with him. I'm torn. What if he knows what my symbols mean or what happened to the city?

What if he knows my parents?

I've never killed someone before. People go to therapy for that kind of stuff. I don't want PTSD. And how will I explain the body to the police?

Hood faces forward as he starts his descent down the rainy road. Based on the revving engine and the bumpiness of the journey, I'm guessing he's in a hurry to get somewhere.

We've just barely started the descent when the truck strikes something in the road. The cabin shakes as we swerve off the dirt road. For a brief moment, everything is still as I float off the back seat.

The car is in freefall.

Another shattering crash and the car rolls. I try in vain to keep my body anchored in the backseat. I tumble inside of the washing machine car. Instead of detergent, glass and metal spin with me. If only I wore a seatbelt.

After two spins, I hit the seat in front of me and land in a pile of glass on the ceiling. The car is upside down. Rain pours in through the broken windows, pooling on the roof beneath me. I think to run, but

Hood is already crawling out of the window and climbing the embankment.

At the top of the slope, a figure peers down at the wreckage. He wears a tan coat and a bushy beard. The man has a build of a... Lumberjack? *Could it be?*

I watch through the empty window frame, but the rain obscures my view. It's too dark to be sure. The new arrival is carrying something in his hand. He raises his arm at Hood, and gunshots burst from the barrel of a pistol.

Hood shudders as the bullets strike him in the chest, but somehow, he keeps walking. A bullet snaps his head back, but Hood doesn't break stride. I can't believe my eyes. *He should be dead! Very very dead!*

A flash of lightning splits the night, vibrating the air. It's indistinguishable from the roar of thunder. I tuck my head between my arms for protection. Wet glass sticks to me like glitter. Not even a second goes by before the next flash illuminates the car. The thunderclap rings like cannon fire. Then another. For a brief instant, the glass shards sparkle like a chandelier.

I twist my neck out of the broken window to get a better view of the scene. Lumberjack looks hurt. He stumbles toward Hood, holding something at his side. It isn't a gun this time; it's a... sword?

Who brings a sword to a gunfight?

Hood lifts his arm. Another deafening flash illuminates the night. Electricity arcs in the air between them, crackling and sizzling. I blink. Colors swim before my eyes. When my eyes adjust to the darkness, I find a body lying facedown in the dirt. It's Lumberjack. He doesn't move. Steam rises from his lifeless body.

He's dead.

Yet miraculously, Hood remains on his feet. He slowly walks back to the wreckage, seemingly unharmed. Any hope of my rescue is dashed in an instant. I lay in the crumpled cabin, utterly stunned. I just witnessed a man getting struck by lightning. I witnessed a man getting shot in the head and live.

I don't breathe. I pray Hood didn't see me moving. I lay as still as possible, clutching my birthday gift beneath my coat. I'll need the element of surprise. I don't know if this will work, but it's my only hope. I only have one shot.

Hood eerily makes his way down the embankment. His cloak flows as he walks, blending his steps into a continuous glide. He moves across the grass to the car. He's almost here.

Without pausing, Hood reaches into the car and drags me out by my sweatshirt. As soon as my head clears the wreckage, I swing the dagger.

The knife slides into Hood's stomach with sickening ease. The hilt strikes his belly button just as lightning strikes. Light explodes inside my head. Everything is white.

Then, darkness. The darkness you only find deep inside your mind.

Chapter 4

Rose

I stand alone on the wooden float with my dead parents. Their portraits sit on either side of me in memory of the fallen king and queen. The rest of the float is neatly embellished with ivy and marigolds. They were my mother's favorite flower.

Two white show horses tug my float forward through the fields. In front of me, a long row of floats inches its way toward the royal plaza like a giant centipede.

The city is designed like a circular spider web. The palace and royal plaza are in the center of the web. From there, a dozen spider silk roads branch out to the ring—the border of the web. Then, dozens of roads run circles around the city, connecting everything together.

As we enter the ring, hundreds of people line the side of the road, shouting and cheering and fighting for a spot along the street. Parents hold children on their shoulders to give them a better view. Grey chalk clouds blossom in the air as children throw handfuls of a dusty powder. It's a Remembrance Day tradition. The grey chalk symbolizes the ashes of the fallen. The dead have always been cremated in

Cavernum. Everyone assumes it's because there's no room for a cemetery within the walls, but I know better. The tradition originates from an ancient fear—demons can't possess ashes.

I take a deep breath. *Everything will be fine.* Royal guards hover around my float like guardian angels. They never wander more than a few feet from me.

I try to hide my nerves the best I can. I smile and wave as I scan the edge of the unruly crowd. Guardsmen walk with the parade, keeping the spectators at bay. They make me more nervous than the crowd. Any one of them could be here to kill me. To make matters worse, the float directly in front of mine is in honor of the fallen guard. A black flag with a red circle flaps in the wind. A dozen guardsmen cheer from the float and throw sweets to the crowd. Normally, their proximity would have been an extra safety measure, but today it only puts me at risk.

I wish Antai were here. He has to direct security from the rooftops, which are restricted to guard use only. They provide fast, traffic-free travel and a safe vantage point to patrol the city. Dozens of small bridges connect the rooftops throughout the entire city. Antai oversees security for the east parade, the one I'm participating in. There are three other parades coming from the south, north, and west. They'll all meet in the royal plaza for the main event.

I study each guardsman, searching for a flaw in their uniform. As far as I can tell, everything seems normal. No sign of an imposter.

Music from the royal orchestra echoes through the street. They're only three floats ahead of mine. I spot my violin tutor in the front row of the string instruments. Right now, it seems much more appealing than riding alone.

I take another deep breath and focus on the children. As always, the children in the ring are energetic and unrestrained. They jump up and down, screaming for attention and tossing ashes on the living. Poor things. Most of them stay cooped up at home while both parents work in the fields. All they need is some extra attention.

I wave at a little girl and blow a kiss to a boy who can't be older than six. He grins shyly and ducks his head back into his mother's dress. His mom doesn't seem so amused. Most laborers don't fancy the royal family. To them, I represent everything they don't have. I'm the reason their children are starving.

Mixed in with the crowd are the protesters, most of which are drunk. They hold wooden signs painted with equalist propaganda. Those who aren't holding signs hold bottles of homemade booze instead. Others shout insults from the camouflage of the crowd. —"We won't keep feeding the king!"—"Equal pay for equal work!" —"Share the amulets!"— A few are more threatening. —"Down with the tyranny! Kill the king!"—

Suddenly something slaps my arm. A red liquid oozes down my elbow. "Seriously?" I wipe the rotten tomato off my arm just as another hits me in the back. From both sides of the street, laborers toss rotten fruit at me. *How dare they?* I'm their princess. Their advocate. How can they mock me like this?

I won't allow it. Fortunately, I'm wearing my amulet. My grand-father spent many afternoons teaching me how to use it. One thing he stressed above all else was how to defend myself.

I clutch my amulet in one hand and hold the other out in front of me. Suddenly, the air around me ripples, distorting my surroundings like ripples on a pond. The shimmer in the air is almost unrecogniz-able. Still, I know it marks the surface of an energy shield—an invisible barrier of pure force.

A man chucks a rotten apple at my face. I don't so much as flinch as the apple splatters a foot from my nose. It smashes against what appears to be a wall of glass. Ripples cascade around me, expanding from where the apple struck.

Several more tomatoes collide with the energy shield before the protestors lose interest and return to their insults. —"You feed those horses better than you feed us!"—"If you're not careful, princess, you'll end up like your parents!"—

I refuse to make eye contact with the protesters. Instead, I scan the rooftops overhead looking for Antai. Dozens of guardsmen spy down from the parapet. They all have a clear shot at me. One guardsman in particular stares at me without blinking. His hand hovers dangerously close to his holster. I feel uneasy.

I look at the royal guards, searching for assistance. Have they noticed him too? They all seem preoccupied with the crowd. Octavian walks along the opposite side of the road. He wrestles a drunk man to the floor who has been throwing trash and shouting. No one else is concerned about the suspicious soldier up above. I want to call out to Octavian, but I don't want to make a scene.

When I turn back to the rooftops, the guardsman is gone. Sweat trickles down my underarm. I scan the alleys and the road. Everything seems as it should be. I just need to calm down and stop overreacting. Focusing my energy back on being princess, I smile and hold my head high. We're passing under the inner wall now. Commoners replace laborers on the side of the street.

My thoughts wander to the portraits of my parents. Would they be proud of me right now? Would they like my speech? I wish Grandpa were here with me on the float. I feel so vulnerable standing here alone.

Someone waves at me from the top of the inner wall. It's Antai. He grins at me, leaning over the parapet. When I smile back, he winks. I wonder if he sees me blushing.

Antai follows my float from the rooftops, keeping pace with the horses. I can't keep my eyes away from him, but every time I look, he's looking somewhere else. His eyes dart from one side of the road to another. I can't be mad; he does his job well. I feel safer already.

The core isn't as hectic as the ring. No one carries signs or curses at me. And no one throws rotten fruit. The children calmly point and smile as the floats pass.

BOOM! An explosion silences the crowd. I flinch so hard my tiara almost falls off my head. Panic seizes me by the chest. I debate jumping from my float. I flinch at the sound of another explosion. Up ahead, teenagers are throwing firecrackers into the street.

Relax, Rose. It's just kids. I take another deep breath and try to calm my startled heart. I'm too paranoid. *Everything's going to be fine,* I tell myself.

As the floats near the royal plaza, the roar of the crowd engulfs me. Thousands of citizens are packed into the courtyard. The laborers dominate the crowd, both in numbers and in vigor. They stand shoulder to shoulder, their children perched on their shoulders. Unfortunately, their company is tainted with protesters demanding justice.

Commoners gather on nearby balconies to watch. Several elite families accumulate along the edges of the crowd, avoiding the masses. In the center of the plaza stands a tower of hay bales and dried timber. Nestled in the center of the structure are several bodies wrapped in white linen—deceased laborers from the previous day. They'll be burned as the grand finale—a ceremonial cremation. *From dust we came and to dust we shall return.* It's tradition.

The floats part the Red Sea of viewers and park themselves in front of the palace wall. A concrete stage has been constructed for the purpose of addressing the public. It's a shoulder height block of concrete built directly into the outer side of the palace wall.

Next to the stage sits the gallows—a wooden platform with three long ropes. It's more of a scare tactic than anything, but every now and then, a severe crime forces Grandpa to hold an execution. It happens more often than I'd like to admit.

Once the floats stop, everyone begins dismounting. Octavian gives me his hand and helps me down. Most parade participants find places in the crowd, but I join the city officials onstage. There's a seat with my name on it towards the back of the stage. On the seat next to mine, the name 'Alfred' is crossed out, and 'Antai' is scribbled underneath. I smile at Antai's handiwork. Much better than sitting next to some crusty, old politician.

I try to find Antai on the rooftops surrounding the plaza, but there are too many guards. Every soldier in the sanctuary must be here.

They line the edge of the plaza and barricade the palace gate. Several guards on horseback gallop through the crowd. Most importantly, a blockade of royal guardsmen encircles the stage to keep the crowd at bay. I'm in good hands.

Antai's seat is still empty when the ceremony begins. Chancellor Bolo from the high council leads the event. He's a round man with almost no hair, somewhat resembling an overgrown baby. As kids, Antai and I called him Chubby Chancellor and Baby-face Bolo.

Bolo greets the crowd and gives the yearly statistical report. Afterward, the orchestra bursts to life, and everyone sings the Cavernic Anthem.

> *Blessed beauty, promised land*
> *Bestowed by God's redeeming hand*
> *Guarded from the evil beast*
> *On this holy land to feast*
> *Bless Cavernum, God we pray*
> *Bless us each and everyday*

I mouth the words to the beat of the anthem. As much as the music enthralls me, singing is not one of my strong suits.

Once the anthem ends, each guild is given a few minutes to present in preparation for the upcoming dividing. The blacksmiths demonstrate how a sword is made and have a mock sword fight. Horse trainers leap on rippling show horses. Seamstresses display elegant ball gowns. My music tutor performs a classical piece on the violin. Next, the healers present, then the architects and the chefs. None of the laborers are represented. *What is there to say about growing corn?*

Antai takes his seat halfway through the carpentry guild. I can tell he's stressed. He must be as worried for his speech as I am for mine. As commander of the eastern quadrant, he's been selected to present for the guard. I'm excited to hear him speak, but he doesn't strike me as a poet. Then again, maybe the people don't want to hear from a poet.

Throughout the entire event, Antai scans the crowd. He's worried about more than just his speech. I take his hand and squeeze it. He squeezes back, but his furrowed brow never falters. Always watching. Always alert.

I lean in close. "I bet you 100 bars I'll get a standing ovation."

Antai sneers in mock disgust. "Please, a commoner makes more than that. Whoever gets the loudest cheer gets a homemade meal from the loser... tonight!"

"Deal!" I'm not much of a cook, but Nevela will help me if I lose. I already know Antai's favorite: stuffed chicken and gravy.

Antai stands and replaces the lawyer guild onstage. I stare at his back, trying to imagine his facial expressions as he speaks.

"Hello, Cavernum!!!" His voice booms over the crowd, amplified by his amulet. The crowd matches his intensity. Everyone stomps their feet in response. I can't keep the grin off my face.

"I'm Antai Elsborne, commander of the eastern quadrant. If you haven't heard of me, that's probably a good thing. Most of my acquaintances live in the pit." He smiles, and the crowd chuckles on cue. "Don't worry, I promise I'll try not to bore you like some people." Antai gives an exaggerated glance at the lawyer guild official. The crowd erupts in another wave of laughter. I already know I've lost the bet.

Antai grows serious. "As much as I'd love to tell you more about myself, today's not about me."

A few female screams burst from the crowd. "Tell us more!" I roll my eyes. I would probably be thinking the same in their shoes.

Antai pretends he didn't hear, preserving his thoughtful gaze. "Today we celebrate the fallen. We celebrate all those who've lost their lives in the great sanctuary of Hogrum. They were just like us. Farmers and craftsmen, healers and lawyers. The only thing separating us from them is a wall and those who guard it."

Antai takes a deep breath. The subtle sound is amplified over the audience, capturing them with emotion. I'm impressed. He's a natural onstage.

"I hope today we can take a moment to remember those we've lost. Friends, brothers… parents."

The last word is spoken so softly it tickles my ear and tugs at my heart. I know the crowd feels it as well. Every mother in the audience seeps concern.

"As we remember them and what they meant to us, I hope they remind us of why we fight today. Not just of the danger, but of the reward. As we remember what we've lost, let's remember everything we've been given: peace, stability, safety, love. I hope we remember those who protect us from the threat outside the wall. Those guardsmen who risk everything to give us the gift of safety. I hope we remember those who gave their lives that we might laugh and love and live. That is the greatest gift. Let us not forget!"

The crowd stomps their feet and screams. Antai raises one hand in the air, and the crowd hushes for him. "For you brave souls out there, we'd love to have you at the flats this Friday for the guardsman trials. We need your help to keep this city safe. Joining the guard is the best choice you'll ever make."

Those words play on repeat in my mind. Will it be the best decision ever? I try to imagine myself in Antai's uniform. Can I see the guard being my life? The idea both thrills and terrifies me.

Antai is loving the attention. He grins at the audience until they hush once more. "Thank you all for listening and for being here today. I hope you've enjoyed it as much as I have. Now, if you'll give a warm welcome to a few of my good friends, we'd like to thank you all with a little demonstration." The crowd roars its approval.

Several guardsmen climb onto the stage, amulets bouncing as they dance over to Antai. The orchestra begins playing a catchy tune. The guardsmen take turns, demonstrating the power of dominion. Fire streams from one man's fingertips in a rainbow of colors. Another guardsman melts sand into bubbling lava and sculpts it into a curvy glass woman. The crowd goes wild.

With the help of the amulets, they have complete control over the elements. The displays of power are mesmerizing. But I know that it comes at a price. Their amulets aren't as powerful as mine. Using dominion quickly saps their strength.

It's Antai's turn. He strides directly off the end of the stage, waking on an invisible runway. His feet hover just inches above the tallest heads. With each step, transparent ripples extend out from his boots as if he's walking on a thin layer of water. Girls rush to touch his hands. They adore him. Antai is a celebrity.

I have to admit it's impressive. My amulet may be stronger, but I doubt I could do the same with such ease.

When the music stops, the guardsmen bow together, and all I hear is the roar of the audience. Although most laborers despise the guard, they're a crowd favorite in events like this. The guardsmen migrate offstage, and Antai goes with them. I know he wants to be on the rooftops where he can supervise security. He feels more in control up there.

Finally, it's my turn to speak. I take my place at the front of the stage. The crowd stops cheering. They stare with empty, doubtful eyes. *I'll definitely be making dinner tonight.*

I take a deep breath. I've practiced my speech dozens of times in front of Nevela. I just need to relax. If only I had a podium to hide behind. I feel so exposed.

"Hello, people of Cavernum. My name is Roselyn Malik, grand-daughter of King Dralton Malik." My voice projects, but not as loud as Antai's. "My grandfather gave me the opportunity to address you all this Remembrance Day in his place."

Silence. The audience doesn't seem to care. I can't blame them. I would rather hear Grandpa speak too. He's the most powerful man in the sanctuary.

"Today is a special day. For most of us, it is a sad day. No amount of celebration can hide the pain we feel. I feel it too. As many of you did, I lost loved ones in Hogrum—my parents. Most of you know them better than I ever will. They left a legacy of love and compassion. They loved Cavernum and what it stood for. For peace... for freedom." The crowd begins chatting amongst itself. It's like I'm speaking to a bunch of school children.

"Today, Commander Elsborne spoke of the great fight to maintain this city we cherish. I would like to speak about another fight: a war that is raging inside these very walls. A war we are losing. I am talking about a battle against hunger and starvation that continues day after day. A battle against disease. A battle against hopelessness. Today, I want to speak directly to the residents of the ring." The chatter dies, and eyes turn to me. I have their attention.

"We are not blind to the battles you fight every day. We hear your chants from the palace. We desperately want to help."

Some shouts of disapproval erupt. —"Then share your food!"— "You just want to use us!"—

Deep down, I know it's partially true. We need all the laborers we can get for planting and harvesting. Without machinery, everything has to be done by hand. But even in the winter, when the workload is light, there are no jobs to fill. There's no space to build new schools. There's no room for more blacksmiths or more shops. We need space, but the wall shatters any hopes of expansion.

I continue. My amplified voice drowns out the complaints. "We don't address these issues because it means admitting defeat. We tried rooftop gardens and failed. We tried expanding underground and failed. We need to build schools, but we have no space. We need more farmland, but we have no space. In the past 50 years, our population has doubled, but our city hasn't."

A man towards the front lifts an equalist flag into the air. A red upside-down pyramid flaps in the wind. It represents a reverse hierarchy. He faces the crowd and shouts, "There's enough food, but you gorge yourselves in the palace. What we need is equality!" Several cries of agreement cascade over the crowd. I'm starting to lose my audience.

Guilt gnaws at my gut like a parasite. I think of my violin and books being shipped into the city. How much food could fit instead? I think of the royal kitchen. How many children could it feed?

I'm almost yelling now. "I've thought very hard, and I'd like to propose a possible solution." The man reluctantly lowers his flag. Once again, I have their attention. "This last year alone, 15 guardsmen have died in the beyond. It's a dangerous job, but I know that more than 15 laborers die every month from starvation and sickness alone. Although dangerous, the convoy brings valuable resources that can save us.

The world out there has an excess of everything we need: food, vaccines, clothes. And the only way to get them is to leave the sanctuary. We need more guardsmen if we wish to make that possible. So, as princess and heir of Cavernum, I'm proud to announce that this year, we will be accepting twice as many recruits for the guard and devoting twice as many guardsmen to the convoy. We plan on increasing supply convoys from monthly to weekly trips."

It takes a moment for the crowd to register what I've said. Leaving the sanctuary is taboo, and the elite are very suspicious of it. A few laborers stomp their approval, but not all of the protesters seem so thrilled.

The lead equalist lifts his flag back into the air. "That's it? What about the rest of us? We're already divided! Where's our equality?" His drunk buddies echo his disdain. Others from the crowd join in. —"Where's our food? Where are our amulets?"— The man with the flag begins chanting. His laborer buddies join in, echoing his words.

"We want equality! Down with the hierarchy! We want equality! Down with the hierarchy!"

The chant is contagious. It spreads through the audience like wildfire. Soon, the entire crowd is a seething mass of chanting laborers. They pulsate like a swarm of angry bees, swaying together to the rhythm of the chant.

"We want equality! Down with the hierarchy!"

I raise my voice. "Listen! Please, list—" The roar of the crowd is too loud. I'm not finished, but it's useless to continue. I stand speechless before the crowd as debris rains down on the stage. They throw whatever they can get their hands on.

A chunk of concrete shatters onstage a few feet to my left. A cob of corn whizzes past my ear. I know I should run, but a part of me doesn't want to. I shouldn't have to run from my people. They're supposed to adore me, not chase me off the stage.

The bottle is mid-flight before I notice it. It tumbles through the air, careening straight at me. But that isn't what scares me most; a flaming cloth streams from the neck of the bottle. It's a beggar's bomb. As soon as the bottle breaks, the contents will instantly ignite. I want to run from the makeshift bomb, but my mind is faster than my feet. I only have time to raise my arms.

Just before the bottle strikes me, it shatters against the transparent surface of an energy shield, sending ripples through the air. Flames erupt against the unseen barrier, flinging glass in all directions. I watch in horror as the burning liquid rains down on the front row of protestors. The fiery liquid coats their skin and sets their hair ablaze. Almost instantly, screams of agony pierce my ears.

I don't care if they hate me; I can help them. I dash to the edge of the stage and jump down to the plaza floor, directly behind the blockade of royal guardsmen. The closer I am, the easier it'll be to exert dominion.

Clutching my amulet in one hand, I reach with my mind until I feel the flames at the edge of my conscious. I command the fire to dissipate and dispel the heat into the surrounding air. Immediately, the flames flicker out like candles on a birthday cake, one protester at a time.

I expect to see grateful faces but find rage instead. The man closest to me glares with bloodshot eyes. His face is spotted with second-degree burns. The bottle was the final kick to the beehive, and I'm standing before the swarm.

The equalist with the flag raises his charred arm and screams. "Freedom is bought with the blood of the beaten!" With that, the crowd charges.

They don't get far before the guard intervenes. The royal guards around the stage extend their arms in unison, forming a ten-foot wall of transparent energy. A second later, the mob collides with the energy shield. They beat their fist into the wall, sending ripples through the air. Others continue to hurl projectiles over the invisible barrier at the diplomats onstage.

One grungy man pours beer onto the base of the cremation tower and sets it ablaze. Another burning bottle collides with the guards' float engulfing it in yellow flames. Chaos erupts onstage as the city officials scramble for cover.

I stumble back and heave myself onto the stage. The farther I am from the mob, the better. From my vantage point, I can see across the entire plaza. Guards everywhere flee the clutch of the crowd. In the center of the mob, a lone guard on horseback frantically maneuvers his horse toward the perimeter. The laborers around him lunge at him like a hoard of hungry zombies. He clings desperately to the horse's neck as dozens of hands claw at his legs.

I cover my mouth. I can't believe what I'm seeing. Several equalists grab hold of the horseman's leg. They drag him off the horse's back, and the crowd swallows him whole. I can't hear him scream over the roar of the crowd.

At the back of the plaza, another horseman is ripped from the saddle and disappears into the sea of bodies. A laborer raises the guard's gun above his head like a trophy. He fires several shots into the air as the mob cheers him on.

Several gunshots ring out from the rooftops as guards take matters into their own hands.

"Stop! No lethal force! Hold the perimeter!" It's Antai's voice. I spin around and spot him on the palace wall behind me. He turns, and our eyes meet for just a second. Then, he disappears beyond the edge of the wall. *Where is he going? Why is he leaving me?*

Frantic screams pull my attention back to the crowd. The cremation tower is now a 30-foot pillar of fire. As the base of the tower is reduced to ashes, the tower starts to lean. The mob tries to run, but there are too many bodies. I watch as the flaming hay bales topple onto the crowd, scattering ashes and embers on the unlucky laborers. I hear their screams, but they're too far away to help this time.

I finally come to my senses. I search for an escape route but find none. The mob has formed a semi-circle around the stage. The only escape is to fight through the mob or climb over the palace wall to safety. Part of me wonders if I could use dominion to lift myself over the wall, but I'm afraid to try. I've never attempted something so complex before, especially not in the middle of a riot. If I somehow lost control, it would be a long fall from the top of the wall.

The mob continues to press against the energy shield. I can hear guards grunting from the effort. I know they can't maintain the shield for long. Using dominion is exhausting, especially a barrier of that size. But the guardsmen have no choice. It's the only thing protecting the city officials from a certain and violent death. And the mob isn't tiring. They use their bodies like a battering ram, charging the wall in a single wave and throwing themselves against it.

I flinch as someone grabs my arm. It's Octavian. He starts walking, tugging me towards the back of the stage. "We gotta move, princess. It's not safe here. Antai's almost here with the ladders."

Antai! I knew he would come back for me. I join the other officials by the wall. They crane their necks up the face of the wall, waiting for salvation. The group is frantic. Two women from the seamstress guild are hugging each other and sobbing. Meanwhile, a cluster of guards on the wall are shouting words of encouragement.

Finally, Antai reappears on the wall. He's carrying a long wooden ladder over his head. Two other ladders are being carried close behind. Antai stops on the portion of the wall above us and lowers the ladder to Octavian, who secures the base. Once stable, Antai clambers down the rungs.

"Everyone up as fast as you can," Antai demands. "Go, go, go!"

He doesn't need to ask twice. I've never seen officials move so fast in my life. Courtesy is tossed out the window. They push and shove to be first in line, scurrying up the ladder like their lives depend on it.

I turn my attention to Antai. His head is craned back as he orders the guardsmen on the wall. "Don't shoot unless absolutely necessary," Antai commands. "If they step foot on the stage, open fire. I repeat, defend the stage at all costs."

Antai fixes his eyes on me and pushes through the officials. I'm hoping for a hug, but he grips both my shoulders and scans me up and down. When he sees I'm fine, he finally pulls me into a tight embrace. It only lasts a moment.

"What are you doing, Rose? You should be on a ladder already. We need to get you out of here."

"Let them go first." I point to my amulet. "If anything happens, I'll have a better chance than them." I'm not a guardsman yet, but I've trained enough to take care of myself.

Antai glances at the edge of the stage. With each ram of the crowd, the mob inches a little closer to the stage. The soldiers are drenched in sweat and shaking from the strain.

"We don't have long, Rose. They won't last until everyone's over the wall. You need to get out of here."

I open my mouth to disagree. Out of nowhere, a brick crashes onto the stage between us, shattering into a hundred tiny shards. My body responds before I can stop it. I jump back, shrieking. If the brick had landed a few feet to either side, it could've killed one of us.

Antai hardly flinches. He grabs my hand and drags me towards the ladders. He shoves an official aside and guides me to the left-most ladder of the three.

"Go!" he commands. "Please, go!"

I obey. Antai holds the base of the ladder as I climb. I'm glad he does; the ladder wobbles and flexes with each step. I look down at Antai, who encourages me with one of his finest smiles. It's exactly what I need. I climb as fast as I can, placing one hand over the other. *Thank goodness I'm wearing flats.*

Hand over hand, I pull myself up the ladder. I'm only a few rungs from the top now. The guard above me outstretches his hand. I reach for it just as a bottle shatters on the wall to my left. I instinctively turn my back to the flames as I'm showered in a burning liquid. The pain is immediate. I scream as the fire gnaws at the skin on my left arm. On my back, I feel the warmth of the flames eating my dress. The world spins.

The next thing I know, I'm falling. I lose my grip on the rung, and I plummet towards the concrete stage. Flames from my dress billow around me. Fear and dread fill my chest. I squeeze my eyes and wait for my bones to break onstage. Instead, the air rushing past me grows thick, tugging at my clothes and hair. It almost feels like falling through water.

Then, I hit the floor.

I must have fallen thirty feet, but the impact only feels like five. The air whooshes from my lungs, and my head whips back against the concrete. It hurts, but not nearly as bad as the burns.

Antai is at my side in an instant. Whatever he did to slow down my fall has also extinguished my dress. But my skin still burns like acid. I curl into a ball on my right side and suck air into my lungs.

For the first time today, I see fear on Antai's face. His hands hover over my battered body, but he doesn't dare touch me. "Rose, are you alright?"

I'm certainly not, but I nod anyway. I don't trust my voice enough to speak.

Another beggar bomb shatters on the other side of the stage. It makes a puddle of yellow flame several feet wide.

Antai hardens his gaze. "I'm sorry, but we need to move now. If I put you on my back, do you think you can hold on?" I nod as tears stream down my cheeks. I just want the burning to stop.

Antai gingerly slides one arm underneath my armpit and lifts me onto his back. I wince as I wrap my arms around his neck and straddle his back. The world around me shimmers as Antai forms an energy shield to protect us. He's not taking any chances.

Without hesitation, Antai starts up the ladder. He climbs with one hand and uses the other to support me. I can feel his back muscles flexing with each rung. Before I know it, we're halfway to the top. Someone in the crowd shouts something, and in a matter of seconds, the debris is directed at us. A tin cup deflects off of the shield. A glass bottle shatters in the air above me. I press my face into Antai's neck. *Thank God for Antai.*

I peer down from Antai's back as the mob surges one last time. Without warning, the crowd bursts through the invisible barrier and buries the guardsmen in a stampede of bodies. A few lucky guards abandon the perimeter and dive onto the stage for safety.

The guards on the palace wall raise their weapons, and for a brief moment, the mob hesitates.

Why? Why are they doing this? Don't they know it's suicide? They have no weapons. *Why even try?*

A protester shouts at the top of his lungs. "Equality!!!" Then, they charge the stage.

I turn away as machine gun fire erupts from the wall above me. A moment later, Antai pulls us over the parapet, and I lose sight of the stage. Still, the machine gun fire echoes around me, and it doesn't stop.

In the end, I can only think of one explanation: *maybe they don't care if they die. Maybe, they prefer it.*

Chapter 5

Matt

I toss and turn under my favorite blanket. Strange memories churn inside my head, a thrashing river of pain and fear. The dreams are so vivid, I can almost hear the thunder. I can almost feel the stinging in my neck.

I reach up and rub my throat. The tiny spines of stitches prick my fingers like a cactus. My eyes flutter open, and I shove off the blanket. I'm lying in my bed in the same clothes as last night, except I'm dry and my boots are missing. The alarm clock on my nightstand reads 4:38 pm.

Shoot! A whole day has gone by. The last thing I remember is Lumberjack lying dead and Hood pulling me from the car. I certainly didn't walk here. Whoever saved me must've carried me home. They're likely still here.

I slide my hand beneath my shirt and clutch my necklace in my fist. Relief floods through me. I scan the room and find my dagger lying on my dresser by the closet. A cup of water rests on my night-stand. I drink it furiously. The lukewarm water washes away the fire in my throat. Half the water trickles down my neck as I try to drink lying down.

The cup is empty before I'm satisfied. Hunger claws at my stomach. I would give anything for some of Judy's homemade lasagna right now. I lay there in silence for a few moments listening for any sign of my savior.

Silence.

I run my fingers over the stitches again. They curve in a big U shape, matching the shape of dentures. Stitches also dot my arms, I'm guessing from the car crash. The glass cut me pretty good. Whoever stitched me up is probably a good guy. Aren't they? They left my knife on the dresser. They gave me water and tucked me in bed. I don't feel in danger. I'm in my own house after all.

I wish Judy were here—that she would turn the corner with my breakfast, and everything would be back to normal. But that would be a daydream even on a normal day.

Hunger finally forces me from bed. I prop myself up on my elbow just as a large burly man walks through the doorway. His head almost scrapes the doorframe. I freeze. So does the man. His caramel eyes look puzzled. They're buried in a nest of brown facial hair. He wears the same tan coat from the day before.

Lumberjack survived!

Lumberjack breaks the silence. "Don't move."

I don't even know if I can. My body aches as if I've just finished a marathon. Lumberjack steps out of the room and returns with a chair from the kitchen table. He carries another cup of water as well. I gratefully sip it while Lumberjack spins his chair backwards and sits facing me. His legs straddle the back of the chair like an oversized cowboy.

His voice is deep and airy. It thunders from his massive chest. "I'll bring in some food in a minute. I bet you're pretty hungry. But first, I need some answers."

I nod, afraid that if I speak, Lumberjack will turn from good cop to bad cop. I set the half-empty cup back on the nightstand. I think this is more of a half-empty moment than half-full.

"What's your name?" Lumberjack grunts.

I wince as I sit up and lean against the headboard. "Matt. What's yours?"

Lumberjack ignores me. His voice is monotone, almost emotionless. "What were you doing in the sanctuary?"

The sanctuary? "You mean that... place?" I don't know what to call it. A city? Ruins? "I just followed you in through the fence. I was out hunting, I swear. I've never gone through the fence before."

Lumberjack narrows his eyes. I worry he doesn't believe me.

"I left my ATV outside the castle. I swear. I can prove it to you." I ramble.

Lumberjack sits statue-still. He's good at this. I'm beyond intimidated. I can tell this isn't his first interrogation. I wonder what he does when he doesn't get answers.

Lumberjack points at me. "Where did you get those tattoos on your shoulder?"

I glance at my shoulder and shrug. "Honestly, I don't know. I've had them since I was a baby. I swear."

Lumberjack's eyes narrow even thinner. I can't blame him. My whole life sounds ridiculous. I wouldn't believe me either.

Lumberjack leans in closer. "Well, who gave them to you? Babies don't tattoo themselves." He never raises his voice or seems angry. Just cold.

I hate admitting it, especially to strangers, but today it's my alibi. "They left me on the doorstep, my parents, I mean. Or at least I think it was my parents. I don't even know who it was or who my parents are. Judy—she's my adoptive mom—she said I already had the tattoos when she found me."

His icy, lumberjack voice softens to a cold slush. "And the dagger?" Lumberjack nods his head towards the knife on the dresser.

"Was that with you the whole time too?" It's less of an accusation now and more of a question. I nod again, confused why any of this matters.

Lumberjack watches me with his beady brown eyes. I don't know what to do, so I stare back. "How long has it been since they left you?" He grumbles.

"18 years ago, yesterday. Why?"

Lumberjack doesn't speak for a long time. It can't be more than a minute, but it feels like forever.

"Can you at least tell me what's going on and why you're in my house?" I plead.

"Do you know anything about Adamic?"

I squint. "A damn what?"

Lumberjack cracks a smile and turns his chair around. Maybe he is a good cop after all.

"Adamic. You know, like Adam and Eve. The language of the gods. What's written on your shoulder and back."

My face lights up. I pull up my sleeve until my entire shoulder is exposed and point at the symbols.

"This is called Adamic?"

When lumberjack nods, I untuck my necklace from my shirt. "This too?"

"Two for two, keep it up." His flat tone makes it hard to tell if he's being sarcastic or genuine.

"What do they say?" I beg. These are the questions I've had my whole life. And all of a sudden, some stranger shows up with all the answers.

Lumberjack shrugs. "Nobody knows exactly. It's an extinct language. No one has spoken it for thousands of years, and only a handful of people know what they mean and how to write them." He pauses, as if debating on sharing a secret. "Your parents must have been very powerful people."

My interest is at a peak. I can't hold back the questions any longer. "Do you know what they do? The tattoos."

Lumberjack ignores my question. "None of this is going to make sense for a while. It's a lot to explain. I'll make you a deal. You tell me everything that happened to you yesterday, and then I'll answer any questions you have."

It's the easiest deal I've ever made. I eagerly begin with the elk. I mention Judy and the cancer and the hunting. I talk about the truck and the castle and the strange man with the tattoos. Everything. The more I say, the more outrageous everything seems. I start to doubt it all myself. Yet, here sits Lumberjack as evidence. He doesn't seem the least bit surprised by my story.

Occasionally, Lumberjack stops me and asks for extra details. Weird things like, "Did you hear thoughts that weren't your own?" and "Did your body ever feel out of your control?"

When I finally catch up to the present, Lumberjack simply grunts his approval. It's my turn to ask questions. I have so many I don't even know where to start. I ask the first thing that pops into my head. "How did you know where I live?"

Lumberjack points to my wallet on the nightstand. "Your wallet was in your pocket. I read your driver's license."

"Oh." I feel stupid for wasting one of my questions. I scoot forward in bed and swing my legs over the side. Immediately, the room begins to swim. Darkness creeps in at the edge of my vision. I reach for the headboard to stabilize myself.

"Take things slow," Lumberjack advises. "You had some of your soul drained by the feeder. It'll take a few days to feel back to normal."

"Ummm, what do you mean my soul was drained, and what's a feeder?"

Lumberjack sighs his annoyance. "This will take some explaining. Let's see. Well, me and you, we're Adamic—direct descendants of Adam. We have…" he pauses, searching for the right word, "dominion, or power, over the Earth. Elements, animals, you name it."

I raise my eyebrows and point to my necklace. "I'm Adamic, and this is Adamic?"

"It's like French; it's a language and a people."

When I nod, he continues. "The language is older than the Earth. It was used to command the elements, but no one has spoken it in thousands of years. Only the written language remains. We have amulets, like yours, that are written in Adamic. They allow us to exercise dominion without speaking."

I nod even though I'm lost. The more I learn, the more complicated things become.

Lumberjack speaks slowly, picking his words carefully. "Soul-feeders hunt the Adamic like me and you. Some call them the children of the devil. They feed off our dominion and use it to control the elements. The more they feed, the more powerful they become."

I feel the stitches again on my neck. "So a vampire did this? To suck my soul and use it to control the elements?" It sounds completely insane.

"I was a refugee like you when I was a kid," Lumberjack says. "I know it's a lot to take in. Just give it a few days, and it'll all make sense."

"And they can control the elements?" I almost feel embarrassed asking. The adult in me is skeptical, but the child is beyond excited. I always dreamt of flying as a kid. "What kind of things can they do?"

Lumberjack leans back in his chair and crosses his legs. "Depends on the person. Even with an amulet, most people can't do much. It takes years of training. I've seen telekinesis, matter manipulation, electric currents..."

My mind flashes to last night. "You mean the lightning… and the taser?

Lumberjack grins a toothy grin. "Hurts, doesn't it?"

I nod. "Does that mean you have an amulet too?

Lumberjack pulls out a silver amulet from the neck of his tan coat. It's a golf ball-sized sphere. The symbols encircle it, creating a continuous chain of Adamic. They're identical to the ones on my necklace:

I don't know what to think. Either this guy is crazy, or I'm crazy... *Or* it's all true. I don't know which I prefer. Part of me wants to ask for proof, but it seems so childish. I have stitches in my neck and a night of memories as proof.

Lumberjack gets bored of the silence. "I can show you if you like."

I sit up straighter, my imagination churning. "Yes, please."

Lumberjack grins like a child, which looks out of place in his thick, manly beard. He seems like a completely different person from his interrogator self. He picks up the water cup, sticks his hand inside, and tips it upside down.

No water hits the floor.

Lumberjack pulls off the cup, revealing a thick congealed liquid clinging to his hand. The water crawls up and around his fingers, paying no heed to gravity. Suddenly, with a crisp crackle, the water solidifies into a misty glass. An inch-thick glove of ice encases his hand.

Without delay, Lumberjack raises his hand above his head and swings it down. The roar of sizzling bacon fills the room as his hand leaves a cloud of steam in the air. He rests his dry hand back in his lap as the steam cloud disperses into nothingness.

A simple "wow" escapes my lips. I've never seen anything like it.

Lumberjack looks pleased with himself. "Maybe someday I can teach you."

Is that an offer? Could I really do that someday? I feel as ordinary as anyone, but the possibility seems too good to pass up. "I would like that." I point at Lumberjack's wrist. His sleeve partially covers a black tattoo. I noticed it earlier, but I've been too afraid to ask. "Is that Adamic too?"

Lumberjack pulls up his coat sleeve revealing two Adamic symbols.

"It's called an Adamic bond." Lumberjack explains. "It's like a key that allows me to use my Amulet. Only powerful Amulets have them. They're bonded so that only the owner can use them if they fall into the wrong hands. Every bond is unique. You have one too—on your shoulder.

I look at my shoulder with new understanding.

The tattoo is a key. That's why it matches the amulet so perfectly. "Does that mean mine is powerful too?" I ask.

Lumberjack smiles. "Like I said, your parents must have been very powerful people."

A new cloud of curiosity envelops me. "And the feeder. Why did he have them all over his face?"

"Not just his face," Lumberjack corrects. "His whole body. It's Adamic armor. Only an Adamic weapon can pierce it. And only a few of them still exist." He motions toward the dagger on the dresser. "You have quite the inheritance."

I sit open-mouthed as I try to digest what I just heard. "And the tattoo on my back? What does that one do?" I ask.

Lumberjack opens his mouth and closes it again. It's clear he doesn't want to discuss it. "That one's a little more complicated. I can't really tell you exactly what it does. I've only seen it a few times." He lets out a short sigh before he continues. "I've only seen them on devil-worshippers."

I'm stunned. *What does that even mean?* Is he suggesting my parents were…?

Lumberjack seems to read my mind. "I'm not saying anything about you or your parents; that's just what I've seen. But other people might get the wrong idea if they see your tattoo. You'll want to keep them covered. All of them." Lumberjack checks his watch. "More questions?"

I'm not satisfied with my previous answers, but I can tell Lumberjack wants to change the subject. "What's that sanctuary place we were at? The city at the power plant?"

Lumberjack holds back another smile. "There's no power plant, kid. That's just a lie we made up to keep out any wanderers. That place is Hogrum, or at least what's left of it."

When he sees my open-mouthed stare, he continues. "It was a sanctuary—a city protected by Adamic to keep out the feeders. There are sanctuaries all over the world. We have another in Washington state. Another in France. They're the only safe place for Adamics like ourselves."

I can't hold back my questions. "What happened to Hogrum?"

Lumberjack casts his eyes at the ground. When he looks up, they seem different. Sad, maybe even regretful. *He isn't emotionless after all.*

"Normally, Adamic spells are unbreakable," Lumberjack sighs. "No one knows how they broke down the walls. Feeders killed everyone and destroyed the city. It's been deserted for 18 years. There were only a few survivors."

I can't believe what I'm hearing. If my parents took me to Judy's, maybe they made it out alive. But if they survived, why didn't they come back for me? My hopes hover in limbo between hopeful and hopeless. I try to push the image of my dying parents out of my head. *Or maybe they were the ones attacking?* I like that idea even less.

Finally, I ask what's been on my mind since I woke up. "So ummm, who are you?"

Lumberjack grins through his beard. "I'm Zane. I'm the guardian over immigration."

I only need to raise an eyebrow to ask Zane to translate.

"Guardians are what they sound like: guardians of the sanctuaries. We have the strongest amulets, and we're the highest-ranking members of the guard. It's like the police force. I'm in charge of bringing supplies and refugees back to Cavernum—that's the other sanctuary in Washington."

I think for a moment. One thing still puzzles me. "So, if Hogrum is deserted, why were you going back?"

I see his eyes droop again. I wish I didn't ask. The room becomes cold and awkward.

"I'd rather not talk about it," Zane mumbles. "You're just lucky I found you when I did."

I hope I'm not pushing my luck, but my curiosity compels me. "How did you know where to find me, anyway?"

"I heard a gunshot and went to investigate. I saw you getting dragged by the feeder. To be honest, I thought you were dead. I've never seen anyone survive a feeding."

"What happened to the feeder?"

"He got away. But you did a number on him first. His blood was all over your blade. You probably saved both our lives."

"And these feeders, where do they come from."

Lumberjack groans. "That is a long story, a story I don't have time for." He glances at his watch. "I know you have lots of questions, but this will all be explained to you in Cavernum. My plane leaves in a few hours for Seattle. From there, it's only a few hours to the sanctuary. If you want, you can come with me. They'll be other refugees like you. You'll learn all about your heritage. I can give you some time to think about it, but I need to know soon if you're coming."

My gut twists. It's the same feeling that haunts me every day. The feeling of being trapped with nowhere to go. "Thanks, but I can't. I have to take care of Judy. I'm the only one she has." Still, I can't lose this opportunity. If I'm being honest with myself, I don't know how much longer Judy will last. "If I choose not to go today, can I still come in a few months?"

Zane sits in silence a few more moments. "What if I agreed to cover the medical costs? Then, would you be interested?"

"Wait? Are you serious?" I can't believe it. For years, it's been the sole cause of so much stress, and all of a sudden, some stranger offers to pay for everything. I think back to his beat-up truck. "Can you even afford that?"

"Trust me. Money isn't a concern." He picks up a quarter from my desk and palms it in his fist. When he opens his hand, the quarter gleams solid gold.

Amazing!

Zane already knows he's won. He stands up from his chair and strides for the door. "I'll bring in some food now. You think about it."

Zane leaves me alone as I eat the Mac n cheese he made. Despite my hunger, I don't pay much attention to the food. Nervous snakes slither around in my stomach. Judy has been running through my mind the whole meal. Will anyone visit her if I leave? How will she take the news? What will I even tell her? I know I'll have to lie. I've done it so much; why should it be a big deal now?

But what if I don't go? Will I be able to pay the bills on my own? Will I ever find Zane again? Will another feeder find me? That last thought makes me shiver. And then there's the possibility of learning to use my amulet.

I ask myself the questions.

Will I regret it if I go?... No. It will be hard, but I won't regret it. More than anything, we need the money.

Will I regret it if I stay?...... Yes. Definitely yes. I'll never get answers. I need to know where I come from and who I am.

My mind is made up, but that doesn't make leaving any easier. I still have to break the news to Judy. That will be more painful than anything from last night. Zane tells me what to bring, and I pack my bags. The hospital will be our last stop before the airport.

It's time to say goodbye to my best friend.

I wear a sweatshirt to cover up the stitches on my arms and neck. I don't want to have to explain those to Judy. I've been rehearsing my lie the entire ride to the hospital. It has gaps, but I can't think of any other way. I don't have time to tell the truth. We have to be at the airport in 30 minutes.

I twist the stainless steel handle and creak the door open just wide enough to slip through. Judy is asleep on the hospital bed under a thin blanket. She breathes so softly. The rise of her chest is barely visible. I never want to wake her when she's like this. The pain can't reach her in her dreams.

I pull up a chair until my knees touch the hospital bed. I poke Judy on the shoulder. She stirs but doesn't wake. I poke her again. Her eyes stay shut.

"Can't you see I need my beauty sleep, Matt? I've got a long way to go if I want to impress one of those doctors." She opens her eyes and sits up.

I smile, but I can't bring myself to laugh. I dread this more than anything. "Hey, Mom." I don't know what else to say. All I can think about is the lie that's been maturing in my head. And the painful truth that I'm leaving. My smile droops back toward the floor. I start to lose my resolve. *Maybe I should stay after all.*

Judy toggles with a remote, and her bed slowly lifts her to a seated position. She takes one look at my solemn face and matches it with her own. "What's wrong, Matt? Everything okay?"

"No… well, I don't know. I have to tell you something."

Judy is now as worried as I am. "Of course, dear. You can tell me anything."

I swallow. "I… I got accepted for a scholarship."

Judy's eyes light up. Her wrinkled face stretches into a massive smile. "Matt, that's wonderful! That's so great. Is it for CSU?"

I shake my head. "It's in Australia, and the program starts in two days. If I accept, I'll have to leave tonight."

Judy is shocked. She sits back in her chair and bows her head.

I hate seeing her like this. "I don't have to go if you don't want me to. I can stay."

Judy looks up. She's actually smiling. "Do you have to pay for anything? Do you need money?"

"No. It's all-expense paid," I assure her. "It even comes with a stipend that should be enough to cover your medical bills."

Judy's eyebrows shoot to the sky. "Oh, wow! That's too good to be true."

For a second, I think she's onto me, but then she beams at me like never before. I haven't seen her smile like this in months. "This is wonderful, Matt. Oh, I'm so excited for you. It's perfect. You're going to be the best researcher they've ever seen. You're going to help so many people. You already make me so proud."

I'm both relieved and puzzled. I wouldn't exactly call it 'perfect.' "You're really okay with it, mom? I won't see you for at least a few months. Are you sure you don't want me to stay?"

"Of course I'm okay with it. I'm going to miss you like crazy, but I'll be so much happier with you studying in Australia than wasting your life away in the woods."

I nod. I figured she would say that, but it still doesn't make leaving any easier. I check my watch. I don't have much time. "Mom, someone's outside to take me to the airport at seven. I have to leave in ten minutes."

Judy doesn't seem upset in the slightest. She extends her arms, and I hug her as tightly as her frail body can take. She clasps her hands over my ears and kisses me on each cheek. "Oh, Matthew, you're everything I ever dreamed of and more. Have I ever told you why I named you Matthew?"

"I always thought you named me after the doormat."

We both laugh. It feels good to share one last happy moment together. I'm going to miss this so much. Tears push at the back of my eyes. I can't let myself cry if Judy isn't even crying. Moms are supposed to be the emotional ones.

Judy takes me by the hand. "Matthew means 'gift from God.' Dave and I prayed for years for a child. When we found out I couldn't have kids, we were devastated, but I still didn't give up. I prayed and prayed for a miracle. We thought about adopting but could never afford it. 20 years I prayed. When Dave died, I completely gave up. I was so mad, Matthew. I was mad at myself, and I was mad at God. He never gave me a baby, and he took my husband away from me. And then, out of the blue, you show up on my doorstep, this beautiful little baby—a gift from God. Being your mother has been the greatest gift God has ever given me."

I don't say anything. What if this is the last time I ever speak to her? A single tear hangs on my lashes.

Judy squeezes my hand with all the strength of a dying woman.

"I've always wanted to give you the world, Matt. I know I haven't been able to do that. I've worried for weeks and weeks about you, praying you'd get the scholarship. I would be devastated if you gave up your dreams to stay with me. This is an answer to my prayers, Matt. I want you to go. All I ask is that you call me as much as you can and tell me everything."

Zane told me there are no phones in the city, but I'll find a way. "About that, Mom… the research facility is in the desert, and they say I won't have service while I'm there. But I'll call as much as I can. I promise."

I don't want to leave. I want to tell her everything, but I'm out of time. "Thank you so much, Mom, for everything. I'll be back before you know it." I lie. "When I get back, I want to see you doing push-ups."

We hug one last time, and after a simple "I love you", I walk out the door. I turn back and Judy waves through the hospital room window.

As much as it hurts, it went much smoother than I anticipated. The fact that Judy is happy for me makes it so much easier. My heart swells with gratitude just thinking about her.

I'm not sure if God exists, but I've been praying for a miracle too: that Judy will recover. Maybe Zane is an answer to my prayers after all. If he can shoot lightning from his hands, why not cure cancer.

I promise myself I'll find a way.

Chapter 6

Rose

When I finally awake, sunlight gleams through the seams of my drapes. By the looks of it, it's early morning. I'm wrapped in a cocoon of silk sheets. I claw my way out and dangle my feet off the edge of the bed.

I'm no longer wearing my maroon dress. I'm in a silk nightgown. The soft fabric swoops low on my chest and falls down to my knees. I look at my arm. White bandages spiral from my shoulder to my wrist. *So, it wasn't a nightmare after all.*

The events from yesterday feel like a hazy dream. The speech, the riot, the burn. The last thing I remember is Antai carrying me to the healing loft. I must have fallen asleep before the healing was complete.

Frustration burns within me. I should be out training, but instead, I'm lying in bed like a cripple. I only have three days until The Dividing. I can't waste a moment.

Tap. Tap. Tap. The knock is so quiet I can barely hear it. "Come in Nevela, I'm awake," I call out.

Nevela eases the door open and slips inside. She smiles when she sees me sitting up. "Morning, princess. You look well-rested. How do you feel?"

"Good, I guess." I stand up and bend my arm. No pain. I spread my fingers and curl them into a fist. The skin feels tight, but still no pain.

Nevela watches me anxiously. "Does it hurt?"

"Not really. It's a little tender, but it's bearable." I peel the bandage off my wrist. Fresh pink skin peeks back at me. It's missing my normal almond complexion, but I'm relieved. The healers did an incredible job.

"Madame Santone said she wants you back again tonight for more treatment," Nevela informs me. "She said it'll help with the scarring."

"Did they say if I'll be healthy for The Dividing?"

"I think so. She said you'll make a complete recovery." Nevela leans a little closer. A wide grin spreads between her cheeks. She glances at the bedchamber door before whispering. "Are you still thinking about joining the guard? That would be so brave after everything that's happened."

I try to keep the frustration from my face. "I don't know. Maybe… probably. It just depends."

Nevela opens her mouth to respond, but I cut her off. "I don't really want to talk about it right now."

"Oh, okay." Her smile disappears, but she doesn't take offense. She skips to the door. "You must be starving. I have breakfast waiting for you in the kitchen. I'll go fetch it. Be back in a jiff."

"Wait," I stop her just as she's reaching for the door. "Is everyone okay? Did any officials get hurt at the riot?"

"Everyone's fine. A few officials were injured, but none died."

"What about Antai?" I ask. "He's alright?"

Her girly grin returns. She gives me a teasing smile. "Antai's perfectly fine. He's already come to check on you twice today."

"Where is he now?" I ask.

"He's in a meeting with the guardians. They should be done any minute."

The guardians? Relief pours through me. That means Grandpa is back from the beyond. That means he's safe.

Every time he leaves on a trip, I worry he won't return. The beyond is a dangerous place. I know my Grandpa can handle himself, but no one is invincible. Not even a guardian.

Nevela takes my silence as permission to leave. "Be right back, princess." She opens the door.

An old man is standing in the doorway, his fragile frame bent over a wooden cane for support. His long gray hair is pulled into a ponytail with the help of several copper bands. Wrinkles clutter his face like old tree bark, weathered from years of survival. A beautiful black and gold robe hangs from his bony shoulders. It's embellished with layers of intricate stitch work to please the eye. Most stunning of all, an ornate bronze amulet hangs around his neck.

He's the most powerful man I know.

Nevela falls to her knees and bows her head. "Your majesty. I wasn't expecting you."

Grandpa waves his hand in the air. His gentle voice is deep and syrupy. "Good morning, Nevela. Please excuse us for a moment."

Nevela bows and scurries down the hall. Grandpa shuts the door behind her, and I run into his arms. He squeezes me astoundingly tight for such an old man. He speaks into my shoulder as we hug. "Antai told me what happened. I'm sorry I wasn't there for you." As he stands, he adjusts the crown upon his head. Its solid gold frame is inlaid with precious jewels. I've never seen him without it.

"It's alright," I breathe. "I know you don't leave because you want to. Besides, Antai kept me safe." The very fact that he asked Nevela to leave tells me he has something serious to say. "How was Lycon? Is everything alright?"

"I'll have to tell you about it later," Grandpa says. "The high council has called an emergency meeting to discuss the riot. They want you to join us."

"Me?" I'm shocked. Not even Antai attends the high council meetings. Other than being princess, I don't hold any official titles. I have no reason to attend.

"You're of age now," Grandpa reasons. "You won't have a vote yet, but I recommended that you come and observe the meeting. It won't be long before you preside over the council. Your father did the same when he was your age."

I don't know if I'm ready to face the high council. It was my speech that sent the crowd into a frenzy. *What do I have to contribute?*

Grandpa senses my hesitation. His expression softens, and all I see are his unblinking brown eyes. I feel his expectations dissolve. "If you prefer, Rose, you can pass on this one. I'll tell them you still don't feel well. They'll understand."

No. Deep down, this is what I want. I swallow my doubts and straighten my shoulders. "I'll go. When's the meeting?"

"Get dressed quickly," Grandpa replies. "It starts in ten minutes."

The high council meeting is located in the uppermost room of the eastern tower. By the time we arrive, we're already several minutes late. Two guardsmen stand outside the rustic oak door. They both drop to one knee as we approach from the stairwell.

"Rise," Grandpa commands. "Is everyone accounted for?"

The guard on the left replies. "Yes, your majesty. They're ready to begin."

"Excellent." Grandpa gives me one of his fatherly smiles as the guards push open the door.

Conversation inside the room falls silent, and everyone jumps to their feet—a sign of respect for the king. The diplomats stand at attention around a rectangular, marble table. At the head of the table is Grandpa's seat. It's a granite throne adorned with streaks of gold and precious jewels. On one wall of the room is an intricate map of the city. The other side is a glass wall with a grand view of the western quadrant.

Grandpa lowers himself onto the throne and signals for the other diplomats to take their seats. I sit in the empty chair to his left and search for friendly faces. No one is smiling.

Including my own, I count 11 chairs around the table. Four are for guardians, six are for diplomats, and one for myself. Strangely, one of the chairs is empty. Then, I remember: Zane is out with the convoy.

I recognize several of the council members. Chancellor Gwenevere sits across the table with her face pulled into an angry scowl. Her ear is covered in a white bandage. To my left, small red scabs dot Chancellor Quine's face—from glass shards, no doubt. Apparently, I wasn't the only one injured during the riot.

Grandpa addresses the council with a courteous nod. "Thank you all for coming on such short notice. I'm glad to see everyone is safe and able to attend. Zane won't be able to join us today. He's still with the convoy in the beyond. Hence, five votes will become our new majority. Any questions before we begin?"

Silence.

Grandpa gestures towards the back of the table. "Excellent. General Kaynes, would you mind reporting for the guard?"

"Of course, my king." General Kaynes stands and crosses his arms behind his back. He's wearing a long black robe embroidered with the silver zigzags of Adamic armor. He has a face like a dagger, with sharp cheekbones and a pointy nose. His dark robe contrasts with his pale, blonde hair. It's pulled into a small bun on the top of his head.

General Kaynes holds his head high and dignified. "I'm sure you are all painfully aware of the riot yesterday." He exaggerates a glance at Chancellor Gwenevere, and I suppress a laugh. "Fortunately, the guard managed to protect all of the officials onstage. However, three guardsmen were killed, and another three were critically injured. We have six men in custody who are ready to stand trial."

"How many civilian casualties?" Grandpa asks.

"18, your highness. Almost all of them were equalist protesters. Another 30 or so were injured."

Grandpa nods.

"It should be noted," General Kaynes continues, "that there was an attack the night before the riot. Several guardsmen were slaughtered, and their uniforms and weapons were stolen. Our original suspicion was that the princess would be the primary target.

All eyes fall on me. I wish I could melt into my chair and disappear through the cracks in the floor.

Kaynes raises his index finger in the air. "However, we were very wrong. The parade was only a distraction. While our guards were focused on the riot, equalists attacked the southern guard tower and looted the armory. They killed six of our men. Fortunately, most of our weapons were distributed for the parade, but our losses were still significant. They stole 19 pistols and 11 assault rifles. They also took all of the uniforms and amulets: 15 each." General Kaynes reports everything very factually. He doesn't seem embarrassed or apologetic. I wish I could be more confident like him.

Chancellor Gwenevere huffs her disgust. She has a wiry frame and bird-like features. Her beak nose is too big for her face, and her eyes are sunken and hollow. She speaks in a shrill, demanding tone. "How is it that your men can't handle a band of unskilled laborers?"

"Chancellor, please try not to offend the dead." General Kaynes chastises her like a child. "My men were shot in the head. Some were burned. These were not your average protesters. They were armed and trained in dominion."

Tension grows in the council room, but Chancellor Gwenevere doesn't back down. "Do you have any leads?"

"One of my captains pursued them to the sewer tunnels. They escaped inside."

The sewer tunnels? In Cavernum, the sewer is built into an underground cave system. Raw sewage flows underneath the city and out of the sanctuary. But I understand the implications. The sewer connects to a much larger tunnel system—a labyrinth of unexplored caverns.

"And where are they now?" Chancellor Gwenevere demands.

General Kaynes shrugs his shoulders. "Still down there, I presume. Laborers are the only ones who work the sewer. They know the tunnels better than anyone. It makes sense that the equalists would take refuge underground. We're going to find them, but it'll take some time."

"Hiding like rats!" another diplomat chimes. "Typical!"

Chancellor Gwenevere huffs her disgust once more. "Well, perhaps if you guardians actually guarded the city like you're supposed to, these things wouldn't happen. What business did you have in the beyond anyway?"

Grandpa lifts his cane and cracks the tip of it against the stone floor. "Enough! We didn't come to watch you two bicker. This should be a discussion, not an interrogation."

Chancellor Gwenevere turns her head to the window and falls silent. General Kaynes finally takes his seat. I can tell grandpa is frustrated. His jaw protrudes slightly, pushing his lips tight together. He exhales loudly. "We are a council. So please, let's council for once. The equalists are becoming a serious threat. For the first time, they're making offensive attacks against us. What should we do about it? Any ideas?"

For a moment, no one speaks.

Chancellor Quine raises his hand. He is an average-sized man with thin almond eyes and a big mouth. Other than his receding hairline, he seems fit and young. I've known him since I was a kid. He has a daughter my age. I used to play with her when I was a little girl. It's weird to think that I'll be his queen someday.

"Yes, Chancellor Quine?" Grandpa asks.

He clears his throat. "Perhaps we are giving them too much freedom. If they don't have holidays or celebrations, they won't have time to plan attacks and cause riots." A few council members nod their agreement.

Grandpa looks appalled. "Isn't that the very reason they're rioting in the first place? The more we take from them, the more desperate they'll become.

A sinister smile appears on General Kaynes' face. "What if we turn them against each other? We offer 500 bars to anyone who can give valuable information regarding the equalists. Names, locations, whatever it may be. The laborers are desperate enough to testify for money. They'll get their bars, and we'll get the equalists. Win-win." Heads bob around the table.

Chancellor Gwenevere scrunches her beak-like nose. "It's not that simple. What if they feed us false information? They could lead us in circles or set up an ambush."

"We'll only give payment after a tip proves useful," General Kaynes explains. "And if a tip proves false, they'll get lashings. That should deter lying." More nods of agreement.

Chubby Chancellor Bolo sits on the far end of the tables. He raises his hand. "Won't the laborers be afraid to snitch? Should we try to provide a way to give anonymous tips?"

Chancellor Quine shakes his head. "If it's anonymous, we'll have no way of punishing a false tip. Like General Kaynes said, we need accountability to deter lying." He swivels his head as he speaks, addressing the entire council. "As long as we pay them enough, laborers will come forward. Money is a strong motivator."

"Excellent," Grandpa announces. "If anyone else has any concerns or questions, please speak now."

Silence.

"We'll continue with a vote. All in favor, please indicate." Around the room, council members raise their right arm to the square. Immediately, I can see it's a majority.

"Any opposed?" Grandpa asks.

Chancellor Gwenevere is the only one who raises her arm. She doesn't seem to mind playing devil's advocate.

"Eight to one. Very well then. We'll announce the new policy immediately," Grandpa declares. "Any other ideas before we commence with the trial?"

Chancellor Gwenevere shoots me a quick glare. "Are we still moving forward with the princess's proposal? We all saw how the laborers reacted. Why do it if the laborers don't want it?"

I'm speechless. I didn't think I'd become a topic of debate. I don't know what to do except look at my grandpa for support.

General Kaynes speaks first. "Don't be dense, Chancellor. Those men had their minds made up from the beginning. They would have complained if the princess offered them free room and board. If you go out and talk to the youth in the ring, you'll get a completely different response, I promise you."

General Kaynes glances my way and flashes me a quick smile. Relief washes through me. It feels good to be defended. Maybe my speech wasn't so bad after all.

"I agree with the princess," says an unusually deep voice to my right. It's General Katu. His skin is the darkest shade I've ever seen —beautiful, deep ebony. His ivory eyes and teeth seem to glow neon white. He's small for a guardian. But he's lightning fast.

"We need more men for the convoy." General Katu argues. "Zane loses more men than he can replace. The feeders are gaining numbers. They are working together. We must gain numbers too."

Chancellor Gwenevere rolls her eyes. "You've handled the feeders in the past. Why are they suddenly such a problem?"

I know she's getting on Grandpa's nerves. Every time she talks, his hands squeeze around his cane. He's sitting on the edge of his throne. "Chancellor Gwenevere," Grandpa speaks with a voice like gravel. His impatience is hidden under a mask of formality. "Considering that you've never in your life laid eyes on a feeder, let me explain a little about them. Normally, they behave like any other predator. They hunt the weak. They look for the injured or the young—the elderly, children, babies."

At the word 'babies,' Gwenevere flinches, yet she maintains eye contact with Grandpa in some sort of prideful power struggle.

"Unless they're desperate, a feeder seldom attacks a guardsmen. They avoid a fight if they can, and they always hunt alone." Grandpa explains. "However, in the last few months, something's changed. They're working together now. Hunting in large numbers. Organizing attacks. Just this past month, a pack of them ambushed one of our trucks. We lost an entire team of guardsmen in one day. In the last few months, we've lost more men than the last few years combined."

Chancellor Bolo looks doubtful. He rubs his chin as if he is scrubbing a potato. "Your excellency, I want to make sure I heard you right. You're saying those savage man-eaters are strategizing against us? That they're working as a team?"

"It shouldn't be that surprising," General Kaynes scoffs. "They invaded Hogrum in one unified attack. What makes us think they can't do it again?"

Grandpa nods. "We fear someone might be leading them. Bribing them or manipulating them somehow. We're hoping if we can cut off the head of the snake, the feeders will return to their normal activity." Grandpa points his face at Gwenevere. "If you must know, that is why we left the sanctuary this last week. We were following a lead in Lycon regarding feeder activity."

Chancellor Gwenevere opens her mouth to retaliate but closes it again. She can't think of a comeback. I fight to keep my lips from pulling into a smile.

Grandpa leans back in his chair. "My hope isn't to worry you all about your safety. I simply wish to express the complexity of our task as guardians. We have as many problems outside the sanctuary as we do inside. Maybe more. Now, let's return to the previous concern: the convoy."

After a short silence, Chancellor Quine raises his hand again. "Might I remind everyone that we ran out of antibiotics last month. My daughter had a fever for three days. If it wasn't for the healers, she would've died. I agree with the princess; we need more supplies."

"We almost ran out of ammunition as well," Katu adds.

"Then why do we keep bringing in refugees?" Gwenevere demands. "We could bring an extra truck full of supplies instead."

Grandpa grips his cane with white knuckles. "That is not a topic of debate." His voice is laced with warning. I don't blame him. His wife was a refugee, as was my mother. Grandpa has always had a soft spot for refugees. His emotions may cloud his judgment, but I would do the same in his shoes.

"Any last suggestions about the equalists?" Grandpa changes the subject, his voice returning to its normal, calm tone.

General Kaynes catches my eye. He's smiling at me from across the room. "I would love to hear what the princess thinks. She's already had such good ideas."

All eyes turn on me. I'm a cornered animal with nowhere to run. I look at Grandpa. He encourages me with a nod. "You may speak, Roselyn."

I try to think of an easy way out, but nothing comes to mind. I swallow hard. I've thought a lot about this, but only as a personal reflection. I don't know if I'm supposed to, but I stand, trying to look as dignified as possible. I open my mouth and words tumble out.

"The equalists are gaining numbers and weapons, but they're still only a fraction of the laborers. Lots of laborers still think violence is radical. We have to use that to our advantage."

The more I speak, the quicker the words fall from my lips. "If we retaliate now, we'll only push more laborers to join the equalists. However, if we reach out to the laborers and show them that we're on their side, they might question their cause. With a few simple compromises, we just might avoid a war."

"And what would you propose?" Chancellor Gwenevere sneers.

I'm secretly glad she asked. The idea has been floating through my mind all day. "Lots of people were injured during the riot, some were supporters of the equalists, but not all. Some were just innocent bystanders caught in the crossfire. I suggest we temporarily open the palace infirmary to treat their injuries. Then, instead of being the enemy, we become the hero. And the very people trying to kill will realize we're on the same team."

Chancellor Quine laughs a maniacal cackle. "You want to invite those savages into the palace, the very place we're trying to defend."

"Hear me out," I plea to the council. I know I won't get another chance like this for a long time. "I think it would be virtually risk-free. What if we check them for weapons at the palace wall and keep guards in the infirmary? There won't be enough laborers to cause any trouble, and we'll send them straight home after treatment. If we don't reach out to them first, the riots won't stop. They'll only get worse."

Katu stares at me thoughtfully before addressing the council. "I'm with the princess. They won't trust us until we trust them first."

Chancellor Gwenevere rolls her eyes. "This is ludicrous. When the enemy is weak, it's time to deliver the final blow, not invite them in and tend to their wounds."

General Katu shakes his head in frustration. "Why fight an enemy when you can make a friend instead?"

Chancellor Bolo slams his fist on the table. "Not a chance! I don't want those brutes anywhere near me. No picker is a friend of mine."

"I say we vote on it," General Kaynes suggests.

Grandpa sits a little straighter, surprised by the sudden turn of the discussion. He raises his hand. "All in favor, please manifest."

To my surprise, hands rise around the room. I count 6. I can't believe it. In an instant, my idea is approved. It's actually approved.

"Any opposed?"

Gwenevere, Quine, and Chancellor Bolo raise their hands in defeat.

A thin smile creeps on Grandpa's face. It's subtle, but he can't hide his amusement. "It's official. I'll inform the medics, and we'll announce it in the ring immediately."

Grandpa sweeps his gaze around the room. "Any last concerns that need to go before the council before we proceed."

No one speaks.

"Excellent. General Kaynes, we're ready for the prisoners."

General Kaynes nods and quietly leaves the room. After a brief silence, he returns. A moment later, two guardsmen enter the room escorting a line of six prisoners in chains. The prisoners are all men, ages 25 to 50. They're still wearing the same clothes from the riot. Blood spatters each of them from head to toe. I can't tell if it's their own blood or someone else's.

General Kaynes lines up the prisoners in front of the city map. They seem miserable. Exhaustion is painted on their blood-stained faces. One prisoner's eyes find mine. I almost don't recognize him. It's the man who held the flag during the riot. The one who interrupted my speech. Now, his eyes are hollow. Passion is replaced with hopelessness. In some weird way, I feel sorry for him. I push the pity out of my head. *He deserves this! He almost killed me!*

General Kaynes returns to his seat, and one of the guards steps forward. He begins by pointing to each prisoner and stating his name. Most are refugee names I'm not familiar with, like Bill and Steven. There are too many to remember.

The guard pulls out a small sheet of paper and reads it aloud. "These prisoners are charged with the following crimes: noncompliance, inciting a riot, assault and battery of government officials, attempted murder of government officials, and murder of guardsmen Taiku Lorain, Joto Kans, and Pocheni Toz. Each of the prisoners was caught and detained in the very act. The proposed punishment is death by hanging."

The guard tucks the paper into his uniform and steps back against the wall. "The prisoners may now present their case." They must be too poor to provide a lawyer. I'm not surprised. Lawyers aren't cheap, especially for a case this big.

I wait for a prisoner to plead his innocence, but no one speaks. No witnesses testify. No questions are asked. They simply stare in silent rage at the council. *Why are they giving up?* I don't understand it. Finally, after a long pause, the equalist who held the flag mutters, "Burn in hell."

"Very well." Grandpa frowns his disappointment. He turns to the council. "Any final concerns before we vote?"

A few heads shake from side to side. The room remains silent. "All right then." Grandpa's voice is stale, devoid of its usual vigor. "All in favor?"

In unison, 9 hands float into the air.

Grandpa sighs. "It's unanimous. We'll hold the execution in two days." I can tell he doesn't enjoy this. If anything, he loathes it. "Who would like to direct the ceremony?" It's tradition that a council member leads the execution ceremony and reports the final verdict.

No one volunteers. I can understand why. It sounds like a terrible job.

Chancellor Gwenevere gives me an eerie smile. "Perhaps the princess would like to direct the ceremony. If she can attend a council meeting, why not an execution?"

Grandpa narrows his eyes at Chancellor Gwenevere. "I don't think that's fitting, Chancellor. She's barely of age."

General Kaynes drums his fingers on the edge of the table. "Your majesty, perhaps the chancellor has a point. The entire sanctuary saw the princess fall from the wall. There are rumors in the ring. Some say she died from the fall—that the equalists killed the princess. They view it as a victory. Perhaps it would be strategic to have her direct, to put an end to the rumors."

The thought makes me sick. I've only witnessed a few executions, and always from a distance. I won't last up close. I can't be the one to announce the verdict. I can't.

Yet if I ever become a guardian, this will be my life. Arresting criminals. Punishing them. Enacting justice. *How will I ever become a guardian if I can't direct an execution?*

Grandpa shakes his head. "I see your point, but I just don't think that would be appropriate."

"I'll do it!" I blurt the words before I can change my mind.

Grandpa's eyes double in size. Whether with surprise or concern, I'm not sure. I meet his gaze with the bravest face I can muster. Eventually, he nods to himself. "Anyone opposed?" Grandpa asks.

No one raises their hand.

"Very well," With the help of his cane, Grandpa lifts himself to his feet. "It's settled. Roselyn will direct the execution in two days. Council dismissed."

My hand hovers above the gold foil. This is my third time attempting to write the Adamic spell. It's a simple lantern spell, but I'm not having success.

Grandpa sits next to me in an old oak chair. He watches over my shoulder and analyzes my every move. "Remember, Rose, the creation of the symbols matters as much as the final product. Remember the order," he nags.

"I know. I know." He's told me a thousand times. If I don't draw each symbol in the correct order, in the correct way, they won't have a binding effect. In English, you can write a word infinite ways as long as it looks the same. But Adamic is different. Each line of each symbol has a specific direction and order and speed and style. It's frustrating, to say the least. A single error can ruin the entire spell.

For centuries, scholars have been trying to imitate the Adamic spells without success. Even though they can replicate the appearance of Adamic, the symbols don't form binding spells like they're designed to. But Grandpa is an adalit—one of only a handful on Earth who is literate in Adamic. Even though he can't pronounce the words, he can understand the meaning of most symbols and form his own written spells. And the best part is, he's teaching me everything he knows.

I've already finished the sun—the symbol for light. Now, I'm etching the looping symbol of eternity, careful not to lift my chisel. There are no distractions as I work. We're inside Grandpa's personal library. It's the only place he's willing to discuss Adamic. It's filled with his personal collection of Adamic books and symbols. He doesn't allow anyone entrance except me, and only during our lessons.

When I finally finish, I hold up my foil.

I squint my eyes. The symbols should be glowing, but I don't see any light. It's supposed to create an eternal lantern. The dungeon is full of these symbols, illuminating the underground tunnels. I jump up from my chair and pull the drapes shut, plunging us into darkness. The foil still doesn't glow.

"Ugh! What am I doing wrong?" I groan as I pull open the drapes.

Grandpa smiles at me from his chair. He squints at the symbols in puzzled amusement. "You're getting close. That time I didn't see any obvious errors. I'm sure you'll get it soon enough. It just takes practice. It took your father months before he completed his first spell."

Frustration clouds my mind. I've already been trying that spell for almost three months. I'm just wasting my time while I still have so much to figure out before The Dividing.

I slump back into my chair. "Can we take a break, please?"

"Of course." Grandpa gives me a sympathetic look. "Worried about the dividing?"

I haven't told him yet that I want to join the guard. If I do join, I'll be demoted to a commoner. I'll go to training in the core. I won't return to the palace unless I get promoted to an officer and become an elite again. Not to mention the danger. I won't be able to have my guards with me 24/7. All of my worries press on the inside of my chest, making me feel ill.

I shrug. I still don't really want to talk about it. The last thing I want is an argument with Grandpa.

"Rose?" Grandpa gives me a stern 'spit it out' kind of look.

"Really, it's nothing," I assure him. "Don't worry about it."

"Okay. We don't have to talk about it." Grandpa folds his arms across his chest and scans his eyes over my body. "Your arm looks a lot better." He comments. "I can't even see the scars. It shouldn't give you any trouble for your orchestra tryout on Friday… or competing for the guard."

My head snaps up. "Who told you?" It must have been Antai. He tells my grandpa everything.

Grandpa chuckles to himself. "Octavian told me you've been sneaking out every morning to go shooting. I figured it wasn't for orchestra practice. I just wish you would've told me sooner."

"Why? So you could talk me out of it?" My voice is more bitter than I intended.

Grandpa looks appalled by the thought. He shakes his head slowly. "I don't want to stop you, Rose. I want to help you. When I was your age, my father wanted me to become a lawyer in the lower courts. He thought it would prepare me better for kingship. But I wanted to join the guard. I would've never been happy cooped inside the palace all day. Now that I'm old and I look back, I'm so glad I didn't listen to him." He sighs. "I only wanted you to join the orchestra because I thought it was your dream."

"It still is my dream," I say. "I love the orchestra, but I want to make more of a difference than beautiful music. I want them both."

"I wish there was a way," Grandpa sympathizes. "But you can't have your cake and eat it too."

"Ugh, I can't decide. What do you think I should do?" More than anything, I want someone else to make up my mind for me.

Grandpa laughs quietly. "Did you listen to anything I said? I want you to do what you want to do. It doesn't matter what I think."

"But what if I don't know what I want?" I exclaim. "I want to do what's right, but I don't know what that is anymore." I don't want to hurt Grandpa, but I can't keep these feelings bottled inside any longer.

"Even if I get accepted in the guard, I might never become an officer. I'll probably never become a guardian. What then? I'll be a commoner. I don't know how to fix the sanctuary. I don't know how to please the people like you do. They tried to kill me, Grandpa. You didn't see them yesterday. They charged like starving animals. They were willing to die. How am I supposed to fix that?" I bury my head in my arms and mumble into my hair. "Maybe someone else should rule."

There's already talk in the palace that Antai should rule when the king retires. Antai is his apprentice, after all. Or maybe one of the chancellors.

Grandpa lifts my chin until my eyes meet his. He has a sad, caring look on his face. The face of a loving father.

"Rose, no one expects you to fix the sanctuary. I can't do that. My father couldn't do that. No single person can do it on their own. What Cavernum truly needs is someone who cares about the people. Whether you want to be queen or not isn't up to me. But if you choose to accept the crown, I know you'll be a better leader than I've ever been. You proved that today in the council meeting."

"But what if someone else would make an even better ruler? Isn't it my obligation to let them lead?"

Grandpa has that look in his eye that he gets when he wants me to pay attention. "Rose, sometimes there's no right or wrong. There are just decisions—two right answers. And you get the lucky job of choosing how you want your life to be. I can't do it for you. And I wouldn't want to even if I could. Life would be pretty dull if there was only one right way to live it."

"And if I choose the guard...?" I ask. "You know it's not that simple."

"Then you can compete in disguise and keep your amulet hidden. When we feel it's safe, I can announce your true identity to the sanct-uary. If it's what you want, we'll make it work." Grandpa assures me. He always knows just what to say. Already I feel lighter. Less stressed.

"Okay. Thanks, Grandpa. That helps a lot." I want to change the subject away from myself. "What about you? How was your trip? You never told me what happened in Lycon."

At first, Grandpa doesn't respond. I'm not even sure if he heard me. He purses his lips and looks around the study. Suddenly he sits upright in his chair. "I have something important to show you. Tell me what you can make out of these symbols." He picks up a piece of paper and a pencil and quickly begins scribbling Adamic characters. I study each symbol as they form.

"Well?" Grandpa asks. "Any ideas?"

I point at the last symbol. "That's the symbol of humanity, but I'm not sure about the other two." I point at the first. "That's the symbol for God's power—the all-seeing eye. But it's upside down?"

"That's because it represents the devil," Grandpa announces. "It mimics and perverts the power of God." He gives me a look that tells me he's not joking. Chills run down my spine. He points to the middle symbol. "This is a symbol you've probably never seen. It means supremacy or dominion."

I combine the symbols in my head, trying to make sense of them. "Dominion over mankind?"

"By the power of the devil," Grandpa adds.

"I don't understand?" I confess. "This is devil worship. What does this have to do with Lycon?"

He meets my gaze with apologetic eyes. He wouldn't be showing me this if he didn't have to. He lays his cane across his lap and takes a deep breath like he always does when he tells a story.

"A few days ago, the king of Lycon requested our help. A few of their soldiers were going rogue, attacking their own men. One tried to kill the king. He almost succeeded. People said they were in a trance. That they were... possessed."

I know where this is going. I've heard the stories. Myths of men that can steal your body. Men who can enter your mind and take control. They fill history with bone-chilling tales. Stories of dream-eaters and skinwalkers. Folktales to scare children at night.

"But demons are extinct," I argue. "They were all killed in the great flood. You told me yourself when I was little. It's written in our history."

The look Grandpa gives me unsettles my soul. "I thought so too, but I'm afraid we were wrong." He points to the symbols he drew on the paper. "In Lycon, we eventually captured the man who was controlling the soldiers. He had these symbols tattooed on his back. I saw them with my own eyes."

The implication of what Grandpa has just revealed courses through my mind, scattering my thoughts. *Demons aren't extinct. Demons are alive!*

Grandpa gives me a look that sends shivers down my spine. His tree bark skin creases with dread. "Roselyn, I've never lied to you, but I haven't told you everything I should have." He lowers his gaze and falls silent.

"Grandpa, what are you talking about? What haven't you told me?"

He lifts his head, taking a deep breath. "It's time I tell you the truth about Hogrum... the truth about your father."

Chapter 7

Matt

A large bump in the road jostles me awake. It takes me a second to remember where I am. I've been riding in the truck for at least a few hours. By now, it must be sometime in the early morning. We must be getting close.

The flight from Colorado was quick. I slept through most of it. But now I'm riding on a windy road in the back of a semi-truck. The cargo area has been decked out with rows of leather bus seats drilled into the floor. Most of them are filled with other refugees like me. A slight breeze blows through gaps in the aluminum walls. The deeper into the mountains we drive, the colder it gets. Even with all the bodies, I need a sweatshirt to stay warm.

At the back of the truck, two guards sit in silence. Each one has a machine gun cradled in his lap. I can't tell if they're there to keep us in or keep the feeders out.

The truck takes a sharp turn, and my duffel bag slides under my seat. It holds the rest of my belongings: Some clothes, some cheap sneakers, and some photos with Judy—just the necessities.

So far, the ride has been lonely. Everyone else has someone to talk to. An Asian family across from me whispers in an unfamiliar language—maybe Mandarin. A young couple cuddles in the front of the truck while the mom whispers to her baby. Behind me, a little girl sleeps on her brother's lap. And then there's me, sitting all alone with a bath towel as a pillow.

I pat my empty chest through my shirt, feeling where my necklace would normally rest. I'm naked without it. Zane confiscated it before I was loaded into the truck. He snatched my dagger too. Supposedly, no weapons are allowed in the sanctuary. Zane claims they're a liability and only the guard can possess them. *So much for the second amendment.*

I'm not happy about it, but fighting is useless. I want to be on Zane's good side. So far, he's my only friend—if I can even call him a friend.

I already miss my house and my city. Most of all, I miss Judy. I start to feel sorry for myself when the small boy in front of me starts to cry. He's young, maybe 7 years old. His mother pets his hair and tries to soothe him without success. She keeps whispering apologies to the other passengers.

I feel sorry for them. They look dressed for the beach, and I don't see any luggage. The boy only wears a blue Disney t-shirt with some jean shorts and flip flops. My heart aches for him. I don't see a man with them. I know how hard it is to grow up without a dad.

I look around the truck. It has a solemn feel, like a funeral. No one wants to act too happy because others are mourning their losses. Everyone here has abandoned their homes. Everyone here has lost something. Confusion and fear are everyday emotions. *Maybe I fit in better than I thought.*

The boy in front of me begins shivering while he whimpers. I look down at the sweatshirt I'm wearing. It's my sweatshirt from summer biology camp freshman year. It reads 'I *heart organ* biology.' I know I have an extra coat in my bag. I don't need two. I pull off my sweatshirt, careful not to catch the thread on my stitches. Leaning forward, I tap the boy on the shoulder. "Excuse me," I whisper to the little boy who looks up with wide eyes and a puffy nose. "I have an extra sweatshirt if you want it. It'll be a little big on you, but it's pretty warm." I lay the sweatshirt over the back of the seat and sit back before they can refuse.

The boy looks to his mom for approval. She looks like she might cry. The woman tenderly takes the sweatshirt in her arms. "Thank you. We didn't have time to take any clothes. We can give it back when we get to the sanctuary."

I shake my head. "Don't worry about it, really. I have another. I won't miss it at all. Keep it."

She thanks me one last time before devoting her attention to her son.

I smile as the mom pulls the hoodie over the boy's head. The boy pulls his knees to his chest and tucks them inside the waistband of the sweatshirt. Then, he pulls the strings of the hood to tighten it over his face. He sniffles once or twice from inside the hood, but I don't hear crying. Satisfied, I reach for my bag to pull out my spare coat.

"Holy crap!" The voice has a Spanish accent. The startled whisper originates from behind me. "Dude, your neck."

It takes me a second to realize the voice is talking to me. I twist in my seat and lock eyes with the guy behind me. His copper eyes stare at me in awe. He's short with straight, black hair and dark brown skin. A faint mustache stains his upper lip. He has a roundish face that looks about my age, and a gold catholic cross dangles from his neck.

The boy points at my stitches. "Is that from a feeder? That's crazy." His sister still sleeps on his lap, undisturbed by the one-sided conversation.

Despite his mild accent, he speaks English smoothly and quickly. His boldness catches me by surprise.

"Uh, yeah. I got bit yesterday," I mutter.

His eyes double in size. "Frick man. How'd you survive? I've never even heard of that."

I shrug. "I guess I just got lucky." At the mention of feeders, some other passengers tune in to the conversation, ears perked. I'm not a fan of the extra attention.

"Do they really have sharp teeth?" the boy asks. "I heard they're like razors."

"I didn't really get a good look," I confess. *They sure felt like razors.*

Before I can turn around, the boy changes the subject. "That was nice what you did for that kid. I thought it was cool. My name's Diego." He looks down at the girl on his lap. "This is my sister, Mary."

"Nice to meet you. I'm Matt." I consider turning back around but decide against it. "Where are you from, Diego?"

"Los Angeles. But I was born in Guatemala if that's what you mean." He hesitates for a moment before continuing. "Do you have family at the sanctuary?"

I shake my head. "I didn't even know it existed until yesterday. My adoptive mom thinks I'm going to school in Australia." I scoff at how ridiculous it sounds. "What about you? Any family there?"

"Yeah, I lived there with my family when I was little, but I haven't seen them since my parents split. That was..."— He pauses as he counts in his head. —"six years ago."

Diego looks down at his sleeping sister as he whispers loudly. I'm pretty sure everyone on the truck can hear him. "My older brothers and my other sister stayed with my dad while Mary and I left with my mom. That is, until we got attacked last week. We ran, and we didn't stop until the police found us. A guardsman showed up the next morning." He watches his sister in a hopeless daze, replaying the events in his mind. "My mom is still missing, though. The police said they couldn't find her."

I don't know why Diego is telling me all this. We just met. But I feel like I have to match his tragedy with my own. Like it's my personal duty to make Diego feel better.

"I'm sorry, my parents are missing too. I was left as a baby. I'm hoping I'll maybe find them in the sanctuary. Maybe your mom will show up too."

Now Diego is the one who seems taken aback. "Dang dude, I'm sorry. That's rough."

An awkward silence wavers in the air as I think of something else to ask. "I like your cross," I say.

"Thanks." Diego stares solemnly down at the gold around his neck. "It was my mom's cross. She got it at her first communion. Her parents were catholic." He leans toward me, almost pushing his sister off his lap. "Hey, does it hurt when they feed? When it bit you, I mean? I heard they actually feed on your thoughts and memories."

"Ummm." I don't know what to say. The truth is, it had. It hurt like hell. I think of Diego's mom. More likely than not, she died from a feeder bite. I glance at Mary. Her eyes are shut, but I wonder if she's secretly listening.

"Not really," I lie. "I just felt really sleepy really fast. It wasn't so bad."

"Oh." Diego relaxes a bit and sits back in his chair. He seems relieved with the answer. "Thanks."

I face forward again and lean against the wall to sleep. Suddenly, the day ahead doesn't seem so lonely. No matter what happens today at the sanctuary, at least I'll have a friend. I have a feeling I'll need all the friends I can get.

I step out of the truck onto a sandy, dirt road. Diego and his sister climb out after me.

Amazing! An endless field of grapes and corn surround us. Off in the distance, a stone city teeters on the mountain top. It looks just like Hogrum, except the road is well kept, and the field is filled with healthy grapevines. The sun is still hidden behind the mountain, and already workers are shuffling down the road and taking their places in the field.

One worker in particular looks at me and doesn't look away. He nudges the two workers next to him and points right at me. As a group, they change course and begin walking my direction. Diego noticed them too. He stares at the workers in disbelief.

"Dad?" Diego calls. "Jorge! Javier!" He takes a step toward the workers and breaks into a run. Mary takes off after him. They embrace for a long time on the road. I can hear Diego's voice, but I can't make out what he's saying. Their joyful tones tell me everything I need to know.

Something hurts deep in my chest. I wish I had a family like that —someone waiting to greet me and take care of me. All I have is Judy, and I left her for dead. The guilt chews at my gut.

As Diego catches up with his family, I watch the sun slowly settle over the city. It was one of my favorite things to do back home; dawn was my favorite time to hunt. Other passengers linger around me. No one has given us instructions, so we wait. I look for Zane, but I don't see him anywhere.

Workers trudge past me as they unload crates from the other trucks. They ramble to each other as they work. I only hear bits and pieces, but it's enough to catch my attention. Something about a riot. A massacre. Guards firing on a crowd. I don't know how much to believe.

After a few minutes, Diego and Mary join me by the truck. "Who's excited for orientation?" Diego asks in mock excitement.

I furrow my brow. "You're not going with your family?" Sure, we're friends. We chatted most of the ride here. But if I were suddenly reunited with my dad, I wouldn't leave his side for anyone.

"I can't," Diego confesses. "Their shift in the field starts in a few minutes. But I'll see them later today. Besides, I can't leave my new bestie to orient himself." He slaps me on the back, and with that, we join the crowd of confused refugees.

A lady struts down the road toward us. She's a tall, lanky woman with black hair and thin square glasses. I can tell from her velvet jacket that she's not here to unload crates. "Hello, everyone. Welcome to Cavernum. I'll be your tour guide this morning. If you follow me, we're ready to begin." Her voice is informative and professional.

She starts back the way she came without looking to see if we follow. "This is what we call the flats." She gestures with her hands as we walk down the dirt road. "It's the lowest altitude of the sanctuary and wraps around the entire city."

The fields are dotted with workers. There are more than I initially thought. Hundreds of them. They're out carrying water and picking fruit. Some look as young as 12 or 13, while others are bent over with age. I swear one lady has to be at least 90.

"They're so young." I marvel. "Shouldn't they be in school?" *Or a nursing home.*

Diego kicks a pebble as we amble through the fields. "A lot of poor families will send their boys to work if they need the money. My brothers started when they were fifteen." He gives me a defiant glance... an angry glance. "That's why my mother left with us. She didn't want me ending up like them. She calls it slavery. She doesn't think it's worth living within the walls."

I'm stunned. That's child labor. That's supposed to be illegal. "Do they work all day?" I worry.

 Diego stares over the fields. His brothers and dad are out there somewhere. "They get a break at noon. Just two hours to eat lunch and rest when it's hottest, and then they go till sundown. Every day except Sunday."

I don't hide my disgust. "That sounds terrible. What about labor laws? What about worker's rights?"

"I know. It sucks." Diego shakes his head with conviction. "I'm not ending up out there, Matt. I don't care what I do, I'm not going out there with them. If they try to send me out there, I'll leave the sanctuary. I'd rather die."

"Hey, I'm with you." And deep down, I know I mean it. I'd go back to Judy. She wouldn't want me in the fields my whole life. It would break her heart. I didn't abandon her for this.

We pass a tall wooden post on the side of the road. Chains dangle from the top of the post, ending in metal cuffs. Our tour guide passes it without uttering a word.

"What's that?" I ask Diego.

"A whipping post." His voice is bitter. "When people break the laws, they get whipped. These posts are all over the sanctuary."

"You're serious?"

Diego nods. "I've seen it. It happens all the time."

I shuffle to the side of the road as a horse trots by. A man is perched on its back in a black police uniform. A wide-brimmed leather hat sits crooked on his head. He watches the workers with beady hawk eyes. I almost expect him to be holding a whip. The workers pick faster under his gaze. They seem tense. Afraid. Now, I understand why.

Our tour guide pauses next to some workers gathering grapes. "Cavernum is actually built on the nutrient-rich soil of a dormant volcano. For centuries, we've been known for our abundant crop production. We grow all of our crops inside the sanctuary, so our workers are safe from… outside dangers." She avoids the word feeder as if it were a curse word. "We grow everything from corn to broccoli. Whatever we can't grow is imported from the beyond."

Now is my chance to get more answers. "What was Hogrum like?" I call out.

Guide Lady searches for the source of the voice. When she finds me in the crowd, she smiles. "Great question. Hogrum and Cavernum were sister sanctuaries—built by the same prophet. Hogrum, however, was primarily a mining sanctuary. It was built on top of a rich gold deposit in Colorado. They were known for their beautiful jewelry and amulet production. Most of the amulets in Cavernum actually originate from Hogrum."

"Couldn't they just make gold with dominion?" I ask.

Guide Lady shakes her head. "Alchemy is a powerful and rare form of dominion. Anciently, it was almost unheard of. Mining was a much more practical option. However, as our understanding of chemistry has grown, alchemy has become more common. Today, much of Cavernum's gold is created by our guardians."

More questions tumble through my mind. Were my parents amulet-makers or merely the recipients? All I have is speculation.

Our tour guide marches onward towards the city. Diego and I follow at the back of the pack. After about a mile, the dirt path transitions into a bustling cobblestone road. Just like Hogrum, the stone buildings blanket the mountain like pine trees. Except for a few towers and the castle, the buildings look almost identical, rising with the incline of the mountain. Each rooftop is interconnected by a series of ramps and small bridges. In the distance, I can see policemen patrolling the rooftops, peering down at the roads below.

The road begins to tilt in front of me, and the ascent begins. It's one giant case of dejavú. Everything is almost identical to Hogrum. Excitement buzzes inside me. I take a deep breath and follow the tour group into the shade of the urban forest.

My amazement only grows stronger with each step. It feels like I'm in an old western movie. People hurry in all directions. Most men wear beards on their faces. Their clothes are colonial: crude cotton shirts and leather boots. Girls wear simple, plain dresses. And everyone is dirty in one way or another.

"Please tell me they have showers here," I beg Diego.

"Sorry, dude. Not that I can remember. I think we used buckets."

Maybe the city isn't as great as I thought.

"Welcome to the ring!" Guide Lady announces. "It consists of the outermost ring of the city and has the cheapest housing. Most labourers live here for its close proximity to the flats."

I have a feeling they aren't living here by choice. The sour smell of urine burns my nose. The streets are filthy. The bottom floor of the apartment buildings is lined with rundown shops selling bread and fruit. Flies hover in the air. I try not to stare as a naked toddler squats down and pees in the street. The weirdest part is, no one seems to care. *Where are her parents?*

It's noisier than I expected. Especially for six AM. Vendors shout from the shop windows, advertising their goods. In front of another shop, a dead pig hangs from its hind legs. A butcher slices its throat, spilling blood on the sidewalk.

I spot two policemen strolling down the opposite side of the street. Their faces are clean-shaven, and modern pistols hang on display from their waists. Their crisp, black uniforms seem out of place among the colonial outfits. As they walk, the colonials cross the street to avoid them. No one makes eye contact, and conversation hushes to a whisper. The tension is palpable. I think of the whipping post. *I would be afraid too.*

Just as it had in Hogrum, a large wall arcs over the road up ahead. The archway is the width of a two-lane highway. Not that any cars would ever be driving in the sanctuary. I have a feeling the people here don't even know what a car is.

Guide Lady stops in front of the wall and points to the giant symbols carved into the wall. "These symbols are Adamic. They form a powerful spell that protects us from the beyond."

I stare in awe. There are too many symbols to keep track. They stretch endlessly along the wall in both directions.

△◉⚡☰☄◇◈△✤》‡◉△

"What do they mean?" I blurt.

Guide Lady laughs. "I wish I could tell you, but only an adalit can read Adamic. In Cavernum, the only adalit is King Dralton, and even his knowledge is limited. These spells are some of the oldest and most complicated in existence. Not even the king knows exactly what they mean."

She turns back to the crowd and directs us towards the archway. "As you pass through the wall, you might feel a strange sensation. Don't be alarmed, it's only the wall's energy field. In the sanctuary, each wall functions independently. Even if one were to fail, the others would remain intact.

The guards at the gateway nod to our tour guide as the group passes underneath the arch. As I step through the gateway, I feel the hairs stand up on my arms. A slight breeze rushes across my entire body like a wave of static electricity.

Amazing.

"Welcome to the core," Guide Lady announces. She seems excited to be out of the ring. Everyone does. "The core includes the entire center of the sanctuary, except for the palace. It's where the middle-class citizens live and work."

The core is a huge step up from the ring. Not only do the streetside apartments have balconies, but they are decorated with small potted plants and furniture. Here, the colonial-style dress is mixed with modern blue jeans and t-shirts. Most people walk in worn sneakers instead of the leather shoes I've seen in the ring. A man jogs by in Nike exercise clothes. Bakeries and restaurants line the street. It seems like a completely different world from the ring we just left.

"Make way," a man shouts from the driver's seat of a horse-drawn carriage. People press to the side of the street to allow the carriage to pass. A girl smiles at me from the carriage window. I smile back.

"It's like everyone is Amish," Diego laughs. "They don't even know what they're missing."

I'm thinking the same thing. "No music. No movies. No micro-waves. I don't know how long I'll last." The sanctuary doesn't seem to offer much except protection. But is safety worth giving up the world?

As we walk, Guide Lady blurts out random facts about the sanctuary. "Cavernum is named after the labyrinth of caverns that run underneath the sanctuary. Lava tubes formed from cooling magma millions of years ago. Recently, the tunnels have been adapted into a sewer system for the city."

Up ahead, a sliver of the castle looms between the buildings. Just a hundred yards, and we'll be in the giant courtyard I remember from Hogrum. As I step into the plaza, the castle opens up before me.

Dozens of spiraling towers twist into the sky. Most of my view is blocked by the castle wall, but from what I can see, it's magnificent. The castle is so much more elegant than I remember from Hogrum. Spacious balconies extend from each floor adorned with gardens and fountains and beautifully kept hedges. Huge stained-glass windows glitter in the sunlight. How could they have possibly built it without tractors and cranes? It seems impossible.

I gaze at the castle wall in awe, half expecting to see a bomb crater where I did in Hogrum. Here, police are guarding the entrance, and workers are coming and going. There isn't a crack in the flawless stone surface.

What could possibly destroy a city like this?

Guide Lady spins around and gives a proud smile to the refugees. "Welcome to the Royal Plaza. And as you can see, we're right next to the palace. Unfortunately, the palace won't be part of our tour today. It's home to the elite citizens of the sanctuary. Master craftsmen live there along with healers, lawyers, politicians, as well as high ranking guardsmen."

I shuffle deeper into the enormous plaza. It's filled with row after row of makeshift tents selling every type of good imaginable. I see baskets and soaps and tools and blankets. Women and children amble between the shops, eyeing the products and bargaining for the lowest price.

Guide Lady gestures at the tents. "Whenever there isn't a scheduled event, the plaza doubles as the central market. The finest craftsmen in the city sell their products here." She points at the ground. "This plaza was built over a colossal cavern. Underneath our feet is an old dueling stadium. Before the guardians chose apprentices, contestants used to duel for available guardianships. Now, it's only used by the guard for graduation assessments."

She directs the group towards the far side of the plaza. "The final portion of orientation will begin shortly at the plaza stage." She points to a concrete stage built into the side of the castle wall. "Please make your way over, and I hope you enjoyed the tour."

As we approach the stage, men in dirty clothes scrub blood stains from the stone floor. *So, it wasn't a rumor after all.* My eyes settle on a wooden structure next to the stage. Three long ropes hang above a wooden platform. Each ends in a head-sized loop. I've seen enough old western movies to know what it's used for. Whoever the king is, he won't be earning my vote next election.

The tour group huddles around the stage, insignificant compared to the massive concrete structure. We're barely enough to form two rows. Once everyone is settled and the stragglers catch up, a woman steps onto the stage. Her pale face beams with enthusiasm. She smiles a little too wide, showing more gums than teeth. Her amber hair twirls like flames in the breeze, but she doesn't seem to notice. She strides to the front of the stage and calls out to the crowd, her voice surprisingly loud for such a fragile woman.

"Hello, everyone, and welcome to the great sanctuary of Cavernum!" She pauses a moment while the conversation dies down. She waits, frozen like an overjoyed mannequin, chin up and chest protruding.

"I'm Zifra, head of integration. I'm the one in charge of helping you all settle in, so if you have any questions feel free to ask me or one of my—"

"Why are we here?" A man shouts from the back, his hands cupped over his mouth. "Where will we live?"

More join in. —"Tell us about the massacre."—"Are we safe here?"—

Zifra's smile stretches thinner. "I know you've all had a long night and probably have lots of questions. But..." She stares towards the outspoken man. "—the fewer people interrupt me, the quicker I can present, and the sooner you can begin your new lives."

She pauses with her superficial smile, challenging the crowd to interrupt. When they don't, she continues.

"Now, some of you are familiar with the sanctuaries and our history, but by the looks on your faces, I can see that most of you don't fully understand why you're here. It's now my pleasure to share with you our history. To help me, I would like to invite the royal theatre to join me onstage."

A dozen men and women in tights and eccentric costumes climb the stage steps. They dance to the center of the stage and stand stone still. Offstage, a small band begins playing a calm melody with a violin and harp.

Zifra speaks as if delivering the happiest news on earth. "Listen carefully because this will be your new life, and it's a lot to absorb. Perhaps it'll be easier if I start from the beginning... the very beginning."

I strain to catch every word. "In the beginning," she begins, "there was the word; and the word was God. When God created the earth, he said, 'let there be light,' and there was light. He commanded the Earth to be made, and it was done. Through the word, he created the Heavens and the Earth. It was a language that the elements understood and obeyed. Today, we call this language Adamic."

She sweeps her eyes over the audience as she speaks, waving her hands with the inflection of her voice. "Through the Adamic language, God created the earth and everything on it. On the last day of creation, God created man."

One of the actors leaps forward and lays on his side. He uses his hands for a pillow as if he's asleep. Another actor skips forward. He wears a white glittery robe and a long white beard. I assume he's supposed to be God.

Zifra continues. "God made the first man, Adam, and breathed into him the breath of life, or the soul."

The actor playing God pulls a handful of glitter out of his robes and blows it onto the sleeping actor. Diego and I look at each other and crack a smile. I can't tell if they're serious or if it's some kind of comedy. However weird it is, it's working. The play has everyone's attention. Even the children watch quietly.

Zifra rants on. "God blessed man and granted him dominion over all the earth. This God-given authority granted us power over the

Earth, from the air we breathe to the fish in the sea. However, in order to use this dominion, man had to speak Adamic."

The sleeping actor wakes up. He dramatically climbs to his feet and looks around.

Zifra continues. "And so, starting with Adam, God began to teach man the Adamic language. Man became fluent, and for a time, man was like God, able to command the Earth. Man spoke, and the Earth obeyed. With a simple sentence, man could move mountains or call down rain."

The actor for Adam raises his hands above his head and mouths silently. On cue, water droplets rain onto the stone around him. Offstage, several helpers fling buckets of water to mimic rain. When the rain stops, two male actors dance forward to the beat of the music. Just like Adam, they're dressed in animal skins and have long, scraggly beards. Suddenly, the music from the band intensifies again.

"It didn't take long until Adam's son, Cain, was tempted by the devil and murdered his brother Abel." The Cain actor pulls a knife out of his sleeve and tiptoes behind Abel. He holds the knife in two hands and lifts it high above his head.

A little boy next to me squirms in his father's arms. "He's behind you!" He squeaks.

Cain pretends to violently stab Abel in the back. The little boy watches in horror as Abel slumps to the floor.

Zifra rants on. "Cain and his posterity were cursed for the sin. God removed their dominion, and they lost the power to command the elements." The God actor dances over and tosses a puff of a dark powder onto Cain.

"Man flourished on the Earth as Adam and Cain both had many children. Cain and his most wicked children grew jealous of the children of Adam and their dominion." To my relief, no one acts out the part about having children. However, a new actor creeps onstage. He wears a black cape and has dark eyeshadow smeared around his eyes.

Zifra's voice grows sinister. "The devil came and tempted Cain once more. He taught Cain that just as the breath of life could be given, it could be taken as well." Cain leaps over to another actor and lunges at him. He buries his face in the man's neck and pretends to bite him like a vampire. The victim shakes dramatically and collapses to the floor.

"Cain murdered a child of Adam and sucked from him the breath of life, becoming the first soul-feeder." Several distracted heads turn at the word 'soul-feeder.' It seems to be a touchy subject for everyone. I rub the stitches on my neck.

"By consuming the souls of their victims, feeders regained dominion over the elements. Once again, they could speak, and the elements obeyed. Eventually, God flooded the Earth to purify it of the wicked soul-feeders."

The helpers offstage start flinging water. Onstage, two other helpers hold the ends of a long blue sheet. They spread the sheet vertically to simulate the rising water of the flood. Gradually, they lift the sheet higher as the actors stand behind. As the blue sheet rises above their heads, they violently pretend to drown. Eventually, the sheet is removed, and only an old bearded man remains. He holds a staff in one hand.

"After the flood, the Adamic language was kept secret. God visited only the most faithful—the great prophets of old. He taught them Adamic and them alone. For centuries, these prophets led our people and protected them."

The actors migrate to the back of the stage, and Zifra takes their place in the center. "It wasn't long before the children of Cain returned to their evil ways. As before, they hunted the Adamic and fed on their souls—dominion and all. They couldn't speak adamic, but by consuming the souls of many victims, they became strong enough to exercise unspoken dominion."

Unspoken dominion? I glance at Diego, who shrugs. Zane used dominion without speaking, but how does it work? I expect her to explain more, but she glosses over the topic.

"The feeders grew in power and used unspoken dominion to murder our kind. They hunted us by the thousands. When we were on the brink of extinction, the prophets created the sanctuaries. They used written Adamic spells to repel the feeders. They also created amulets. Amulets allow us to exercise unspoken dominion without the sin of feeding. The guard was organized and has fought tirelessly to defend our kind ever since."

Zifra motions to the city around her. "While we hid in the sanctuaries, the children of Cain filled the beyond. While some became wicked feeders, most chose not to commit sin. Without dominion in their blood, they weren't hunted by their wicked brethren. They multiplied and filled the earth."

Zifra takes a deep breath. "And so, as the last of the prophets passed away, the spoken Adamic language was lost. Fortunately, the written language was preserved." Zifra gestures to the symbols on the castle wall behind her. "The sanctuaries and amulets live on. To this very day, we have four guardians in Cavernum—our personal guardian angels—as well as hundreds of guardsmen working day and night to protect us." Zifra spreads her arms wide. "The soul-feeders still hunt, but you are all safe here in Cavernum, your new home."

She gazes over the audience as if expecting applause. No one claps. I don't know what to think. If anything, I have more questions than before. *No wonder Zane didn't want to explain it.*

Zifra clasps her hands together. "Any questions? Surely you all have questions." She frowns, anxiously scanning the crowd. "Awww. No questions?"

When no one says anything, I raise my hand. Zifra smiles and points at me. "Yes?"

"How does unspoken dominion work?" I ask. "And how can feeders do it without an amulet?"

Zifra scowls for a second before hiding her disdain. "Oh, don't you fret about that." Zifra coos. "Only the guard needs to worry about dominion. The rest of you shouldn't burden yourself with such knowledge."

I look at Diego, who merely shrugs again. I have more questions, but I don't ask. Something tells me she wouldn't answer them anyway.

Zifra claps her hands. "Wonderful. Now that we've covered some of our heritage, it's time to explain a little more about the inner workings of the city. Unfortunately, the Adamic wall protecting us also hinders the use of electronics. Apart from the imported supplies, we have to grow and make everything by hand. We need everyone's help to accomplish this. In the city, everyone is divided into necessary roles: blacksmiths, bakers, medics, teachers, farmers, the guard." She gestures to a few policemen on the castle wall.

"Etcetera, etcetera, etcetera. Everyone fills a role and receives a fair wage. Even those who have no special talents will find a place in the fields. The children grow up learning and preparing at a young age for the role of their choice. When they turn 18, they have a chance to compete for available apprenticeships. Those who aren't selected, all find a place as laborers."

Unrest settles over the crowd as they realize the implications of what Zifra has said. Men begin shouting. "I'm a computer programmer, you expect me to work in the fields?"

"How will I watch my children?" Shrieks a woman holding a baby. Two small girls cling to her shirt, pulling it down into a dress.

Zifra loses her smile as she tries to appease the crowd. I can see her lips moving, but I only hear the angry accusations of the men around me. Suddenly, red-hot flames hiss high above the crowd. Heads tilt skyward as the stream of fire sweeps above the crowd, radiating heat like a bonfire. It quickly dissolves back center stage, receding from a policeman's hand.

I blink. The crowd is equally stunned. No one has spoken since.

Silence ensues as the man lowers his hand back to his waist. He's average height, maybe an inch or two shorter than me. And he looks older, maybe late 20's. He smiles a friendly, apologetic smile to the women in the front row and steps silently aside, giving the stage back to Zifra.

I watch as he retreats next to the stage with his partner. All the policemen today look like they were shaped by the same cookiecutter. They all have short hair and conservative demeanors. But the fire guy is different. His hair is longer and dyed a light grayish color. He has bold black eyebrows, and his eyes glow a silvery white. He gives off a different vibe than Zifra. More confidence, maybe. More power. More genuine.

Zifra resumes her rambling. "I promise everyone will find a place in the city, and it may take some getting used to, but we will be here around the clock to help you settle in. I think you'll all see Cavernum is a wonderful place. Those of you 18 and older will have the pleasure of being divided this week and can start settling into your new roles."

This week? Whispers cascade through the gathering.

Diego leans in close. His mouth is pulled tight with worry. "Crap man, I don't know any tricks. I just worked at McDonald's over the summer. I'm going to get sent to the fields. They'll get one look at my skin and send me to pick grapes."

I'm not sure if he's joking or serious. I decide not to laugh. "Maybe we can both be bakers or something. It can't be that hard."

Diego pats his belly. "No way, bro. Pastries won't be good for me. I need something active like one of those security guards."

I nod. I refocus on the stage as Zifra gives her closing remarks, thanks the audience, and steps off the stage with a curtsy. A new face steps forward, only it's the same policeman as before: Sparky the fire bender.

Fireboy smiles before he speaks, a subtle thanks to the audience for paying attention. "Hello, everyone, I'm Proticus Tyre, the new head trainer of the guard." He pulls out a piece of paper with notes. "I'll be reviewing a few safety policies for you folks." He stands awkwardly still in the center of the stage, holding the sheet of paper at his waist. I don't think he's done a lot of public speaking.

"We have three walls in the city, the outer wall, the inner wall, and the palace wall. Travel in and out of the inner wall is unrestricted. But the palace wall is heavily guarded and off-limits. And most importantly, no one is to leave the outer wall, under any circumstances. If someone really wants to leave the sanctuary, they can ride out on the convoy. It now leaves weekly. Understood?" A few heads bob up and down, and Proticus nods his own satisfaction before continuing.

"Also, for your own safety, we have a city-wide curfew from dusk to dawn." As soon as the words leave his lips, complaints tumble through the crowd. Proticus raises his hand. As he speaks, the whispers hush to listen. "As you may have noticed, electronics don't work inside the walls. Without streetlamps, the streets quickly become… hazardous. We don't mean to inconvenience any of you, I promise. It's just a matter of public safety. I think you'll all find that you prefer going to bed earlier. You can't get much done here after dark, and the sun rises early.

Now, as head trainer, I'm also in charge of the selection process for the guard. As Zifra explained, those of you 18 and older will be divided this week. The Dividing takes place in two days. Everyone under 35 will qualify to compete for the guard. Law enforcement and military officers are especially encouraged. For those of you debating the guard, let me just remind you that the only ones with the privilege of using amulets are the guardsmen. It's the chance of a lifetime. I hope to see you all out at the trial field on Friday. It's the best choice you'll ever make."

I'm already convinced. The guard is my only chance at learning dominion. If I make it in, I can get my amulet back. And maybe I'll learn enough to save Judy. It's my only hope.

Zifra returns to the front of the stage. "Before you leave, it's important you return here at four o'clock this evening to receive documentation. Without documents, you cannot receive payment or join a guild. Thank you for listening, and we'll see you at four."

"C'mon." Diego grabs me by the shoulder. With his other arm, he holds Mary's hand. "You can eat lunch with us. My family would love to meet you."

Chapter 8

Rose

The truth about Hogrum? About my Father?

I don't understand what he's implying, so I wait for Grandpa to explain. He takes another deep breath. "18 years ago, there were rumors in Hogrum. People spoke of an adalit. They said he was evil; that the devil taught him himself. They said he was reviving the demon cult. Your father had completed his Adamic lessons, so I sent him to investigate..." Grandpa looks down and lets his words hang in the air.

Already, I'm puzzled. "Wait? You always told me we were visiting family."

Grandpa meets my gaze with a political mask. I don't see tears, but I see the anguish in his charcoal eyes. "Technically, you were visiting your aunt. At the time, Violet was 8 months pregnant with you, and she wanted to stay with her sister. Your parents planned on coming home before you were born, but the mission lasted longer than we planned." He pauses again, wrestling with his memories. "For the first few weeks, I thought everything was fine, but then your father sent me this letter." Grandpa removes an old weathered note from his robe and hands it to me. I tenderly open it.

Father,

I won't say too much in case this letter is intercepted, but I'm afraid it's worse than we thought. They've integrated themselves into the entire sanctuary. They have people in places of power. They've even infiltrated the high council. I'm trying to earn their trust, but they're wary. Please don't send assistance. They are already suspicious of me. With a little more time, I think they will learn to trust me.

Sincerely,

Zezric

"They, as in the demons?"

Grandpa nods. "It gets worse. A week later, I received this letter." Gingerly, he sets the note before me, like flowers on a grave. I snatch the letter and read.

Father,

I have terrible, terrible news. Roselyn was born, a beautiful, healthy girl, but Violet has fallen ill. She's lost too much blood from the birth. The healers are afraid she won't survive. I know you'll wish to help, but you must stay put. I'm getting close to a breakthrough. Your arrival would only put me in jeopardy.

Sincerely,

Zezric

My mother, ill? Dying? Why had I never heard this before? I imagine my mom, bleeding out as she holds me for the first time.

"Tell me there's more," I beg.

Without a word, Grandpa sets the next letter on the table.

Father,

I must be brief. The demons are preparing to attack. They've told me of their plans, things I can't discuss over letter. Hogrum is in danger, father. We're all in grave danger. I'll be returning to Cavernum at the end of the week. Please wait until then.

Zezric

P.S. Violet passed away last night.

The last sentence cuts me to the core. *Feeders didn't kill her, I did!* If I hadn't been born, maybe, just maybe, she'd still be alive.

I crinkle the note in my now clenched fist. "Why didn't you tell me?"

"Because I was afraid you would blame yourself, just as I have. It makes no difference, Rose. This knowledge changes nothing."

I imagine my father, scared and alone, surrounded by demons and danger, fearing for the life of his newborn daughter. My poor father, given a life and stripped of another. I'm filled with a sense of urgency. It's as if my father is there right now. It's as if there's still time to save him.

"Then what?" I demand.

Grandpa sighs. "I wanted to go to him, but I was afraid my arrival would put him in danger, so… I waited. The weekend came and went, and Zezric never returned."

I sit rigid in my chair. I wrap my arms around myself and try to breathe steadily. It's the only thing that keeps me from crying.

"Then what?" My voice cracks, but Grandpa doesn't notice. He's wrestling with his own emotions. I can see the regret on his face. The guilt in his eyes. He speaks slowly, like a corpse. I've never seen him so discouraged. *He really does blame himself.*

His voice trembles quietly. "I prepared the troops immediately. We left the next morning, but I was too late. When we arrived, the walls were already toppled. We didn't find any survivors in the sanctuary. A week was spent burning the bodies—thousands and thousands of them."

"Do you think the invasion had to do with the Adalit?" I ask.

"I'm convinced," Grandpa says. "The only thing strong enough to destroy an Adamic spell is Adamic itself. I can't think of any other way."

I squeeze myself tighter. I feel my pulse rising. I've never asked this question before, but after reading what I just read, I have to know. I need closure. "Did you find their bodies?" I ask.

Grandpa looks at me with wide, watery eyes. He pauses, and already I know the answer. "I'm so sorry, darling. We found your father in the palace. He was dead when I arrived. Your mother, we never found. They likely cremated her remains before the attack."

I grit my teeth and let anger wash away the despair. *Demons did this! Demons killed my father!* "Tell me everything," I seethe through clenched teeth. I know it's not Grandpa's fault, but he's the only one around to blame. "How did he die?"

I don't stop to consider how painful this must be for Grandpa. His hands shake in his lap as he responds. "Zezric was... we think he was caught in a blast. His injuries were... extensive."

I release my clenched fists. At least the feeders didn't get to him first. He died fighting. He died a hero.

"What else?" I don't know what I'm looking for, but I want to know every detail.

Grandpa looks down at the table and takes a deep breath. "There's one more thing you should know." He points to the symbols he drew for me: the demon spell. "When I found your father, I found these symbols tattooed on his back."

I open my mouth, but no words come out. *No! Why?... Why?* A storm of emotion blows through me. Doubt. Betrayal. Confusion. Admiration. "He had to!" I insist. "He had to earn their trust. He did it to earn their trust, didn't he?"

Grandpa wraps his arm around me. "I know," he soothes. "I don't have a doubt in my mind, Rose. Your father fought them to his dying breath. I just want you to know everything. No more secrets. You deserve the truth."

I sit up and rub my watery eyes. I feel the anger returning. "Why do it?" I beg. "It just doesn't make sense. What does an adalit gain from destroying a sanctuary? He can make his own amulet if he wants one. He already has power. What else could he want?"

Grandpa struggles to his feet. "I have a guess, but I hope I'm wrong." He reaches for a book on the nearest bookshelf. The title is handwritten: 'Adamic Folklore by Titan Malik.'

Titan Malik is my great-grandfather. In his day, he was a famous Adamic scholar and a powerful king. He single-handedly created the dividing process and put an end to a bloody civil war. But that was in his prime. Now, Great-grandpa Titan is only a crazed shell of the man he used to be. His mind is corroded, and most days, he doesn't know his own name.

Grandpa sets the book gingerly down on the table. "Remember this?"

"Of course! It's the one you used to read me when I was little."

Grandpa smiles at the thought. "My father wrote this book when I was young. He used to read it to me every night before bed. It contains an entire history of our people. From Adam and Eve to the flood, to the creation of the sanctuaries. On the last page, my father mentions something that has puzzled me for years."

Grandpa opens up to one of the last pages and begins reading aloud. "For a time, the great prophets ruled the sanctuaries with the power of their godly tongue. As adalinguals, they had complete mastery of the Adamic language. They could create or destroy with a simple word. Pieces of their language were recorded as holy text, but the prophets refused to pass on the spoken language. When they died, Adamic died with them, leaving only written remains."

None of this is new to me, but Grandpa seems convinced. He keeps reading. "Some ancient records, however, indicate that Adamic was preserved in its entirety: both written and spoken. The prophet Valventis desired to preserve Adamic until a future day of righteousness. He devoted his days to creating the Book of Life—a manuscript containing the entire Adamic Language. It was said to contain all the knowledge of Godliness.

According to the records, Valventis sealed and hid all of his writings. Unfortunately, the prophet never disclosed the location of his Library. For centuries, men have searched in vain for the Lost Library of Valventis. However, the rumors are ancient, and none know for certain if The Book of Life truly exists. As for myself, I am a believer."

Grandpa slams the book shut in his hands and looks at me with excitement in his eyes. I raise my eyebrows at Grandpa. "Don't you think that's a bit of a stretch?"

"Perhaps, but it's the only motive I can think of."

"Did you ever ask Titan about it?"

"My father was a very secretive man," Grandpa recalls. "I've asked him a hundred times, but he's never said a word about it. He refused to even acknowledge my questions."

It sounds absurd. "You're telling me that a prophet made instructions on how to speak Adamic, and that an adalit destroyed Hogrum looking for it?"

"I don't know if the library actually exists," Grandpa admits. "Nonetheless, I believe the Adalit is searching for it." Grandpa holds up his finger. "If it does exist, we have to protect it at all costs."

The implications are outrageous. With knowledge of the spoken language, there's no limit to one's power. The prophets of old could move mountains, raise the dead. They became like God. If an adalit got his hands on the full language, there's no telling what he could do.

"Promise me this, Rose. Promise me you won't take off your amulet under any circumstances. It's the only thing that will protect you from a demon."

"A demon? Grandpa, what are you talking about?"

Grandpa takes off his amulet and lays it on the table where I can see the symbols clearly.

Grandpa traces his finger along the symbols as he translates. "Protect the soul and anchor it to the body." He rests his finger under the first symbol. "This protection symbol is powerful. It doesn't just protect you from the strain of dominion, but it also protects against outside influences. As long as you wear your soul-anchor, you're protected from possession. Promise me you will."

"Alright. I promise."

"We have to be cautious, Rose. These are dark times. If the Adalit can make one demon, he can make others. Not to mention amulets and adamic armor. He can create an army."

"You can make an army too," I counter. "We have the amulet vault. And you could always make more."

Grandpa shakes his head. "We'd never win a war with feeders. We only have so many men. But the world is full of potential feeders. Billions of them. They'd outnumber us. It'll never stop until we kill the Adalit. He'll just keep making more."

"How do we find him?" I ask.

"We might not have to," Grandpa corrects. "If he didn't find what he was looking for in Hogrum, he won't stop until he finds it. He'll invade every sanctuary…"

I gasp. "—Until he gets to us."

I wander through the hallway, searching for a distraction. The marble floors are polished to perfection. They reflect the black soles of my slippers and the steady swing of my limbs. Despite my best efforts, my thoughts wander to Antai. I still haven't seen him since the riot. He's been on duty all day. I've yet to thank him for saving my life.

I pass the central staircase with its intricate banister and glass chandelier. I should go to the library to finish my studies, but the magnitude of Grandpa's revelation still weighs on my mind. Instead, I start for the music room. It has, and always will be, the sanctuary of my soul.

To my delight, I find the music room deserted. The stage is empty except for a single grand piano. The piano bench calls my name.

I take a seat and slip off my shoes. It's easier to play the pedals barefoot. There's no sheet music, but I don't need any. I composed this song myself. I press the keys, and familiar vibrations fill the air.

The song starts slow and solemn, but gradually transforms into a cacophony of emotions. My ballerina fingers dance gracefully over the sharps and flats. The gentle resistance of each key is calming—almost nostalgic. A simple melody fills my ears and silences the outside world. My worries dissolve. The tension in my mind goes slack.

The music rocks me from side to side like the changing tide. Time seems to disappear. Finally, I hold down the last note until the piano grows silent. After such a song, the silence is almost sweet. Music would mean nothing without silence.

Normally, music brings me clarity, but now I'm only more confused. How can I leave this behind? Music is my dream. Music is my life. But it can't be everything. There's so much I want to see. There's so much more to life than a piano.

The orchestra or the guard? How do I choose?

I rest my hands back on the keys. I'm about to play when footsteps skitter behind me. Nevela runs down a row of theatre seats and scampers onto the stage. She's panting like a dog and clutches a piece of paper in her hand.

"Princess! Oh, I'm so glad I found you." She holds out the note to me with an unusually large smile on her face. "It's from the commander."

I don't have to ask which one. I snatch the note from her hand and unfold it.

Dear Rose,

I apologize for being so busy today. I've been dying to see you. Meet me on the observation deck of the west tower at sunset. Come hungry and wear what you normally would for a date.

    Sincerely,

    Antai

A date? An actual date with Antai! I can't believe it. I've never been on a date before. My birthday was only weeks ago and courting under-age is strictly forbidden. But now that there's nothing stopping him, Antai has finally asked me.

Nevela jumps up and down, shaking her fists. "What is it, princess? Oh, please tell me!"

"Antai asked me on a date. At sundown." I look down at my clothes in disbelief. I'm wearing yesterday's dress, and my hair is a tangled mess. "I can't go looking like this."

Nevela takes me by the hand and tugs me towards my chambers. "Don't worry, princess. I've been planning for this night ever since your birthday. I have just the dress. Tonight, Antai won't be able to resist you."

The observation deck is a tiny balcony at the very top of the west tower. It's the highest point in the entire sanctuary. When Antai and I were little, we used to always go there to play. We would write notes on paper gliders and throw them off the tower.

Butterflies flutter in my stomach as I climb the staircase. I feel overdressed, but Nevela insisted. I couldn't bring myself to turn her down. I'm wearing a knee-length gold dress with gold pendant ear-rings. My dress hugs me tight at the waist and falls into a low V across my back. With Nevela's help, a crown of braids weaves around the back of my head. My lips are brushed with blush pink lipstick, and my eyes are lightly shaded in gold. According to Nevela, it highlights my hazel eyes.

At the top of the steps, I pause and take a deep breath. I take one last look down at my outfit. *Please like it.* Then, I push the door open and step out onto the observation deck.

The view is breathtaking. Soft pinks and oranges are painted across the clouds as the sun sets over the adjacent mountain peak. Antai is seated at a tiny cast iron table just big enough for the two of us. Several small candles are dispersed across the table and around the deck.

I suck in a breath. "Antai, you shouldn't have." The table is piled with assorted fruits—a delicacy in Cavernum. I spot strawberries and mangos and pineapples and bananas—most of which have to be imported. Best of all, a bowl of melted chocolate sits on the center of the table.

Antai jumps to his feet. He's wearing his formal officer uniform. Black slacks and boots with a black suit coat and red lapels. A gold medal of achievement hangs from his left breast pocket. I can tell he's nervous from the way he tucks his hands into his belt.

"A deal's a deal." Antai grins. "It may have been riot chanting, but it sure was loud." He looks me once over, his face blooming into a dazzling smile. "You look amazing. Really amazing." He says it softly. Almost shyly.

My face turns red. Antai's not one to openly compliment. He usually hides his affection in jokes. But right now, he's being so direct, so vulnerable. I'm flustered. I rush into his arms and squeeze him as tight as I can. He gingerly lets his hands fall to my waist and pulls our bodies tight together. I tuck my head into his neck and breathe in his cologne—the subtle scent of cinnamon.

"Thank you for everything. For saving me… for tonight. This must have taken you forever."

Antai lets go and directs me to the table. "Nah, it was nothing." He pulls out the chair for me as I sit down. "I was actually going to do all this anyway, I just thought I'd invite you to be polite."

I laugh. If Antai could have it his way, a roasted pig would be on this table instead.

Antai takes his seat. "I'm sorry I've been so busy. After the riot, we did a full sewer search for the equalists. It took all day."

"Did you find anything?"

Antai gives me a disgusted look. "You don't want to know the things I found."

My jaw drops open. "You didn't have to walk in it, did you?"

Antai flashes a relieved smile. "Not this time, but I saw a sewer rat bigger than a piglet."

"Do you think they're really down there?" I muse.

"Hard to say. The tunnels go so deep. We barely scratched the surface. Honestly, they could be hiding an entire army down there, and we'd never know. If there are people down there, they have to be getting food somehow. We're going to put guards at all the sewer entrances and starve them out."

"Sounds like a good plan." I glance at the fruit. It's almost as distracting as Antai. "So... how does a date normally go?" In an ideal world, my mom would've taught me everything there is to know about dating, or maybe an older sister. But I don't have either, and Grandpa isn't much help.

Antai rubs his hands together. "I was thinking we would eat some fruit, chat for a bit, then we can lay back and watch the stars if you don't mind breaking curfew?" He points to a pile of blankets that I didn't notice before.

"That sounds perfect."

Antai looks down at the table. "Please, dig in."

I dive for the strawberries first. I dip one up to its neck in chocolate and plop it into my mouth. "Mmmhhh." It's dark chocolate—my absolute favorite. The bitter and the sweet combine so perfectly. I'm almost certain I'm drooling.

"This is perfect, Antai." I mumble through a mouth full of chocolate. I look out over the balcony at the city. It's bathed in a pink glow as the sun sets. A slight breeze pulls at my hair. *It's literally perfect.*

I dip a slice of pineapple in the chocolate and take a bite. Antai does the same. He smiles as I take an especially big bite of mango. Then, he does the same. Formalities aren't necessary with Antai. It's just me and my best friend.

"Remember when we used to come here as kids?" he asks.

"Of course! Remember when you spat off the edge and hit old man Zancus?"

Antai nods. "And he chased us all the way to the garden. If King Dralton hadn't found us, Zancus would've skinned me alive."

"I miss those days," I say. "Everything was so simple. We didn't have to worry about anything."

"A lot has changed since then," Antai admits. "I heard you were invited to the high council meeting, and you convinced them to open up the infirmary to the laborers. How'd you pull that off?"

I fake a serious face. "Bribery. It's the only way to pass legislature."

"No, really." Antai laughs after swallowing a bite of banana. "I heard Chancellor Gwenevere won't even leave her chambers. She's too afraid she'll catch poverty."

I laugh back, but my laughter quickly fades. I remember I have to direct the execution tomorrow. I've been dreading it ever since the high council meeting.

Antai looked down at me with his soft brown eyes. "You okay, Rose?"

I've stopped eating, and Antai has noticed. He's always been too observant for his own good. That's what makes him such a good commander.

"Sorry. I'm... just thinking." An understatement. I'm overwhelmed. Ever since my lesson with Grandpa, I can't get my parents out of my head. Not to mention The Dividing is in two days.

"About what?" Antai urges. He puts his elbows on the table and leans forward. It's hard to believe, but he looks even more handsome up close.

I sit on the edge of my seat and empty my lungs. I might as well tell him the truth. "Just everything. The council, The Dividing... you."

Antai's eyebrows twitch at the word 'you'. He smiles. "Don't worry, Rose. It'll all work out. All of it."

Antai emphasizes the last sentence. Is he referring to himself? To our relationship? Either way, it doesn't make me feel better. When he tells me not to worry, it just makes me feel like he's dismissing my concerns. "You don't know that," I say. "So much could go wrong. Just think of this week. I almost died at the riot."

"But you didn't," Antai reminds me. "Besides, we caught the protesters, and tomorrow they hang. Good guys win again."

He speaks about it so casually. Most of the equalists have families to feed. They acted out of desperation. I don't want to argue about it. This is supposed to be a romantic date. Besides, Antai is right. They killed innocent guardsmen. *They deserve to hang. Don't they?*

"So, have you chosen a guild yet?" Antai asks.

"Not yet, but I might be leaning towards the guard. I finally talked to Grandpa, and he said I can compete in disguise. That way, I won't be at risk."

Antai's face is doubtful. His lips press together.

"What?" I demand.

"I don't know, Rose. Maybe the guard isn't the best idea."

"What do you mean? You're the one who trained me every day. After all that, you're saying I shouldn't even try?"

"That was before the riot. You said it yourself, Rose. You could've died."

I don't like how he uses my words against me. "Well, like you said. I didn't."

"Don't forget they have guard uniforms, Rose. They could be anywhere. Anyone. It's just not safe."

"I'll be fine," I insist. *Why can't he just let it go?*

Antai's voice has lost its tender tone. "Don't be blind, Rose. You don't even know the danger out there. The riot was only one day in public. Imagine a lifetime. Those were only protesters. Imagine a pack of feeders. You won't get lucky forever."

Blind? Lucky? Now, I'm really upset. He's treating me like I'm helpless. Like I'm nothing without my bodyguards. I turn my back to him and stare out at the fading sunlight. The sun has now dropped behind the mountains. I use my silence like a weapon against him. It drags on. I can hear Antai exhale loudly.

"I'm just worried about you, Rose," Antai mutters. "The thought of you getting hurt terrifies me. When I saw you burning, I almost lost it. If anything ever happened to you in the guard, I don't know what I'd do." My heart softens. He's showing his vulnerable side again.

"You can't protect me forever, you know."

Antai offers a half-grin. "You're still alive, aren't you? So far, so good."

I'm not in the mood for jokes. "I can't hide in the palace my whole life, Antai. The queen has to be able to defend herself. She has to be able to go outside and visit the people." It's the same argument every time. I hate it.

"You really think you can do better than the royal guard. If you get accepted, you'll be a cadet, Rose. The very bottom of the food chain. With a guardian by your side, no one will be able to touch you."

I don't want a babysitter my whole life. For once, I want to be independent. "Well, maybe I don't want a guardian by my side."

Antai looks like I slapped him in the face. The pain in his eyes hardens into anger. He grits his teeth. "Then why are you even here?" He demands. He gestures angrily at the table and balcony "What's the point of all this if you've already made up your mind?"

The stairwell door opens, and a guardsman steps onto the roof.

"What do you want?" Antai barks.

The soldier hesitates. "S-sorry to interrupt, commander, but we've received a new tip. A man in the ring claims he knows where the equalists are hiding. He's offered to guide us through the tunnels. The guardians want to meet immediately to discuss a plan of action."

Antai's eyes widen. His head swivels back and forth between me and the messenger. "Tell them... tell them to start without me." Antai decides. "I'll be there as soon as I can."

"It's fine, Antai. Just go." I mutter. I try to keep my voice steady. I'm done arguing for tonight. I just want to be alone. I push back my chair and climb to my feet. As I look down at the table, I instantly regret it. The food is set up so nicely. He did all this for me. He had a whole night planned. But I'm not thinking clearly. My emotions are clouding my judgment.

I can't take it back now. My pride won't let me. I'm already on my feet and walking towards the stairwell. I wait for Antai to stop me, but he doesn't. He bites his tongue and watches me leave without a word. I'm running down the stairwell now. I'm so frustrated I want to scream. This night was supposed to be perfect. It could have been perfect, but I ruined everything. I run all the way until I'm safe in my chambers. I collapse onto my bed, bury my face in my pillow, and scream as loud as I can.

Nevela comes running from down the hallway. She's already asking questions before she's in the room, her voice soaked with excitement. "I didn't expect you so soon. How'd it go? Did he kiss y—" She stops as soon as she sees my face.

"I just want to go to bed," I cry. I wrap myself in the sheets and close my eyes, begging sleep to overcome me. Without a word, Nevela removes my shoes for me and blows out the candles.

I replay tonight's argument over and over in my mind, waiting for sleep to end my mental anguish. Tomorrow is the execution. Tomorrow, five lives will end at my command.

They deserve this, Rose. They chose this.

Deep down, I'm not so sure.

Chapter 9

Matt

I follow Diego into another alley, but every street looks like the last —tan stone and trash.

"My feet hurt," Mary complains. "Are you sure you know the way?"

"We're close," Diego assures her. He does a double-take before charging down a small alley. "Just a little bit further."

Diego leads us down an even smaller alley. Foot traffic has cleared a small path in the scattered trash. *Do people really live here?* It looks like a third world country. Wooden boards have been placed to cover up holes in the brick walls. Nails jut from the wood at random. I can hear yelling coming from inside.

Diego stops at the top of a staircase that leads underneath the building. It looks like a basement entrance. At the bottom of the steps, darkness peers through the cracks of a wooden door. A gaping black hole marks where the doorknob should be. Thick metal chains wrap through a hook on the doorframe and disappear into the doorknob hole.

"This is it," Diego announces. He starts down the steps, and Mary follows. I linger in the alleyway. I already feel like an intruder.

"Abuela?" Diego calls. "Javier? You guys in there?" He pounds his fist on the door, shaking the chains. The shuffle of feet approaches, and with a jingle, the chains are dragged back into the hole and out of sight. The door cracks open, revealing a wrinkled, round face with bulging brown eyes. The eyes barely come to the height of the missing doorknob.

"Diego! ¡Mi hijito! Come in. Come in." The woman pushes the door open and waves her arm in a frantic circle. Her voice has an accent identical to Diego's. "When your father told me you were here in the sanctuary, I thought the sun had cooked his brain." She pulls Diego into a hug.

With the hunch in her back, she only comes to Diego's chin. Her long silver hair is braided and hangs nearly to her knees. Mounds of wrinkles are piled on her puffy cheeks. The rest of her body is hidden under a simple white dress. "María, is that you?" Abuela cries, peeking around Diego's shoulder. "When I last saw you, you were just a little girl. Look how beautiful you are now." Abuela shuffles over to Mary and clasps her arms around her.

Abuela lifts her eyes and finds me watching from the stairwell. "What are you looking at! Get lost!"

I flinch. "Uhhh..." I open my mouth, but I don't know what to say.

Diego comes to my rescue. "No, Abuela. This is my friend, Matt. He has nowhere to go, so I told him he could stay with us."

Her wrinkled face gets even more wrinkled. "You disappear for years and bring back another mouth to feed. We barely have enough for ourselves."

"That's enough, Mom." A man's voice calls out from deep within the home. "Tell them to come into the kitchen. We're almost ready to eat." The voice doesn't share the usual Spanish accent.

Abuela huffs and retreats into the darkness without another word. I hesitantly descend the steps into the apartment.

"Diego? Is that really you?" It's a girl's voice. She comes running down the hallway and dives into Diego's arms in a whoosh of black hair. "Mary, get in here!" She grabs Mary by the arm and pulls her into the sibling group hug.

I stand as still as I can, hoping no one notices me. I awkwardly watch from the doorway until the group hug disassembles.

"Isabela!" Diego exclaims. He holds her by the shoulders as he stares at her face. "You're so old."

She has especially big almond eyes and a wide bridge of her nose. She's pretty—very pretty, not that I would ever admit it. She's Diego's sister after all.

"You look… you look just like Mom." Diego gasps.

The mood grows solemn. Isabela pulls Diego back into a hug. "Dad told us what happened. It wasn't your fault."

"Lunch is ready." The same manly voice interrupts from down the hall. Diego breaks the hug and nods at Isabel. Together with Mary, they head down the hall to the kitchen. I follow an awkward distance behind them.

The kitchen is a small square room with a round dinner table in the center. Three ceramic pots are on the table with a pitcher of water. Instead of chairs, short wooden stools surrounded the table. A tiny window lets in just enough sunlight to see. The kitchen looks oddly empty without a fridge or a sink. Something smells delicious—almost like bacon. I find the source. A small wood-burning furnace is the only appliance in the kitchen. It's positioned by the wall. Inside it, a chunk of mystery meat is sizzling. An exhaust pipe slithers from the top of the stove to the window, directing the smoke into the alley outside.

"Take a seat, please." The dad directs from his seat on a stool. "We're ready to eat." His voice is the same manly voice I heard from the hallway.

He's a short, fit man—much slimmer than Diego, likely from his time in the field. His hair is buzzed almost to the skin. It makes him look tough. He wears a tattered cotton shirt that is now more yellow than white. A deep five o'clock shadow blankets his chin and neck. More than anything, he looks tired.

Two other boys sit at the table, brothers by the looks of it. They look like Diego, but skinnier and older. If I had to guess, I'd place them in their early twenties. Their clothes are equally soiled, and their arms are browned by the sun. They watch me with suspicious eyes.

Isabela takes a seat next to Abuela. Mary grabs the seat next to her. I sit on the last stool between Diego and his dad. It's as comfy as it looks, which isn't very. Without warning, the dad holds out his hands and bows his head. Everyone else does the same. I catch on and cautiously take the dad's and Diego's hand.

"Oh, God," The dad begins before I can close my eyes. "We're thankful that my son and daughter could be brought home to us safely and that none of us were harmed in the riot this week. We're thankful for this food and for our safety in the sanctuary. Your name be praised, amen."

"Amen," the family echoes. Immediately the older brothers snatch the pots and scoop a serving of corn and beans onto their plates.

"Who's your friend, Diego?" The dad smiles and nods my way. "Why don't you introduce him to the family."

Diego pauses halfway through serving himself beans. He points in a circle around the table. "You already know Mary. This is my sister Isabela. That's Jorge and Javier. That's Esperanza, but we just call her Abuela. And that's my dad, Enrique. Everyone, this is Matt."

After a short echo of hellos, Isabela leans forward with eager eyes. I can tell she and Diego were close. "Tell us everything, Diego," she sings. "Where have you been? What have you been doing this whole time?"

Diego shrugs. "Not much. Just going to school in LA. Working a little. Not much has happened to be honest. What have you guys been up to?"

The dad looks proudly at Isabela. "Isabela got divided last year. She got a sewing apprenticeship at Mr. Williams's factory.

"He only chose her so he can stare at her all day," Jorge teases. "He put her desk closest to his office."

"Shut up," Isabela snaps. "I make more than you do in the fields."

"Hey, that's enough." Enrique intervenes. A small smile creeps onto his face. "It's a shame you don't look like your sister, Jorge. Then, maybe we could afford dessert."

Diego snickers, and Abuela lets out a thunderous laugh. She holds her fork high in the air as she speaks. "A beautiful woman is worth her weight in rubies."

I'm enjoying this. So this is what it's like to have a big family. I've always wanted siblings. Or at least a brother.

The corn and beans finally reach me. Already, the pots are almost empty. There wasn't much to begin with. I scoop less than a handful of each and pass it to Enrique. I watch as he takes even less and passes it back to Jorge for a second round. When the meat comes around, Enrique passes it without serving himself any.

Isabela notices. "Dad, c'mon! You have to eat."

Enrique shrugs it off. "Eat up. I'm on a diet." He smiles at his own joke.

Isabela rolls her eyes and takes a bite of the meat. "Mmhhh! This is delicious."

Enrique shrugs off the compliment. "You know what they say: hunger is the best sauce."

"Is this roast?" Isabela grows concerned as she peers at her meat. "Dad, how did you afford this?"

Enrique just smiles. "Mr. Johnson offered it to me half-off for fixing his door. I had to take him up on it."

"Well, it's good," Jorge reports though a mouthful of seconds. "You should fix his door more often."

I try to eat my food slowly. I don't want to be the first one done. I notice Mary staring at her plate. I feel bad for her. She barely knows her siblings. She probably feels as out of place as I do.

"Pass the beans, please," Diego asks.

I reach for the pot in the middle.

"Whoa! What happened to your neck?" Enrique gasps.

I reach up and feel my neck. My fingers come back wet. The stitches are swollen and oozing a clear liquid. They itch and burn like a dozen bee stings.

"I... uhhh—" I feel my cheeks getting warmer. Everyone is staring at me.

"He got attacked by a feeder," Diego proudly explains. "One of the guardians saved him."

Eyes grow wider around the table. Isabela leans forward timidly. "Can I see the marks?" She asks in a soft voice. I reach for my collar.

"No!" Abuela slams her fist on the table. "There will be no talk of feeders in this house. I won't stand for it." She sweeps her eyes over the table, daring someone to disobey, which they don't. The only sound is Jorge and Javier munching on their corn.

Diego shoots me a glance and spins his finger around his ear where Abuela can't see it. I turn my head to hide my smile. At least I'm not the only one who thinks she's crazy.

"What are you going to choose for the dividing?" Isabela asked Diego, trying to revive the conversation.

Jorge swallows a mouthful of corn. "I know Mr. Rockwell is looking for some more hands for city custodial. It's the same pay as the fields, but he's a fair boss. It'll be less sun. I would take it if I were you."

Diego plays with the corn on his plate. He doesn't seem too excited by the offer. "Actually, I was thinking about maybe trying the guard."

Reactions vary around the table. Javier laughs. Enrique purses his lips. Abuela chokes on her beans and mutters something in Spanish.

"No grandson of mine will be a guardsman. Didn't you hear about the massacre? They shot unarmed civilians. They're murderers." She clenches her fork so tight her brown knuckles turn white.

"They'll do anything to keep us oppressed," Jorge agrees. "I heard they have hundreds of amulets in the palace, but they lock them away to keep us powerless. You really want to be a part of that, Diego?"

Javier snorts. "Just let him try it. He'll end up back in the fields anyway."

"I think he could do it," Isabela says. "Dad made it, didn't he?"

Diego whips his head toward his dad. "What? I never knew you were a guardsman!"

"Well, you were just a toddler at the time. And it wasn't for very long."

"He got kicked out for refusing orders." Abuela croaks. "He wouldn't whip a little boy, and they decided he wasn't cruel enough to be a guardsman."

"Is that true?" Diego peers at his father in disbelief. Something tells me that Abuela has a knack for exaggerating.

Enrique sighs. "He was just a kid, maybe six or seven. They caught him stealing herbs from a street vendor. Turns out, his brother was sick. He earned ten lashings, and I refused. He was Jorge's age at the time. I couldn't bring myself to do it. They dismissed me the next day with no explanation." Enrique doesn't sugarcoat anything for Diego. His face still shows signs of resentment. "Even if you make it in, Diego, you might not want to stay."

"Is it hard to get accepted?" Diego asks.

Enrique thinks for a moment. "It's not easy. Luckily for me, I had a knack for dominion. That was my ticket in."

Abuela proudly lifts her chin. "We may not be rich, but we're full-blooded Adamics. Our bloodline is as pure as they come."

Diego looks back at his dad. "Is it true what Jorge said about the king and the amulets?" Diego asks.

Enrique nods. "The king is an adalit after all. If he wanted to, he could make guardian amulets for every one of us. But he's a coward. He's afraid that if the people get any kind of power, they'll overthrow him. So, he keeps them all locked away. As for the guard, he makes sure to keep their loyalties bought."

Diego seems torn. "But the pay is ten times what I'd make in the field. Don't we need the extra money?"

"We do just fine," Abuela shouts. "All we need is each other." Her voice rises with her emotions. "We just got you back, we can't lose you already!" The table falls quiet. No one dares take another bite.

"This is exactly what happened with your mother," Abuela cries. "She decided life wasn't good enough for you here. You were too good for the fields. Too good for beans and corn. She wanted more, and look how it ended up. She's dead, and nothing's ch—"

"Mother!" Enrique's tone is threatening, almost scary. "Enough!"

He's too late. With a loud creak, Diego pushes back his stool and storms out of the kitchen. Isabela throws a needle-sharp glare at Abuela before jumping up and running after him.

I don't know if I should chase after them too or stay in my seat. I'm starting to wish I'd eaten at the refugee center.

"Thanks a lot, Mom," Enrique sighs. He slumps defeated in his chair.

Abuela doesn't back down. "We need to learn to be happy with what we have. Problems always come when people start wanting more."

Enrique hunches with his chin on his fist. "Well, if you're not careful, we'll lose the only thing we do have: our family."

Abuela huffs to herself and crosses her arms in front of her chest.

"Besides," Enrique mumbles to himself. "There's nothing wrong with wanting more."

Jorge and Javier wolf down the rest of their food. "Can we be excused?"

Enrique nods, and they escape into the side room. Part of me wants to follow them—to get out of range of Abuela's judgemental eyes.

Now it's only Abuela, Enrique, Mary, and myself at the table. Abuela stands and collects the dinner plates in her arms. "Come on, María. Let me show you how we do the dishes. The water basin is outside." She leads Mary by the hand down the hallway and out the front door.

And then there were two. Enrique leans back in his chair and sighs extra loud. He seems exhausted. Defeated. I feel bad for the guy. I've seen enough to know he's a good man.

"You have a beautiful family," I say.

Enrique is speechless. His mouth hangs slightly open. It's the first sentence he's heard me speak.

I quickly fill the silence. "I grew up an only child. I never knew my dad. It was kinda rough. They're lucky to have you. You're a good dad." I don't know if it's too personal, but I hope it helps.

Enrique looks at me with a newfound curiosity. "Thanks... and thanks for watching out for my boy."

I nod. "Honestly, he's been the one taking care of me. I have no idea where I would be without him."

Enrique furrows his brow. His parental instincts kick in. "Do you have anywhere to stay in the sanctuary? Any family?"

I don't want to be a burden, but I don't want to lie either. "No. It's just me."

"They have refugee centers, but they're not the safest," Enrique advises. "You're better off staying here with us. We have a few extra blankets. It's a little crowded, but you can stay in the boys' room if you want to."

"That would be nice, thank you." I want to say more but don't know what. Enrique is still a stranger, and it's a bit awkward being alone with him. The silence drags on.

Enrique gives me a friendly dad smile. "It gets easier," he assures me. "You'll get used to this place eventually. Do you have any questions about orientation? I know they don't do the best job."

"Actually," I lower my voice in case Abuela returns. "I'm still kind of confused about the whole feeder thing. Why they feed and on what? I don't really get unspoken dominion either."

Enrique smiles at me as if he was expecting the question. "They don't like to explain much about dominion to the lower class. Knowledge is power, and they like to keep us stupid." I can hear the frustration in Enrique's voice. "They explained what Adamic is, right?"

"Yeah, mostly."

"Okay, let me see if I can connect everything." He seems excited to be of service. I no longer feel like such a burden. Enrique snaps his fingers. "Okay, I got it."

As if on cue, Diego and Isabela walk through the door. "Sit down, Diego," Enrique says. "I was just about to explain dominion to Matt. If you really want to join the guard, you'll need to know this." Diego and Isabela plop down on the stools without a word. I have a feeling this isn't an everyday conversation.

"Now, exercising dominion is made up of two parts: the dominion itself and communicating with the elements. Except for the descendants of Cain, all of Adam's offspring inherit dominion. It flows in your veins. It's intertwined with your soul. But dominion alone is not enough. You need to communicate that authority for anything to happen. You with me so far?"

I nod. With each word, I feel my curiosity being quenched like a terrible thirst.

"In the past, people spoke Adamic to communicate with the earth —the famous language of the gods. It was the only language the elements understood. That make sense?" Diego and I both nod in unison.

"Good. Now, remember what I said about dominion requiring two parts. That means that the children of Cain, even if they learned Adamic, couldn't control the elements. They lack the authority. If you teach a parrot to speak Adamic, it can't control the elements. Make sense?" He's going slow, but things are starting to connect. Little by little.

"Now, when the Adamic language was lost, there was no way to communicate dominion. At least not easily. The only alternative was to communicate soul to soul."

"Soul to soul?" I echo. "What do you mean by that?"

"The soul is probably a new concept. It contains your mind and thoughts."

"Like the brain?" I ask.

"Mhhh, not exactly. The brain is just the bridge between the soul and the body. But the soul isn't limited to the body. It can go beyond. To communicate dominion, the soul can be stretched into its surroundings. It can reach out beyond the body to communicate directly to the elements. But, stretching the soul has consequences. It can damage the soul's connection to the body. Tear it. Destroy it even. They say it's a painful death."

"That's why they use amulets?" I guess.

"Exactly." Enrique snaps his fingers. "Amulets protect the soul from being damaged. Maybe I can simplify this." He runs his palms over his Velcro stubble as he thinks. "Okay. Let's say exercising dominion is like making light. If you try to do it without an amulet, your soul is like firewood. You can burn it to make light, but it will get destroyed in the process. With an amulet, the soul is like a rechargeable battery. It still gets weakened quickly, but it doesn't get completely destroyed. It can recharge with time and rest."

"What about soul-feeders?" The words slip out of my mouth before I can stop them.

Enrique hesitates. He gives a sad glance at Diego. "Feeders consume the souls of the Adamic, dominion and all. Just like we eat meat, and it becomes a part of us, the souls they consume become a part of them and make them stronger. Without an amulet, exercising dominion still damages the soul of a soul-feeder, but it's like having ten logs of firewood instead of one. They can burn nine logs and still be fine with the one they have left. That's why they're so dangerous. After feeding enough, they can make a bonfire much more powerful than a battery, stronger than an amulet even. That's why we hide in the sanctuary. Even with amulets, it's not safe out there."

I know those last words are directed at Diego. His dad just wants him to be safe, and safety means staying inside the sanctuary. Diego won't lift his eyes from the table. I know he's thinking about his mom. None of this could be easy to hear after what happened to her.

"But the children of Cain are safe, right?" I ask.

Enrique nods. "They have souls, but no dominion. If a feeder fed on a child of Cain, it would be like wet firewood. It just wouldn't burn. The feeders usually just leave them alone."

"And what about guardians?" I wonder. The question has been on my mind ever since Zane confiscated my amulet. He said it was powerful like his.

Enrique looks at me and laughs. "You don't waste any time, do you? Ambition; that's good. I hope it takes you farther than it did me." He looks off into the corner of the room as he thinks. "Guardians are the exception. They have special amulets. They don't need to recharge like the rest of the guard. They're like the sun. Unlimited power for life. But don't get your hopes up. Only the best of the best are chosen."

I nod. It may not be the best time to ask, but I have so many questions. I don't know when I'll get another shot like this. "If I understand everything right, almost everyone outside of the wall is a descendant of Cain, and they all can become feeders?"

"Technically yes, they can, but becoming a feeder isn't easy. They'd have to find an Adamic and consume his soul. No one becomes a feeder by accident."

I try to imagine Judy commanding the elements. Feeding for power. The idea seems ridiculous.

I form another question in my head and take a deep breath. "So, if the Adamic and non-gifted both can't use dominion without an amulet, wouldn't they both have equal incentive to become feeders? Wouldn't the Adamic become feeders too?"

"Blasphemy!" A raspy voice roars from the hallway. Abuela comes storming into the kitchen while signing a cross over her heart. She points her index finger at me like a gun. "Never speak of such satanic things in this home again, or I'll throw you out myself!"

I don't dare move. I sit frozen in my seat, looking to Diego for help. Diego stares back, equally stunned. Abuela storms up to me until her finger trembles inches from my nose. "No Adamic would ever commit such an unforgivable sin. To even speak of it invites the devil."

"Mom, leave the boy alone," Enrique asks politely. "I brought it up. No one will mention it again. I promise."

She glanced at Enrique and back at me. Her finger slowly lowers to her side. "I'll be in my room," she hisses. Her dress billows behind her as she flees down the hallway and into one of the side rooms.

Enrique waits until Abuela is out of earshot. He looks Diego square in the eyes. "You still want to be a guardsman?"

Diego shrugs. "I guess." He lacks his usual excitement.

Enrique stands up from his stool and grabs his hat from a hook on the wall. "There's an execution tomorrow in the royal plaza. It starts at six o'clock. I want you boys to go see it. If you're still confident after the execution, you have my permission to join the guard."

Diego's usual smile slowly slithers back onto his face. "You'll really let me join?" He jumps up and wraps his arms around Enrique. "Thanks, Dad. You won't regret it."

Enrique slips on his boots and pulls his hat over his head. "Don't thank me yet. I'll see you boys tonight."

He stops at the edge of the kitchen. "Oh, and Matt, the answer to your question is yes."

Chapter 10

Rose

The crowd is bigger than I anticipated. There must be at least a few thousand, but not nearly as many as Remembrance Day. They wait in quiet anticipation for the execution to begin.

The crowd is mostly commoners and elites. The laborers can't afford to miss work, and today is no holiday. It's strange to think that the riot was only three days ago. The bloodstains have been scrubbed from the plaza, but the memories are burned into my mind… and my arm.

Grandpa, Antai, and a few other officials are seated next to me on stage. They'll be right by me in case something goes wrong. I spot Zane a few chairs down. I'm glad he's back safe from the beyond. He's one of my favorite guardians. He's wearing jeans and a red flannel. That's what I like most about him. He's genuine. He doesn't put on a show for the other diplomats.

The prisoners kneel next to the gallows, chained from head to toe. The executioner patrols the structure, eagerly checking the knots. When he's satisfied, he trots down the wooden steps and pulls a lever underneath the platform. The floor of the gallows suddenly swings on a hinge until it's hanging vertically. Had someone been standing on the platform with a noose around their neck, they would have plummeted several feet until the rope snapped taut. It's designed to break the victim's neck on impact. It's quicker that way and more humane for the prisoners. Yet every now and then, a prisoner survives the fall and is slowly strangled by the rope. It's a terrible sight to see.

As soon as the floor is latched back into place, the executioner gives a nod. Grandpa looks at me, and I take a deep breath. It's time.

I walk to the front of the stage and unfold my script. Everything I have to say is written before me. It's short and to the point. I only have to get through it without fainting. I clear my throat.

"I am Princess Roselyn Malik, reporting for the high council. Yesterday morning, these men were brought before the council to be judged for the following crimes." I read the list from top to bottom. I look out over the crowd and try not to think about what's about to happen. "In the name of the high council, these men have been found guilty on all accounts and are condemned to death by hanging, to proceed immediately."

A wave of cheers erupts from the crowd. A few people boo. I think I hear someone weeping as well.

"The execution will proceed in the following order." I try my best to pronounce each name loudly and clearly. They deserve that much. It will likely be the last time they hear their own names. "James Hill. Spencer Madison. Quonos Wryke. Vygil Limnah. Bill O'brien. Steven Walsh."

I turn my body towards the gallows and speak directly to the prisoners. "According to the law, you will each be allowed one minute to give your final words."

I look down at my paper. I don't want to read the last paragraph. It's a warning directed to the equalists, none of whom are here to listen anyways. But I know I must. Every execution ends with the same admonition. It's tradition.

"Let these men stand as a reminder that justice cannot be avoided. The law is set, and those who defile it will pay for their crimes. There are only two options: obedience and life, or rebellion and death. The choice is yours."

I sigh a breath of relief and take my seat. I'm done with my speech. Now begins the hard part: watching the execution.

The executioner leads the first prisoner onto the gallows by his shackles. It's the flag man from the riot. He lifts his head high and shouts his last words. "The only crime I've committed is defending myself. You are the real murderers." The prisoner jabs his finger directly at Grandpa and I. "You people have condemned us to death in the fields. I've watched my brothers and sisters die. Some from infection. Others from exhaustion. When we're too tired to plow the field, you beat us like dogs. You starve us, and then you beat us when we steal bread. Obedience is suicide. If we submit, we starve. If we fight back, we're hung. You say we have a choice… What choice? Death by starvation or death by hanging. No matter what we choose, we die.

But mark my words: you can't kill us all. Your tyranny is almost over, and when we rise against you, there won't be enough rope in Cavernum to hang you all."

The prisoner steps back and allows the executioner to place the noose around his neck. He closes his eyes and holds his head high. He doesn't show a morsel of regret. The executioner pulls a lever, and he falls through the floor. I turn my head and hear a faint crack. It was his neck. When I peek, he's swinging motionless, already dead. The crowd cheers.

I try not to look at the body. I've never seen one this close before. I can see his eyes bulging and the crease in his neck from the rope. My stomach lurches, and I look away. I already know I'll have nightmares tonight.

The body is still swaying when the next prisoner is guided up the wooden steps and onto the platform. He stands next to the first body and delivers a similar speech. I can hear him shouting, but the words don't register. My stomach is queasy, and I can't think straight. Then, the trap floor drops, and he sways next to the first. The crowd cheers.

The third prisoner looks absolutely terrified. He stands quivering on the gallows. He opens his mouth to speak, but no words come out. Finally, he bursts into tears, a dark circle of urine expanding around his groin.

The executioner slips the noose around his neck, and the floor collapses beneath him. His sobs are instantly silenced by a sharp snap. His suffering is over.

All three ropes are now occupied by the dead. There's a long pause as the bodies are cut down, and three new ropes are tied onto the wooden beam.

My stomach is folding into knots. I lean forward, tuck my head between my legs, and suck in air. It helps a little. I notice Antai watching me from his seat to my left. His brow is furrowed with worry. I don't care about our fight last night; I wish he were sitting next to me.

I hear words from the fourth prisoner, but I keep my head between my legs. I'm afraid if I raise my head, I'll vomit in front of the entire audience. I hear the creak of wood and the snap of a rope, but I don't raise my head. I can't bear to see the body. The crowd goes wild. Another speech is given, and prisoner five is hung. All I hear is my heart thumping in my chest. One word snaps me out of my trance.

"Daddy!"

It's the voice of a child. A little girl. Her voice is frantic and fearful.

"Daddy!"

I find her in the crowd. She stands directly in front of the gallows and reaches with outstretched fingers. Only her mother's arms keep her from running to her father. She's so young—maybe six years old. Strands of hay colored hair stick to her wet cheeks in a tangled mess. She calls to her father as he's led up the wooden steps of the gallows.

Something in me breaks. I can't stand to see her suffer like this. She's innocent. I don't care what her father did, the girl doesn't deserve this. She's the one being punished here, not the father. The prisoner will be dead in an instant, but the girl will feel the pain of this moment for the rest of her life.

The last prisoner stands tall on the gallows. He doesn't take his eyes off of his daughter. "Sarah, can you hear daddy?"

The little girl bounces up and down as her dad smiles at her longingly. It's the last time he'll see her. My chest gets tight, and water pushes on the dam that is my eyes.

"Sarah, listen closely. I want you to know how much I love you. More than the moon and the stars. More than anything. Please, please don't forget that!" he begs.

His daughter listens with wide, eager eyes. She obviously adores him. She soaks up every word like a sponge.

"I'm so sorry. I just wanted to give you a better life. Everything I did, I did because I love you. I hope you can forgive me someday. I know it won't be easy for you. But I pray someday you'll understand."

I feel as though the prisoner is speaking to me. My heart is ripping in my chest. Feelings I've hidden deep inside are suddenly rising to the surface. My dad gave his life to try to keep me safe. He would do anything for me. And now he's gone. The ache is almost unbearable.

His expression shifts, and now he's speaking to his wife. The woman squats behind her daughter and hugs her from behind. Her cheeks are striped with tears, but she's acting brave. I doubt she has many tears left to cry.

"Honey," the prisoner cries, his voice raw with emotion. "I'm so sorry you have to do this alone. Please forgive me. I'll be waiting for you on the other side. I love you… I'll love you forever."

With those last words, the mother clasps her hands over the daughter's eyes. The next thing I know, the noose is slipped over the prisoner's head, and the executioner pulls the lever.

As his body starts to fall, I squeeze my eyes shut. I hear the rope go taut, but I don't hear the usual crack. The crowd gasps.

I peek my eyes open just enough to see his legs kicking.

No! Please no! Not him. Not with them watching. He survived the fall, and now he's slowly strangling. This time, no one cheers.

The wife finally loses it. She hugs her daughter's face in her chest and screams. I've never heard a cry so full of pain. So heart-wrenching. The crowd is silent as the prisoner struggles against the rope. I squeeze my eyes shut, but I can't escape the scene before me. The wooden beam creaks loudly as he kicks his legs in the air. I can hear him gurgle. His wife screams long and loud. "Noooooooo!!! You monsters!!!"

This isn't right. I've never considered it before, but I'm convinced of it now. Hanging a father in front of his family is wrong. Executions are wrong. They've always been wrong.

I can save him. The solution is suddenly so obvious. The gallows are only a few meters from the stage, and as always, I'm wearing my amulet. With a simple thought, I can sever the rope. *I can set him free. I can save him.*

I wrestle with the thought in my mind. No one has to know it was me. Any of the guards could do the same. There would be no way to pinpoint it on me. And if they try to hang him again, I'll just keep cutting the rope. *This could actually work. I can save him.*

Then, I notice it: the silence. The creaking has stopped. I open my eyes and find the prisoner hanging limp. Dead.

No, no, no! I'm too late. I could've saved him. I could've saved her father. *He died because I hesitated. He died because of me.*

Suddenly, I'm choking on my emotions. My throat constricts, my breath coming in gasps. I squeeze my eyes shut, but the damn finally breaks.

I could have saved him. I could've, but I didn't.

I run up the stairs, my feet slapping the stone in a flurry of footsteps. All I want to do is be alone with my emotions. I need time to think.

I turn down the hall to the royal wing of the palace. I duck my head to the floor as I pass a servant boy. I don't want him to see my red eyes. A princess should never cry in front of her subjects. Out of the corner of my eyes, I can see he's carrying a bowl of food. What looks like large clumps of oatmeal are smeared down the front of his shirt. I already know who's at fault.

Part of me wants to ignore him and go straight to my chambers, but I know I shouldn't. I wipe my eyes and try to look like a lady. "Excuse me?"

The servant graciously bows. "Princess, how may I serve thee?" He's young, somewhere in his mid-teens. But he's confident and composed for such a young servant.

"Did my great-grandpa do that?" I ask, pointing to his mess of a shirt.

"Yes, princess. He's rather feisty today. He refused breakfast and lunch as well."

I hold out my arms for the bowl. "If you don't mind, I'll see if I can get him to eat." Titan doesn't remember much, but he does remember his wife, who I apparently resemble. She died years ago, but Titan has no recollection of her death. As long as I play the part, I've always been able to calm him down.

"Why thank you, princess. That is most kind of you." The servant hands me the half-empty bowl of oatmeal and bows before leaving. I carry the bowl down the hall and turn into Great-grandpa Titan's chambers. His room is spacious with a high ceiling and a large fireplace. On all sides, the walls are lined with bookshelves. He was a real scholar in his day, but 'his day' was decades ago.

Titan sits in a large sofa chair in front of the cold fireplace, a pile of oatmeal pooling in his lap. Two servants hover around him, coaxing him as they would a child. "Lord Titan, as soon as you change your shirt, you can take a nap for as long as you like. Please let us help you."

Titan stares blankly at the fireplace. His pale gray hair clings to his scalp in patches. His leathery skin is more gray than brown. The worst are his eyes. Usually, they're sunken and lifeless, but every now and then, they fill with madness and delusions.

I step into the room. "Hello, Titan, I missed you."

At the sound of my voice, Titan slowly turns his head. When he sees me, he smiles and pats his lap. "Clarinda, come sit." He wheezes. His voice is hoarse and scratchy.

"That's all right. I'll pull up a chair." A servant carries over an extra chair and mouths the words 'thank you' before receding into the background.

"Why aren't you eating?" I ask. "These poor men are trying to help you."

Titan pouts his lips. "I don't want to eat; I want to die. You never come anymore." Guilt tugs at my heart. He's right. I've been so busy I haven't visited in weeks. The poor old man misses his wife.

"Clarinda, do you still love me?" Titan asks out of innocent fear.

"Of course I do," I assure him. "How about this? If you eat all of this oatmeal, I'll stay with you the rest of the hour."

Titan smiles and grows quiet. I take it as a yes. I feed him the first spoonful like a baby, and he opens wide. When the oatmeal runs down his chin, I scoop it up and plop it back in his mouth. Within a minute, the bowl is empty, and it's time to keep my end of the bargain.

"What do you want me to read?" I ask. Every time I visit him, Titan asks me to read the same book: Clarinda's journal.

Grandpa points to the fireplace, and I spot the journal on the mantel. It's a hefty book, over two inches thick. A bookmark is placed on Titan's favorite entry: his wedding day. I've read it to him dozens of times, but every time I return, he doesn't remember. There is still so much of the journal I want to read.

"Is it alright if I read somewhere else today?" I ask.

Titan shakily points to his bookmark and grunts.

"Please, Titan. Can I read something new? Is that alright?" Titan stares blankly ahead, which I take as a yes. I flip to a random page in the middle and begin reading loudly so Titan can hear.

January 8, 1943,

This last week was terrifying. The laborers have become insatiable. The things they've done are unspeakable. Titan never thought it would come to this, but he was wrong. They've committed the unforgivable sin. God, have mercy on us all. Even now, they chant outside the walls. We've been trapped in the palace for almost a week now. We're running low on food. Any who try to leave risk death at the hands of the laborers. The guardians are getting impatient. They want to open the amulet vault, but Titan forbids it. They claim the extra amulets will give us the upper hand, yet Titan fears they will fall into picker's grasp. Even more, he fears God's judgment has finally befallen us for our sins. The only option is to repent.

–Clarinda

Risk death? Unforgivable sin? Clarinda was obviously terrified of the laborers. But why? Even without the amulets in the vault, the rebellion was no match for the guardians. *Why was she so afraid?*

I've studied all about the Blood Rebellion with my tutors. The laborers rebelled by the hundreds and surrounded the palace. The guardians could've wiped them out. Fortunately for them, King Titan was merciful.

I keep reading.

January 11, 1943

What a wondrous day it's been. The rebellion is over. Rather than open the vault, Titan bargained a compromise. Today, everyone from all classes gathered in the plaza for Titan's announcement of a new social caste. He calls it "The Dividing."

151

Children are no longer confined to the social class of their birth. Now, classes are determined by merit alone. Everyone has an opportunity to raise their social standing. When they heard the news, the people of Cavernum were ecstatic. I can still hear them celebrating from my chambers. The elites weren't so pleased, but sacrifice is necessary to reconcile past wrongs. The pickers no longer fight against us. It's days like these that remind me why I married Titan. He'll do anything to make the world a better place. I'm so lucky to be his queen.

- Clarinda

When I look up, Titan looks puzzled. "Did I do all that? I don't remember." His voice sounds so hopeless. It hurts me to see him like this. I wish I could've known Titan in his glory days. The Titan who revolutionized the sanctuary.

"You really did," I say. "You avoided a war and united the sanctuary."

A blissful smile spreads across Titan's face. His eyes drop half shut. "I must've been a good king."

"One of the greatest," I assure him. I flip a handful of pages and pick a random entry.

July 01, 1956

This week has been wondrous. Titan took me to visit our sister sanctuary of Hogrum. When we arrived, we were graciously greeted by King Rotum and offered a guest room in the palace. While Titan did his archeological research in the gold mines, I spent most of my days with Queen Jozy. Such a kind-hearted woman. We shopped at the jewelers market and I brought home some beautiful gold earrings. Our stay was brief, but Titan says we'll be going to visit more sanctuaries soon. He's been working on a special project lately. He doesn't like to talk about the details, but whatever it is, it's all he thinks about. We don't converse like we used to. I feel awfully lonely. But I know he has his reasons. He says he's getting close to a breakthrough. I hope he finds it soon so things can return to normal. Either way, I hope we can visit Hogrum again soon.

– Clarinda

After what Grandpa told me yesterday, I can't help but think of the Lost Library. I crane my head and gaze around the room. I don't see any of the servants. It can't hurt to try.

"Titan, I need to ask you something. Did you ever find what you were looking for in Hogrum?"

Titan stares blankly ahead. Once again, his eyes are empty. A drop of drool spills over the corner of his mouth. I need to try harder. I lace my voice with false affection.

"Titan, my love. Listen to me please. Did you find what you were looking for in Hogrum?"

Ever so slowly, Titan nods his head up and down. Part of me wonders if he even knows what I'm saying. From what I've read in the journal, Titan kept his wife in the dark. But maybe now with his feeble mind, he'll tell me something. "Can you tell me what you found, my love? What did you find?"

Titan continues to stare into the fireplace. I can't find any hint of understanding in his hollow eyes.

I lower my voice. "Titan, did you find the Lost Library?"

Suddenly, Titan's head jerks to meet mine with wide, wild eyes. "I told you to never speak of that place again!" he seethes. "You promised me you wouldn't! Why did you break your promise?" His voice is as loud as his tender throat can muster. His fists shake angrily in the air in front of him. "I knew I should've never trusted you. It must stay hidden. You'll kill us all. You'll kill us all!" He reaches for my wrists with his claw-like hands, but I leap from his grasp.

The other servants come rushing into the room. "What happened? What's going on?"

"I don't know," I lie. "He went mad as I was reading."

"Never speak of it again," Titan hisses, spittle spraying from his lips. "It must stay hidden. You'll kill us all. It must stay hidden!"

Titan tries to stand, but the two servants easily hold him down in his chair. "Titan, please calm down," they soothe. "You're safe. There's nothing to be afraid of."

"Maybe I should go," I say. "I think I'm upsetting him."

"I'm afraid you're right, princess," the servant agrees. "Perhaps come back later when he forgets all of this."

I hurry out of the room and leave the servants to wrestle with my deranged great-grandfather. I have to tell Grandpa what just happened. Titan basically confirmed it. It really exists.

Titan found the Lost Library. *The Book of Life exists!*

Chapter 11

Matt

As soon as the last body is hung, the crowd begins to disperse. I stare in disbelief as they cut down the last three bodies. Real bodies. This isn't Hollywood special effects. They just killed real people.

"This is messed up, dude." Diego's eyes are wide with disbelief. "Maybe my dad is right. I don't know if I can do this, Matt."

I try to sort through my feelings. In Colorado, we had the death penalty, but only for the worst of criminals. Supposedly, those men killed police officers, but from the speeches I've just heard, it almost sounds justified.

"No wonder your mom left," I finally mutter.

"I'm thinking about it, dude. I'm this close to going back." He holds his thumb only an inch from his index finger. "This close!"

"What now?" I ask. It's getting later in the evening, and the shop-keepers are starting to pack up. My neck still itches and burns and I just want to lie down and sleep. "I'm guessing this place doesn't have much of a nightlife."

"Yeah, we should probably head home now. I don't want to get caught outside after dark. Jorge missed curfew once, and he still wears the scars."

We don't get far before I hear a scream behind me. "Thief! That picker stole my cake," a woman wails.

I turn around to see a skinny boy sprinting straight at me. He runs with a football-sized loaf of bread tucked under his arm. Two policemen are in pursuit, but they're quickly falling behind. One of them points at Diego and me. "You two! Stop him!"

I freeze. So does Diego. The boy runs right in between us and weaves his way into the dispersing crowd. Within a second, he's completely out of sight.

The cops stumble to a stop in front of us and huff to catch their breath. One is a bulky man with a weightlifter's build. The other is just your average Joe. They search the crowd for another second before turning their anger on us. The average Joe of a cop shouts with a nasally tone. "Damn ringlings! Why didn't you stop them? They ran right past you!"

Diego looks at his shoes. I lower my gaze as well. I've met people like him before. As long as we submit, he'll eventually lose interest. All he wants is someone to yell at.

Average Joe steps uncomfortably close. His face is inches from mine. "Did you want him to get away? Huh?"

I don't respond.

He steps up to Diego and sticks out his chest. "Why'd you let him go? Huh? Was this a picker helping out a picker? You wanted him to escape, didn't you?"

"We were just minding our own business," Diego quietly replies. "We don't want any trouble, sir."

The cop steps even closer. "Well, you found it, picker. Aiding a criminal is punishable by lashings. You better convince me that your innocent real fast, or I'll have you flogged." His partner stands silently next to him with his arms crossed. He doesn't say anything, but his muscles do the talking.

"We don't want any trouble," Diego repeats.

The cop narrows his eyes at Diego's neck. A portion of his necklace is visible above his collar. "Is that gold?" The cop asks.

Diego nods.

A greedy grin grows on the cop's face. "Show me."

Diego retrieves his gold cross and gingerly lays it on the outside of his shirt. Average Joe stares hungrily at the necklace. "Hmmmm. That would probably convince me... unless you prefer the whip."

"Please don't do this," Diego begs. "This was a gift from my mom. Please don't take it." Anger boils inside me. These men are bigger thieves than the boy stealing bread.

"What's it gonna be?" the cop demands.

Diego slowly reaches up and lifts his cross off his neck. Average Joe reaches his greedy hands to take it.

A shadow falls over my head. "Something wrong, boys?" I know that voice. I spin around and find Zane towering behind me in a classic lumberjack flannel.

"General." The cop snaps to attention with his chin held high. "These two aided a thief in his escape. We were questioning them before making an arrest." He confidently reports.

"Really?" Zane turns to me. "Matt, is that true?"

"No, sir," I say with a smile.

The cop's jaw falls wide open. He looks back and forth between Zane and me in disbelief.

"Hmmm." Zane pretends to be puzzled. He scratches his beard and turns to the cop. "That's weird. They said they didn't do it. But you said they did. How odd."

"S-sir, they let a thief run right past them. They didn't even try to stop him."

Zane's sarcasm disappears. Now, he looks angry. "Whose job is it to catch criminals, theirs or yours?"

"Ours," Average Joe admits.

Zane steps closer, towering over the cop. He uses the same tactic of intimidation the cop just used on us.

"So, who really let the thief get away?" Zane growls. "Them or you?"

"Me, sir. Forgive me, sir."

"Good," Zane breathes in his face. "Now, get out there and do your job. If I see you stealing from refugees again, I'll send you to the pit. Get out of my sight!"

The two policemen turn and speed walk away as quickly as they can. An elderly man in a nearby shop claps his hands. He must have been watching the whole time.

Zane smiles and laughs. "Man, I hate those guys. If they give you trouble again, just let me know. I have a feeling they won't."

"Thank you so much, sir." Diego rambles. "I don't mean any disrespect if you're not, but aren't you a Guardian?"

Zane chuckles. "Something like that."

"This is Zane," I inform Diego. "He's the Guardian that saved me."

Zane frowns at me. His eyes jump from my face to my neck. "Hold still, Matt." Zane puts his hand on my forehead and tilts my head to the side, exposing my feeder bite. "Demons, it's getting worse. You should probably get that bite checked. I'm heading to the palace right now. I can take you to a healer if you want."

"Ummm, sure." I feel bad leaving Diego, but my neck has been itching like crazy, and I can't pass up a chance to see the palace. I look at Diego. "How do I find your house when I'm done?" I wait for Zane to invite Diego as well, but he doesn't.

"Just go," Diego insists. "I'll wait for you here, and we can walk back together."

"It shouldn't take long," Zane assures me. "But it'll be dark soon, so we better hurry."

"Alright, I'll meet you here," I tell Diego. "See you in a bit."

Zane starts across the plaza, and I hurry to catch up. He's such a strange man. How does he always show up just in time to save me?

Zane waits until I'm walking at his side. "What did you think of the execution?"

"I'm not a fan," I confess. "It seems a bit extreme." *Very extreme.*

Zane sighs. "Yeah, I'm not a fan either. Sometimes you just have to grit your teeth and look the other way."

"Why doesn't someone change it?" I ask.

"Not everyone on the council agrees with you and me. But the king has things moving in the right direction. Cavernum is far from perfect, but it's sure come a long way from where it was. Change takes time."

As we approach the palace gateway, two policemen in white uniforms straighten their backs.

"He's with me," Zane announces as we pass the guards. As I step through the gateway, I feel the static wash over me. The hairs on my arms stand up, sending shivers down my spine. We cross a long stone driveway lined with elegant fountains and perfectly manicured hedges. Two more guards stand at the castle entrance. They open the door as we approach.

"I have a meeting I'm late for, but I'll show you where to go." Zane leads me up a marble staircase and down a long hall lined with landscape paintings and fancy sculptures. I quietly follow after him as we climb two more staircases.

Zane points in front of him. "Down this hall, first staircase on your right. Tell them I sent you." Zane starts the opposite way before I can respond.

"Thank you!" I call after him. He raises his hand in acknowledgment but doesn't turn around.

My head throbs as I climb the last staircase. I reach the top and stop at a small doorway. Rather than a door, multicolored beads block my view. They hang from the door frame forming a curtain of privacy. I make a slit in the middle of the bead curtain and peek inside.

"Come in," Coos an older lady. She wears a knee length white dress, like a nurse from the 50's. She's a plus sized woman with poofy gray hair. Wiry glasses rest on her stumpy nose. Every few seconds, she sucks on the pipe in her teeth and blows smoke out her nose. *So much for health laws.*

Just like the police I've seen, a red symbol is sewn on her shoulder. I know this symbol well. It's a staff with two snakes coiled around it—the international symbol of medicine.

I walk through the doorway, and beads pour over me like a waterfall. I stop just inside the door. The room is big and covered with dozens of knee-high leather cots. All but two of them are empty. On one side of the room, an old man lays on one of the cots like a mummy. On the opposite side of the room, a particularly large man is getting treated. A breeze blows through an open window, clanking wind chimes and blowing the curtains. Daylight from the setting sun bathes the room in orange. Everything gives me 70's vibes—peaceful and psychedelic.

"Ummm, I'm looking for the healing loft." I speak softly, trying not to disturb the other patients. "Am I in the right place?"

The woman takes one look at me and scowls. "I'm sorry, but the loft is reserved for elite citizens only. All commoners must go to the infirmary on the main floor." As she speaks, the woman straightens a blanket over a leather cot.

"Zane sent me, he said you would be able to help."

The lady stands up and rolls her eyes. "And why would he do that?"

I pull down on my collar and point to the exposed stitches. "He wanted me to get this checked."

The lady chokes on her pipe and coughs smoke. "My goodness. Is that what I think it is?" She stares at me as if I'm a walking corpse. "Well, sit down. Please, sit down." She scurries through a different door of beads into a back room. I sit down on a cot in the middle of the room. As soon as my butt hits the plush leather, I realize how exhausted I am—like a long day of hunting, except without my ATV to ride on.

Almost immediately, the gray-haired woman returns with a young girl trailing behind her. The new girl wears a matching white dress with the snake symbol on her shoulder. A silver amulet bounces on her chest as she walks. She's short, maybe a foot or so shorter than me.

Her blonde hair falls in wavy locks over her shoulder and sways with each stride. When her green eyes meet mine, her slender lips curl into a beautiful smile.

I smile back.

"This is Kendra. She's a first-year healer, but she's the top of her class. She'll be taking care of you tonight." The lady introduces her, placing a hand on her shoulder. "And Kendra, this is…"

"Matt. Nice to meet you." I hold out my hand and shake Kendra's. *Do the people here shake hands?* I'm not even sure.

The gray-haired lady speaks as she slowly backs away from us. "Well, I'll leave you two be. Call if you need anything, Kendra."

Kendra doesn't waste any time. She's obviously done this before. "Alright, Matt, before we begin, I just need to ask you a few questions." She bombards me with a flurry of questions. "How long did the bite last?… Did you lose consciousness?... Rate your pain from one to ten." I answer all her questions quickly and precisely.

Coming up behind me, she takes a closer look at the stitches. She cringes and frowns at me accusingly. "It's definitely infected. Did you do these yourself?"

"No, Zane the guardian did them. Why?"

"They look terrible," Kendra laughs. "Those guardians think they're masters at everything. Be right back." She returns with a box of surgical tools and a tube of white paste. She squirts the paste over the wound and begins cutting the threads and pulling out the stitches.

"The cream is to numb you, but this still might sting a little. We need to remove the infected fluid before the healing can begin." She covers my neck with gauze and squeezes my neck. I cringe. Why does the cute girl have to deal with my infected neck puss? *So much for a good first impression.*

"That should do it," Kendra announces after dabbing the wound with gauze. She pours something onto my neck that stings like fire. I grit my teeth and tense my arms.

"Sorry, that was to disinfect. The worst is over. Now I just need to stitch you up, and we can finish with the healing." She holds up a long curved needle and works a thread into the loop at the base. I sit quietly as she works the needle through my skin, re-stitching the wound. Each prick of the needle stings, but it's bearable. Her soft hands lightly tickle my neck as she works.

She finishes quickly and returns the supplies to the back room. When she returns, she's carrying something shiny. A gold, pear-shaped amulet is bundled in her curled fingers. Two symbols are engraved on the surface.

"All your vitals seem fine, and your wound is clean, but I'll heal what I can just to be safe. Can you lie down on your back for me and put this on?" Kendra lays the amulet gently in my hand. "This will amplify your soul and make it easier for me to communicate with you. Just make sure you're touching the amulet with your skin. It needs skin contact for the spell to take effect."

I comply. The necklace provides a familiar weight on my chest. Its symbols are identical to the one Kendra is wearing. I wondered where my own amulet is now. Maybe locked somewhere deep within the castle.

I look up at Kendra as she sits on the edge of the bed and leans over me. She places her delicate hands on my chest. "Now, I just need you to relax and try not to fight anything. Try focusing on your breathing, and I'll do the rest."

But I have questions. "How does it work? The healing?"

"Well, healers are able to speak to the body of patients, just like the guardsmen speak to the elements. But we don't have dominion over other humans, so we need permission first. With permission, a healer can build tissue, remove toxins, connect bones, basically anything. They can even give some of their soul to help sustain someone near death. Pretty remarkable, right?"

"Yeah," I agree as ideas spin in my head. Before I can ask more, Kendra closes her eyes.

It begins as a faint sensation in my neck. The skin along the stitches tingles and quivers. I watch her face as she works. Her mouth hangs slightly open, and her eyes squeeze tightly shut. Her hair dangles in the air above my face.

I can't help but wonder what she's thinking—what it's like to heal someone. As I watch, I feel something on the edge of my thoughts: Concentration. Effort. I can feel the strain of healing through Kendra. She's scanning my entire body now looking for damage. I sense a hint of something else: attraction… desire.

I blush and turn away. The thoughts disappear almost instantly. But were they her thoughts or my own? Except they weren't really thoughts, more like emotions. Did she feel it too? Kendra keeps her eyes shut. If she did, she hides it well. I close my eyes like instructed and focus on my breathing. I don't feel anything else. Maybe it's all in my head.

Kendra opens her eyes and stands up. "That should do it. You seem healthy to me. If you did lose dominion to the feeder, you recovered quickly. If anything, you seem stronger than most."

I sit up. "Ummm, great. Thanks."

Kendra looks out the window. "Hmmm, it's already sundown. Looks like you'll be staying in the palace tonight. You can't be in the streets after curfew."

Shoot! I promised Diego I would meet him. All I can do is hope he made it home before curfew.

Kendra motions to the cots. "You can stay here until sunrise. I'll bring you a blanket. Is there anything else I can do for you?"

"I just have a quick question. Can a healer do this with a child of Cain? Would it still work?"

Kendra thinks for a moment. "I suppose so, as long as you can communicate with their soul and earn permission. They don't need dominion to be healed. The healer is the one who does all the work."

"What if they're about to die?" I ask.

Kendra purses her slender lips as she thinks. "It would be difficult, but I suppose the healer could breathe some of their soul into the patient. It's a method used to revive someone near death; we call it the breath of life. I suppose you could do the same with a child of Cain."

"Really? Like reverse soul-feeding?" I wonder.

Kendra frowns at the thought, obviously disturbed. She shrugs. "I suppose so, but I wouldn't word it like that."

A deep, grizzly voice flows from the other side of the room. "No, that's a perfect explanation." He's a large, middle-aged man. Only a round belly stains his muscular build. His nose is oddly small for his face, and a thick brown mustache shades his devious grin. He lounges under the hands of an elderly asian woman.

"Healing is the exact opposite of soul-feeding," he says confidently. "With soul-feeding, one selfishly attacks the other's soul and strips them of life. With healing, one selflessly gives their own soul for nothing in return. One is directed with consent, the other is a violation." He doesn't even flinch as the healer feels up and down his chest. She continues with her eyes squeezed shut, hardly disturbed by the man's comments.

"Polar opposites," he concludes, his eyes settling on me. "Kendra, would you mind introducing me to your new friend. I don't believe we've met."

Kendra stands up straight. "Matt, I'd like you to meet Commander Noyan. He's in charge of the royal guard. Commander Noyan, this is Matt, a new refugee from yesterday's convoy.

"Welcome to Cavernum." The healer's hands bounce on his belly with each word. "You must have had quite the welcoming party. Not many refugees spend a night in the palace."

Kendra nods at my neck. "He was bitten by a feeder. Zane brought him in."

Commander Noyan raises his eyebrow, looking at me in disbelief. "Zane? As in General Zane? Is that so?"

There it is again. Why is it so surprising that Zane helped me out?

Commander Noyan points with his ogre-like finger. "You, my boy, are one lucky lad. Not many survive a feeding. That's one trophy of a scar you'll have."

I shrug. "That's what they tell me." I don't feel very lucky. But I won't admit that to this man. He seems friendly enough, and I want to keep it that way. "I can't complain," I lie. "A night in the palace has its perks."

Commander Noyan glances at Kendra and bursts out laughing. He grins and points to the old healer above him. "I could say the same myself." He barely finishes the sentence before the laughter bursts through his lips.

As if on cue, the woman opens her eyes and calmly clasps her hands in front of her. "I am finished, Commander Noyan. I will see you again tomorrow." I can see the sweat beads on her forehead. Whatever she was healing, it was no walk in the park.

Commander Noyan thanks the woman as she retreats through the curtain into the side room. "How old are you, boy? You getting divided this week?"

I opened my mouth to answer, but Commander Noyan blabs on. "You've gotta be what? 18, 19?" He reasons, eyeing me up. "Good height, strong build. Lots of potential. Got any idea what guild you wanna join?"

I only have to think for a moment. "I've always wanted to go into medicine. Maybe I could be a healer or a medic," I muse.

Commander Noyan slaps his hands on his belly. "Bwah, that feeder bite has gone to your head, son. Healing is a woman's sport. You, my boy, need to join the guard."

Kendra clears her throat. "I think he would make a great healer." She looks at me with her sea-green eyes. "We could use some more men around here."

Kendra is smiling at me in a way I'm not used to, but I like it. Maybe Cavernum isn't so bad after all.

"Honestly, either one sounds great," I confess. "Which one is easier to get into?"

"Neither is a walk in the park," Commander Noyan says. "There's not very many healers in Cavernum, and even less apprenticeships.

The guard is definitely your best bet. They even say they're accepting twice as many recruits this year. A decision of the princess."

That's all the persuasion I need. "Sounds good to me," I say. "Where do I sign up?" I'm a decent hunter. *How hard can hunting men be?*

Commander Noyan jostles his belly. "The trials are tomorrow in the flats. Some of my men will be officiating. Meet me here at sunrise, and I'll send you with them." He holds out his hand.

I shake it. There's no going back now. Tomorrow, I'll fight for a place in the guard. Tomorrow, my fate will be decided.

Chapter 12

Rose

Six hours have passed since the last body was hung. Already, the memories haunt my dreams. I see a body hanging limp, swaying in the wind. His back is facing me. The crowd cheers as the face slowly spins into view. I gasp.

The body has Antai's face.

I awake with a jolt. The sheets tangle knots around my sweaty body. I kick out of the blankets and sit on the edge of my bed. It's late, maybe midnight. I strike a match and light the candle on my nightstand. On the bright side, Nevela left me a glass of water. I sip it to wet my throat.

I don't want to lay down, afraid I'll fall back into the same wretched dream. I'm no stranger to the nightmares. They follow every execution. They haunt me for days until the memories fade. But I have a feeling today's memories will linger for much longer. My mind drifts back to the execution. The sound of creaking wood. The snap of the rope. Trying not to think about it only makes me think about it more.

I slide out of the sheets and step into my slippers. I unhook a robe from the closet and slip it over my nightgown. Finally, I unbolt the lock on my door and slide into the dark hallway.

I leave the candle on my nightstand. I don't need it to find my way. I make this trip often. My slippers make only a soft scuffle on the marble floor. It takes a few minutes to make my way to the central tower of the palace. I step out onto the terrace and suck in the sweet scent of roses. According to Grandpa, I'm named after these specific roses. This garden was my mother's favorite place in the palace.

The tower garden is the second largest garden in the sanctuary. Not to mention, it has a view of the entire plaza. I spend most of my sleepless nights up here, and they aren't few.

I walk to the edge of the railing and peer out over the city. Torches light the streets like lightning bugs in a spider web. It's breathtaking. The serenity of the night calms me. I stare up at the sky. Stars blanket the night like a million gleaming snowflakes. Thanks to the curfew, the city is silent. I lean on the concrete railing and close my eyes, listening to the crickets and the rustle of leaves.

"Can't sleep?"

I nearly jump out of my slippers. A small shriek escapes my lips. I turn from the railing and find a boy looking at me from the shadows of a cherry tree. He sits alone on a bench. It only takes me a moment to decide he's not an assassin. He's tall and lean, but he's not dressed the part. He's wearing clothes from the beyond: slim jeans and a jacket with a zipper. His wavy hair swoops to the side and curls at the tips. He seems to be about my age, maybe a little older.

I take a deep breath. My cheeks burn red with embarrassment. "What are you doing here?" I demand. "It's after dark."

The boy's mouth falls open, and puzzlement pulls on his eyebrows. He stands up from the bench. "Sorry, I didn't mean to scare you. If I'm not supposed to be here, I can leave. This is my first day in the city. Where I come from, everyone goes to bed a lot later. I just came out here to think."

My suspicions wash away. He must have come with the convoy. He's an outsider—a refugee. He's likely been chased from his home by the same beasts that keep us holed up in Cavernum. I try to imagine being in his shoes. In a new place. Confused. The poor boy must be overwhelmed.

"Normally, it's not permitted, but I do it all the time," I confess. I turn and look out over the city. The only city I've ever seen. "It's beautiful, isn't it?"

"I've never seen anything like it, that's for sure," the boy says, a tinge of disappointment in his voice. He takes his seat once again on the bench and nods at the empty oak next to him. "You can sit down with me if you want. There's plenty of room."

I hesitantly take a seat as the boy extends his hand. "My name's Matt."

I shake his hand. "Matt? Like a rug?" Refugees always have the strangest names.

The boy laughs at my question. "It's short for Matthew. Like from the Bible. Don't tell me you've never heard of it?" The boy called Matt looks at me like I'm crazy.

"I've heard of it," I assure. "Just never met anyone with the name."

"Hmmm," he thinks vocally. "It's a super common name where I'm from. Like John or Chris."

I can't help but laugh. "I've only heard of those names in books."

"Okay. What names are popular here then?

I don't even have to think. "Normal names like Krim, Zylon, Xanter."

Matt laughs again, his voice light and humming with amusement. It ends quickly, making me wish I could hear it again. "Those sounds like space names from a sci-fi movie."

I tilt my head. "What's a sci-fi?"

Matt smiles again. He finds joy in my confusion. "I keep forgetting you guys don't watch TV. It's a movie genre. It stands for Science fiction. Like spaceships and Star Wars."

I nod my head despite being utterly clueless. I don't like knowing less than a refugee, but I'm awfully curious about the beyond, and Matt seems to be an expert.

"And what's your name?" Matt asks. "Padmé? Katana?"

"It's R- It's Lynn," I lie. Matt may be new to Cavernum, but I still have to be cautious. Now that I'm closer, I can see his face more clearly. He has prominent cheekbones and full, soft lips. A small cleft in his chin is the only bump on his smooth jawline. He's taller than I initially realized. Sitting down, my eyes only come to his lips. I try not to stare at them as they move to shape words. He's handsome in a different way than Antai. Not quite as rugged. I almost want to use the word 'beautiful.'

"Nice to meet you, Lynn. We have that name too. It's actually pretty common." Matt smiles at me like an old friend. Are all refugees this pleasant?

"My mother was a refugee," I explain. "Her name was Violet— after the flower. My dad wanted to name me Zendal, but my mom liked the beyond names better." I want to tell him that I'm named after a flower too, but I'm already trapped in my lie.

Matt tilts his head back to look at the palace spires. "This place is amazing. Do you live here?"

For a second, I panic. A commoner wouldn't be taking a nightly stroll in the tower garden wearing a silk nightgown. I need to change my alias and fast.

"All my life," I brag. "I'm one of the Princess's handmaids." I make up the lie as I go, using Nevela as my model.

"Is that what you chose for The Dividing?" Matt wonders.

I try not to laugh at the notion. I think silently as I blend reality with my lie. "My parents died when I was little. In exchange for food and clothes, I live as a palace servant."

Matt looks at me, horrified. He wouldn't make that face if he understood.

"It has its benefits," I explain. "Servants receive better education than most. I get to live with the princess until The Dividing. And I'm not completely alone. My grandpa lives in the palace as well."

"Why doesn't he just take care of you?" he asks.

"It doesn't work that way. Grandparents rarely live to see their grandchildren divided. My grandpa is the exception. It's much easier on an orphan if they adapt to the palace while they're young."

"When do you get to choose a job?" he asks.

"I get divided tomorrow."

"No way! Me too." Matt leans forward on the bench. "What job are you going to choose?"

I sigh. "I think I'll join the orchestra guild. It's an elite guild. And it's what my mother did." I list the benefits, trying to convince myself it's what I want.

Matt looks at me with doubt in his eyes. "You don't sound very excited."

He's not wrong. Deep down, I want to choose the guard. I can't be confined to a lifetime of palace living. I want to see the world. Go on convoys. Experience the beyond. But I can't tell all this to some random boy... Can I?

"I am excited," I say. "I just... I'm interested in the guard as well, and I can't make up my mind. I've been going back and forth all week."

"The guard? Really?" Matt raises his eyebrows in surprise. He's just like everyone else: doubtful.

"I can do it," I insist. "I shoot better than most guardsmen. I'm trained in dominion. And girls have been accepted before."

Matt holds up his hands in defense. "No, I don't doubt you. In America, lots of girls are soldiers. It's just... I want to join the guard too. It would be cool to have a friend." He smiles until his dimple is visible in the moonlight.

Now, I'm the doubter. Children train their entire lives for the guard. Matt doesn't stand a chance. "It's not easy, Matt. They test combat and fitness and marksmanship and dominion. Have you ever exercised dominion before?"

Matt looks out over the city. "No. Not exactly." The smile on his face slowly fades. "But I've had a lot of practice with guns. I know how to shoot." He looks back at me with a humble softness in his eye. "I'll just have to hope it's enough."

"And what if it's not?" I say. I've been asking myself that question for years. *What if I'm not enough? What if I fail somewhere along the way?*

Matt thinks for a second before answering. "I almost didn't come out here to Cavernum. My mom is sick at home. Until this week, I'd never heard of Adamic or feeders or anything. But this guardian guy came and offered to take me. I knew if I didn't go, I would regret it. I had to at least try."

Matt stares directly into my eyes. His eyes are a bright glacier blue. He's so close, so genuine. It takes my breath away. "And even if I don't get accepted tomorrow. Even if I go straight home, it'll be worth it. I'll never have to wonder what could've happened." Matt shifts his gaze to the sky. "The only thing worse than failure is knowing you never tried. That's what my mom always told me."

No one speaks for a moment as I soak in what Matt just said. He's right. I can't live my life wondering what could have been. Maybe someday, when I'm queen, I'll hire Matt as an adviser. The thought makes me smile.

Matt continues, undiscouraged by the silence. "If you had to choose between the guard and the orchestra, knowing you would succeed in both, which would you choose?"

I barely have to think. "The guard." It's barely a whisper. But I know it's the truth. "I want to join the guard."

Is the decision really that easy? Matt has a way of making it so simple. Of making me forget my fears. But what if I don't make it? Doubts begin to creep back in. *If Matt can take the risk, then so can I.* The more I analyze it in my head, the more sure I become. I have to at least try.

I don't care what Antai or anyone thinks. "Tomorrow, I'm going to join the guard."

"Good!" Matt exclaims. "Now, maybe you can teach me how to exercise dominion?"

Chapter 13

Matt

I wipe the sweat from my forehead. The clearing is packed with hundreds of 18-year-old kids. They called it the flats. The sun is rising higher, and it's already getting hot out here.

I search the crowd for a friendly face. I can only think of two: Diego and Lynn. Every time I spot a girl with hickory brown hair, my heart leaps, but none of them are her. *Maybe she chose the orchestra after all.*

I can't find Diego either, and The Dividing is about to begin. Everyone has already received their wristbands: a small leather strap with an identification number. The number 124 is branded into mine.

My eyes wander across the field. Next to a beat down barn, a dozen kids are competing for the horse trainer apprenticeships. I watch as they ride in circles and guide the horses on foot.

A sturdy hand slaps me on the shoulder. A familiar Guatemalan accent fills my ear. "Dude, what happened last night? You never came back. I barely made it home before curfew." A bracelet reading #405 adorns Diego's wrist. He wears tattered high school gym shorts and a baggy blue t-shirt. Already, a dark blue stain soaks his underarm like the rising tide.

"Sorry, Diego. I spent the night in the palace. They wouldn't let me leave after dark," I explain. "I'm glad you're here though. I was worried you chickened out and went looking for a desk job."

"Are you kidding me? No way, José. I was just waiting under that tree." Diego points to a lone tree at the edge of the clearing. Two girls are standing in the small patch of shade it offers. Diego cracks his knuckles. "You ready to guard stuff?"

"As ready as I'll ever be." The banter helps keep my mind off of what lies ahead. We're only yards from the shooting range. Empty wooden tables are lined up before a sea of metal targets. I don't spot any guns yet. That's what I'm most looking forward to. If anything will set me apart, it'll be my marksmanship.

A loud voice silences the crowd. I spin and find the speaker standing on the roof of the armory. It's Sparky the fire bender again. Next to him stands a shorter guardsman with red lapels on his uniform. He wears a medal on his chest and a scowl on his face. He seems special, maybe a leader of some kind.

Sparky stands on the edge of the roof and yells to the crowd. "Hello everyone, I'm Proticus Tyre, head trainer, and welcome to the guardsman trials. Please gather in close because The Dividing is about to begin. You all have a wristband with an ID number. We'll use it to score you throughout the trials. There are a lot of you today. Almost 500 competitors. Sadly, only 50 of you will be accepted."

The man with the medal steps forward. He doesn't introduce himself. His voice is deeper than Proticus. More commanding.

"Unfortunately, not all soldiers are created equal. Today is designed to highlight your individual strengths and weaknesses. We want to see not only the skills, but the qualities that will make you a good guardsman: resilience, strength, determination. We want to find the 50 of you with the most potential to succeed. The fate of Cavernum depends on it.

Today's dividing consists of four trials. They test fitness, combat, dominion, and marksmanship. We want to see your best effort; this will be your only chance to prove yourselves. Might I add, anyone caught cheating will be automatically eliminated. Understood?"

A murmur of agreement echoes through the crowd. The soldier with the medal steps back from the roof's edge, and Proticus reclaims the spotlight.

"First off, we'll have a simple fitness test. If you look way down on the other side of the field, a guardsman is standing with the black and red flag of the guard. The red circle symbolizes the wall you will defend."

I squint. The black flag looks like a bug on the horizon, twitching and squirming beneath the blazing sun. A brown dirt road stretches toward the flag through a shoulder-high field of corn.

"Fitness isn't only physical, but mental as well. We need soldiers who can push the limits of their bodies and show self-mastery. The task is simple. Race around the flag and finish back here to record your number. It's a mile total. Understood?"

I look at the other competitors around me. Half of the kids are wearing a type of leather moccasin shoe. Fortunately, I'm wearing my modern running shoes like the elite boys. My odds look pretty good.

A gunshot rings out, and I scramble to follow the crowd. An elbow smacks me in the ribs. I hold out my forearms to shield me as I run. Almost instantly, Diego is lost in the stampede. I worry about the kid. He's a lot stockier than the Cavernum boys. A lot rounder as well.

I pump my arms and try to break free of the masses. A skinny boy in moccasins runs past me. Then another. Then another.

By the time I approach the flag, a stampede of twig-legged competitors are passing me on their way back. My shirt clings to my sweaty back, and the dust coats my throat. I scramble past the flag and start back towards the armory. My lungs burn.

I don't understand. Before Judy's cancer, I was one of the fastest runners on my football team. But those were sprints, and this is a mile.

Here, all the kids look built to run. They don't have electronics: no cars or TVs or phones. They must spend all day on their feet.

As I cross the finish line, a man with a clipboard jots down my ID number and place. I finished 176th. I'm in the top half, but I know it's not enough. Only 50 are accepted. I need to find a way to stand out.

I stand by the finish line, waiting for Diego. More and more boys finish. I start getting nervous. Finally, I spot him in the last group of boys. He crosses the finish line, and Clipboard Man records his place: 480th.

"It's not that bad," I try to console. "We still have 3 more events. You'll be fine."

"Are you kidding me? I'm pretty sure a girl on crutches passed me."

I laugh. "Don't feel bad. That girl was hauling ass."

"I'm serious. I can't end up in the fields," Diego insists. "I almost got last place. What are they feeding these kids?"

I crack another smile. "GMO free, organic vegetables."

Diego ignores me and trudges off after the crowd. He's not in his normal cheery mood.

We follow the crowd to another part of the clearing. The ground is bare except for a dozen circles formed out of hay bales. Inside each circle, the ground is covered in a thick layer of hay. Each circle stretches about 15 feet across. It looks like an abandoned petting zoo.

Proticus climbs onto a hay bale and calls out to the crowd. "Welcome to the second trial: the combat circle. This trial is the most rigorous and most dangerous. In the guard, hand to hand combat is inevitable. You must learn to act fast and react to your opponent's actions. Quick thinking is essential in a guardsman.

In this trial, each of you will be assigned two competitors as opponents. You will be given padded gloves and will fight to subdue your opponent. The match will end when someone verbally surrenders, or when they are physically unable to fight. A guardsman will be assigned to each combat circle as a judge. The judges will decide when a fighter is subdued.

No biting, scratching, or using any form of weapon other than your fists. If you remove the gloves, you'll be disqualified. Listen for your number, and you will get assigned to a circle. Understood?"

I'm genuinely nervous. I've never fought anyone in my life. Football is the closest I've come to any type of combat, and yet they expect me to play gladiator with a bunch of colonials.

Diego slaps me on the shoulder. "Don't be scared. They're like little sardines. You'll do fine."

"I guess." Something tells me these little guys are scrappier than they look. "I feel bad for whoever has to fight you."

Diego smiles at my compliment. He may not be the fastest runner, but he's sturdy and strong.

Proticus shouts the first round of numbers, and the brawls begin. Each circle has a small crowd of its own. The kids ooh and aww with every big hit. Diego and I watch from the sidelines. A beefy kid with a shaved head knocks down a skinny boy with one punch to his jaw. The judge ends the fight almost immediately. I see the boy spitting blood after.

The next set of numbers are called. I watch two lean boys battle it out for almost a full minute. First, they pummel each other with their fists. Then, they roll around in the hay, fighting to pin the other. Eventually, one boy climbs on top of the other and punches his opponent's face until the judge pulls him off. The crowd cheers him on.

The fights go quickly, and before I know it, a judge calls number 124. I step into the circle and pick up the gloves on the ground—faded leather with a thick cotton pad over the knuckles. The fingertips are left exposed for grabbing. I take a deep breath and slip my hands into the warm, sweaty leather.

The judge calls number 225. A skinny kid climbs into the ring, his nostrils flaring as he gives the air a few playful jabs. Brown hair caps his head in a hideous bowl cut. It looks like he's wearing half a coconut on his head. Most important, he's shorter than me and a whole lot lighter. He almost looks skinnier than Judy.

"Matt, come here!" Diego calls from the side of the circle. I rush over, worried the judge will get impatient.

Diego grabs me by the shoulders. "Listen. You're taller than him, and you have a longer reach. Don't let him get too close. Just keep swinging, and you'll win no problem. Okay?"

"Got it." I like the plan, and I like my odds. I turn to the judge and square up to Coconut-head.

"You know the rules," rambles the judge. He stands between Coconut-head and me. "Keep it fair and keep the gloves on. When I drop my hand, the fight begins." The judge raises his hand and lets it fall.

For the first second, no one moves. I bounce on my toes, ready to swing at the slightest flinch. Coconut-head does the same. He holds his fists in front of his face and dances a foot closer. I stay on my toes, waiting for the perfect moment. *Just a little closer… Almost there.*

He dances forward, and I swing for his face. I clench my jaw expecting impact, but at the last second, his coconut of a head twists out of reach. He's faster than he looks. Much faster. I take another jab, but Coconut-head zips away. He's a fly, harmless and irritating. He buzzes around the edge of the ring before darting closer. I swing, but he flees at the first sight of motion. He doesn't even try to hurt me. He's only trying to stay alive.

I keep advancing until he has nowhere to run. Like a fly on the glass, I have him backed against the hay, ready for smashing. This is my chance. I take a step closer and throw my weight into one last punch. Coconut-head rears back, and his leg kicks up. I see the blur of motion below, but I'm too slow to stop it. His foot catches me directly between the legs.

I let out a tortured gasp as the pain grips my groin. I double over and fall to my knees for support. My stomach lurches into my throat, and my insides feel scrambled.

"Watch out!" Diego warns.

I lift my head just as a foot slams into my stomach. I tip on my side and struggle to suck in air as the judge intervenes. One kick was all it took. One impeccably placed kick. The judge records the loss as I climb shamefully out of the circle, still clutching my lower abdomen.

I hear the spectators laughing. Laughing at the irony. The tiny fly won. David just kicked Goliath in the nuts.

Diego covers his mouth. "You okay, dude? That was a real ball-buster."

"I'm fine," I bark, but it's obvious that I'm not. I collapse to the ground and sit hunched in a ball as the pain subsides.

Diego stifles another laugh. "It's okay, dude. My Aunt Petunia couldn't have kids either, but she still lived a long and happy life."

Before I can offer a comeback, the judge calls number 405. I force myself to stand and follow Diego to the circle. I wish him luck, not that he'll need it. Like my match, his opponent is nothing but bone. If my opponent was a fly, Diego's is a gnat.

The match is over in seconds. As soon as the judges' arm drops, Diego starts swinging and doesn't stop until the boy is on the ground. The crowd cheers as Diego raises his arms in victory. I almost feel sorry for the scrawny boy. He took a few to the face and fell straight on his butt. I know the embarrassment of failure.

Watching the fights only makes me feel worse. One boy gets pummeled in the face and walks out with a disfigured nose. Another boy gets hit in the mouth and loses several teeth.

These kids aren't criminals. They don't deserve a beating. But I don't want to get hurt either. I have no choice but to fight. Before I know it, my number is called again. I step into the ring and slip on the gloves. I look up and freeze.

"Lynn? What are you doing here?"

It's the girl from last night. She wears athletic leggings and a loose-fitting tank top over her sports bra. Even after the race, she looks stunning. Her hair is pulled into a ponytail, and her eyes shine like honey.

Lynn hides her surprise better than me. "I liked your advice. I decided to join."

"You know her?" Diego exclaims from the edge of the circle.

Lynn slips on her gloves and inserts a rubber mouthguard between her teeth. "Can we talk after, please."

Why don't I get a mouth guard? I take my place, and the judge reviews the rules. Lynn whispers to me. "Don't go easy, or they'll mark you down. Just trust me." She glances over her shoulder. I follow her gaze and spot the guardsman with the red lapels and the medal. He stands a few feet from the circle, facing Lynn and I. His steady gaze makes me uncomfortable.

I nod. I don't want to hurt Lynn, but I can't afford another loss. At least I won't damage her beautiful smile.

The judge drops his hand.

I swing first, but Lynn is ready. She ducks and delivers a blow to my ribs. The blow forces a grunt of air from my lungs, but I'm otherwise unharmed. Confidence surges through me. I skip forward and swing twice, my second jab catching her on the ear. Lynn stumbles but keeps her balance.

I step forward and fake with my left. Lynn raises her gloves in front of her eyes to block and I swing hard with my right, crashing around the cotton and into her jaw. With a grunt, she tumbles onto her back in the hay. I have a chance to pummel her, but I can't bring myself to do it. In a second, she's back on her feet and advancing.

"Take her down," Diego calls. It's perfect. I can wrestle her easily and pin her without hurting her. As Lynn approaches, I calculate my next few moves.

I swing for her face, and Lynn ducks. Before she can punch at my stomach, I lunge forward and wrap both of my arms around her in a bear hug.

Rather than pull away, Lynn leans into my chest. She tucks her chin to her chest, plants both feet, and jumps. The crown of her head collides with my chin in an audible thunk. My head whips back, and the world spins.

The crowd cheers.

I land on my back in a pile of hay. The world swims circles around me. When my vision settles, Lynn leans over me with her fist hovering before my face.

I've lost again.

At the judge's word, Lynn helps me to my feet. I'm both impressed and humiliated—but mostly humiliated. Two consecutive losses. I spit to empty the blood from my mouth. My chin is bleeding too.

The guardsman with the medals jots something down on his clipboard and laughs to himself. Whatever it is, it isn't good news for me.

"Sorry about that. Here, come with me." Lynn takes me by the arm and guides me to an extra hay bale away from the combat circles. I take a seat on the straw and rub my jaw.

"Look up, please," Lynn directs. I tilt my head back until I'm staring at the sun. She bites her tongue as she studies my chin. "It doesn't look too deep. You shouldn't need stitches."

I don't know if I should be mad or grateful. She told me not to go easy after all. "Thanks. I—"

"Matt, who the heck is this?" Diego interrupts. "She whooped your butt, dude." Diego flashes a smile at Lynn. "I'm Diego. Nice to meet you."

Lynn laughs, enjoying the attention. "I'm Lynn. A pleasure."

"Number 405!" a judge shouts.

"Crap." Diego backpedals away from us. "I don't want to be rude, but I'm up. Wish me luck." Diego jogs over to the centermost combat circle and steps in with a particularly tall kid—even taller than me. The boy wears athletic shorts and a tight spandex shirt. His clothes highlight his excellent muscle mass. He has sleek blonde hair, and his face reeks of confidence.

"Oh no," Lynn gasps. "That's not good."

"What?"

"That's Vyle, an elite from the palace. In his first fight, he broke a competitor's knee. They had to carry him out on a stretcher."

Before the fight begins, Vyle strips off his shirt and throws it to a buddy. *Showoff.* He's ripped. Not just workout strong, but Calvin Klein model strong. His shoulders are huge and his abs, chiseled. The gathering is larger than normal. They want to witness a slaughter. I have to warn Diego.

"Diego, he's good! Be careful!" I yell over the crowd.

Diego rolls his eyes. "I kinda noticed."

Vyle hears me too. He waves at me with an arrogant grin on his face. "Don't worry. I'll try to keep this brief."

The judge raises his hand and drops it to the floor. Vyle charges swinging fast and often. Diego keeps a wide stance and takes the blows with his gloves. Block. Block. Duck. He's quick for his size. Surprisingly quick.

Vyle feigns with his left hand and follows with a right hook. It catches Diego in the jaw, but he manages to keep his footing and blindly counters with a blow to Vyle's eye. Vyle staggers back and charges again with a rapid series of jabs to Diego's face. Diego tries to counter, but his fist falls short. Another blow catches Diego in the temple, and he stumbles back.

Vyle charges again. Jab. Jab. Left hook. Jab. He finishes the series with a kick to Diego's knee. It connects. Diego winces but holds his ground. He's tough, but all things considered, I don't like his chances. Vyle has a longer reach and is always on the offensive. It's only a matter of time.

As Vyle charges again, Diego plants his feet. Vyle swings with his right, but Diego ducks underneath and tackles him at the waist, landing on top of him in a pile of hay. In a flurry of limbs, Diego wraps his thighs around Vyle's throat. With his hands free, Diego grabs Vyles arm and twists it behind his back. Vyle's free fist bounces weakly off of Diego's legs. He thrashes helplessly against Diego's tree trunk thighs as his face fills with blood.

One kid in moccasins whoops. The crowd begins stomping its feet.

One second. Two seconds. Vyle doesn't tap.

Diego holds him like a hungry boa, squeezing tighter and tighter. It's only a matter of time.

Five seconds. Six seconds.

Vyle's head is now a ripe tomato. His eyes look ready to pop out of the socket.

Eight seconds. Nine seconds.

"Enough!" It's the guardsman with the medals. Diego opens his legs, and Vyle sucks in a gasp. The crowd goes silent.

The judge promptly peels Diego off of Vyle, who scrambles to his feet. The redness in his face refuses to leave. "You're going to regret that, ringling." He kicks over a hay bale and storms away with a group of elites.

The guardsman with the medal laughs and offers his hand to Diego. "Nice work," he mutters before walking to the next circle. Diego is speechless. He slowly walks over to Lynn and me.

"Did you guys see that?" he gasps, still out of breath.

I slap Diego on the back. "Where did that come from? That was awesome."

Diego beams. "I wrestled in high school. My coach taught me that one."

"You just made a fool out of an elite," Lynn praises. "And not just any elite, that's General Kaynes' son. His dad is a guardian on the high council. Best of all, Commander Elsborne witnessed the whole thing."

Diego brushes the hay from his gym shorts. "Who?"

Lynn points to the guardsman with the medals. He's facing the other way watching two more competitors fight. "That's Antai Elsborne, commander of the eastern quadrant and the king's apprentice. If he liked your performance, you're in for sure."

I wish I could say the same about myself. Commander Elsborne watched me get spanked by a girl. The trials are already half over, and my odds aren't looking too good.

The competitors gather back by the armory in a single mass. Once again, the shooting range is just a stone's throw away. I'm drawn to it. But something is different this time; metal necklaces lay strewn on the various wooden tables, each one with a unique shape and pattern. They glitter silver and gold in the sunlight.

Proticus climbs the ladder onto the roof of the armory. Once again, he stands on the edge and calls out to the crowd.

"Welcome to the third trial: a test of dominion. As descendants of Adam, we are all blessed with dominion over the Earth. When mastered, dominion becomes our greatest weapon. All of you will now be given the opportunity to use an amulet to demonstrate your potential. You each will be permitted 30 seconds. Use it wisely."

The competitors are divided into ten lines. One line for each amulet. My friends and I are separated into different lines. I'm assigned to the third line with competitors number 101-150. Diego and Lynn are in lines 9 and 10. I inch forward in line, replaying Lynn's council from last night. *Reach out with my mind? Speak to the elements?* It sounds completely crazy, but the possibilities excite me. *What if it actually works?*

I watch the competitors struggle with the amulets. One boy lets out a grunt as he lifts a small stone with his mind. Another squints his eyes and waves his arm. Nothing happens. It's the same for most of the lower class. *At least I won't fail alone.*

A bright flash from table one catches my eye. A wave of orange flame crashes into the dirt of the shooting range. I stand on my toes to get a better look. Vyle stands behind the table, clutching an amulet in his hand. Another wave of flame erupts in front of him. The competitors in his line cheer.

With a flick of his wrist, Vyle launches a pebble across the range. A moment later, the pebble shatters against a steel target with a high-pitched ring. The judge next to him offers a short clap and marks something on his clipboard. I don't have to read it to know it was a high score. Another elite holds steps forward. Flames stream from his hand like a firehose. Something tells me this isn't their first time.

I'm up next.

I step up to the table and tuck my head through the golden loop of an amulet. I take it in my left hand to ensure skin contact.

"You have thirty seconds," the judge reminds me. "You may begin."

I try to follow Lynn's instructions. I approach the table and focus all of my attention on the tiny stone, trying to force it with my mind. I imagine it lifting off the table. I can picture it so clearly in my head.

Nothing happens.

I try again. *C'mon c'mon c'mon.*

Nothing.

I try to speak to it in my head, the words echoing off my skull. *Move! Please move!*

Still nothing. I'm running out of time. *I'm failing!*

I change my tactics. I stare at the rock, imagining it melting—forming liquid, molten lava. I picture it in my head until I can almost see it. *Melt!* I scream the words in my head. *Melt!*

The rock remains whole as my confidence melts instead. I glance at the judge. He bows his head as he scribbles something on his clipboard. I find myself staring at the top of his head, wondering what he's writing. My eyes are drilling a hole through his skull, searching for the contents inside. Will he fail me? Is my score the lowest possible? Does he know how hard I'm trying?

A sense of boredom fills me. A wave of pity swells until it fills my head. *Poor kid. Another for the fields. At least he's strong. He might actually last a few years.*

The thought invades my mind without warning. I drop my amulet and suck in a breath. As soon as I do, the thoughts vanish.

"Times up," the judge mutters as he scribbles one last note on the clipboard.

I wander away from the range in a daze. The sense of pity lingers in my head. But it isn't my pity, it's the judge's. I heard his thoughts —not in the form of a voice, but as an emotion. It's as if I thought them myself.

"Matt," Diego calls as he and Lynn approach. "You should've seen her. It was crazy."

Lynn smiles shyly. "It was nothing."

"Nothing?" Diego exclaims. "She lifted the judge into the air. You should have seen his face."

"You didn't do so bad yourself," Lynn teases. "For a refugee."

Jealousy grows in me. It sounds like Lynn and Diego are bound to be accepted. Meanwhile, I'll get sent to the fields to plant seeds for the rest of my life. And then there's Judy. If I don't learn how to heal her, she'll die.

"How did you do, Matt?" Diego asks.

"Not so good," I laugh. I try to shake it off, but my smile soon fades. Frustration boils inside me. I've failed again. With my total performance, I have to be ranked at the very back of the pack. Maybe I'll be seeing Judy sooner than I thought.

Lynn comes to my rescue. "You said you were a hunter, right? There's always trial four. You just have to get someone to notice you."

She's right. *There's always hope.* That's what Judy would say.

When the last of the competitors finish, Proticus resumes position on the roof. "I hope all of you are happy with your performance in the last three trials. The time has come for us to finish with the trial of marksmanship. Although dominion is a powerful tool, it has its weaknesses. It's only effective close range, and it burns energy quickly. More often than not, survival depends on your ability to hit a target when it matters most. Marksmanship saves lives.

Each of you will be given a single magazine for both a pistol and a rifle. The pistol will be used on close-range targets, the rifle for long-range targets. We will be looking for both speed and accuracy. When you're finished, please stay in the area to receive the results of The Dividing."

Once again, I'm separated from my friends. I wait in line 3 as the ear-splitting gunfire begins. The sound engulfs me like some kind of horrific fireworks accident. They don't offer ear protection, not even for the shooters.

It only takes a minute to realize I'm in trouble. The competitors are quick with the pistols. Even the laborers skip from one target to another. I've never trained for speed shooting. It's always been a single target, long-distance, one-shot hunting. Here, the farthest target is half a football field away. Not exactly my idea of marksmanship.

The competitor in front of me empties the rifle clip and leaves the gun on the table. It's my turn. I step forward as the judge places two fresh magazines on the table. He nods to let me know he's ready. I slide a pistol magazine into the base of the gun and aim it at a target 15 yards away. I squeeze the trigger.

The steel plank twitches and as the lead clanks against the target.

I jerk the pistol to the next target at 15 yards. Clank. Clank.

25 yards. Clank. Clank

35 yards. Silence. A puff of dirt is the only trace of the bullet.

I missed.

I aim at a row of targets 20 yards away and rapid-fire down the row.

Clank. Clank. Clank. Miss. Clank. Clank. Miss. Miss. Miss.

9 out of 15. Not terrible for speed shooting, but not good enough. I drop the empty pistol and slam the magazine into the rifle. I press the stock tight against my shoulder and peer through the tactical scope. The magnification is a lot weaker than my rifle at home, but it's all I have. I kneel and rest the rifle on the edge of the table for extra support. I settle the crosshairs on a target in the farthest row and pull the trigger twice.

Clank. Clank.

I move to the next target at 50 yards.

Clank. Clank.

I'm slower than the other competitors, but at least I'm accurate.

I search for a target farther than 50 yards, but there's nothing. Only dirt and hay and the grapevines behind that. I aim at another target at 50 yards.

Clank.—

"Help! Heeelp"

I barely hear the sound over the roar of gunfire. It's a frantic scream. A woman's scream.

A lone horse gallops past the far side of the shooting range at full speed. Two other horsemen are already in pursuit, lassos in hand. They're gaining slowly but have a way to go before they catch up to the runaway horse.

"Ceasefire," the commander shouts from the armory roof. He peers at the scene with curious concern. The gunfire trickles to a stop, and the competitors watch the scene in silence.

"Heeelp!"

I struggle to pinpoint the source of the scream. It sounds like it's coming from the runaway horse. I don't notice until Proticus points it out. He holds binoculars to his eyes. "Commander! There's a woman being dragged."

I quietly press the rifle to my eye and peer through the scope. The horse is now galloping belly-deep in corn sprouts. I can't see the girl, but the saddle sits crooked on the horse's back. I spot something stuck in the stirrup. It's an ankle. The rest of the leg disappears into the corn.

I wait for someone to do something, but no one moves. *Why don't they stop the horse with dominion?* I remember what Proticus said: it's only effective at close range? *What a useless superpower!*

Proticus peers through the binoculars again. "Commander, she's going to hit the canal. They won't reach her in time."

I scan the field ahead of the horse, and sure enough, a stone canal runs perpendicular to the horse's path. It's only 200 yards in front of the horse, and less with every second. I imagine the scenario in my head. The horse will clear the gap in one easy leap, but not the girl. She'll be dragged straight into the canal at full speed.

Someone has to do something. I look at the commander. He taps on his holster. His face is scrunched in thought. I turned back to the horsemen. They're closer now, but not close enough. They won't reach her before the canal. I'm sure of it now. She's going to die.

150 yards.

If no one else is going to act, I'll have to do it myself.

100 yards.

I can only think of one solution: shoot the horse. Finally, this is my kind of shooting; a single shot to take down the beast. Normally, I wouldn't shoot at a moving target, but I have no choice. I set the sights center-mass and slowly rotate the gun to match the horse's speed. Even if I only injure the horse, it should be enough. I have to try.

I take a deep breath and squeeze the trigger.

BANG!

The horse keeps running.

50 yards. I adjust the gun one last time and take another deep breath. *God, help me!*

I pull the trigger.

Chapter 14

Rose

I try not to stare at Antai, but I'm craving one of his winks. It's so hard to keep my eyes off him, especially after the letter.

A thin paper crumples inside my pocket. I found it underneath my door before leaving for the trials. The message is short:

Dear Ringling,

I'm sorry about what I said the other day. I want you to know that I do think you would make a great guardsman, an amazing one actually. We need more soldiers like you. I only worry because I care about you. I can't imagine how dull and meaningless my life would be if anything happened to you. I want you to be safe. But even more than safe, I want you to be happy. Choose what makes you happy, Rose. And, If you do choose the guard, I would love to see you at the flats today.

Love Antai

It's no sonnet, but I love Antai's letters. I just wanted to run to him and fall into his arms.

Instead, I pull my eyes away from Antai and watch the range. I promised Grandpa I would stay undercover. That was the condition.

I can't believe how smoothly everything has gone. I placed 81st in the race, won both of my combat matches, and wooed the judge with my dominion. Only one trial remains. I shuffle forward in line. I'm almost up.

My attention drifts back towards the armory. Antai is standing on top. He looks so handsome in his uniform. His face is clean-shaven, and his hair is neatly combed to the side. The red stripe on his shoulder demands attention and respect. Antai scans the crowd. Watching. Observing. For a brief moment, his eyes lock with mine. It's faint but unmistakable; he winks.

Butterflies erupt in my stomach. I try not to blush. Not that anyone else is watching me. I'm as ordinary as everyone else.

In the line next to mine, Diego steps up to the table. I watch as he fires at the closest targets one at a time. He's shaky and slow, but he manages to hit half of the targets. With his performance in the combat circles, Antai might just accept him. He always loved the underdog.

I stand on my tippy-toes and find Matt waiting in line at the other side of the range. A ping of sadness burrows into my heart. Matt isn't going to get accepted. Diego maybe, but not Matt. The thought makes everything a little less sweet. The boy who convinced me to join will get sent to the fields. *Maybe if I ask Antai, he'll let him in?*

No. Antai isn't one to make exceptions, especially not for a boy. Antai is already over-protective. I don't need him to be jealous too. I don't know why it bothers me so much. Matt's only a refugee after all. We'll probably never speak again after The Dividing. Even if he does get recruited, we'll likely end up in different districts under different captains. *Why do I even care?*

I step up to the table and load the pistol. I follow Antai's advice, alternating from close to medium range targets. The steel rings with each hit.

Clank. Clank. Clank. Clank. Clank. Clank.

"Ceasefire!"

It's Antai's voice.

I empty the chamber and set the pistol on its side. The gunfire around me ceases almost immediately.

Then, I hear it. A faint cry floats on the wind. A desperate and terrible cry. The kind that leaves your throat bloody. I squint down-range. I can see a horse galloping on the horizon. Two horse-trainers follow close behind on horseback. They're almost directly behind the range now. A stray bullet could easily kill them.

I step back from the table. Gunfire often makes the horses jittery. It's not unusual for a horse to escape from the coral. Especially with a bunch of amateurs at the reins. But that doesn't explain the scream.

"Commander!" Proticus gasps from the roof. He holds a pair of binoculars to his face. "There's a woman being dragged."

I spin and squint again. Without binoculars, I can't see any sign of the woman. The growing corn stalks are too tall. My heart races faster.

"Commander, she's going to hit the canal. They won't reach her in time."

A million thoughts spin through my head as I search for a solution. I press my hand to my chest.

Grandpa insisted I keep my amulet with me at all times. I hid it in the only place it won't be noticed: my bra. But even with a soul-anchor, dominion won't save the girl. Dominion from this distance is almost impossible.

I glance at Antai. He'll think of something. His eyes are riveted on the fleeing horse. He doesn't move. No one moves. The horse trainers aren't fast enough.

200 yards from the canal.

100 yards from the canal.

Reality weighs down on me. The girl is going to die. My heart pounds in my chest. I feel like I'm back at the execution. Only this time, there's nothing I can do.

BANG!

A single gunshot erupts to my left. My hand instinctively reaches for my amulet. I spin to the source of the gunshot, my adrenaline rushing.

It's Matt. He's kneeling next to the table a few rows to my left. A thin wisp of smoke trails from the muzzle of his rifle.

Is he insane? What is he thinking? Matt fired during a ceasefire. Acting contrary to orders is a colossal mistake in the guard. At best, he'll be expelled from the trials. At worst, he'll be flogged.

BANG!

Matt fires a second shot, a thin-lipped smile forming on his face. His grin disappears as two guardsmen tackle him to the floor. Matt tries to sit up—another foolish move. A guard extends his hand, and an electric jolt forces Matt onto his back.

"I s—" Another shock silences Matt.

Don't hurt him! I open my mouth to shout but close it instead. As long as I'm in disguise, I can't act as princess. I'm a commoner now. I'm powerless.

I remember the girl and spin back to face the shooting range. It's too late. The two horse-trainers have dismounted next to the canal. The runaway horse is gone. I can't help but imagine the girl at the bottom of the canal, mangled or dead. Even if she survived, she'll likely never ride a horse. Or walk. The thought makes me sick. I force myself to turn away.

"He hit the horse!" Proticus gasps from the rooftop. "He actually hit it!" Antai snatches the binoculars from Proticus and scans the horizon. I look too. Something is moving in the corn reeds just yards from the canal. I can't believe it. It's the runaway horse. It limps away from the canal, favoring its back leg. Understanding settles on me. I feel so stupid.

"She's alive," Antai announces to the crowd. "They're coming back."

I cover my eyes with my hand to shield the blinding sunlight. Antai is right. The two horsemen are galloping back towards the armory. The horseman on the right carries a limp body in his arms. It's the girl.

Matt shot the horse! Matt saved her!

Antai climbs down the ladder from the rooftop and points to a medic. "Go see if they need any help." He points at a guardsman. "Prepare a carriage for travel to the palace. She might be in critical condition." The medic takes off on horseback with a pack full of supplies.

Antai turns back to Matt, who is held on his feet by the two guardsmen. Dust clings to his back, and blood drips from his split chin. The wound has reopened from the scramble. Antai marches up to Matt until their faces are only inches apart. Matt stares back unblinking. Everyone else holds their breath.

"That was bold, recruit," Antai spits at Matt. "I could have you flogged for that." I know it's just a face. Antai likes being intimidating.

Matt looks Antai in the eyes. *Bold indeed.* He holds his tongue. *Bold and smart.*

"What's your name?" Antai demands.

"Matt, sir… Matthew MacArther"

"Well, Matt, it took guts to take a shot like that. Quick thinking, initiative, not to mention skill. We need men who can follow orders. But we also need men who can think for themselves."

Antai's speech is interrupted by the clomping of hoofs. The two horsemen arrive accompanied by the medic. The girl lies unconscious in the horseman's arms. Her legs hang limply off one side of the horse's back. I grimace. Her left ankle is twisted at a gruesome angle.

The man holding the girl shouts as the horse skids to a stop. "It's my daughter. Her saddle broke mid-jump. Her leg is pretty bad and her head too. She needs a healer."

I recognize him immediately from the high council. It's Chancellor Quine. He must've been watching his daughter compete for a horse-trainer apprenticeship. Lavana is his only child, after all. He wouldn't miss it for the world.

Chancellor Quine lowers his daughter to a medic before dismounting. I catch a glimpse of Lavana's back. Her shirt is shredded, and long lacerations color her back with red. I'm relieved that she's not awake to feel it.

Chancellor Quine follows at her side until the carriage leaves for the palace. The worry is like a weight on his face, tugging his eyebrows and dragging down the edges of his lips. "I'll be right with you, Lav." He whispers though he knows she can't hear him. Once she's out of sight, he puts on a diplomatic face and turns to Antai. "That was one hell of a shot, commander. Which one of your men can I thank for saving my daughter's life?

Antai smiles and walks over to Matt, who stands stiff as a board. With a smile, he slaps his arm around Matt's shoulders.

"Chancellor Quine, I'd like you to meet Matt, our newest addition to the guard."

I pull my blankets over my head, but I can't escape the noise. It's relentless. I've never heard a girl snore so loud in my life. She sounds like a feral hog.

Only three other girls were recruited this year. They're now my roommates. I'm lying in my new bed—a fraying twin mattress. I roll over, but metal springs dig into my ribs. My neck aches, and the wool blanket itches like Poor Man's Rash. Above it all, my throat is a dried-up creek, and Nevela's not here to bring me a glass of water.

I can't take it much longer. Morning should have come hours ago. I sit up and look out the window. It's still pitch-dark outside. *Ugh!* I want to scream. I already hate it here. I miss my king size bed and my silk sheets and my maid.

After the results were announced, those of us accepted were given the rest of the day to say goodbye to our old lives. I ate dinner with Grandpa, had one last Adamic lesson, and carried my things to the guard tower. To my disappointment, Antai was on assignment all day. I still haven't spoken to him since our disagreement.

I stare at the underside of the bunk above me. *This is my new home.* I don't know if I'm excited or horrified. We sleep on the 5th floor of the eastern guard tower. When we graduate from training, most of us will rent houses in the core. Until then, we're stuck here.

Muffled voices penetrate the door. There is some kind of commotion in the hallway. I tilt my head to hear. Suddenly, the door to our room bursts open. Proticus stands in the doorway, a kerosene lamp in hand. "Rise and shine, girls. Get dressed and meet me on the top floor in five minutes. We have work to do." Then, he disappears back into the hallway to wake the next room of recruits. I can hear him repeating the same exact message to the boys next door.

A girl moans in the bunk above me. I groggily roll out of bed and fumble in the dark for the matchbox. I strike one and light the lamp on the dresser. Another girl climbs out of bed and slams the door shut. "Demons! At least close it on your way out."

A third girl descends from the other bunk bed. She has straight red hair and a face full of freckles. Her silk pajamas are pink with white polka dots. I recognize her from the palace. Her father is Judge Lumb, chief judge of the Upper Court, but I can't remember her first name. She gives the girl who slammed the door a dirty look. "Geez, ringling. You don't have to slam it. Have some manners."

The girl who slammed the door furrows her brow. She takes a deep breath, and her face slowly relaxes. "My bad. It won't happen again." She has skin like dark honey and black bangs. Her petite body is dressed in grey cotton pajamas. I feel bad for her. She's the only ring-born in the room.

She catches me staring. "Sorry, I'm not much of a morning person. I promise I'm not usually like this. I didn't sleep well. These mattresses are terrible."

The redheaded girl scoffs. "Sounded like you slept just fine to me. Your snoring kept me up all night. And don't act like your bed at home was any better. What did you sleep on, straw?"

The laborer girl stands stunned in the center of the room. She takes a step towards her dresser, but her anger gets the best of her. "You know what? I'm done trying to be nice. I deserve to be here as much as the rest of you, so get off my back." The other girls look at each other and snicker. That was precisely the reaction they were hoping for.

The laborer girl silently storms to her dresser. I want to say something to her, but she's already getting dressed. I hurry to do the same. I slip off my pajamas and throw on my new training uniform: joggers and a spandex shirt. The material is imported and fits me like a glove. Everything is jet black. Even our socks and shoes. The red circle insignia is sewn onto the shoulder of my shirt, and my name is stitched over the left breast to match. It reads: **Lynn**

The redheaded girl and her high-born friend are ready first. They rush out the door without so much as a goodbye. I pull my hair into a ponytail and adjust my amulet in my bra. I start for the door but stop. The laborer girl is frantically pacing the room barefoot. Her shirt reads: **Velma**.

"Everything alright?" I ask.

She climbs on her hands and knees and peers underneath the beds. "Everything's fine. Just go."

"Are you sure?" I ask. She's carrying her socks in one hand, but I don't see her shoes anywhere. "Did you lose something?"

Velma stands up. "Are you deaf, purebred? I said I'm fine. I don't need your help."

I place my hands on my hips. "What did I ever do to you?" I demand.

"Nothing!" Velma yells. "That's the problem. Your people do nothing for us. Absolutely nothing. So don't try to help me now as if you care. Just go."

I open my mouth and close it again. I want to tell her that she's wrong. That I've tried everything to help her kind. I want to tell her that she's only in the guard because I made them accept twice as many recruits. But even If I could tell her, she wouldn't listen. She wants action, not words. So that's what I'll give her.

I scan the bare floor of the tiny room. If the shoes were here, they would be in plain sight. Her shoes didn't just disappear. They were moved. Something tells me I know where they are. I march over to the redhead's dresser and start yanking open drawers. I find black uniforms, makeup, and some jewelry, but no shoes.

I have to think like a bully. *If I stole her shoes, where would I put them?* I have an idea.

I step into the hallway. It's empty except for a few stragglers rushing by. I walk down the hall and into the girl's washroom. It's a small room with a row of toilets against the back wall and a few tubs for bathing. It smells awful. The toilets are no more than concrete seats with holes in the center. Each tub has a hand crank to pump water from below. For Cavernum's standards, the bathroom is quite nice, but it's nothing like the luxury of the palace.

I scan the room. No sign of any shoes. I walk over to the tubs and look inside. Sure enough, two black shoes soak in a puddle at the bottom of the tub. I let out a sigh of relief. *At least it wasn't the toilet.* I pick up the shoes and hold them in my hands. I reach with my mind and speak to the water.

Evaporate. I command, guiding the water with my mind. In a rush of steam, the water flows out of the shoes and into the air. The steam disperses, and the shoes are left looking like new. I feel the inside of the sole; it's dry to the touch. Satisfied with myself, I hurry back to the dorm room. I push the door open and hold up the shoes by the strings. "Are you size 6?"

Her eyes narrow with suspicion. "Where did you find them?"

"In the washroom," I say. "You're welcome."

The laborer girl grabs the shoes from my hand, her facial muscles contorting with rage. "Those little witches! They took them, didn't they? They're trying to get me kicked out." She pulls on her shoes and storms past me. "C'mon!" She bolts for the stairwell, and I run after her. We're late. Very late.

The stairwell is lit by a small window on each floor. I peer through the window as I jog past. Dawn is just beginning to light the sky above the fields. I clamber up the stairs to the next landing and push through the door. I emerge in a wide room. At the far end of the room is the armory service desk. A long, waist-high counter stretches from wall to wall. Behind the wooden counter are rows and rows of shelves. It's like a library, except with rifles and pistols instead of books. One wall has amulets hanging like merchandise in a jewelry shop. The two guards behind the desk scramble to attend to the mass of eager recruits. Those already serviced linger against the side walls, admiring their new amulets.

The redheaded girl spots us and frowns at Velma. Her shirt reads: **Crasilda**. She looks at Velma's shoes and forces a face of relief. "You finally made it." She mocks, her voice laced with fake distress. "We were worried something happened to you."

Velma doesn't say a word. She doesn't even look at them. She simply holds up her middle finger and walks to the back of the line. Crasilda is dumbstruck. She stares after Velma with her mouth agape. I doubt she's ever been flipped off by a laborer before—or by anyone.

I tighten my lips to withhold a laugh and join Velma in line. She acts unladylike in the most dignified way. She's fearless and confident—rare traits for a laborer. No wonder she got accepted.

Proticus eyes us from his spot by the counter. His appearance is hypnotizing. His steel gray hair forms a perfect wave on his head and highlights his brilliant silver eyes. His skin is flawless, and his teeth gleam unnaturally white. I expect him to approach and scold us for being late, but he doesn't move. He's a lot more lenient than Antai would've been. Or maybe he's just soft. Considering his bleached teeth and manicured hands, I lean towards the latter.

I find Matt and Diego in the corner. Diego laughs at something Matt said and slaps him on the shoulder. I can't believe they both made it in. They were the only refugees accepted.

The line moves slowly. Velma looks back at me and brushes her frizzy hair out of her face. She rubs her hands together and shifts her weight from side to side. "Ummm... thanks for finding my shoes down there." She casts a fiery glare at Crasilda. "I still can't believe they hid them in the washroom. My mom said the palace-born are cruel, but I didn't expect this."

"We're not all like her," I say. My thoughts turn to Nevela. She's the sweetest. She only ever wants to help. And Antai, he always does what's right.

"Well, it looks like you're the minority," Velma sighs. After a moment, she regrets it. "I'll umm... I'll tell my mom about you. She'll be glad to hear you're not all as bad as she thinks." Velma stops talking and stares past me just as a finger taps me on the shoulder.

I turn and look straight into Vyle's cloud grey eyes. It's as if a thunderstorm is brewing just below the surface. His face is growing a thin layer of blonde scruff, and his hair is slicked back with incessant amounts of hair oil. He grins and speaks with a confident voice. "Excuse me, but do I know you from somewhere? You look awfully familiar?"

I swallow and try to suppress the panic rising within me. I smile back and pretend I'm speaking to a stranger. "No, I don't believe we've met," I say. It's a lie of course. I spoke with him at the harvest feast last Fall. We danced for one song before Antai swooped in and saved me. Not to mention, he's seen me perform in the orchestra on multiple occasions. But I hardly resemble my old self. "Perhaps I look like someone you know. People tell me I have one of those faces."

Vyle smiles, leaning in closer. "I don't think so. I wouldn't forget a face like yours."

He's flirting with me! I realize. He's not ugly, but I'm miles away from interested. "Well, I certainly don't remember yours," I say. I hear Velma snicker behind me.

For a moment, his smile disappears, but he manages to mask his anger. "You're high-born, aren't you? Surely we've met in the palace?"

I shake my head. "I was a maidservant. I lived in the royal wing and hardly ever left. I really don't think we've met.

Vyle is doubtful. "Are you sure?"

"She said she doesn't know you," Velma grumbles. "Take a hint."

Vyle's voice turns sour. "Shut up, picker. No one asked you." He turns back to me. His brow softens back into a pretentious smile. "Either way, I'd like to get to know you, Lynn. Just think about it." He retreats back toward his group of friends.

Velma shakes her shoulders. "Ugh, good riddance. That guy gives me the creeps." Before I can agree, Velma points behind me. "You're up."

I step up to the service desk and write down my fake identification number on the record sheet. The guard behind the desk hands me a small gold amulet. I trace the amulet with my finger. It's barely the size of my thumb. The Adamic symbols are faint and small.

Velma picks up her amulet. She cradled it in her hand like a newborn baby. Except for the trials, this is likely the only time she's ever touched one.

"Does anyone still need an amulet?" Proticus calls. He's standing in front of the door to the stairwell. No one speaks up. "Good. Then training begins now. Follow me and hustle. And try not to trample anybody. It's going to get dark."

Proticus throws open the door to the stairwell and disappears inside. The recruits chase after him in a tight single-file line. I run after the boy in front of me and scurry down the steps as fast as I can. I count down the floors as we descend. Five. Four. Three. Two.

The flood of recruits runs right past the exit on the ground floor, following Proticus down into the dark. There are no more windows on the walls. We're descending underground... deep underground. With each bend in the stairwell, it gets darker and darker. The steps continue to descend into the earth. 30 steps. 40 steps. 50 steps. The air grows stale. I can barely see the next step in front of me. Still, we run deeper.

It's pitch-dark now. I blindly place each foot as fast as I can without tripping in the dark. I bump into the kid in front of me, and some boy slams into my back. I can't take it anymore. I touch my hand to my amulet.

Light!

I speak the words with my mind, and a soft white glow illuminates the bodies around me. A few other recruits whoop their approval. Behind me, another boy touches his amulet and does the same. Still, the steps continue into the earth. I've lost count now. The air is getting cooler and cooler.

I take another bend in the stairwell. The steps finally flatten into a long circular tunnel. A subtle yellow light shines from the tunnel's end, outlining the recruits in front of me. They charge towards the light, sweeping me forward in a river of men. I have no choice but to move with the flow of bodies. Suddenly, the tunnel opens before me, and I suck in a gasp.

I let go of my amulet and stagger into a giant cavern. It's the size of the palace ballroom, maybe bigger. Jagged earth walls arch high overhead. Adamic symbols are carved across the cavern walls.

Each symbol emits a yellow glow, bathing the cavern in shadows. *It's just how Antai described it.* The cavern stretches forward, sloping downward into a stoney beach. A large underground lake floods the remainder of the cavern. The water sits completely motionless, reflecting the yellow light like a mirror. The murky black water conceals everything underneath.

Just like Antai said, the cavern isn't empty. One corner of the cave is filled with weights and gym equipment. Another side has foam pads strewn on the floor for combat training.

Movement catches my eye toward the center of the cavern. Diego waves at me with an excited grin on his face. Matt stands next to him and motions for me to join them. I quickly make my way over.

"What is this place?" Matt asks. "It's amazing."

"It's a lava cave," I say. "I've read about them, but I've never actually been in one."

"It's so cool," Diego gasps. He points at the pool. "How deep do you think it is?"

I shrug. "Who knows. It could be miles. These tunnels stretch under the entire sanctuary. Sometimes they flood from rainwater."

"Everyone on me," Proticus calls as the last recruits shuffle into the cavern. The recruits flock to him, eager to receive instructions. I follow Matt towards the forming congregation.

As we walk past Vyle, he points at Diego and whispers to his friends. "Watch out, picker coming through." He puffs out his cheeks and holds his arms in front of him, forming the shape of a large belly. He pretends to waddle, and his posse snickers on cue. Crasilda stands next to Vyle and laughs with the rest. *No wonder the palace-born have a bad reputation.*

Proticus casts a scolding look at Vyle before addressing the recruits. "Alright, kiddos. Welcome to the guard. Now that you're officially part of the program, we can get a little more friendly. I'm Proticus, but my friends call me Tick. And I highly recommend you be my friend."

Proticus looks right at Vyle. "I don't care who you were before the trials, laborer, elite, refugee. I don't care if your family is royalty."

I nervously cast my eyes around me, but no one looks my way. Most eyes turn to Vyle instead.

"Starting now, you're all recruits of equal rank. You're team-mates. So get to know each other. The guard is a team effort. No one can guard the sanctuary by themselves, not even a guardian."

Once again, heads turn towards Vyle. Why wouldn't they? He's the son of a guardian after all. Right now, I'm Lynn the nobody.

Proticus shouts on. "You have to learn how to work together and trust each other. I recommend you start making friends if you haven't already."

I glance at Matt. He's already smiling back at me. His wavy hair is disheveled, but he looks good in his training uniform. The black doesn't quite compliment him like it does Antai's darker complexion. Matt would look better in blue. The thought makes me smile.

Tick continues. "For the next 3 months, it's my job to teach you how to fight, act, think, and live. We'll be covering all of the skills from the trials as well as strategy, combat protocol, and more. Just because you made it in, doesn't mean you can slack off. Everything is a test. You will still be assessed, and at the end of 3 months, your score will decide your rank and your first assignment. The recruit with the highest score will be immediately promoted to lieutenant—an elite citizen."

Recruits whoop their excitement. A boy puts his hand in his mouth and whistles.

Proticus smiles. "Exciting, I know, but it'll only be one of you. So work hard. After your three months with me, you'll work under the supervision of a senior partner to finish your training in the field. In the guard, we always work in pairs. Any questions?"

"Just one," Velma says as she raises her hand. "Where are we exactly?"

"This—" Proticus sweeps his hand in front of him, "—is the trench! This is where we'll do most of our training. Down here, we don't have to worry about civilian casualties or catching the sanctuary on fire."

Another boy raises his hand. His shirt says: **Klinton**. He has curly brown hair that only partially covers his protruding ears. Thick rimmed black glasses magnify his innocent brown eyes. "Do we get time off to see our families?"

Tick nods. "Monday through Saturday, you're mine. Day and night. Sunday's, however, are your free days. Spend them however you want. Sundays are also paydays; you should all get your first payment next Sunday after you complete a full week. Once you finish your training, you'll work a regular shift and have even more free time for whatever else you guys do. Family, girlfriends, you name it."

Proticus scans the crowd one last time. "Excellent. Let's begin. Today, we're going to start with what's most difficult for recruits: dominion."

Tick lifts his amulet off his chest and holds it out for all to see. "Who can tell me what type of amulet this is?"

Silence. No one raises their hand. I want to answer, but I know I shouldn't. A maidservant wouldn't know about amulets, and I have to play the part.

"No one?" Tick challenges.

"It's an amplifier," Vyle shouts.

Proticus points at Vyle. "Correct! And Vyle, why is it called an amplifier?"

"Because it amplifies the soul of the wearer enough to exercise dominion."

Proticus nods his approval. "Exactly. Before I teach you kids how to exercise dominion, you need to understand something very important: amplifiers only amplify. In order to control the elements, you must speak to them, and that strains the soul. Even with an amplifier, you'll still strain the soul to some degree."

Tick points to his bicep. "The soul is like a muscle. It gets tired. After a workout, it needs rest to heal and recover. It has its limitations, but like a muscle, the more you exercise it, the stronger it gets.

I'm here to teach you to use dominion as efficiently as possible. Most trained guards can exercise dominion at a range of 20 feet, but just because you can, doesn't mean you should. Closer objects place less strain on the soul. Smaller objects place less strain. Control is always better than power. Once you weaken the soul in battle, you'll be virtually defenseless."

None of this is new to me. Grandpa already taught me almost everything there is to know about dominion. I'm still learning to put those principles into practice, but according to Grandpa, I've mastered the basics.

One of Vyle's elite friends raises his hand. His head is shaved on the sides, and a silver ring loops between his nostrils. His chest reads: **Zander**. "What type of amulets do guardians use?" he asks.

"Good question," Tick says. "Anyone know?"

Matt slowly raises his hand. "Is it called a soul-anchor?"

Proticus raises his eyebrows. "Yes, it is. Very good, Matt. And what's the difference between the two?"

Vyle blurts again. "Soul-anchors shield the soul completely and let guardians exercise dominion indefinitely."

"Very good," Proticus says. "Soul-anchors are extremely powerful. Unfortunately, there are only four in the sanctuary—one for each of the guardians. The only other soul-anchors that we know of are in the other sanctuaries: Lycon, Beskum, and Desmelda."

Wrong! There are far more than four. A soul-anchor is safely tucked inside my bra this very moment. Not to mention all the others in the palace vault.

Zander raises his hand. "My dad says the king can make soul-anchors. Is that true?"

Proticus tilts his head from side to side and chews his lips. "Yes, technically, that is true."

Another boy in the back shouts. "Why doesn't he make more so we can have more guardians?"

Proticus silences the recruits with his hand. "All I know is, if the king can make amulets but chooses not to, he must have good reasons for it." A few recruits anxiously raise their hands, but Proticus quickly changes the subject. "What else is special about soul-anchors?"

To my surprise, Matt raises his hand again.

"They're bonded to their owners with Adamic, so only the owner can use them."

How does he know that? Matt is a refugee, and that's not common knowledge.

"Yes, that's correct," Proticus admits with apparent confusion.

I sneak a glance at Matt. There's something mysterious about him. Something secretive. He knows more than he should. Not to mention, he survived a feeder attack.

"Alright," Proticus continues. "Two ground rules before we begin. One: go slow. It's easy to overexert yourselves. I've seen recruits end up in the infirmary for trying something crazy. If you're new to

dominion, only try commanding objects very close and very small."
He holds his thumb an inch from his index finger.

"Two: no fooling around. Like I said, dominion is dangerous. If
anyone uses dominion against another recruit, they'll have their amulet
privileges revoked. Understood?"

Everyone nods.

"Be safe, but give it your all. Remember, dominion is your most
powerful weapon. Mastering it is your best chance to climb the ranks."

Proticus holds up his hand as if he remembered something
important. "Some advice: don't get frustrated if you struggle with
dominion. Dominion isn't all or nothing. It has a spectrum. Those of
you with pure bloodlines will have an easier time with dominion. In
the guard, we refer to you as full-bloods. Those of you of mixed
descent will find it harder to perform the same tasks. We refer to you as
dry-bloods."

Proticus sighs. "Please don't blame yourself if you struggle, it may
not be your fault. Just do your best. There are lots of great positions in
the guard for dry-bloods, so don't freak out. I'll separate you into
groups according to your abilities."

Proticus organizes us into three groups using the scores from the
trials. Matt is placed in group one, Diego in group two, and I'm placed
in the third with Vyle and his friends.

I listen as Proticus instructs Matt's group. "Don't try to command
the rock as a whole. Elements aren't like animals or people. Elements
are fluid. A rock can be broken or melted or changed in infinite ways
and remain the same element. Instead, speak to the tiniest particles that
make up the rock. Those are what will obey you. As much as the rock
changes, the elemental particles will always remain the same."

I find myself nodding along with his instructions. It's good advice.
I watch as Matt picks up a rock from the floor and tries to move it with
dominion. It doesn't budge. Maybe I can tutor him later.

Proticus joins my group last and leads us to the pool of water. "You
guys are a bit more advanced with dominion, so I decided to give you
something a little more challenging: I want you guys to freeze the

water. There are two ways. You can take the heat out of the water, which will cause it to automatically freeze, but this requires a lot of energy. Instead, try commanding the water to form ice crystals directly. Give it a shot. I'll be back in a few minutes if you need help." Proticus strides back towards group one. Matt's rock is still in the same place. *He'll get it eventually,* I think. *Hopefully.* Some people just never figure it out, even guardsmen.

I walk to the lake's edge until my toes are inches from the water. I close my eyes and reach out with my mind. I speak to the water molecules, willing them to stop flowing and align.

Freeze.

The water obeys. Crystals slowly form on the surface, expanding and growing. The crackling of ice fills the room. Two other boys join in until a sheet of ice stretches several feet from the shoreline.

The boy next to me drops to his knees and rests his hands on the floor. He winces and holds his head in his hands. Poor guy. He overexerted himself already.

Thanks to my soul-anchor, I feel fine. I could have frozen the entire shore by myself if I wanted to, but I decide against it. I can't do anything to raise suspicion. Instead, I watch Vyle linger by the lake. He unfreezes a tiny portion of ice and joins his friends. They don't seem tired at all. Maybe they think they're too advanced for such a simple task.

The new recruits quickly tire from the exercises. A skinny boy in group one faints. The rock he's levitating topples to the floor. More and more recruits sit down from exhaustion. Diego lays down on his back in the middle of the room. His small belly peeks out of the base of his shirt. I smile at the sight.

Matt, however, hasn't moved an inch. He still stares intently at his rock. He's persistent. Or maybe stubborn is a better word.

Eventually, Proticus claps his hands. "Alright, that's enough for today. Everyone upstairs and return the amulets. You can all rest after some firearm training. You'll get another chance tomorrow."

Recruits slowly climb to their feet and follow Proticus back into the darkness of the tunnel. Once I'm inside the tunnel, I wait for Matt and Diego. Matt still stubbornly stares at his rock. At first, Vyle follows the recruits towards the exit, but he stops once he's between Matt and the tunnel where I'm standing. As the last few recruits file past me, Vyle and his two friends march towards Matt and Diego. One is the bald recruit, Zander. The other, a boy named Croyd, has dark skin and thick lips. His short hair curls in tiny spirals. He's slim and walks with a bounce in his step.

They're now the only ones in the trench. Something tells me they aren't there to mingle.

Chapter 15

Rose

I press my body against the wall of the tunnel, hiding my head in the shadows. I peek my eye around the corner until only a sliver of my head is visible.

Diego is frozen with fear as the gang approaches. He turns and nudges Matt on the shoulder. They're the only ones left in the trench. Matt's eyes bulge when he sees Vyle. His head swivels around the room, searching for an escape. Diego tries to make a move towards the stairwell, but Vyle intercepts him and shoves him toward the back of the cavern.

"Please. Stay for a second. We just want to have a nice chat." Vyle lies.

His two friends form a semi-circle around Matt and Diego, who both backpedal until they're on the shore of the lake. There's nowhere to run. They're pinned between the gang and the murky, black water.

Vyle shoves Diego again. "You see, ringling, you ruined my day yesterday. I said you would pay for that, and I'm always a man of my word."

Diego puffs out his chest. "Take off that amulet, and I'll ruin your day again."

Vyle keeps his composure. "Don't fool yourself. You're just an outsider. A nobody. Let me guess. Daddy got eaten by a feeder."

Diego glares at Vyle. He's an open book.

Vyle smiles. "No? Then maybe it was Mommy!"

"Shut up!" Diego grumbles through gritted teeth.

Vyle grins wider. "Did you try to save her? Or did you run away?"

"Shut! Up!" Diego demands. His hands ball into fists at his side. I know Vyle's strategy. If Diego swings first, Vyle can retaliate in 'self-defense.'

Matt hasn't said anything. He watches Vyle with a furious fierceness in his eyes. He doesn't blink.

"I bet she was plump like you. Nice and juicy with sweet, savory blood. A feeder feast."

It's hard to bear. I can't imagine how Diego must feel. His face is red, and his knuckles white.

Vyle leans in closer. "Did she scream for long? Did she beg for mercy?"

Diego lurches forward and spits in Vyle's eye. I want to cheer him on, but I hold my tongue. I can't get involved. I can't bring attention to myself.

Vyle maintains his grin as he wipes the spit with the back of his hand. "Maybe I'm wrong. Maybe she was eye candy. A real looker." He turns to Zander. "Do you think they ate her right away, or did they have fun with her first?"

Matt swings. His fist collides with Vyle's eye with an audible thunk. Vyle's head snaps back, and he lands on his butt on the rocky floor. His face turns sour.

Vyle leaps to his feet and charges Matt. Matt leans left, dodging Vyles jab. Vyle swings with his left, but Matt steps back, just out of reach.

Right hook, dodge.

Left jab, dodge.

Matt seems to move before each punch begins. He twists to dodge a kick and jabs Vyle in the nose. He follows with a lunge and clasps his hand onto Vyle's amulet.

I see it coming before Matt does: Croyd charges with an outstretched hand. Electricity crackles against Matt's side, and with a cry, he crumples to the floor. He tries to stand, but Croyd kicks him in the stomach.

"Don't leave any bruises," Vyle reminds.

Diego follows Matt's example. He dives at Vyle's amulet, but Vyle is faster. Vyle catches him by the wrist and sends electricity surging through his arm until he's convulsing on the floor.

"Toss him in the water and freeze the top," Vyle commands. "Let's teach him what real choking feels like."

Zander and Croyd grab Diego by the wrists and ankles, dragging him towards the shore of the lake. Diego tries to resist, but he's already weak from the dominion training. Not to mention the electric jolt. He doesn't put up much of a fight.

Matt struggles to his feet. With the wave of Vyle's hand, Matt is thrown back to the floor by an invisible force. I can't take it any longer. I storm out of the tunnel and into the cavern. "Put him down!"

When Vyle sees I'm alone, he turns his back to me. "Move along, princess. This is between us and them." I cringe at the word 'princess,' but Vyle doesn't seem to notice. *It's just a nickname,* I tell myself.

Vyle's buddies look a little more nervous. They look to each other for assurance. Vyle waves his arms at them. "What are you waiting for?" Together, they carry Diego the last few steps to the water's edge.

I run across the trench until I'm on the shore next to Matt. "Let him go, or I tell Proticus everything that happened."

Vyle turns to me and laughs. His eye already has a slight purple hue. He steps forward, pointing at Matt. "His knuckles are bleeding. My eye is bruised. Who's Proticus going to believe? A bunch of pickers or the son of a guardian. I'll have you all kicked out of the guard by nightfall." Vyle turns to his minions. "Dunk him."

With a grunt, Zander and Croyd heave Diego over the lake. I reach with my mind, speaking to the water.

Freeze!

Instead of a splash, the crisp crackling of ice fills the air. With a grunt, Diego slaps onto a thick slab of ice and slides several feet across the surface.

Zander stares open-mouthed, backing away slowly. Croyd touches his hand to his amulet. Vyle does the same.

If they want a fight, I'll give it to them. I speak with my mind. My hands tingle as blue sparks crackle and jump between my fingertips.

"Enough!" The voice comes from behind me. Proticus stands in the opening of the trench. He doesn't look happy.

"You're all coming with me! NOW!"

I fight to keep my heavy eyelids open. I lay in my bed and stare at the underside of the top bunk. The guard tower is quiet, and I'm exhausted after everything that's happened today.

I squeeze the folded paper tight in my hand. During dinner, Antai slipped it to me in the cafeteria. It reads:

Dear Ringling,

Meet me on the roof as soon as everyone is asleep. I gave the guards a few hours off. We'll be alone. Wear your training uniform just in case. I have to tell you some things.

Love,

Your secret admirer

Ps. Destroy this paper.

I'm still fully dressed in my training clothes, waiting for my roommates to fall asleep. I listen to their breathing, trying to decide whether they're conscious or not. I lay in silence until Velma starts snoring.

It's time.

I shimmy out of bed and slip on my shoes in the dark. I wait for the next snore to open the door. The creak of the hinge is hidden by the grumble of Velma's breathing. The hallway is pitch-dark. I'm tempted to use my amulet for some light but decide against it—too risky. Instead, I trace my hand on the wall as I blindly make my way down the hallway. My hand dips over the curves of each door. Matt and Diego are sleeping in one of these rooms. I wonder if they're already asleep.

I make my way up the stairwell to the rooftop. After a small pause to build courage, I crack open the door and peek my head out. The rooftop is a flat concrete square that overlooks the flats. The fields are eerie at night. The moon reflects off the top of the corn reeds, hiding whatever might lurk within. Off in the distance, the tiny glow of torches dot the outer wall. On the other side of the rooftop, the city looms. The streets of the ring are dark and deserted. The palace is barely visible above the surrounding buildings. It's strange to see it from this angle. I've never been beyond the palace walls at night.

"Hurry up," Antai whispers. He sits on the edge of the roof with his legs dangling over the edge. I scurry over to him as quietly as I can. Antai takes my hand and helps me sit next to him on the ledge. The height makes me nervous, but I know I'm safe. Antai won't let me fall.

His smile gleams in the moonlight as he looks me over. "You know, I've never been so fond of a training uniform."

I wipe the hair out of my face and take a deep breath. "I'm so sorry about the other night. I didn't mean what I said. I was just stre—"

"Shhhh. Don't worry about it. I'm sorry too. Let's just forget it ever happened. This can be our new first date."

I like that idea. "Are you sure no one will see us?" I ask.

"Positive." Antai checks his wind-up watch. I don't know how he can make out the numbers in the darkness. "No one should be back here for another hour, and if they're early, I'll yell at them until they leave."

I laugh. I've seen him do it before. Antai can be quite terrifying when he wants to be.

Antai looks up, and I follow his gaze. "Look at the stars," I gasp. Out here, away from the palace lights, they're a million times more stunning. They cover the sky with brilliant white spatters. I smile to myself. It's a perfect redo of the first date—stargazing on the roof.

I cuddle next to Antai and rest my head on his shoulder. "I can't believe I'm a guardsman. What am I doing, Antai?"

"A pretty good job by the looks of it." His voice is confident and assuring. "You were amazing out there. Keep it up, and you'll get ranked first in class for sure. Next thing you know, you'll be back in the palace with me."

I nod. My mind wanders to when Antai was in training years ago. I hardly saw him. When will I see Grandpa? Or Nevela? I already have so much to tell them.

Antai squeezes my hand as he looks down at me with his maple brown eyes. "Really, you were amazing. I'm sorry I tried to talk you out of it."

I gasp. "Am I hearing an apology from the great Antai Elsborne?"

"I mean it, Rose. I'm sorry. You're already a great guardsman. You had the second-highest score from the trials."

"No thanks to you," I tease. "You paired me with two of the biggest guys to fight."

Antai holds up his hands. "Hey, don't blame me. Those were orders from the king. He's worried that when he announces who you are, people will accuse us of rigging the trials. He wants the odds stacked against you."

"Fair enough. Consider yourself forgiven." The last thing I want is suspicious subjects. Antai smiles and looks up at the stars. I squeeze my face into his neck. "The trench was just how you described it."

"Amazing, right? How was your first dominion lesson, by the way?" Antai asks. "What was the topic?"

"Freezing water. It was good. We froze the surface of the lake."

"Wow." Antai's eyebrows leap in surprise. "Proticus doesn't waste any time." He chuckles to himself. "Did I ever tell you we skinny-dipped in that lake our last night of training?"

"No!" I gasp. "You never told me that."

Antai smiles at the memory. "Yeah, well. I was a tad reckless back then."

Jealousy wells inside me. I wonder if there were any girls there, but I don't ask.

Antai slips his fingers into mine and squeezes my hand. "I'm so excited for you to finish training. Just wait until the graduation party. You're going to love it." He looks into my eyes and grins proudly. "Maybe you'll end up a captain in my quadrant."

"I hope so," I say. I relish the sound of Antai's breathing as we sit in silence for a few moments.

"What did you think of the refugees?" Antai asks. "They put on quite a show."

For some reason, the question makes me nervous. But why? I can have friends other than Antai.

"I like them. What did you think?"

"Well, I've never seen a shot like that before," Antai marvels. "They didn't score very high, but they have potential for sure. Proticus agrees."

I'm relieved. Matt went from a nobody to a celebrity in minutes. After he saved Lavana, word quickly spread that he survived a feeder attack. Diego told anyone with ears.

"So, who beat me?" I ask. "Who got first?"

"The Kaynes boy, Vyle. What do you think of him?"

"He has a pretty wild temper," I say. "Honestly, I think he's trash."

Antai shrugs. "I had a temper too. Besides, his dad taught him well. He shot a stone faster than a bullet. I don't know many captains who can do that."

Antai always sees the best in everyone. Especially me. And I love that about him. But this time he's wrong.

I shake my head. "He's not like you. Today, he used dominion on the refugees. He tried to drown Diego. If I didn't stop him he would've done it."

"Hold on?" Antai sits up straight and looks down at me. "You fought Vyle today?"

"Well, no. Not exactly. I was about to, but Proticus showed up."

"You got caught?" Antai grumbles and rubs his fingers over his scalp. "What if someone recognizes you, Rose? You can't bring attention to yourself."

"It's not a big deal," I say. "You're overreacting."

"What was your punishment?" Antai asks.

"I don't know yet. Proticus said he'll give it to us tomorrow."

Antai purses his lips. "You have to be careful, Rose. You can't risk your cover, especially not for some refugees you don't even know. Let them fend for themselves."

"What would you have done?" I ask. "Let him drown?"

Antai sighs and relaxes his shoulders. "I guess not. I'm just… I'm worried about you, okay? The equalists still have our uniforms. If anyone finds out who you are…" The sentence hangs in the air. "Are you wearing your amulet day and night?"

"Yes. You don't need to baby me."

"I know. King Dralton wanted me to check. Someone broke into the palace last night and murdered our informant. He was supposed to guide us through the tunnels this week."

I'm stunned. "What? How'd they get in?" The palace is supposed to be impenetrable.

"We don't know," Antai admits. "King Dralton thinks it might have been someone on the inside. We're already questioning the royal guards." Antai clears his throat. "But that's not all. They also ransacked your chambers. Nothing was taken. Grandpa is convinced it was you they were after."

I still don't understand. "But… Why me?"

"Like it or not, Rose, you're powerful. In a few years, you'll be leading the entire sanctuary. They won't give up until you're out of the picture. This is only the beginning."

I sigh. No wonder Antai is so worried. My thoughts return to the riot. "Sometimes, I don't want to be queen," I confess. "I wish we could just explore the world and forget all about Cavernum."

Antai brushes a strand of my hair out of my face. "Someday, I'll take you. When the sanctuary doesn't need you anymore, we can see the world together. I promise."

I believe him. As far as I know, Antai has never broken a promise. But will there ever be peace in the sanctuary? Will I ever be able to leave? I have my doubts. For now, hope is enough. I sit there with my head on Antai's shoulder for several minutes. I never want this to end. If only we could sleep here on the rooftop.

Antai sighs. "You should get to bed. You need your rest, and the guards will be back soon enough." Antai stands and helps me to my feet. He looks at me with his big brown eyes. They gleam in the city's glow. His dark eyebrows and perfect smile. His lips are so close; I stare at them. They move closer. He closes his eyes as his lips approach mine. They're about to touch.

What if someone sees? I panic and pull away.

Antai opens his eyes. "Rose, what's wrong?" His face falls in disappointment.

"Nothing. It's not that I don't want to. It's just that… what if someone sees us?"

A glitter of hope returns to Antai's face. "A commander kissing a new recruit. Now that would be quite the scandal," Leaning in close, he whispers in my ear. "Let me know if you see anything."

His lips brush softly against my cheek. They pause as he gives me a tender kiss below my ear. His lips leave a lingering warmth on my skin. Or maybe I'm blushing. I let my cheek lean into his lips, but Antai takes a step back.

"Night, Rose. I'll see you again soon."

I want to reciprocate. I want to kiss him back, but don't know how. I reluctantly retreat towards the stairwell. "Night, Antai. Thank you. It was nice. Really." I open the door to the stairwell and disappear inside.

He kissed me. He finally kissed me.

Chapter 16

Matt

I watch as the last of the recruits disappear inside the stairwell on their way to the trench. I want to follow them so badly. Rumor has it, today's lesson is on heat manipulation.

Instead of following the other recruits, I stand silently in the armory hallway next to Lynn and Diego. After yesterday's scuffle, Proticus hardly said a word. He told us he would determine our punishment tomorrow—which is now today. He already left Vyle and his gang in the cafeteria kitchen. They'll be scrubbing dishes for the next hour.

Proticus turns his attention to us. "Alright, kiddos, follow me, and I'll show you your assignment." He leads us behind the armory service desk and down a long row of rifles. There's a small door on the back wall. Proticus opens it and gestures for us to enter first.

The room looks like a factory assembly line, with a matching smell of paint and metal. Several tables are cluttered with spare rifle parts and tools. On the back wall, a single window overlooks the city.

Proticus points to a table in the corner. "I need those rifles cleaned and the cartridges loaded. When you finish, you can oil the barrels. If you have any questions, ask the guard at the service desk."

Lynn clears her throat. "Sir, how long do we have to do this? We're missing valuable instruction."

"Call me Tick," he reminds us. "And a typical sentence for this type of violation is one week."

"One week?" I gasp. "But we didn't do anything. They attacked us. You didn't even ask our side of the story."

Tick sighs. "Look, guys, I know you didn't start anything with Vyle. Knowing him and his family, I wouldn't doubt for a second he came after you first."

Lynn shakes her head. "If you know we're innocent, why are we being punished?"

Tick sighs again and glances at the doorway. "I wish it were that simple. As far as General Kaynes is concerned, I didn't see Vyle attack you. I saw both parties reaching for their amulets, but I didn't see who started it. General Kaynes is a reasonable man, but if both parties aren't held accountable, I'll be in trouble."

"But it was self-defense," Lynn argues, shaking her arms in frustration. "If I hadn't been there, they would've drowned Diego. Shouldn't they be expelled?"

Tick shakes his head. "Listen, even if I had the power to expel Vyle, I wouldn't. I know he has his problems, but it's not his fault." Tick glances again at the doorway and lowers his voice. "He was raised that way. General Kaynes rewards cruelty and punishes weakness. He takes out his anger on his sons, and they do the same to whoever they can. If no one ever shows Vyle what mercy is, he'll end up just like his brothers."

Lynn frowns and bites her lip. "But General Kaynes is a guardian. He's a good man, isn't he?" She speaks as if she knows him personally.

Tick shrugs. "Depends what you call good. Sure, he's a good guardian. He's good at protecting the sanctuary, but he's violent and cruel. I've seen him torture feeders before killing them. He likes to watch them suffer. That doesn't sound like a good man to me."

Lynn scrunches her nose. I expect her to argue, but she only nods.

Tick sighs. "I'm sorry, guys. I know it's not fair. I'll be back within the hour. I'll tell the guard at the desk to let you talk if you want. Try to make the most of it." With that, he strides out the door.

I exhale my frustration and pick up a rifle from the table. Dried mud is wedged into the seams of the stock. I grab up a washcloth from a bucket on the floor and start scrubbing. "Well, this sucks."

"It could be worse," Diego insists. "I could've died."

I stare at the muddy gun and washcloth in my hands. I'm not in the mood to count my blessings.

Diego isn't giving up. "I'm just saying we have it pretty good in here. I'd rather be loading bullets than working in the fields with my brothers."

"He's right." Lynn agrees. "We got off easy. General Kaynes could've dismissed us from the guard. We'd be picking right now."

I know what's really bothering me. It isn't the punishment; it's how helpless I feel. Sure, I made it in the guard, but only by luck—because I saved some politician's daughter. I still can't even use dominion. While everyone else is learning to make fire, I'm slaving away in the armory storage closet. Now, I'm going to fall even more behind. How will I ever save Judy if I can't use dominion?

I'm running out of time.

Lynn finishes her second clip and picks up another empty cartridge. She's working at twice the rate of Diego.

I try not to stare. Her hair falls down around her face like a dark curtain. She bites her lip as she works another bullet into the cartridge. At least the punishment has some perks.

There's something different about Lynn. Something more. She's beautiful. And smart. And confident… And she froze a lake solid in an instant. But not only that, she saved Diego and me when she barely knew us. Whatever the reason, she's piqued my interest.

I scrub at a red-stained stock as questions tumble in my head. "While we're here, we might as well get to know each other."

"Okay," Diego agrees, finally finishing his first magazine. "So ummm…"— He glances between Lynn and me with a childish grin. —"how'd you guys meet?"

Lynn doesn't look eager to talk about it. She scrunches her nose and shoves another round into the magazine. "In the palace garden, actually." She picks her words carefully. "The night before The Dividing."

"Lynn grew up in the palace," I add. "She was the princess's maid."

"Oh." Diego's face twists in disgust.

"What?" Lynn demands. "What's wrong with the princess?"

Diego shrugs. "My family isn't a fan of royalty. My dad says they have too much power."

Lynn looks confused. She thinks for a moment before responding. "Who else should have the power? The royal family prepares their entire life to make the best decisions for the sanctuary. Who else would be more qualified?"

How is she defending them? Didn't she see the execution? How can that be right?

Diego speaks softly now. I know he doesn't want to upset Lynn. Especially not after she saved him from Vyle. "Well, in America, we do things differently. The people vote for who they want to lead. If they don't like the leaders, they can vote them out of office. It's called a democracy. The government is supposed to serve the people, not the other way around."

Lynn furrows her eyebrows. "What if the people are ignorant?" she asks. "What if they make bad decisions? What if they don't know what's best?"

Diego shrugs. But I know the answer. "We have a document with all of our rights listed," I explain. "Like freedom of speech and the right to bear arms. That way, no one makes an unfair law."

Lynn scrunches her nose. "Bear arms? What is that supposed to mean?"

"Firearms," I say. "It's the right to own a gun."

Lynn stops working. "Wait? You're telling me that everyone in America can own a gun? And your guard is okay with it?"

I smile. "That's how America started. We rebelled from an oppressive government. You know, 'Give me liberty or give me death.'"

"How… interesting." I can tell from her face she doesn't agree.

After a short pause, Diego changes the subject. "Did you like working for the princess? Do you think she'll be a good queen?"

Lynn sighs. "I hope so. I know she'll at least try." Her voice is thick with doubt. She doesn't sound too confident in the princess.

Diego smiles. "You could always tell her about democracy. Maybe she'll like the idea."

Lynn laughs at the thought. "She's a reasonable girl. I know she'll at least think about it."

I hope she's right. If Lynn likes her, she can't be that bad. The queen was lucky to have a maid like Lynn.

Lynn changes the subject. "So, Matt, you said you were a hunter before. Do you come from a family of hunters?"

I knew this question would come up eventually. "Well actually, I'm adopted."

Lynn raises her eyebrows. Diego's already heard the story on the bus. He focuses on fitting the rounds into the next magazine.

I try to think of the easiest way to explain it. "My adoptive mom isn't Adamic. She found me on the doorstep when I was a baby. We lived in Colorado—right next to Hogrum, actually. I think my birth parents might've died in the attack. That's actually where I was when I got bit—when Zane saved me."

Lynn's caramel eyes double in size. Her jaw hangs open for a slight moment before she recovers. "I-I'm sorry," she whispers softly. She bites her lip as she stares at the magazine in her hands.

Finally, she looks up. "I never met my parents either. They died in Hogrum when I was an infant. We were only supposed to be visiting. Zane actually rescued me too. Only a few of us escaped. I never knew there were other survivors."

My mind whirls. "Zane lived in Hogrum?"

Lynn nods. "He used to be a guardian there. When Hogrum fell, he lost his whole family—his wife and two little girls." Her hands hover above the magazine as her mind drifts. "My Grandpa says he's never been the same since. Every year on Remembrance Day, he goes back to visit the cremation site."

It suddenly makes sense. He was there visiting their graves. That's the only reason I'm still alive. His personal tragedy saved my life. "What was he like before?" I finally ask.

"Happier, I guess. Friendlier too," Lynn admits. "He's nice when you get to know him, but he doesn't usually have a lot of patience for strangers." Lynn smiles at me. "He must really like you to personally escort you to the palace."

I nod. Not only did he take me to the healing loft, but Zane paid for Judy's treatment. *If he isn't naturally a saint, why help me?*

Lynn glances up at me again. "And your mom, what does she do?"

I hesitate. Just the thought of Judy stings my heart. "She used to teach elementary school, but now she's in the hospital in Colorado. I had to leave her there," I confess. "She thinks I'm at a school in Australia."

Lynn looks at me with soft eyes. Those eyes alone make me feel better.

"I don't mean to pry," Lynn apologizes, "but can I ask why she's in the hospital?"

"She has stage four breast cancer."

Lynn raises her eyebrows. "Stage four?"

"It means she's dying," I summarize. All the emotions of the past week catch up with me. So much has happened I've barely had time to think of her. I still haven't found a way to call. "She could be dead right now, and I wouldn't even know it."

I regret the words almost immediately. Diego looks up from his work with watery eyes. It's been a week since the attack, and his mom is still missing. She could be dead right now, and Diego wouldn't know it.

I lean over and put my arm over his shoulder. I offer the only comfort I know: lies. "Hey, she'll make it, Diego. She'll come in on the next convoy. You'll see." I pat him on the back as the tears flow down Diego's cheeks. His shoulders shudder with silent sobs.

Wood scrapes on concrete as Lynn scoots her chair back. She wraps her arms around Diego and me, forming a giant group hug. She offers a feminine comfort that I can't give. Diego buries his face in Lynn's shoulder. Her chocolate hair tickles my nose, filling it with the scent of lavender. I don't want her to let go.

Diego's sobs quickly cease, but no one moves. I still don't know much about Lynn, but for the first time ever, I feel like I belong in Cavernum—like I'm home.

Eventually, Lynn takes her seat, and the conversation resumes. Lynn asks a lot about what life is like beyond the sanctuary. No one brings up parents again. By the time the other recruits return to the armory, I've learned that Diego is deathly afraid of spiders, and Lynn has never tried tacos. Everything with them flows so naturally, the way it did with Judy. *Like family.*

My friends and I join the herd of recruits and follow them into an unfamiliar room on the second floor. It's relatively large, with a single chalkboard on one wall and a line of windows on another. Dozens of wooden chairs surround a few long wooden tables. They're rough and unpainted—definitely handmade.

I sit between Diego and Lynn next to a window in the back of the classroom—as far away from Vyle as possible. I look out the window at the fields below. Laborers work in the distance like tiny ants. The scraping of chalk on the chalkboard grabs my attention.

Tick stands at the front of the classroom and scratches words on the chalkboard. "As guardsmen, you're not just defenders of the sanctuary, but defenders of the law. Before the end of your training, you're going to need to memorize the standard sentence for every crime. And which crimes require a trial. Understood?"

Diego looks at me with wide eyes. "Dude, these are harsh. Like, really harsh."

As the list grows, so does my unease.

1. Theft - public lashings
2. Assault - public lashings
3. Breaking curfew - public lashings
4. Refusal to comply - public lashings
5. Trespassing on palace grounds - public lashings
6. Possession of firearm - banishment/death by hanging
7. Possession of amulet - banishment/ death by hanging
8. Theft of firearm or amulet - death by hanging
9. Murder - death by hanging
10. Treason - death by hanging

The list goes on and on. I can't believe this. Lashings for breaking curfew? Why not a fine? Or maybe a warning? This doesn't seem like justice to me.

Tick finishes writing on the chalkboard and faces the recruits. "For most crimes like theft, your lieutenant will be the one to determine the severity of the punishment. For example, being caught an hour after curfew will receive more lashings than minutes after curfew. Your lieutenant will decide the exact amount. Crimes punishable by death, however, are always referred to the high council. Understood?"

I can't take my eyes off the chalkboard. This has to be a joke. I lean over to Lynn. "Do you agree with this?" I ask as quietly as I can.

Lynn furrows her brow. "What's wrong with the laws?"

"Lashings for breaking curfew," I whisper. "Doesn't that seem a bit… much?"

"More like ruthless," Diego adds from over my shoulder.

A boy to my right leans over. "Well, it's not enough to keep the equalists at bay." He has rich, black skin, and his hair is braided into tight short strands. He reminds me of a young Bob Marley. The name **Daymian** is sewn into his shirt.

Lynn nods her head in agreement. "Just don't break curfew, and you don't get lashings. It's simple and effective."

"Hanging for treason?" I say. "I'm sorry, but that's insane. It sounds like something from medieval times." *Who am I kidding? This is medieval times.*

Lynn bites her lip but doesn't say anything. I can tell she's not totally convinced by the laws, but she's too stubborn to admit it.

I know I should change the subject, but something in me won't let it go. "So, lieutenants decide the punishments, right? Does that mean they can decide no punishment as well?"

Diego turns to Lynn, smiling at the thought. "Is lieutenant high up? Like, how does it compare to a guardian?

Tick hears him. "Raise your hand if you don't know the rank ladder of the guard."

I raise my hand with Diego and a few other recruits. Based on their skinny frames and timid natures, I assume they're ex-laborers.

Tick steps to the clean half of the chalkboard and draws a ladder. "Alright, kiddos, listen up. It's easiest to start at the top. In Cavernum, there are four guardians. They also function as the generals of the guard and hold a spot on the high council. Together, they have complete control over the guard and a voice in all diplomatic decisions."

He scratches a small x on the next rung down. "Underneath the guardians are the six commanders. One commander oversees each of the four quadrants of the city: north, west, east, and south. We also have a commander over the outer wall and another over the palace. Right now, we're in the east quadrant under Commander Elsborne's jurisdiction."

He marks the next rung down. "Each quadrant is divided into districts, each with its own captain. And each district is divided into zones, each with its own lieutenant. Royal guardsmen are also lieutenants. They defend the palace under the instruction of Commander Noyan."

Tick marks a big X at the base of the ladder. "And here at the very bottom are all of you. Subject to all, master of none. If you behave yourselves, when an officer retires, you might be selected to replace them. All officers live in the palace as elites. They get paid triple what you make. So work hard. Remember, whichever one of you is ranked first in your class will automatically be promoted to lieutenant. Any questions?"

"What rank are you?" Zander asks with a stupid smirk on his face.

"Technically, I'm a captain. I worked under General Zane in the beyond before taking this position."

The other kids bustle with excitement. Some shout questions. —"Have you killed feeders?"—"What are they like?"—

Tick smiles and shakes his head. "I'm flattered by your curiosity, but we really need to focus. We'll talk about feeders later in your training."

A short, frantic knock echoes from the classroom door just before it's flung open. A young soldier stands in the doorway, sweat dripping from his face. A crumpled note peeks out of his fist. He leans on the doorknob as he stammers. "Lycon sent a message! Code red!" As soon as the words are out of his mouth, the soldier turns and runs down the hallway. Immediately, Tick drops the chalk and sprints after him. Confusion erupts in the classroom. Lynn sits frozen in her seat.

"Who's Lycon?" Diego thinks aloud. I remember hearing the word recently, but I can't quite put my finger on it.

Klinton answers from the row in front. "Lycon isn't a person, it's a sanctuary in France."

I ask the next obvious question. "What's a code red?"

Lynn finally pulls herself out of the trance. "Code red means imminent danger." She looks at me with wide, worried eyes. "Lycon is under attack."

Chapter 17

Matt

Move! I command in my mind. I squeeze the amulet in my left hand. In my right hand, I hold a tiny pebble in my open palm.

Nothing.

It's no use. I've been trying all day, and I still can't even move a pebble. A defeated sigh escapes me. I've tried everything: controlling water, making fire, moving air. It's all hopeless.

After the code red yesterday evening, we spent the rest of the evening in our rooms as a hundred soldiers left for Lycon. This morning, Tick released us from our amulet suspension. He said we don't have time to waste. Still, he hasn't shared anything about the distress message. According to Lynn, the last code red was when Hogrum fell. I hope this time is different.

I take a deep breath and scan the trench for my friends. The hiss of flames periodically fills the room with an orange glow. By now, half the class has learned to create fire. The bursts of flame fill the trench with heat. Sweat drips off my forehead and soaks into the dusty cavern floor. Vyle and his buddies peel off their shirts and toss them aside. The yellow Adamic lights glisten of Vyle's sweaty, buff back.

Show off.

A few other recruits follow his example. Even if I wanted to, I can't take off my shirt. Zane made it clear that my tattoos have to stay covered. Sharing a room with 3 recruits has been a pain, but so far, I've managed to keep them hidden.

On the other side of the trench, Lynn coaches Diego as a baseball-sized fireball flickers in his cupped hands. A ping of jealousy gnaws at me, tearing at my rib cage. Diego is picking up dominion surprisingly quick. He's been promoted to the advanced group with Lynn and the elites. Meanwhile, I play with rocks alongside eight other struggling recruits. We're the only ones left who still can't do anything.

I watch my friends from across the gymnasium. I stare at Diego, looking past his eyes and into his head. The thoughts come slowly. A feeling of triumph. Concentration.

Fire. The word pops into my mind without warning. A moment later, a sphere of red flame materialized in Diego's hands.

I smile. I can't use dominion on elements yet, but I'm getting pretty good at mind reading. I find Vyle in the crowd. His black eye makes him hard to miss. He narrows his eyes at Lynn from a few yards away. I stare at his face, trying to look past his eyes. Anger, confusion, jealousy. But I feel something else too. Longing, desire, … lust.

Whoa! I blink and try to shake the thoughts from my head. I guess I'm not the only one with the hots for Lynn. To be honest, I'm not surprised. She's beautiful. I catch myself staring more often than socially acceptable. Her smile, her walk, the way she bites her tongue when she concentrates. It's hypnotizing. And sometimes... just sometimes... I find her staring back.

I look at Lynn, trying to see past her eyes. I wrestle in my mind, trying to catch a glimpse inside her head.

Darkness. A large black wall. No thoughts. No emotions. Nothing.

For some reason, Lynn is different. It's like trying to read the mind of a rock. Either she's a cyborg, or she's blocking me somehow. I'm curious to know how, but I'm too scared to confront her about it. I still haven't disclosed my newfound ability, not even to Diego.

I need to focus. Reading minds won't save Judy. I look back at the pebble in my hand, trying to see past the surface. *Rise! Float! Move!*

It doesn't budge.

With a grunt, I throw the rock onto the floor. It bounces several feet and lands by another boy's feet. The boy picks up the pebble and walks over to me. It's Klinton, the curly-haired boy with glasses. He blinks at the pebble and looks up at me. "Don't worry if you don't figure it out. One of my brothers is a guardsman. He's a dry-blood, but he's just fine. They really do have good jobs for us."

"Thanks," I mutter even though I don't mean it. "I'll figure it out eventually." Klinton seems like a nice guy, but he doesn't understand. It's not about the guard, it's about Judy. *Dominion is everything.*

"Okay." Klinton nods. He gets the hint that I don't want to talk. He starts to leave but turns to face me once again. "Well, don't feel bad if it takes you longer." He points to the advanced recruits on the other side of the trench. "They've been practicing since they were little."

I know he's trying to be nice, but it just sounds like he's rubbing it in my face. I swallow my frustration and fake an interested face. "What about you?" I ask. "Were you a commoner before?"

Klinton laughs. "No, I'm high-born like them. My dad is a master painter. He does the portraits for the royal family. But he doesn't know a thing about dominion, so I never learned."

"Why didn't you become a painter too?"

"I would've, but my oldest brother is already his apprentice. The palace only needs so many painters. I thought my odds were better in the guard."

"How many brothers do you have?" I ask. I always wanted a brother.

"Five," Klinton proudly reports. "And one sister. I'm the youngest in the family."

"Wow. Seven kids." That's even more than Diego's family. "Is that normal here?" I ask.

"In the ring, it is. They have a lot of kids. But elites usually don't have very many, two or three at most."

"What do your other brothers do?"

Klinton looks at the floor and drags his foot in the dirt. "Well… actually, they're pickers now. They didn't make it in the guard. I don't see them very often."

"Oh." That wasn't what I was expecting. I try desperately to fill the awkward silence. "Well, I'm glad you made it. I'm Matt by the way."

"I'm Klinton. Here's your rock." He holds out the pebble in his open palm even though there are hundreds on the floor. I take it. Klinton steps back and motions toward an empty corner of the trench. "I'll let you go back to practicing now. Good luck with dominion. If you figure it out, maybe you can help me too."

"Thanks. You too." I say as Klinton wanders away. I squeeze the pebble in my hand. I need to master dominion, but it's hard to concentrate with Tick shouting instructions.

"Fire dominion is one of the most dangerous," Tick warns. "Make sure to direct the heat away from you! It will naturally want to disperse into the environment, including your body. If you don't direct it, you'll end up burning yourself and those around you."

A loud hiss catches my attention from the other side of the training room. A small stream of fire hisses from Vyle's hand. It's only a few inches long and tapers to a point like a welding torch. Cloyd levitates a chunk of granite in front of the flame, and the rock quickly changes from gray to a bright, glowing orange. Molten lava slowly drips onto the concrete floor.

"Yes! That's it!" Tick praises. "Control before power. Well done, Vyle. Well done." The entire class pauses to watch the display. I look down at my rock. I've seen enough of Vyle showing off.

Today's the day, I tell myself. I won't give up until Judy is cured or dead. I have to try. She at least deserves that much.

They say that proximity makes a difference, so I hold the pebble an inch from my chest. *I won't stop until it moves.* I bow my head and fix my eyes on the small stone, trying to imagine it how Tick suggested. I speak to the individual molecules, willing them to move!

Please. Please. Please.

10 seconds.

The hiss of flames stops, and the recruits cheer for Vyle. I keep my eyes on the pebble.

20 seconds.

I command with all the mental concentration I can muster.

Move!

It twitches. It's barely noticeable, but the pebble tilts slightly to the side.

Yes! I can't believe it. It's only a wiggle, but it's something. I'm sure of it. I lean in closer. My face is only inches from the pebble. I refocus and command the rock to rise.

Ever so slowly, the pebble lifts into the air. It stops at eye level and hovers in front of me, quivering slightly. I watch in wonder. A sense of pride washes away the embarrassment of the last few days. I've finally done it. I know it's a small victory, but it's everything to me.

I will the pebble back to the floor.

Nothing. The pebble doesn't move.

I try again, commanding the molecules to fall.

Nothing. The stone remains hovering in front of my face. Suddenly, the pebble lurches, smacking me straight in the eye.

"Ow!" I stumble back and clutch my eye with one hand. The pebble lifts into the air once again and zips across the room. It lands in Vyle's hand.

Laughter erupts from the recruits. All eyes are on me. They've been watching the whole time. My excitement mutates into humiliation. I didn't exercise dominion. Vyle had been controlling the pebble the whole time. It was one giant prank, and I fell for it like a fool.

"Dry-blood!" someone yells.

Croyd cups his hands to his mouth. "Go home, son of Cain!" More laughter.

I lock eyes with Lynn from across the room. She looks at me with sadness. With pity. She was watching the whole time. Why didn't she say something? Why didn't she warn me? Humiliation crushes down on my chest. I'm sick of dominion. I'm sick of looking like an idiot in front of everyone.

A hand touches my shoulder. It's Klinton. "Don't worry about them. They're just jerks." I brush past him and turn toward the exit.

"Shut up and listen up!" The deep voice thunders like a true lumberjack. Zane stands in the opening of the tunnel, looking as stern as I remember him. He wears a tight-fitting tee and faded jeans. His scowl is half-covered by his scraggly beard. I'm not sure which is more impressive: The silver sphere of an amulet that hangs around his neck or the three foot short-sword fastened to his waist.

The laughter dies instantly.

Zane steps out of the doorway and towers over the recruits. "Everyone, gather in." He waits until everyone is in a giant huddle before he continues. "I'm about to tell you some sensitive inform-ation. Many of you will someday give your life for Cavernum. You have the right to know the danger. However, if you repeat this to anyone outside of the guard, there will be dire consequences.

As you've probably heard, soldiers from Lycon sent out a distress signal yesterday. It was a code red—imminent danger to the sanct-uary. We're not sure what that danger might be or if their walls are still intact, but we're preparing for the worst."

I immediately think of Hogrum. I try not to imagine hundreds of feeders tearing through the city... tearing through my parents.

Zane rests his hand on the handle of his sword as he speaks. "King Dralton left for Lycon last night with reinforcements. They'll likely arrive in France sometime today. We're hoping to hear back from him soon. Until then, we need you all to be aware of... certain dangers within the sanctuary."

Zane glances my way. "Perhaps you've heard the history. Accord-ing to legend, Satan taught the most wicked how to pervert Adamic. How to use Adamic symbols to gain dominion over man. Control humans. Possess them. They wear these Adamic symbols in the form of tattoos. You probably know them as demons.

Until a few weeks ago, we thought they were extinct, but we were wrong. Just days before the distress signal, a demon was identified in Lycon. If there is one, there's likely more. King Dralton is worried that demons might already be in the sanctuary."

Diego's eyes bulge. I feel the same. This is some creepy stuff Zane is talking about.

"I thought the walls protect us," Klinton cries.

"They do..." Zane assures, "from feeders. But demons are a totally different matter. They were extinct when the sanctuaries were built and aren't repelled by the wall. As long as they don't feed, anyone can pass through the walls, including demons."

Zander looks confused. "Demons aren't feeders?"

Zane sighs at the technicality. "Sometimes, but not always. Anyone with the demon tattoo has dominion over man. Those tattoos alone define them as demons. That being said, demons, like the rest of us, still need a way to communicate that dominion. To accomplish this, most resort to feeding. However, if a demon has an amulet, he can exercise dominion without ever needing to feed. That was the case with the demon in Lycon."

Velma raises her hand. "Let me get this straight. Feeding makes someone a feeder, and the demon tattoo makes someone a demon. Someone could be one or the other, or they could be both."

Zane nods. "Correct."

"How do we kill them?" Vyle shouts.

Zane sets his eyes on Vyle. "Easier said than done. You won't know it's a demon until it's too late. Once you're possessed, you're as good as dead. You become their puppet. They can make you kill yourself, or they can use you as a weapon to kill others. The best thing to do is to find a Guardian. Our soul-anchors protect us from possession."

Diego leans over to me. "Dude, this is crazy. We're all gonna die." I know he's partly serious. I'm nervous too. I didn't sign up for this.

"Quiet!" Zane commands. "That's not all. We've also encountered feeders with Adamic armor. They wear it in the form of tattoos, sometimes from head to toe. These tattoos are impenetrable. Lightning, fire, bullets, you name it."

Zane unsheathes his sword from its scabbard. The blade is perfectly polished with glittering gold symbols inlaid in the steel. I recognize the symbols from my birthday dagger.

$$\text{\Large ⚡ ⩕ ⩍ ☉}$$

"Only an Adamic blade can penetrate the tattoos, but they're rare. Only the guardians have them. So, if you encounter a feeder with Adamic armor, run and find help. Fighting is suicide."

Impenetrable armor! Fighting is suicide! Now, I'm upset. I'm a guardsman. Where's my Adamic dagger? Where's my amulet? At least with those, I'd stand a chance. Without them, I'll be lucky to survive a few weeks in the guard.

Zane spins the blade in his hand like a toy. "Cutting through armor isn't all this is good for." He looks to Tick. "Which of your recruits ranked first in dominion? Send them up here."

"Vyle, you heard him."

Vyle steps forward from the front row and stands before Zane.

"Make an energy shield. The strongest one you can." Zane says.

Unease flashes across Vyle's face. He hesitates. "But sir, my shield won't—"

"Just do it. I didn't ask your opinion."

Vyle widens his stance and takes hold of his amplifier in one hand. The air shimmers before him like vibrating glass.

Zane grins mischievously. "Not only does an Adamic blade pierce Adamic armor, but it can pierce all types of defenses." He points the blade tip first at Vyle and slowly presses it into the shield. It glides, like a hot knife through butter, directly through the shield. The air ripples around the steel but does nothing to slow the sword. Vyle arches his back and leans away as the sword's tip approaches his nose. The shield dissolves, and Vyle stumbles back.

"You get the idea." Zane slides the blade back into its scabbard. "Don't forget. This is sensitive information not to be discussed outside the guard. I trust you'll keep your mouths shut." Zane nods to Tick, passing him the floor.

Tick clears his throat. "Okay, recruits, return those amulets and prepare for firearms training. Hustle!" I follow the recruits as they file out of the cavern. As I approach the tunnel, Tick holds out his hand. "Not you, Matt. You stay here. Zane wants a word with you."

Zane waits until the last of the recruits are out of the trench. Once he's sure they're gone, he approaches me with a sliver of a smile on his face. "I heard about your little stunt at the shooting range. Congratulations."

"Uh, thanks." My shoulders relax. I was expecting a lecture of some kind.

Zane leads me to a weight bench and takes a seat. He motions for me to sit on a bench across from him. He breaks the silence first. "How were your first few days in the guard?"

Is he asking as a friend or as my boss? I decide to play it safe. "Good," I lie.

Zane doesn't respond. He stares at me with his all-seeing brown eyes. "Tick told me about your little scuffle with Vyle. I heard you gave him what he deserved."

"I guess," I say, trying to hide a smile.

Zane doesn't smile. Once again, his face is unreadable. "I just wanted to ask about something one of the recruits told Tick. He said you used dominion to beat up Vyle. You dodged every one of his punches and kicks." Zane raises a suspicious eyebrow. "He said it was like you knew what he was going to do before he did it."

My heart beats faster. For a brief moment, I consider lying. It would be so easy. I could just play dumb. But part of me is curious.

Maybe Zane knows about my gift. He already knows about my tattoos, and my amulet, and my mom. He's paying for her medical bills after all. If I can trust anyone, it's Zane.

"I don't really know how to explain it," I admit. "If I have an amulet, I can…" I hesitate. Saying it out loud makes it sound even stranger. "—it's like I can read minds. I can feel what people are about to do."

A thin smile appears underneath lumberjack's facial hair. He's not the least bit surprised. Something tells me he's known the whole time.

"Reading minds isn't normal, Matt. The ability stems from the Adamic tattoo on your back. Don't tell anyone else about this. You hear me?"

I nod. I'm well acquainted with secrets. "How does it work?"

"Just like when you use dominion, you're communicating soul to soul. You're reaching out to the edge of a person's consciousness and getting a portion of their most prominent thoughts—what they're thinking that very moment."

"Can they read my thoughts too?" I worry.

Zane thinks for a moment. "Depends. If you stay at the edge of their soul, they shouldn't even know you're reading their mind. But, if you go too deep, the communication can go both ways."

"How do you know all this?" I ask.

"When I was your age, I was just like you. I was a refugee. My parents were sent to the fields, and I had no idea what to do. Then, I met a kid from the palace." Zane smiles at the memory. He speaks slowly, deciding how much of his past to share. "He was… different… secretive. He had tattoos just like you. We became good friends. Best friends, actually. He was skilled with dominion. A real prodigy. When he turned 18, he joined the guard. I didn't know what to do, so I decided to follow him."

It's weird to imagine Zane as a kid. I can't picture the brute without his beard.

"After a few weeks, when I couldn't figure out how to exercise dominion, he pulled me aside and offered to help. He entered my mind with the same gift you have and exercised dominion through me. It felt as if I was using dominion myself. Once I learned how to speak to the elements, it was like riding a bike. Ever since then, it's come naturally."

I try to process what Zane just said, but I can't stop thinking about the boy. Zane actually knew someone like me. Maybe this person can tell me where my tattoos come from. Maybe he knows my parents.

Zane looks at me with a soft expression. "Proticus told me how you were struggling with dominion, and I thought we could try the same thing. But only if you want to."

The decision is an easy one. "Of course!" This is an answer to my prayers. Maybe I still have a chance at saving Judy after all. "What do you need me to do?"

Zane smiles and slips out of his guardian amulet. He swaps it with a smaller amulet from his jeans pocket—an amplifier by the looks of it.

"All you need to do is read my mind while I exercise dominion. Let me know when you're ready?"

I nod. I grip my amulet tight in one hand and stare into Zane's eyes. I look beyond his pupils, deeper and deeper into his head. Emotions rush through me. Compassion. Doubt. Stress.

"Ready," I announce.

I feel it. The concentration. The mental exertion.

Fire.

I can picture what Zane intends just before his hands disappear in a swirling spiral of red-orange flame. The flames lick harmlessly at his skin for several seconds until Zane extinguishes them.

"Your turn," Zane instructs.

I cup my hands in front of me and stare at the air inside them, commanding fire to form.

Nothing happens. I start to doubt if I'll ever use dominion. "Maybe I'm dry-blooded or something."

Zane lets out a single laugh like a bursting bubble. "Ha! Trust me. You're not dry-blooded. Read my mind again," Zane commands. "But this time, go deeper. Don't look with your eyes so much; reach more with your mind. Got it?"

I nod my head. I stare into Zane's eyes, reaching deep. Once again, the thoughts return: concentration, hope, a desire for me to succeed. I close my eyes. I can still feel Zane's thoughts. It isn't sight or touch, but another sense completely. I can see Zane in front of me with my mind. A type of sixth sense.

I lean into Zane with my thoughts, pushing myself deeper into his conscious. With every inch of mental space, a flash-flood of emotions pours over my mind. It's hard to distinguish his feelings from my own. An aching sadness. A heavy sense of responsibility. Zane floats all around me. His memories. His dreams. His goals. I'm swimming inside his brain, drowning in his conscious.

Ready! I try to say the word, but my body feels far away. I can't get the words to form.

Then, I feel it. Zane's mind is reaching out, leaving me alone in the dark. I follow him with my thoughts, stretching into the unknown.

I collide with a new conscious. It's everywhere. This new mind is much simpler than Zane's. It doesn't have emotions or memories. It only has one thought: Obey.

Fire! I speak it directly to the air, and the air responds instantly. I open my eyes. Flames erupt around my hands. Only… they aren't my hands. They're big and calloused. I spot my own body through the flickering flames. I'm looking out of Zane's eyes.

I'm inside Zane's body!

In a panic, I squeeze my eyes shut and retract my mind. The onslaught of Zane's brain is replaced with silence. I'm alone with my thoughts. I open my eyes and gasp a breath in my own body. I look down at my uniform and let out a big sigh of relief. I'm myself again. Only now, my arms feel like lead. Fatigue presses down on me as if somebody turned up gravity. Exhaustion fills my bones with sand.

"What just happened?" I gasp.

Zane ignores me. He's unfazed by the whole event. "You got it. Now try again. Repeat what you just felt."

I obey. I close my eyes and reach out with my mind, driving my conscious into the unknown. Almost instantly, I can feel the molecules all around me, flowing and colliding. The air is alive. Each tiny molecule obeying the laws of nature, moving in perfect unison. I speak in my mind, mentally describing the task to the air.

Fire!

Orange flames burst to life in my hands. The heat spills into my flesh, singeing my skin. I push back with my mind, directing the heat away from my hands. Instantly the pain is replaced with a cool sensation. Triumph swells in my chest, and this time, it isn't a prank. *I actually did it! I used dominion.*

My head spins as fatigue quickly consumes me. The fire in my hands flickers out, and I hold out my arms to regain my balance.

"That's enough for today," Zane decides. "You'll need some rest before you go again. If I have time next week, I can teach you more." He removes his soul-anchor from his pocket and restores it around his neck. He smiles at me, showing teeth for the first time. He's the happiest I've ever seen him. "You did good, Matt. Hopefully, it comes easier now. I have a feeling you'll need it with what's coming."

That last sentence makes me uneasy. Curiosity itches at the back of my mind. "Why couldn't I read minds before?" I ask. "Wasn't my old amulet even stronger?"

Zane scratched at his beard. "Your old amulet was a soul-anchor. Soul-anchors protect the soul from invasion. The spell must block mind reading as well. It could also explain how you survived the feeder bite. If your soul was anchored to your body and protected, it couldn't be consumed by the feeder."

"Does that mean my parents were guardians?" I ask.

Zane shrugs. "Like I said before, your parents must have been very powerful people."

I look at the floor, and my mind spins. The mind reading. The amulet. My parents. I'm missing something. I need to know more.

I gather my courage. "What happened to your friend? The mind reader?"

Zane looks at his boots. His face sags into a frown. "He almost became a guardian at one point, but the high council didn't trust him. Eventually, he was banished. He made some bad choices... chose some dark paths."

Dark paths? What is that supposed to mean? I have a guess, but I don't ask. "Where is he now?"

Zane and I lock eyes. I can sense the pain through his hardened gaze. A deep aching sadness. I felt it personally when I read his mind.

"As far as I know, he's dead." Zane finally manages. "He died a long time ago."

My hopes are shattered. "Oh" is all I can muster.

"C'mon. I should probably get you to the gun range before Tick comes looking." Zane starts for the exit.

"Why me?" I finally say.

Zane stops mid-stride. "What?"

"Why help me?"

The corner of Zane's mouth curls up. "I told you in Colorado that I would teach you dominion, didn't I?"

I'm getting frustrated. Zane is avoiding the question. "That's not what I meant," I complain. "My mom. The healing. Now, this. Why are you helping me so much? And only me? From what I've heard, you're not exactly the type for charity work." I bite my tongue. The last part wasn't supposed to sound like an insult.

Zane sighs. The air whooshes out of his heavy lungs, but he doesn't seem mad. He faces me and sticks his massive hands in his pockets. "That boy I told you about—my best friend. You remind me a lot of him. He did me a lot of favors back in the day. Saved my life more than once. I never got to repay him before he died. I guess helping you feels like I'm helping him."

Zane doesn't wait for my reply. He turns back towards the door. I wrestle with my thoughts as I scurry after him. Everything leads me to the same conclusion. The tattoo. The mind reading. The soul-anchor.

I swallow. I hope I'm wrong, but I have to know the truth.

"Zane?"

Zane coasts to a stop and sighs. I'm testing his patience.

"Yes, Matt?"

"I'm a demon, aren't I?"

Chapter 18

Rose

I lay in my bed, listening to Velma's rhythmic snoring. But tonight, it's not her snoring that keeps me up. It's Antai.

He left for Lycon with Grandpa and the rest of the rescue party. But that was four days ago, and I'm worried sick. If all was well in Lycon, they would have returned at least a day ago, maybe sooner. Worst-case scenarios cloud my thoughts. What if they were attacked? What if something terrible happened? What if they're d-?

Stop it, Rose. They're fine, I tell myself. *They have to be!*

I'm so lost in my thoughts, I almost don't hear it. The delicate crinkle of paper. I twist my head and watch as the white square of a letter slides quietly under the door. Then, silence. I stretch my upper body out of bed in order to grasp the note with my fingertips. I pull the covers over my head and speak with my mind.

Light.

A soft glow, seemingly without origin, illuminates the crinkled paper. It reads:

Dear Ringling,

I just want to let you know I'm fine. We just got back in the middle of the night. I have so much to tell you. I miss you. I promise I'll talk to you soon.

Love,

Your secret admirer.

Elation swells in my chest. I slip out of my covers as quickly and quietly as I can and twist the door handle. I close the door behind me and spot a shadow retreating down the hallway. I tiptoe after him. I'm wearing only a nightgown, but I don't mind. He's seen me in my PJs before.

"Antai." I try to whisper, but it sounds like a shout in the silence. The shadow freezes and spins on a dime. He clears the distance between us in a few quick strides, lifting me into a sweeping hug. In an instant, all my worries fall away. The warmth of his body fills my head and conquers my cares. Neither of us speak for several seconds. I rest my head on his chest and listen to the beat of his heart as he runs his fingers through my hair. He's alive. That's all that matters.

"What took you so long?" I finally complain. "I've been going crazy." I can't see his face in the dark, but the pain in his voice is enough to break my heart.

"Lycon's gone, Rose. It's gone. We've been burning the bodies for the past two days, and we've barely made a dent. The rest of the soldiers are still there." The pain turns to anger. Antai struggles to keep his voice to a whisper. "We didn't find a single survivor. Not in the whole city."

"What?" I lift my head to look him in the eyes. "But what about the walls? They had three guardians."

"I don't know how they did it. King Dralton thinks it was the Adalit. It's the only thing that makes sense. He stayed behind to look for the Book of Life."

Book of Life? "He told you?" I gasp.

"Me and the other guardians," Antai confirms. "It's pretty un-believable. Imagine the evil he could do if he finds it."

"What if we find it first?" I mutter. "Imagine the good we could do. We could end world hunger. Eliminate the feeders. We could fix everything."

"I don't know. No man should have that kind of power." Antai sighs. "Well, I probably should go. We can't risk getting caught out here together. Things will be busy this next week, but I'll see you as soon as I can."

Now's my chance. I've been planning this in my head ever since our date. I go onto my tippy-toes and wrap my arms around Antai's neck. Antai knows just what I'm thinking. His hands guide my waist against his, and his lips fold into mine. They're soft and warm, exactly how I imagined.

Antai pushes my back against the wall, kissing me fast and full of passion. I grab a fistful of his uniform and pull him tighter against me. Everything feels so natural. So instinctive. His lips skim over my neck as he whispers in my ear. "I've been waiting for this for a long time."

I interrupt him with another kiss. "Why didn't you tell me it was this nice?" I arch my spine, pressing back against his body weight.

Antai suppresses a laugh and kisses me softly on the cheek. "Oh, Rose. You're killing me. But I really should go. I'll see you soon. I promise."

"Ahhh okay," I pout. I want this to last all night, but I reluctantly release my grip on his uniform.

He kisses me one last time on the lips. "Night, Rose. I love you."

Before I can respond, his outline fades into the darkness of the hallway. I stand in a daze for several moments before I find my way back to my dorm.

He loves me. He really loves me.

Only one question remains: Do I love him back?

I raise an eyebrow at Matt. "Are you sure you can handle it?"

TIck had everyone pair up in order to practice dominion. Today's lesson is on forming energy shields. To my delight, Matt asked to be my partner. Tick moved him into the advanced group yesterday, but I'm afraid I'll hurt him. Just three weeks ago, Matt couldn't lift a rock with dominion. He's progressed unbelievably fast, but I don't think he's ready for this. Deflecting rocks is one thing, fire is a different story.

"Don't hold back," Matt insists. He holds his arms out in front of him, and a thin ripple in the air lets me know his shield is complete. He widens his stance and nods to let me know he's ready.

I push with my mind, willing the flames to form. I throw them at Matt in a single wave. They collide with the energy shield, splashing outward in all directions. When the flames dissipate, I find Matt smiling from ear to ear. It's nice to see him finally enjoying himself.

"Is that it? I expected more," Matt teases from behind the safety of his shield.

"Fine, you asked for it," I laugh. I won't let him mock me like that. He will bow to his queen.

I push with my mind and send a torrent of fire surging at Matt. The flames, like rushing water, flow in a constant stream. I direct as much heat as possible into the center of Matt's shield. Flames mold around the shape of his shield and spill over the edges. Finally, Matt caves. He dives to the side as his shield dissolves.

I cut the flow of fire immediately. "You alright?"

Matt wipes thick beads of sweat from his forehead and laughs from the floor. "Wow. You weren't kidding. That was hot."

I blush. For a second, I think he's talking about me. *The fire, Rose. He's referring to the fire. Get ahold of yourself.*

I reach down and help Matt back to his feet. I don't know if it's just my imagination, but his arms are bigger than they were a few weeks ago. The weight training is doing its job. Even Diego looks noticeably thinner.

"You're lucky I was going easy," Matt pants. He smiles to let me know he's joking. "I think I'm done for today."

Most of the other recruits are tiring as well. From what I can see, Matt is one of the few to have grasped the concept. Around the room, recruits wave their arms in vain. I don't know how Matt learned so quickly. I can't help but wonder if it has to do with Zane. Thrice now, Zane has asked Matt to stay behind when the rest of us go to the shooting range. Some people say he's getting tutored. But even with Grandpa's coaching, it took me weeks to form my first energy shield. *How does he do it?*

"This is hard," Velma complains. She's paired with Diego, who is also struggling to form any kind of force field. "I don't get how this is supposed to work."

"Alright, kiddos, gather round," Tick commands. "Maybe I didn't explain this as well as I could have. Let's start with the basics. What is an energy shield? What's it made of?"

Everyone looks around, but no one speaks up. Even I'm at a loss for words. I know what an energy shield does, but I'm not quite sure what it is.

"No one?" Tick asks, his head on a swivel. "Alright, new question. What do we have dominion over?"

Velma speaks up. "The elements and the animals."

"More than just that," Tick corrects. "We have dominion over all the earth. That doesn't just include the elements, but the laws that control them. Let's take gravity, for example. It's not an element. It doesn't take up space. Yet it exercises a force on everything. And this force is under our control. Allow me to demonstrate." Tick takes his amulet in one hand and closes his eyes.

At first, nothing happens. Then, I feel it. The pressure of my feet on the floor grows lighter. My stomach lurches. Ever so slowly, my feet lift from the floor. In unison with the other 50 recruits, I drift into the air. One foot. Two feet. I float higher and higher. Only Tick remains anchored to the ground. He stands with his eyes squeezed shut. The feeling is incredible. Complete weightlessness. Helplessly, I start to spin. Then, as quickly as it began, gravity returns, and I drop back to the floor. A few unlucky recruits land on their backs.

Tick opens his eyes and rests his hands on his knees. He's breathing hard. "I'm gonna feel that one in the morning," he laughs. "An energy shield isn't too different from gravitational dominion. Without using elements, it applies a force on anything that tries to cross the barrier—even light. That's what causes the distortion. It allows you to defend yourself without blocking your view of the enemy."

Tick faces toward the weight lifting equipment. "Force dominion can also be used as an attack. It's quick, effective, and difficult to evade." He grabs hold of his amulet and extends his arm. The air ripples so quickly I can barely follow it with my eyes. The brief sound of vibrating glass tickles my ears a moment before the nearest dumbbell is thrown into the air. It cartwheels once before striking the cavern wall. A surprised gasp escapes the recruits.

Tick glances at his watch. "Take a few more minutes to practice your shields. We'll wrap up in five. We have some big things planned for today."

Matt and I wander back to our corner of the trench. Footsteps trail behind us. "Do you mind if we join you, Lynn?" Vyle asks. Zander and Croyd are trailing behind him like uglier versions of his shadow. "I figured you might want someone to challenge you a little more. You deserve more than a dry-blood." He sneers at Matt. Zander and Croyd smile to themselves.

Matt clenches his fists. "Are you sure you're not the one who needs more of a challenge?" He gestures at Zander and Croyd, who glare back at Matt.

Vyle takes a step closer. "C'mon, Lynn. What do you say?"

"Get lost, Vyle!" I snap. I look around for Tick, but he's coaching some novice recruits on the other side of the trench.

Vyle tilts his head, amused. "Don't tell me you're afraid. I'm not going to hurt you." He coos as if speaking to an injured animal.

"I know. You couldn't hurt me if you tried," I sneer.

Matt glances anxiously between us. "He's scum, Lynn. It's not worth it. Just let it go."

Vyle shrugs. "If you can take it, what do you have to worry about? You need someone who can help you push your limits." Vyle reasons.

"He's lying," Matt urgently insists. "He's been saving his energy while we've been practicing. He wants an excuse to hurt you."

Let him try, Rose. If you don't teach him a lesson, who will? My soul-anchor is still safely tucked within my bra. I can feel the metal, now warm against my skin. I have every advantage.

"Fine." I take hold of my amplifier to make it look realistic. With a simple command, the air ripples in front of me.

Vyle takes his amulet in his fist and smiles. Instantly, light explodes between us. A single point of blinding white heat burns into my shield. I squeeze my eyes shut for protection. The heat slams against my shield like a battering ram. The force is greater than the strength of my shield. The heat begins to seep through. My uniform grows dangerously hot. My cheeks burn. For a second, I almost succumb.

I turn my head to the side and press forward with my mind. I can feel Vyle's influence urging the fire toward me. The heat begs me to let it through, but I command it back with all my might. The roar of the furnace between us is deafening.

"STOOOP!" Tick screams.

Suddenly the burning heat extinguishes. Vyle's eyes roll back in his head as he falls face-first upon the cavern floor. An audible gasp is heard from the students. He lays corpse-still as blood starts to pool under his nose. *He strained the soul,* I realize. *He fainted!*

"What did you do?" Zander gasps.

Everyone is staring at me. My legs wobble, and I collapse to my knees. I feel fine, but I have to sell it. I should be utterly exhausted after a display like that. *What if I blew my cover?*

Matt stands protectively over me. He looks down with a blend of confusion and concern. Whispers cascade around the gym.

Tick comes running from across the room. "Zander, run and call a carriage. We need to get him to a healer."

Vyle moans and rolls onto his back. He's waking up. A stream of blood trickles out his nose and over his lips. "I'm fine," he croaks, wincing as he shakily climbs to his feet.

Tick puts his hand on Vyle's shoulder. "You should see a healer just in case. Your father would wa—"

Vyle jerks his shoulder out from under Tick's hand. "To hell with my father." With his sleeve, he smears the blood under his nose. "I said I'm fine. I'm not going anywhere."

Tick takes a step back, hands raised defensively in the air. "Alright, then. We're all adults here. That's your decision to make." He looks around the room. "I think that's enough for today. Return your amulets and hurry to the classroom. I want to have time for today's lesson. The topic is one of my personal favorites. It's time you kiddos learn about feeders."

Chapter 19

Rose

As usual, I sit next to Matt and Diego in the back of the classroom. I'm not too excited for the lesson. I doubt Tick can tell me anything about feeders I don't already know. As the last of the students shuffle in, an old man shuffles into the doorway. The recruits fall completely silent.

Grandpa!

I haven't seen him since he left for Lycon three weeks ago. He's been out searching for the Lost Library, and I've been worried sick.

Tick falls onto one knee and bows his head. "Your Majesty, I wasn't aware of your return. How may I be of assistance?" The formality sounds strange coming from Tick.

"Rise," Grandpa commands. He looks directly at me as he enters the classroom. His cane taps the floor as he shuffles into the room. He looks exhausted. Bags hang beneath his bloodshot eyes. "I was in the area and wanted to see how the future guards of Cavernum are doing. Do you mind if I sit in on the lesson?" His expression is calm and thoughtful.

"It would be an honor, your majesty. The pleasure is ours." Tick's cheeks burn red, and his arms are stiff at his side. "We were about to discuss feeders."

"Mmmh, an excellent topic." Grandpa taps his cane lightly on the floor. "I presume the recruits know what a feeder is. Perhaps we can simply answer their questions."

Tick nods his head vigorously. "Of course, your highness. A wonderful idea." Tick faces us. "You heard the king. What questions do you have?"

The room remains silent. Grandpa sneaks a smile at me before moving his eyes around the room. I know he's only here for me. It's his way of telling me he's safely returned. He could've just sent a letter, but I'm glad he came in person.

"Come on now," Grandpa urges. "Don't be shy around the king. Just shout your questions. I know you all have them."

Croyd speaks from his seat in the front. "Do they really have razor-sharp teeth?"

Tick bobs his head excitedly. "They do. They sharpen their own teeth to make feeding more effective. It's really quite remarkable how they do it," he says. "Everyone has dominion over their own body—or self-dominion as I call it. Feeders are able to use that dominion to alter their own bodies and sharpen their teeth. It's a fairly advanced technique."

"Couldn't have said it better myself," Grandpa praises. "Proticus actually specializes in self-dominion. He's developing a new technique to use in combat. If you're lucky, your class will be the first to learn it."

Klinton timidly raises his hand. "How much blood do they eat? Do they have to feed every day?"

Tick glances nervously at Grandpa before responding. "That's actually a misunderstanding. Contrary to popular belief, soul-feeders don't feed off of blood. As their name indicates, they feed on our souls by absorbing it out of the blood."

King Dralton nods his approval. "Just as the breath of life was breathed into man, feeders essentially suck it out of them. It's possible for a feeder to feed by sucking the soul through the mouth, but it's slower and less effective. Through the blood is a more direct route." Grandpa twists his cane on the floor. "And as for your question, the frequency of feedings depends on the feeder. Soul-feeding doesn't replace normal nutrition. Feeders still need to eat like the rest of humanity. Feeding is merely a means to acquire dominion. The more a feeder uses dominion, the more he must feed to restore that dominion. Could be daily, could be yearly."

"I've heard they live forever," Crasilda comments. "That can't be true, can it?"

Tick looks at Grandpa, who sighs and steps forward. "There's much we don't know about feeders, and that is one detail we don't have clear. It's apparent that feeding can lengthen the life of a feeder. As for how long, we're uncertain. Many scholars think they live hundreds of years. Some say thousands." Grandpa smiles to himself. "My father believed that Cain still walks the Earth."

"Are they hard to kill?" Vyle asks, dried blood clinging to his upper lip.

Tick lets out a short whistle. "I can tell you from experience that they are. But with training, it's definitely possible." Tick glances again at the king. "Your majesty, perhaps you could share your opinion on the matter."

Grandpa nods his agreement. "Most feeders are exceptionally well trained in dominion. Their long lives allow them to master even the most advanced techniques. Your best bet is to eliminate a feeder while it feeds. If it spots you, you'll need to kill it quickly. A feeder will outlast you in battle every time. Once you strain the soul, you're as good as dead." When Grandpa sees the discouraged faces around the room, his gaze softens. "But don't you all worry. Proticus will prepare you well. Listen to him, and you'll all do fine."

After a long silence, Klinton softly raises his voice. "How many feeders are out there?"

"I'm not really sure if we have an answer to that," Tick admits. He turns to Grandpa for assistance.

"I think it's safe to say well into the thousands," Grandpa guesses. "Compared to the non-feeding children of Cain, they make up a tiny percentage, but there's more than enough to put us at risk."

Klinton swallows loudly. "How often do we have to fight them?"

"Often enough," Grandpa sighs. "They tend to reside in big cities where there are more Adamic to hunt. Those are the same places we focus our rescue efforts. Unfortunately, the location of Cavernum is no secret. It's hidden from the general public, but there's almost always a feeder or two lingering around our walls."

The thought makes me cringe. I've always wanted to explore the beyond, but now I'm not so sure.

Velma pipes up from her seat next to Diego. "I've heard they can smell dominion? Is that true?"

"That's a great question," Grandpa says. "Yes and no. They can sense dominion, but not with smell; they do it with their soul. With practice, anyone can learn how."

Matt's chair squeaks as he leans forward. His eyes are riveted on Grandpa, his mouth partly open.

Grandpa continues. "Because we don't have dominion over mankind, we can't do anything more than sense their presence. But with enough practice, one can sense the subtle difference between a child of Cain and a child of Adam. The purer the bloodline, the easier it is."

"Do you know how?" Velma asks.

"I do." Grandpa smiles and sets his cane back on the floor. As he closes his eyes, the room falls silent. After several seconds, Grandpa opens eyes and smiles at Velma. "Your dominion is remarkably strong for your bloodline." His eyes scan the room. "In fact, we have a room full of powerful bloodlines." His eyes linger on me, then on Vyle, then on Matt as well. Velma leans back in her chair, satisfied.

Tick anxiously swivels his head. "Any more questions?"

"Why do they feed?" Matt asks. "What makes them start in the first place?"

Why do feeders feed? That's like asking why the sun is sunny. But grandpa doesn't treat it like a dumb question. He lifts up his cane and holds it in both hands.

"The children of Cain aren't like us. They don't know about Adamic or the breath of life. In order to feed, they must be introduced to the sin by another feeder. They must be taught."

Crasilda bows her head before speaking. "But your majesty, I thought that feeders were solitary creatures."

Grandpa nods. "In today's world, they are. The Adamic are few in number, and feeders hunt alone to avoid competition. First-time feedings are almost unheard of. The few feeders we do encounter have been lurking around for centuries. They consumed their first soul hundreds of years ago, when the world was a very different place. The Adamic were much more plentiful, then, as were the feeders who hunted them.

Not only did they mingle in large numbers, but the feeders formed their own cults. They praised the Devil for teaching them to feed. Then, they taught their children to do the same. The youth were forced to feed, whether they wanted to or not. It was a coming-of-age ritual for them. Some started as young as 12."

Surprised whispers erupt around the room. I'm surprised too. Grandpa's never told me that before.

Diego's jaw falls open. "That's Mary's age," he whispers.

When Grandpa sees my confusion, he purses his lips. "At times, the feeders became quite powerful. The blood sacrifices of the Mayan empire. The feedings at Transylvania. The Salem witch trials. History is full of their evil deeds. Once they got a taste of power, they couldn't give it up. It became an addiction for them. Sadly, many good young people have been forced into the life. Feeding changes them. They lose compassion and sympathy. They lose what makes them human. In the end, feeding becomes their entire existence."

I expect Matt to nod or sit back in his chair, but instead, he opens his mouth. "Do they ever feed on each other?"

It's an odd question, but once again, I'm dumbfounded. If feeders truly are as bloodthirsty as they say, why wouldn't they feed on each other?

"I'm glad you asked," Grandpa beams at Matt as any instructor would a knowledge-hungry student. "But this too has no simple answer. I'll explain it to you the way I understand it. Feeding is not a natural process. Our souls were not designed to consume another. Just as the human body cannot fit another man inside it, the soul does not simply fit inside another without consequences. It tears the soul, shatters it. Transforms the humane into the devilish. What once was a solid soul, becomes nothing more than fragments. If another feeder were to try to consume it, it would slip from their grasp, as sand through open fingers."

Matt furrows his brow and leans forward in his chair. His eyes narrow as he stares at the blank chalkboard. I wish I could know what he's thinking. The class is silent for another few seconds.

Diego slowly raises his hand, as if he's uncertain that he wants to ask. "Excuse me, Mr. King, sir, but what happens to someone who is fed on? What happens to their soul in the next life?"

Grandpa grows still and gazes toward Diego. His lips pull tight, and his eyes are strained with sorrow. "That is a question I've asked myself many, many times." He leans on his cane, the air wheezing from his lungs. "Some scholars think that the souls of the victims are lost forever. That they are destroyed by the feeder, never to live again in the afterlife." Grandpa pushes against his cane and lifts his head high. "I, however, refuse to believe this is true. Other scholars believe the souls are trapped within the feeder in a state of limbo—trapped, but not destroyed. It's believed that when a feeder is killed, the souls it consumed are released into the afterlife. This is what I choose to believe."

Diego nods and says nothing. My heart hurts for him. Matt told me what happened. I hope my grandpa is right, that his mom isn't lost forever. The thought of never seeing my parents again would destroy me.

"I'll take one last question," Grandpa says. "Then, I must be on my way."

Finally, Matt asks what's on his mind. "How often does an Adamic become a feeder?"

All heads turn to Matt in shock. Whispers drift through the classroom. *Why would he ask that?* Feeding is evil. To suggest that an Adamic would commit such a sin is unacceptable. Especially in the presence of the king.

Tick glances nervously between Matt and Grandpa. "The Adamic people were hunted by the children of Cain. We are not the feeders, but the hunted. We—"

Grandpa holds up his hand. "Thank you, Proticus, but I'll take it from here." He steps toward the front row and tries to straighten his hunched shoulders. "Who knows anything about the revolution of 1940—the Blood Rebellion?"

Vyle immediately raises his hand. "It was the bloodiest revolution in our history. The pickers rebelled, and King Titan compromised by creating The Dividing."

"Thank you, Mr. Kaynes," Grandpa says. "My next question is this: how did the laborers get the upper hand? How did they have room to negotiate when they were up against the guard with all of their amulets?"

Everyone else is silent, so I raise my voice. "King Titan was merciful. He established The Dividing because it was the right thing to do."

To my surprise, grandpa shakes his head. "Not quite. I'm afraid the answer is more sinister than that." He leans on his cane as he thinks. "My father went through great lengths to hide this part of our history, but you soldiers are the future of Cavernum. You deserve to know the truth." Once again, I know he's talking to me. I can't help but think of what he told me last week. *No more secrets.*

Grandpa takes a deep breath. "When the revolution began, Cavernum wasn't the place it is now. Every laborer was a laborer for life. They were forced to work, or they were slaughtered. End of story. The laborers had no rights and no hope. That is until a man named Corzone killed a guardsman in the core and consumed his soul. With his soul strengthened, he used dominion to kill and feed on more guards. Then, he taught others to do the same. He led a small army of feeders straight to the palace. Being feeders, they couldn't pass through the walls, of course, so they laid siege instead. They forced my father to negotiate. But it didn't end there." He takes another breath and adjusts his grip on the cane.

"Even after the treaty was made, Corzone and his men couldn't stop feeding. They still craved the feeling of power. Eventually, they resorted to feeding on their own neighbors—killing their families and their friends. It took months for the guardians to hunt them all down. It was a dark time in our history. A desperate, terrible time."

The Blood Rebellion was caused by feeders! Adamic feeders! Why didn't Grandpa tell me this sooner? Everything I thought I knew is suddenly uncertain. *What other lies have I been told?*

"As far as I know," Grandpa sighs, "that's the only occasion of Adamic feeders. I hope for all our sakes we don't live to see history repeat itself."

With that, Grandpa starts for the door. "I must get going now. I trust all of you will keep this information to yourselves. We wouldn't want to give the public any unholy ideas."

Grandpa lingers by the doorway. His eyes meet mine. "I look forward to seeing you again soon. Keep working hard. For all I know, one of you might become a guardian someday." Without another word, Grandpa shuffles out the door.

Tick releases a short sigh of relief and relaxes his shoulders. He gives his watch a quick glance. "Alright, kiddos. Get your pistols from the armory and meet me on the ground floor in five.

"Where are we going?" Zander asks. A few other students echo his curiosity.

Tick grins a proud half-smile. "I hope you learned something about feeders, because today, we're going to the beyond."

Grapevines rush past me on both sides as we jog our way through the fields. An endless sea of clouds cast long shadows over the flats. A subtle breeze shakes the vines and cools the sweat on my face. With each bound, the holster slaps against my thigh. Even on the tightest belt loop, it hangs loosely from my waist. It was made for a man twice my size.

My footsteps fall in sync with Matt and Diego. It's a decent jog to the outer wall, and we've only just begun. Diego huffs and puffs as we run, and Matt clutches his side. They both drag their feet in the dirt.

Matt eyes me accusingly. "How are you not tired? I'm exhausted."

I can't tell him the truth, so I lie. "I was, but I'm feeling a little better. More than anything, I have a headache."

Diego coughs out his words between breaths. "You're lucky. I wish I only had a headache. I can barely move my legs."

Matt is watching me with his gentle blue eyes. "I get the headaches too. They suck. I hope you feel better."

Thank heavens, they bought it. I really need to be more careful, even if it means letting Vyle make a fool of me. Part of me wonders what they would think if they knew. Diego hates the royal family. Would he change his mind if he knew I'm the princess? Or would he want me dead like his family does?

I turn my attention to the flats. All around us, the fields are dotted with laborers. As usual, they're timid and fearful. They peek their head above the grapevines only to cower when I look their way. They hated me as their queen, and now they fear me as a guardsman. *Some improvement I've made.*

We're halfway across the flats. The outer wall looms on the horizon, hiding the forest beyond it. "Hold up." Tick shouts from the front of the pack. "We're going to walk."

Bewildered, I glance behind me. Vyle has fallen far behind the last of the recruits. His eyes are squinted into slits. He holds his head with one hand and clutches his side with the other. He struggles to catch up as we slow to a walk.

"Dude, are you kidding me?" Diego says. "We're slowing down for him?"

"I don't get it," Matt echoes. "Why does Tick baby him so much? Hasn't he been spoiled enough?"

I shrug. "I think it's smart. If something happens to Vyle in the beyond, Tick is responsible. It's safer for all of us if we're rested."

Matt grins. "At least he'll make good feeder bait. We don't have to run faster than the feeders, we just have to run faster than Vyle."

Diego doesn't smile. He wears his fear like a tight mask. "Do you think it's safe out there? Do you think we'll see any feeders?"

Matt doesn't say anything. I see him rub his neck.

For once, I don't feel like the worried one. I rest my hand on my holster. "I certainly hope not. If we do, we'll be prepared."

Matt shakes his head. "I had guns last time. They didn't do me any good."

It's hard to argue with that. Matt and Diego have both experienced feeders firsthand. All I have is my imagination. Maybe this time I should be more worried. "I've never seen one before," I say. "What are they like?"

Matt and Diego look at each other. Each waits for the other to talk first.

"It's okay if you don't want to talk about it," I offer. "I wouldn't want to talk about it either."

Diego kicks at the rocks in the road. "There's not that much to talk about. I barely even saw him. He came in the middle of the night. I woke up to my mom screaming. I ran to her room as fast as I could, but I was too late. A chain was wrapped around her arms and legs. He just stood there, holding her by the neck. He didn't say a word. My mom screamed for me to run, so I did."

He grits his teeth and kicks at the road. "I didn't even try to help her. I grabbed Mary, and we ran. We took a bus straight to the police station, and I told them everything. They sent the police, but they never found her body. We slept in the station that night, and by morning, a guardsman was there to pick us up." Diego hides his hands in his pockets. "Just like that, she was gone. It's my fault she's dead."

Matt gives Diego a gentle shove. "Hey, don't say that. It wasn't your fault. Any one of us would have done the same thing."

Diego stops walking and meets his gaze. "Really? If a feeder had Judy by the throat, would you have left her?"

Matt opens his mouth but doesn't say anything. He slowly closes his mouth.

Diego snorts and turns his back on Matt. "That's what I thought."

What if it was me? What if a feeder had Grandpa or Antai? The answer is clear. *You'd fight, Rose. You'd stay and fight!*

But what if I didn't have my amulet? Would I still fight if I didn't stand a chance? I'm not so sure I know the answer.

I place my hand on Diego's shoulder. "I'm so sorry, Diego. I can't imagine."

"Don't be. You didn't do anything." Diego directs his gaze to the surrounding vineyard. "But if I ever find that feeder..." His fists clench at the thought.

It pains me to see Diego so wroth, but I'm no different than him. If I ever found the demons that killed my father, I'd want them dead. I'd kill them myself if I had to.

"I guess it's my turn," Matt sighs. "He was hiding in the shadows. He grabbed me before I even saw him. He was tall and wore a black cloak. He didn't waste any time. Before I could do anything, he shocked me and bit me."

Matt bites his lip. He doesn't move his head, but his eyes flicker towards Diego. "I don't remember too much after that. The next thing I knew, he was dragging me."

"Dragging you?" I ask. *How bizarre.* "Why did he stop feeding?"

Matt shrugs. "I don't know. He just stopped. Then, he dragged me to his car and threw me in."

His car? That makes even less sense. "Where was he taking you?"

"No idea. Zane showed up before we went very far." His voice is elevating with frustration. "Maybe he was taking me to feed his feeder babies?"

"Why didn't he just kill you?" I wonder. I instantly regret it. This time, Diego scolds me with his eyes. I should know better than to say something so insensitive.

Matt looks appalled at the thought. "You know what? Next time I see him, I'll ask him and let you know."

"Sorry. I didn't mean it like that," I insist. "I'm just thinking out loud. I've never heard anything like that before. It doesn't add up. If he was going to keep feeding, why wait? And if he was going to kill you, why wait? Carrying you around would just be more work for him."

"A mystery," Matt concludes. He obviously doesn't want to talk about it. I think there's something he's not telling.

The sound of screaming interrupts my thoughts. Up ahead, several guardsmen loiter on the side of the road. They tote machine guns and aim them threateningly into the fields. It only takes a second to find the source of the screams. One of the guards drags a woman by her hair through the vines. She flails frantically. "Please! No! Please!"

The guard drags her into the road and tosses her against a large wooden pole in the ground—a whipping post. At the sound of our footsteps, he cocks his head and peers at us, waiting patiently for us to approach. He's tall and muscular with a short mustache and goatee. I'm not a fan of his facial hair, but he's handsome. His shaggy mane of blonde hair flares around his head and falls to his shoulders.

Matt leans in close. "Who's Lion Man?"

I know him from somewhere, but I can't quite put my finger on it. His face is so familiar. Maybe I've seen him around the palace.

The officer smiles as we draw near. "Proticus! You're just in time. And you brought the younglings. How nice."

Tick salutes. "Hello, Captain Kaynes. We're just passing through. We're on our way to the outer wall."

Kaynes! How did I not recognize him? "That's Quill, Vyle's older brother," I whisper to Matt and Diego. "He's the oldest son and his father's apprentice."

Captain Quill waves us closer. "Why don't you stay for a moment? We're about to enact some beautiful justice. It'll be good experience for the recruits. Won't it, brother?"

"Yes, sir," Vyle croaks. He casts his eyes to the road in submission. Something tells me they're not the fondest of brothers.

"Well?" Captain Quill demands.

Tick points toward the outer wall. "Can't. We're already running late. Captain Renshu is expecting us."

"C'mon. Most of my men were taken to reinforce the outer wall." Captain Quill motions toward the whipping post. "I could use an extra hand."

Tick bites his lip and eyes the lady battered woman. It's obvious he doesn't want to stay. "Alright, but only for a minute." He steps next to Captain Quill. "Gather round," Tick commands. "Make a circle."

We form a semi-circle in the road facing the whipping post. The woman whimpers at the base of the post as she shields her face with her hands. She's much older than I initially thought. Scraggly white hair covers her face like a bridal veil. Her bony hands quiver with fear. Behind her, hundreds of laborers cower in the vineyards. They've all paused their picking to watch the whipping. Just like the execution, this is meant to be a display.

Captain Quill pulls a whip out of his belt and steps closer to the old woman. Five thin leather cords dangle from a single wooden handle. The whip is only a few feet long, but it looks menacing. The old woman cringes at the sight of it, hiding her face against the pole.

Tick helps the other guards restrain the woman. He shackles her arms on the opposite side of the pole. I can hear him whispering to her as he locks the cuffs on her wrists. "It'll all be over soon, ma'am. I promise it'll be over soon."

Captain Quill scans the crowd of recruits until he finds Vyle. He holds up the whip. "Brother, how would you like to do the honors?"

"No, thank you, sir." Vyle pleads.

Captain Quill rolls his eyes. "Oh, please. Don't be a coward. Get over here."

"Hey!" Tick says. "He said no. They're not your men; they're recruits. They're here to watch. Nothing more."

Captain Quill ignores Tick. "What happened to your face, brother? A picker got the best of you?"

Vyle glares back but doesn't respond.

"Pathetic," Quill spits. "Father would be ashamed of you."

Vyle waits until his brother turns his back. "Devil," he mutters under his breath.

"What did you say?" Quill spins with his enraged eyes trained on Vyle. "What did you say? Say it to my face!"

"Nothing, sir."

Quill takes a step towards Vyle with his fist raised in the air. "I'll teach you not to lie to your superiors."

Tick intercepts him. He stands in front of Vyle and holds Captain Quill at an arm's distance. "Back off, Quill. He's my recruit. If you have a problem with Vyle, take it up with me."

I hold my breath as Tick and Quill stand face to face. Quill's arm flexes as he grips the whip in his hand. I expect him to swing at any second. Finally, Quill steps back and spits into the dirt. "You better teach your recruits some respect, Proticus. Or they'll have to learn the hard way... me!" A false smile masks Quill's anger. He returns to the whipping post and gives the whip a few practice swings through the air. The leather whistles with each swing. "Raise her up, Proticus," Quill commands. "I'll do this myself."

Tick hesitantly leaves Vyle's side and follows Captain Quill to the woman's side. A rusty chain dangles from the post. It feeds through a loop at the top of the pole and connects to the woman's cuffs. Tick grabs the end of the rusty chain and pulls it, raising the woman's arms high above her head. He waits behind the pole, the end of the chain gripped tightly in his hands.

Captain Quill grabs the neck of the old woman's dress and tears it open along the seam, exposing the upper half of her back. I clasp my hands over my mouth to muffle a gasp. The woman's back is laced with long, pink ridges—the scars of past lashings.

"To all those who can hear my voice, let this be a warning." Captain Quill shouts over the fields to the other laborers. "This woman was found stealing food from the vine. As punishment for theft, I announce her sentence to be 20 lashings."

The woman twists her neck and wails. "It's for my son. He's sick, and he can't work. We have no food."

"Silence." Captain Kaynes swings the whip, catching the woman in the ear. She whimpers and collapses against the pole.

A slender, devious grin grows on Captain Quill's face. He points at the scars on the woman's back. "Seeing that this woman is a repeat offender, her sentence will be doubled to 40 lashings. One flogging apparently isn't enough to change her ways."

Tick shakes his head in disbelief. His brow folds between his eyes as he glares at Captain Kaynes. Even the other guards look nervous. They keep glancing at the vineyards as if the laborers will charge at any moment.

I want to believe this is right, but I can't find a way to convince myself. I've broken curfew hundreds of times, yet I've never been whipped. I deserve to be out there as much as this woman.

Captain Quill raises the whip above his head and swings it down with all his might. This whip cracks against the woman's back, and her muscles clench in agony. Her scream pierces the silence. Captain Quill swings the whip again with a crack. The woman's breath comes in short screams as she wrestles in agony with the chains. The cuffs dig into her wrists, and a stripe of blood trickles down her back.

I can't watch this. It's torture. It's evil. But I can't bring myself to look away either. She stole some food for her sick son. Is that really so wrong? I think of my dad—of the demon tattoos. He was willing to do anything to keep me safe. Anything.

Quill swings his arm again, and the woman whimpers quietly. She slumps against the chains as her knees buckle underneath her. Tick leans against the chains to keep her upright.

The woman tries to regain her footing, but Kaynes whips her again. And again. And again.

"Quill, she can't take 40 lashings," Tick hisses. "It'll kill her. How will that look to the laborers?"

Captain Quill pays Tick no heed. He raises his arm again and swings it down. Again and again.

The woman dangles helplessly by her wrists. "Please, stop." Her voice is so hoarse, it sounds inhuman. Rage boils within me. I feel like I'm back at the execution. *This isn't fair!* The truth digs into my heart. It's undeniable. *This isn't justice.* I have to do something. I have an amulet in my bra. I can stop this.

For a brief moment, I hesitate. *It's too risky. They'll know it's me.* Doubt wrestles with desire. I close my eyes, imagining the execution in my mind's eye. I see the gallows. I see the father hanging by his neck, swaying in the wind. I see his daughter reaching for him. I failed her once. I won't fail again.

I take a deep breath and press my hand to my chest.

Chapter 20

Matt

Again and again, Quill swings the whip at the old lady.

CRACK. CRACK. CRACK.

Every time I look at her, I see Judy in chains. With every swing, I hate the guard a little more.

Tick doesn't look like he's enjoying it any more than I am. He squeezes his eyes shut with every crack of the whip. "Quill, she can't take 40 lashings. It'll kill her. How will that look to the laborers?"

Captain Quill doesn't say a word. He answers with the swing of his arm.

"Please," Old Lady begs. "Stop." Her voice is strangled and weak. The chains are the only thing keeping her on her feet.

Tick let's the chain slide though his fingers, lowering the woman into a heap of mangled flesh. At this point, she's hardly conscious. "I'm done, Quill. I won't be a part of this."

For a second, Quill pauses. Then, he swings the whip at her head, stepping into every swing.

Crack! Crack!—

Just before it strikes skin, the whip snaps against an unseen force. A gasp is heard from the recruits as the air ripples underneath the whip.

An energy shield! Someone used dominion to stop the whip. I look around, expecting to see Zane behind me, but he's nowhere in sight. Diego is grinning from ear to ear. Even Tick has a hint of a smile. Lynn, however, stares ahead with her nose scrunched with concentration.

Captain Quill straightens his back and glares at Tick. He takes a step toward him.

"Whoa, don't look at me." Tick holds up his palms. "I didn't do anything."

Captain Quill turns and faces his men as he seethes. The muscles in his neck bulge and his face twitches. "Who did it?" he screams. The only ones wearing amulets are Quill's guardsmen and Tick.

In a single motion, Captain Kaynes spins and swings the whip at Old Lady. Once again, the whip is repelled inches from her back. In a flurry of rage, Kaynes swings the whip over and over against the shield.

Crack. Crack. Crack.

Each time, the whip sends a ripple through the air. From across the semicircle, Vyle narrows his eyes at Lynn. When he sees me watching, he turns away.

Quill points at his men. "I want your amulets where I can see them! NOW!"

All of his guards scramble to action, laying their amulets on the outside of their uniforms. Quill points at his men with the end of his whip. "If any one of you lay a finger on your amulet, I'll flog you next."

Quill glares at Tick. "That goes for you too, Proticus. I want your amulet where I can see it."

Tick crosses his arms in front of his chest. "I don't answer to you, Quill. I already told you, it wasn't me." He smiles to himself. "Maybe you upset the gods. If you repent now, they might spare you."

"You don't want to cross me, Proticus. I won't be made a fool in front of my men. If you interfere again, I'll take it as an obstruction of justice. I'll have no choice but to take you before the council."

Tick leans his face toward Quill and exaggerates each word with his mouth. "It. Wasn't. Me. You lay as much as a finger on me, I'll knock you out cold."

Quil huffs and raises the whip above his head. He gives his men one last look over his shoulder. None of them reach for their amulets. Satisfied, Captain Quill swings the whip.

With a crack, the leather cord is reflected by another shield. Quill roars and throws his whip on the ground. Without warning, he spins and throws a punch at Tick's face. It connects with his jaw in a sickening crunch.

To my surprise, Tick takes the blow without flinching. His face doesn't budge an inch. Quill, however, lets out a scream and falls to one knee. He clutches his fist in his left hand. Blood swells from a gash on his first two knuckles.

I gasp. *Amazing!*

Tick's face gleams like polished silver—his neck and his arms as well. His skin is no longer flesh, but a smooth metallic surface. Even the hairs on his head are metal—everything except his eyes. Metallic eyelids blink over the white flesh of his eyes. The metal on his face molds into a proud smile, exposing a row of shining metal teeth. "Careful, captain. I wouldn't do that if I were you." His voice reverberates from his throat with a metallic tone. "I've learned a few tricks since our last little scuffle."

Captain Quill scrambles to his feet. He cradles his broken hand as his shoulders shake with rage. Blood drips from his hand, soaking into the soil at his feet. "You'll die for that." Quill touches his mangled hand to his amulet and points the other at Tick.

A bolt of blue electricity surges from Quill's fingertips and strikes Tick point-blank in the chest. The lightning is both blinding and deafening. It buzzes and crackles, casting a blue glow on the surrounding road. I squint to make out the scene. Blue tendrils of electricity crawl down Tick's body and into the dirt. I expect him to squirm in agony, but he stands calmly instead.

Tick takes two quick steps against the flow of electricity and grabs Quill's hand in his iron fist, cutting the flow of the lightning. With a jerk of his arm, Tick yanks Quill closer as he simultaneously drives his metal forehead into Quill's skull.

THUNK!

Quill crumples like a tin can, sprawling flat on the dirt road. When he doesn't move, Tick nudges him with his boot. "I told you."

The gleam in Tick's skin fades, slowly being replaced with his normal tan complexion. He looks at the other guards. "Any of you going to arrest me?"

They shake their heads.

"Good. Then get that woman out of those chains and get her far away from here. I don't want Quill anywhere near her when he wakes up."

One soldier scratches the back of his neck. He shifts his weight from one foot to the other as he stares at Quill's sprawled body. "What do we do with him, sir?"

"Leave him for all I care," Tick says. His eyes find Vyle, and he tucks his lips between his teeth as he thinks. Tick finally sighs. "You know what? Take him to the palace. He might need to see a healer. I don't want this coming back to bite me."

Without another word, Tick marches down the road toward the outer wall. "C'mon, kiddos. Break time is over." I run to catch up with him. I have so many questions.

"That was insane," Diego says from behind me. He falls into place, jogging alongside Tick and I. Lynn follows only a few steps behind us. The other recruits trail behind her. At the very back of the pack, I spot Vyle, still looking winded from his stunt in the trench.

"Seriously, how did you do that?" Diego asks, shaking his head in disbelief. "That was crazy!"

Tick smiles and shrugs his shoulders. "It's a simple technique I'm developing. Once I master it, I can teach you how."

"It looked like you've mastered it to me," I say. "How does it work?"

Tick points at the flesh of his forearm. "I turn my skin into titanium, but I leave my muscles and organs and everything underneath intact. Metal eyes don't see too well," he laughs. "I can turn my bones too, but I've never tried anything more than that. I'm pretty sure it would kill me." Tick looks at Diego. "That's why I haven't taught anyone yet. It's a dangerous form of dominion. Accidentally turn your brain metal, and you might never wake up."

"And it's electric proof?" Diego asks.

Tick smiles wide, revealing his perfectly white teeth. "Because titanium is a strong conductor of electricity, the current flows through the metal and directly into the floor. It passes right over the muscles without any effect." He laughs at the thought. "Quill would've been smarter to use an energy shield."

"Is it hard to learn?" Diego asks.

"It took me a while to get the hang of it, but it's nothing you couldn't learn. The best part about exercising self-dominion is that I never have to communicate beyond my own body. It puts very little strain on the soul. Saved me from feeders more than once."

Lynn pipes up from behind us. "How do you know Captain Kaynes?"

Tick makes room so that Lynn can walk next to us on the road. "Quill and I were divided the same year. Let's just say we didn't get along. He and his friends made sure my life was hell."

"Why's that?" Lynn urges.

"I ranked first in the trials. I beat Quill by a few points. Losing made him furious, especially losing to a laborer."

Diego gapes at Tick with both surprise and respect. "You were a laborer? Are you serious?"

Tick raises an eyebrow. "Is it really that surprising? Do I strike you as a purebred?"

"You don't," Diego assures him. "Not at all. It's just…—"

"Not many ring-born become officers," Lynn cuts in. "Almost none. It's quite a feat."

"Yeah, well, it shouldn't be that way," Tick says. "A little equality would be nice." He picks up the pace.

The outer wall is just up ahead. The road passes through an opening in the wall and continues through the forest on the other side. High up on the wall, I can see guards patrolling. They peer intently at the surrounding forest.

Tick stops a few feet from the outer wall. A thirty-foot archway towers over us. "Everyone, on me and listen up" he calls. "I know most of you have never been to the beyond. It'll be easy to get distracted, but I want you all on high alert. After what happened in Lycon, we can't be too cautious. If I give you a command, you do it. If I tell you to open fire, you do it. If I tell you to run for the wall, you do it. Hell, if I tell you to lay down and play dead, you do it. No questions asked. Understood?"

His face grows solemn as he looks over us. His voice is full of certainty. "I promise you, I won't let anything happen to you today. I'll give my life for you if I have to."

My heart thumps in my chest. I reach up and feel my neck. A small ridge of scar tissue is the only trace of the bite. *I'll be fine.* I tell myself. *I'm safe this time.*

Tick points through the archway at the forest beyond. "I'll go first, then the rest of you follow me." He walks briskly towards the archway. As his body passes through the far side of the arch, the air around him bends and warps. I can still see the road beyond the archway, but the light around his body bends and folds. It looks as though he's passing through a sheet of liquid glass. As soon as he's on the other side, the barrier settles. It's completely unnoticeable. He turns around and stares back at nobody in particular. "Come on! Who's next?"

Without hesitation, Lynn steps forward. She slowly reaches out until her hand disturbs the air. Just like an energy shield, the air ripples. She shrieks, retracting her hand. "It's freezing." She takes a deep breath and steps through the archway. The transparent barrier folds and molds harmlessly over her skin. She turns around on the other side and lets out another gasp. Her eyes flicker over us without recognition.

"Demons! Where did they go?" She asks Tick.

"They're still there. Just watch."

Confused, I step forward. I hold out my hand and step through the wall. I shudder and suck in a breath. A cold weight presses against me from all sides. It feels like stepping through a wave of ice water. It washes over my skin, sending shivers down my limbs. The chatter of the other recruits is instantly silenced.

Lynn's eyes bulge as I emerge from the archway. She smiles and points behind me. "Turn around." I do as she says, and suck in a gasp.

Amazing!

The sanctuary is gone. Completely gone. The dirt road I'm standing on suddenly ends a few feet in front of me. Instead of a wall, a deep, lush forest extends as far as I can see. Thick pine trees grow where I was standing just moments ago.

Suddenly, the air shimmers. A disembodied hand appears from thin air. The hand grows into an arm and shoulder. Diego's head appears, floating in the air. He steps completely into sight and grins from ear to ear. "Dude, that was cold." He turns around, and his jaw falls open. "Holy heck! That's some good special effects."

I walk back to where Diego just appeared and stick my hand forward. The air shimmers as my arm disappears. I lean my head forward, and in a blink, the forest is replaced with the flats of the sanctuary. The recruit closest to me gives me a weird look. Crasilda giggles. I lean back, and once again, I'm standing in the center of the forest. Nothing but trees are in view.

Crasilda materializes in the road with a proud smile on her face. Then, Velma and Croyd. One by one, the rest of the recruits appear at the end of the road.

Crasilda spins and eyes the forest with wonder. "There are so many trees! It's beautiful."

Klinton squints into the forest. "How far does it go?"

I never thought a forest could be so novel and exciting. These poor high-borns have never seen a pine tree up close. Never played in the grass. They've been cooped up their whole lives. I almost pity their lives of luxury.

"Is everyone here?" Tick asks.

A boy with short red hair and a face full of freckles calls out. "I was the last one."

"Good." Tick points at the end of the road where we just emerged. "As I'm sure you've noticed, the spell on the wall camouflages it from view. The camouflage spell only works one way." Tick points up into the air. "You can't see them, but the guards on the wall can see us. They have a huge advantage against intruders. The spell blocks any attacks from the outside, but allows our guards to fire outward against intruders."

"The most important spell is the barrier against feeders," Tick says. "If a feeder tries to go over the wall or tunnel underneath, they hit an impenetrable barrier. For a feeder, entry is impossible. For a non-feeder like you and me, we can pass right through, but that doesn't make it easy to get in. The only entrances are the gateways. If you go off the road and try, you'll hit the wall. So be careful not to get lost. If you lose sight of the road, it's almost impossible to find your way back to the entrance."

Tick starts walking down the road, away from the sanctuary. "Follow me, I have a few more things to show you. And remember: stay alert!"

The crunching of footsteps on the dirt road is uncomfortably loud in the silence of the forest. Friends whisper as we walk. If any feeders are close by, they'll hear us for sure.

Diego is no longer next to me. I spot him in the middle of the group walking next to Velma. They've been spending a lot of time together. I'll tease him about it the first chance I get.

Lynn walks a few steps in front of me. She looks out into the forest with quiet delight. I watch as her eyes linger on a patch of lilies next to the road. The flowers are light pink but deepen to magenta in the center. Her eyes meet mine. Lynn smiles and motions towards the flowers. "That's called the—"

"Shasta Lily!" I say. "It's actually my favorite flower."

Lynn scrunches her nose at me and laughs. "That's your favorite flower? Do you know what it symbolizes?"

"Umm, no. What?"

"Chastity," Lynn laughs. "In Cavernum, we call it the virgin lily."

For a moment, I'm speechless. It's not the answer I expected. "Th-that's not why I like it," I assure her. "When I was younger, my mom planted them in our herb garden. Every night, she made us lily mint tea before bed. Even when she got sick, I would make it for her, and we would drink it in the hospital."

Lynn looks at me with quiet understanding. She's familiar with the sorrow I feel. She points to a patch of yellow flowers beyond the trees. She talks so softly I can barely hear her over the crunching of gravel.

"Marigolds are my favorite, but they don't plant them in the palace. They symbolize the fragility of life. They can't survive the frost and have to be replanted each year. Some think this brings misfortune and death. But my mom didn't believe the superstitions. She only saw their beauty.

My dad..." Lynn looks at her feet then out at the forest. "My dad was a guardsman. My grandpa says he used to come all the way out here every summer to pick marigolds for my mom. I suppose that's why I like them. They remind me of my parents."

We walk together in silence for a moment, enjoying the unspoken support of the other. I want to hold her hand. I want to let her know I understand, but I don't get the chance. Suddenly, a dark figure steps into the road up ahead. My heart races, and I reach for my gun.

"You're late!" the figure calls out. He's a stocky Asian man with a plump face. His hair is jet black, and a thin, curly mustache extends from his upper lip. His voice, a higher pitch than I'd expect, is light and fluffy. "I was starting to think you weren't coming."

"My apologies, Captain," Tick calls. "We had some delays in the flats." Tick turns to us. "Everyone, meet Captain Renshu. He'll be giving us a tour of the communications center. He built it himself."

"Well, I had help," Renshu proudly admits. "It's just up ahead. We had to build it a ways from the sanctuary. Even on the outside, the magnetic field of the wall disrupts our signals if we're too close."

Renshu leads us off the road onto a small dirt trail. "It's just up ahead." He repeats. We follow the path for less than a minute before it opens into a sunstruck meadow. Dazzling wildflowers blanket the thick grass. Renshu stops a few yards into the meadow. "We're here!"

Heads twist in all directions. I only see trees and shrubs and grass. Renshu smiles as we search in vain. "You're looking in the wrong places." He bends over and grabs hold of something in the grass. With a grunt, he swings open a section of the earth, revealing a small hole in the ground. The hole is lined with gray steel walls. Small metal rungs lead straight down into the dimly lit bunker.

Captain Renshu faces us and clasps his stubby hands together. "Welcome to the communications bunker. Inside the sanctuary, electronics are useless. But outside the sanctuary, we take full advantage of modern technology. We have computers, cell towers, radio towers, anything you can think of."

Cell towers! If I can get out here again, I just might be able to call Judy. The thought ignites the dying hope within me.

Renshu looks over the group of recruits. "Has anyone here ever used a computer?"

Diego and I are the only ones to raise our hands.

Renshu radiates relief. He smiles at us with newfound interest. "I assume you're both refugees then."

We both nod.

"Wonderful," Renshu says. "As for the rest of you, a computer can write letters to the other sanctuaries and communicate instantly. If something happens in Veltrix or Beskum, we'll know about it in seconds. Then, we can send a messenger hawk to the palace to alert the king."

"So, you received the message when Lycon was attacked?" Zander snickers. "Little good that did."

Renshu sighs. "Sadly, even with computers, we couldn't act in time. The sanctuaries are too far apart. But the computers are good for far more than distress alerts. We use them to coordinate the rescue efforts of the convoy. That way, we know beforehand if a convoy is approaching or if it's an intruder."

At the mention of the convoy, Diego's head jerks to attention. "How often does the convoy come?" he asks. His hands are clenched at his side.

"It's supposed to come weekly," Renshu says, "but we've been delayed ever since Lycon was attacked."

"When does the next one arrive?" Diego persists.

Renshu purses his lips. "I'm sorry, but that information is only for select guardsmen. We try to keep it random to avoid ambushes."

"Please, sir," Diego begs. "My mom might be on it. I just want to know if she's alive." The meadow grows awkwardly silent.

His face is pained, but Renshu shakes his head anyway. "I'm sorry, but my hands are tied."

Diego's eyes bubble, and he lowers his gaze to hide the tears. Another awkward silence ensues.

Klinton raises his hand timidly. "Uhhh, sir, aren't you worried about feeders out here?"

Renshu squints at Klinton. "Ahh, you must be Kowen's brother. Excellent question. For a long time, I wasn't promoted because I'm a dry-blood. My blood is so thin, they called me bloodless. I can't so much as kill a fly with dominion. But I found that being dry-blooded can be a great advantage. Without dominion, the feeders don't take interest. I have ten other guards in my command, and they're all dry-bloods, your brother included. In my ten years down here, we've never been attacked once."

"What about the children of Cain?" I ask. "Do they ever wander over here?"

"Oh, no. They wouldn't come anywhere near here. We're hours from any of their cities. They think this is private property of the U.S. government. Even if they did, we would know about it. We have cameras on the main road. No one gets to Cavernum without us knowing about it."

"Can we look inside?" Klinton asks.

"Oh, no!" Renshu laughs. "A bunch of recruits around my equipment? I don't think so. If you don't have any more questions, I think that concludes our tour." When no one speaks, Renshu shakes Tick's hand and retreats back into his bunker.

"Alright, kiddos," Tick calls out. "Take a moment to enjoy the beyond. We'll be heading back in a few minutes."

As soon as Tick releases us, Diego distances himself from the group. I start to follow him, but he holds up his hand. "I want to be alone. Just for a little bit."

It's fine with me. I'm not in much of a mood to talk either. "I'll be over here if you want me." I find an empty patch of grass within sight of Tick and sit down on the forest floor. It's damp, but not wet enough to soak through my pants. I stretch out my legs and relish the peace of the forest. It feels so familiar—like home. The green, grassy carpet. The tree bark walls. The vaulted ceiling made of leaves.

For the first time since leaving the sanctuary, I feel myself relax. I lived 18 years before I crossed paths with a feeder; what are the odds I see one today? My eyes wander back to Diego. He's sitting on a toppled log. To my surprise, he's not alone. Velma sits by his side. They sit shoulder to shoulder. It's hard to tell from a distance, but it looks like they're holding hands.

I try not to take it personally. I think of Lynn. If I could talk to anyone right now, it would be her. I search for her in the crowd. She's talking with Daymian. Jealousy digs into my gut. I try to ignore it. There's over 45 boys and only one Lynn. I should consider myself lucky to get any Lynn time at all.

A branch crunches to my left, and I whip my head around. It's only Klinton. He smiles when I see him. "Do you mind if I sit with you?"

"Go for it."

He sits in the meadow next to me and plucks the blades of grass one at a time. "Was it scary living in the beyond?"

"Not really," I admit. "I didn't find out about feeders until I got attacked. If I had known, it would have been different. I guess you could say ignorance is bliss."

"You're probably right." He glances at my neck several times before he builds the courage to ask. "Is it true you have a scar?"

I pull down the collar of my shirt, and Klinton's eyes grow wide. He's like a child, tender and innocent and easily impressed. I can't help but wonder how he got accepted into the guard.

Klinton picks another blade of grass. "It's so peaceful out here. Do you ever miss it?"

"Everyday," I say. "I lived next to a forest just like this."

"Do you think you'll ever go back?"

"Yeah, hopefully soon. My mom lives in the beyond." When I see Klintons confusion, I explain. "I'm adopted. She's not Adamic. But she's sick, and I want to see her before she dies." *I want to save her.*

Klinton thinks for a second. He pushes up his glasses with the back of his hand, and his eyes light up. "You know, my brother works in the bunker. Maybe he could let you use the computer to write to your mom."

It's a nice gesture, but unnecessary. "Thanks, but I actually have a phone. It's a little computer I can talk to my mom with. I left it in my dorm room. If I had known we were coming, I would've brought it. I could be talking to her right now." The thought stirs my gut.

Suddenly, Captain Renshu throws open the hatch in the ground. He pops his head up like a scared prairie dog. Some kind of alarm chirps from the mouth of the bunker.

"Tick!" Renshu frantically calls. "Tick! We have a problem. Something passed the camera a quarter-mile south. It's not one of ours."

Fears flickers over Tick's face. "How long do we have?"

"It's hard to tell," Renshu stammers. "Maybe a minute, maybe less."

Tick is already moving. I've never heard him yell so loud. "Everyone, get to the road!" He shoves the recruit in front of him and drags two others to their feet. "Run! Get to the wall now! That's an order!"

They're coming. Feeders are coming!

Chapter 21

Rose

My feet are nothing but a blur beneath me. My legs burn and my throat is raw. I'm breathing so fast my inhale and exhale are one continuous wheeze.

"Hurry!" Tick yells.

All around me, recruits are running for their lives. It's hard to tell if we're getting close to the sanctuary. I can't see where the road ends and the sanctuary begins.

Panic starts to seize me. I pump my arms faster. *Rose, this is what you've trained for!* I tell myself. I peer over my shoulder and catch a glimpse of movement through the trees. The figure is over 100 yards behind us. It's a feeder, I'm sure of it.

You'll make it, Rose. It won't catch you.

I snatch another glance. This time I see five or six of them running parallel to the road. Each figure is concealed in a black cloak. Two more catch my eye deeper into the trees. *They're everywhere!*

I spot Diego at the rear of the group. He seems utterly exhausted. Matt is right next to him. I know Matt can run faster, but he won't leave Diego's side. He's not the type to abandon a friend.

You have the soul-anchor, Rose. You should be there with them.

I slow my pace and immediately the other recruits are rushing past me. We must be getting close now. Any second, I'll burst into the safety of the sanctuary. We're going to make it.

"Stop!" Tick screams.

I plant my feet and skid to a stop in the gravel. Everyone looks at Tick for a command. He stands at the head of the group, his silver pistol in hand. A few feet behind him, large oak trees bar the path. They mark the entrance to the sanctuary. We're no more than 10 yards away.

Why stop us now? It's right there!

Zander makes a move for the sanctuary, but Tick intervenes. "Stop! Hold your positions! Guns ready! Don't shoot until I give the word!"

I force myself to face away from the sanctuary. Matt stands to my left and Klinton to my right. He staggers his feet and holds his pistol at eye level. I grip my gun in my hand and flick off the safety. The gun has a longer range than dominion does. I'll only use my amulet as a last resort.

The feeders come from all directions. They tear through the forest, leaping over tree trunks and ripping through the foliage. They run without hesitation—without fear. I can't shoot them all, so I pick a feeder to the left of the road as my target. I try to slow my breathing, but with every blink, the feeders are closer.

100 yards… 75… 50…

The feeders are in range now. They claw their way closer, shoulders hunched and noses to the air. The billowing black cloaks conceal every feature but their height. Their faces are nothing but a flurry of dark fabric.

"Hold your ground!" Tick shouts. "Wait for my command!"

I align the iron sights and wait. *Any second now... Any moment.* Still, Tick doesn't give the command. Realization strikes me like lightning.

We're bait! Tick wants to draw the feeders as close as possible. He doesn't want them to know the wall is right behind us.

Time is running out. In a matter of moments, the feeders will bear down on us. We have to run now if we hope to reach the sanctuary in time. I wait for gunfire to erupt from the wall behind us. I wait for something. My heart pounds faster. My hands are slick with sweat. My finger twitches on the trigger and my legs shake, but I force myself to wait.

40 yards... 30 yards... The feeders race towards us. We're out of time. I hear scrambling as one recruit darts for the sanctuary. Several others follow suit.

20 yards. It's too late now. I press my hand to my chest. My only option is to fight.

Fir—

Klinton lets out a battle cry and pulls the trigger.

BANG! BANG! BANG!

The other recruits instantly follow suit like dogs let off the leash. They unload on the feeders as fast as they can pull the trigger. The air ripples in all directions as bullets ricochet into the surrounding trees, yet the feeders stand unharmed.

I hunch my shoulders and form a shield around myself. I wait for them to retaliate, but nothing happens. The feeders don't move. They just stand behind their shield, waiting... breathing. For several tense moments, all I can hear is the ringing in my ears.

Then, I hear laughter. The feeder in front of me pulls back his hood. The corners of his eyes squint, his mouth opening wide as he laughs. He peels off his cloak, and the other feeders do the same. They each wear a crisp, black uniform underneath.

The guard?

"Weapons down!" Tick commands. "Everyone, on me." He faces toward the sanctuary. "Come on out. There's no danger."

One by one, the deserters materialize from the wall. They walk back to the group with their tails between their legs.

"They're guardsmen?" Velma gasps. "Are you kidding me? You let us think we were being attacked?"

The uncloaked guardsmen stand behind Tick. They smile at each other, content with the success of their prank. Tick isn't smiling. He glares at us with a sternness foreign to his face. "I gave you two commands!" he growls. "Hold your ground and hold your fire. You broke both! You fired at guardsmen. You fled to the wall. You abandoned your comrades." His eyes linger on the deserters. "I should have you flogged, each and every one of you."

Daymian steps forward. "But, sir, we thou—"

"Silence!" Tick demands. "It's not your job to assume, it's your job to obey. You disobeyed your commanding officer. I knew you weren't in danger. I knew things you didn't. Your captains won't always tell you everything, but they'll expect you to obey." He glances at Matt. "And if you ever decide to disobey orders, you better be willing to bet your life on it, because you won't get a second chance. You'll be in the fields before you can blink."

Seeing our faces, Tick sighs. "I do this for your own good. You need to learn this lesson early. This time, you won't be punished, but other officers won't be so merciful. If this happens in the field, you'll be expelled. No questions asked." Tick motions toward the sanctuary. "Now go, before I change my mind. And hurry! If I beat you to the trench, you'll be scrubbing the washroom floor tonight."

The recruits race toward the sanctuary, disappearing as they enter the wall. I'm about to take off when I see Tick grab Diego's arm. He speaks quietly and I step closer to listen.

"The next convoy arrives at sunrise a week from today. I hope she's there Diego, I really do."

I look down at the rusty door. Diego can't be serious. There isn't even a handle. The front door is nestled into a concrete wall at the bottom of a small staircase. Runoff from the gutter trickles down the first few steps.

"This is it," Diego says, spreading his arms wide. "Home sweet home."

It's Sunday, our day off, and Diego insisted we come eat lunch with his family. At first I was reluctant, but Antai is working today. I have an Adamic lesson planned with Grandpa, but it's not until tonight.

Velma holds Diego's hand loosely in hers. Matt stands next to me. He's wearing the same clothes he wore the night I first met him: skinny jeans and a zip up jacket. He watches me with his brilliant blue eyes. When he catches my eye, he smiles.

Diego descends the stairs first. The door drifts open when he pushes on it. "Dad, we're here."

"Come on back." A man calls from the kitchen. "Lunch is almost ready. Take a seat; it'll just be another minute."

Diego leads us down the hallway. There's almost no natural light inside the house. I squint to make out the details. The apartment has crumbly concrete walls and a dusty floor. The ceiling is only inches above Matt's head. It feels more like a dungeon than a home.

We emerge into a tiny kitchen at the back of the house. A man is leaning over an iron pot, stirring its contents with a wooden spoon. It smells surprisingly good.

"That's my dad," Diego proudly announces.

"Call me Enrique," the man says. "Go ahead and take a seat. Abuela and Mary will be back any minute with the bread."

Two men burst into the kitchen. They're older than Diego by at least a few years. They look almost identical except one is an inch taller and has a bigger nose. They glance back and forth between Velma and I. "Which one's your girlfriend?" The shorter one asks.

Diego's cheeks flush red. He glances at Velma. "She's not my girlfriend." Then, he turns toward us. "Velma, Lynn, these are my brothers, Jorge and Javier." He points to the taller man and then the shorter one.

Javier smiles to himself and takes a big step toward Velma. He grabs her hand and shakes it vigorously. "Welcome to the family, miss."

"Don't upset her," the other brother warns. He looks at Diego and grins. "She's a guardsman. She'll have you flogged."

"Don't worry," Velma says casually. "I try not to flog on the Sabbath."

Jorge and Javier look at each other and burst into laughter. "I like her. Well done, Diego," Javier says.

Jorge shields his mouth with his hand and pretends to whisper to Diego. "Pssst. Did you kiss her yet?"

Velma holds her chin high and grins. Diego had kissed her. Velma came back from their date last Sunday and told me all about it. He took her on a carriage ride through the fields and kissed her in the flats. Not my idea of romantic, but Velma seemed to love it.

When he sees their reaction, Jorge pouts his lips. "Awwww, did my little baby brother get his first kiss."

"Jorge! Leave the girl alone," Enrique scolds, taking off his apron. He sets the pot on the table and grins to himself. "Just because you'll kiss anything with lips doesn't mean you can tease your brother about it."

Jorge holds up a finger. "I'll have you know, I've changed my ways. I'm going exclusive now with Stephanie Rogers."

Enrique exaggerates a surprised face. "My eldest son is finally courting a woman?" He presses his palms together and looks to the ceiling. "Let it be known, God is still a God of miracles."

Jorge rolls his eyes and cracks a smile. He turns to Velma, pointing at his dad with his thumb. "Trust me, you don't want this guy as a father-in-law? I mean look at him, his jokes are terrible."

A girl skips into the room and wraps her arms around Diego. Her black hair is healthy and full. She wears a short black skirt and a plain white blouse. She turns her attention to Matt. "Hey, Matt. Welcome back." She leans in and gives him a quick hug.

Diego gestures at Velma and then me. "This is Velma and Lynn, some friends from the guard. Everyone, this is Isabela."

"Any friend of Diego's is a friend of mine," Isabela sings. She pulls us each in for a hug—a custom I'm not used to with strangers. Elites aren't so fond of affection.

The door creaks open down the hall and an old woman enters with a young girl. They both cradle a fresh loaf of bread. The old woman shuffles into the kitchen and slaps the bread on the table. A long gray braid trails behind her like a tail. Her brown, cracking face is knitted into a permanent scowl. She snarls at Diego. "Three guests? Does this look like a restaurant to you?"

"Hey, he's paying for this meal," Enrique says. "He can bring as many guests as he likes."

Abuela waves her arms at the table. "Where will they sit?"

"Let me worry about that," Enrique says. "I'll stand if I have to. It's better for digestion." He casts us a half smile to remind us that we're welcome. "C'mon. Let's eat."

We sit elbow to elbow around the table. My knees are pinned between Matt's and Velma's, and my stool wobbles if I lean to either side. No one else seems to mind.

Enrique looks around the table. "Jorge, would you say grace?"

"Sure." Jorge holds out his hands, and everyone forms a giant hand-holding circle.

Matt gingerly takes my hand in his. They're bigger than Antai's, softer too. My mind lingers where his skin touches mine. Matt closes his eyes and bows his head like the rest. My eyes linger on his face. His sharp jawline. The way his wavy hair curls over the top of his ear. When I realize what I'm doing, I close my eyes.

"Oh, God," Jorge prays. "We're grateful for this day we've been given. We're grateful for our family and that we can rest and recover this Sabbath day."

I open my eyes. Around the table, I only see the top of each head. Everyone except Matt. He watches me with those piercing blue eyes of his. Whereas Antai's eyes are deep and soothing, Matt's are bright and electrifying. For several seconds, his eyes tarry. He doesn't blush or turn away. He only smiles.

I can't help it. I smile back. I like the attention. I like Matt. I'm flattered that he's so interested in me. He's capable and kind. And he's handsome. I can't deny that. But he's not Antai. He'll never be like Antai, and that makes me uncomfortable. I can't relax around him. I'm always afraid he'll make a move and I'll have to reject him.

Ever so slightly, I feel his hand twitch. He slowly closes his eyes and dips his head. He didn't wink. Antai would've winked.

Jorge prays on. "We're grateful that Diego and his friends were accepted into the guard. We're grateful that Diego has a girlfriend."

Javier snickers and Jorge grunts as his dad elbows him in the ribs. He laughs and quickly concludes. "Thank you for this food and please protect us from danger. Amen."

"Amen," everyone echoes. Immediately, Javier snatches the pot off the table and starts to shovel it into his bowl. It's a stew—beef, carrots, and potatoes embedded in a thick brown paste.

Isabela motions at Velma and I. "So you're both in the guard as well?"

We nod.

Abuela scoffs. "Women don't belong in the guard. They belong in the kitchen. You should leave the fighting to the men."

Enrique rolls his eyes. "Please, Mom. Don't be ridiculous."

"It's not ridiculous," Abuela bellows. "If women are meant to be soldiers, then tell me why there has never been a woman guardian. Hmmm?" She puffs out her chest as if it's irrefutable evidence. "Men simply make better soldiers, and women make better caregivers. Have you ever seen a man breastfeed a baby? It's because God made women to care for the children. That's just the way it is."

"I disagree," Velma says.

Around the table, surprised faces turn towards Velma. She fearlessly elaborates. "I think some women do make better soldiers than men." She gestures toward me. "Lynn is the very top of our class. She's a better soldier than any recruit her age, your son included. I wouldn't be surprised if she becomes a guardian someday."

Abuela studies Velma for a moment. "Fair enough. I still think your kind could spend more time raising families and less time stuffing their faces."

Velma's jaw swings open. After a second she laughs. "Oh, no. I'm not high-born. I grew up in the ring, the 8th district actually."

Abuelas piercing gaze slowly morphs into admiration. "Hmmm." She lowers her eyes and takes a bite of stew.

Enrique leans forward. "I work the flats by the 8th district. Who's your father? Maybe I know him?"

"Eric Venderson."

Enrique's face lights up. "Eric! You're kidding. How's his leg? I was with him when the plow caught him."

"He's fine. He's walking again. He should be back to work soon."

Enrique nods. "Good. I'm glad to hear it. Tell him I hope to see him soon."

"I will."

Abuela sets down her fork and eyes the youngest sister. "Maria, you haven't touched your food?"

Mary sits with her hands in her lap and stares at her bowl of stew. Her spoon is still untouched at the side of the bowl. "I'm not hungry. I don't feel very good."

Abuela reaches over and presses her hand to Mary's forehead. "She feels warm."

Enrique furrows his brow with worry. "Mary, why don't you go lie down for a bit and we'll save you some food for later. I'll be in after dinner to check on you."

Mary nods and recedes out of the kitchen and down the hall.

"Poor girl," Abuela says. "She's still not used to the water."

I'm not surprised. The water in the ring is putrid. Most laborers develop antibodies, but refugees often fall ill.

Enrique stabs a chunk of stew with his fork and directs his attention to me. "So… top of your class? That's no small feat." He looks me over and hesitates for a moment. "You're high-born, I assume?"

"I am." I can already feel the tension. Diego told me himself, his family doesn't like elites. What would they do if they knew they were eating lunch with the princess? I take another bite of beef.

"She's not just high-born." Diego says. "She was the servant to the princess."

I gasp, inhaling stew into my lungs. I cover my mouth, but I can't hold it in. My lungs squeeze, and to my horror, a mist of stew sprays out my nose. I'm mortified. I can't find a napkin anywhere. My eyes water, and I struggle to suppress another cough.

No one is eating. Their spoons hover in front of their mouths as they watch me struggle. Enrique jumps to his feet and hands me a rag from the kitchen. It's dirty, but I'm desperate. I wipe my mouth and cough violently into the rag to clear my airway.

Abuela narrows her beady eyes at me. "I apologize if the food isn't as good as you're used to in the palace."

Frustration boils within me. No matter what I do, I offend them. Yet, Velma doesn't even have to try. She connects with them simply because she's ring-born.

"No, it's delicious. I promise." I manage between coughs. "It just went down the wrong pipe."

Abuela rolls her eyes. "It's no wonder you're first in your class. The princess probably made sure of that. The whole system is rigged."

I brush the hair out of my eyes and put on a brave face. It's my turn to stand up to the old witch. "With all due respect, I had to work hard to get into the guard. I worked for my spot. It wasn't given to me because I'm high-born or because I knew the princess. They recruited me for the same reason we all got recruited: because I can protect us."

Abuela looks at me and cackles, exposing missing teeth. "You grew up in a palace full of guard officials. Of course you can protect us. You had every opportunity to learn. I bet all your palace friends were recruited too. Now, think how many ring-born were accepted. Two or three? How can you sit here and tell me that's fair?"

I look to Matt for support, but he doesn't say anything. He's thinking. After a moment, he frowns at me and shrugs. *He actually agrees with her!*

"She has a point," Velma says. "You definitely had an advantage."

I shake my head. "I was at the shooting range every single morning. I ran to the flats and back every day. Sometimes two or three times. I earned it."

"Do you hear yourself?" Velma says. "Do you know how expensive the shooting range is? I went to school in the morning and I cleaned the stables in the evening. It took me weeks to save up for a single box of ammo. Between all that, and cooking and cleaning, and caring for my sisters, I didn't have time to train or run. It's a miracle I got accepted. It's a miracle Matt and Diego got accepted. We were the lucky ones. But you weren't lucky, you were privileged."

I want to argue, but I can't refute it. Deep down, I know she's right. I had an advantage. If I hadn't trained with Antai—if I hadn't been tutored by Grandpa—I wouldn't have been accepted. I'm a guardsman because I'm high-born. The realization sinks deep into my mind. I grow quiet. I don't want to talk about this anymore.

Abuela opens her mouth to say more, but Enrique stops her. "Give her a break. She was only a servant. Don't take it out on her." But he's wrong. I'm the princess. This is my problem. If I don't try to fix it, who will?

Isabela changes the subject. "Tell me about the training. What did you do this week?" I'm grateful to be out of the spotlight.

"We learned how to make force fields." Diego beams. "And we visited the beyon—"

Tap. Tap. Tap.

A knock echoes through the house. Isabela leaps to her feet and skips down the hall. "I'll get it. It might be Jason." She opens the door and steps back.

A man is standing in the doorway in white dress shirt and slacks. I recognize him as a palace servant. "I have a message for Lynn."

All eyes fall on me. I slide off my stool and hurry down the hall. I feel their eyes on my back all the way to the door. "I'm Lynn. What is it?"

"Your grandfather requested your presence immediately. I have a carriage to take you as soon as you're ready."

I feel judgement burn into the back of my head. I face Diego's family. They all gape at me in utter confusion. I too am at a loss for words. How do I explain this? Technically, nothing should be too suspicious. A message for a high-born isn't unheard of, nor is a carriage escort. "I... uh..."

"Go ahead," Enrique urges. "We understand. You're welcome back anytime."

Relief washes through me. "Thank you. Everything was delicious. Really."

Matt studies me. I can see the curiosity in his eyes. Perhaps a hint of suspicion. I meet his gaze. "I'll see you guys at training tomorrow."

With that, I follow my escort out the door. A carriage is parked at the mouth of the alley. It's painted black with a silver frame and spokes. White curtains shield the cabin from the noontime sun. The servant walks briskly down the alleyway and opens the door to the carriage. I climb inside.

"Hey, ringling. I missed you."

Antai sits on the far side of the carriage. He's dressed in an officer uniform and his hair is slicked to one side. A dashing smile erupts over his face. On the seat next to him, a pair of my white high heels rest on top of a folded cream dress.

I hover in the doorway, searching for words. "What are you doing here? I thought you were working."

"I am working. The king sent me to get you." He takes my hand and, as the carriage lurches into motion, guides me to the seat next to him. He kisses me once, softly and sweetly. I lean into the kiss and rest my hands on his shoulders. I expect him to pull me onto his lap, but he leans away instead. His smile disappears. "The high council called an emergency meeting. Commanders are invited as well, so I'll be going too."

"Is it about Lycon?"

Antai nods. "That's part of it." I wait for him to explain more, but he doesn't. He's not acting like himself. His demeanor is all business. I can tell he's stressed about something. Nervous even. My mind flashes back to Remembrance Day when Antai was worried for my life. He's acting the same way now.

"Antai, what is it? You can tell me."

Antai sighs. "There was another incident in the palace last night. A guard was killed outside your chambers."

Killed? "Did they catch the killer?" I gasp.

Antai shakes his head. "He escaped. They don't have any leads so far."

My heart pounds in my chest. He's still at large. If he got into the palace once, he can likely do it again.

Antai sees my concern. "King Dralton insisted I escort you. He thinks it was an inside job. He doesn't trust anyone right now. And neither do I."

My mind is a mess of unanswered questions. I can't help but wonder what would've happened if I were sleeping in my bed last night. *You'd be dead, Rose. Or worse, tied up and tortured.*

I lean back against the chair. "When does the meeting start?"

Antai glances at his watch. "Two minutes ago." He tosses the cream dress onto my lap. "Get dressed fast, I promise I won't peek." He flashes me a strained smile before turning to face the wall. He's trying to be playful, but his heart isn't in it. He's too distracted. Even now, his fingers drum on his holster.

I kick off my shoes and wiggle out of my shirt and pants. It feels odd to be so close to Antai in my underclothes. Almost exciting. Part of me wants him to turn around. To admire me. To want me. But he's too noble. His head never turns in the slightest.

I struggle to squirm into the cream dress. Every bump in the road threatens to knock me over. Finally, I pull the straps over my shoulders and rest my amulet on the outside of my dress. The dress is nice, but it doesn't exactly match the white heels. Antai must have picked them out himself. "Done," I say.

Antai turns around and grins at me. For a moment, his worry disappears as his eyes skim over me. "You look perfect."

"Thanks." I sit down next to him. It's a long shot, but I ask anyway. "Did you bring my makeup or a brush?"

Antai grimaces and shakes his head. "Sorry. There wasn't time."

For a commoner, I look great, but the high council will notice. My hair is flat and I'm only wearing mascara. "You should have brought Nevela." I complain. "She would have me powdered and ready in no time."

Antai's eyes flicker at me and avert to the corner of the carriage. He opens his mouth but doesn't speak right away. He shifts his hips to face me. He has a strange look in his eye. A cautious, delicate look. The kind of look you make when telling a child that their dog died. Antai swallows hard. "Rose, there's something I need to tell you."

My heart sinks in my chest, weighed down by dread. I should have known. Her room is connected to mine. They wouldn't be able to see her face in the darkness. If an assassin was looking for me, it would be easy to mistake Nevela for the princess. The more I think about it, the more fearful I become. I force the words out of my lips. "Antai, tell me she's alright? Tell me they didn't hurt her."

For a moment, he hesitates. "I'm not sure."

"What do you mean you're not sure?" I beg.

"They took her, Rose. They kidnapped Nevela."

Chapter 22

Rose

I stumble up the staircase as fast as I can, my bare feet slapping against the cold stone. My dress is crunched in one hand, and my high heels dangle from the other. Antai strides a few steps ahead of me, trying to hurry me along.

When we reach the top, the guards snap to attention. "Welcome, princess. Welcome, commander. The meeting is already in session." They politely wait for me to slip on my shoes. Then, they push open the double doors and the voices inside fall silent. Every eye in the room is now on us. I've never seen the high council room so crowded. All 12 seats of the council table are occupied and several extra chairs line the perimeter of the room. The other commanders are already seated along the window. "Take a seat," Grandpa commands from his throne. "We've only just begun."

I follow Antai to an empty seat by the window. Behind me is a stunning view of the city, but I'm not in the state of mind to enjoy it. All I can think about is Nevela. If she's alright. If she's scared. If she's even alive.

"Commander Noyan, you were saying?" Grandpa asks.

Commander Noyan stands and straightens his wrinkled uniform. His shoulders are broad, and a dirty brown mustache clings to his upper lip like a stubborn coffee stain. His face is drained of its usual gusto. "Last night, we had an incident in the palace. I was patrolling the royal wing when I found one of my men on the floor. There was a knife in his back, and his amulet was missing."

Chancellor Gwenevere narrows her beady bird eyes. "How does someone kill a royal guard with a knife?" She interjects. "They must have been within striking distance?"

"The real question is how they got through the palace wall," Chancellor Quine exclaims. "I need to know my family is safe here."

"Demons!" Commander Noyan bellows. "You wouldn't have so many questions if you'd let me finish." He composes himself and lowers his voice. "The palace walls were secure. I can assure you of that. We believe the attacker was someone on the inside: most likely a royal guardsman or a member of the palace staff. Someone who knows the palace and how to avoid the nightly patrol. Someone who could've approached the guard without raising suspicion."

Commander Noyan wipes a drop of sweat from his brow with the palm of his hand. He takes a deep breath. "It's important to note that the guard was found directly outside of Princess Roselyn's chambers. We think that the princess was ultimately the target of the attack."

"This is madness!" Chancellor Quine cries. His face is flushed, and strands of his brown hair hang down like bangs. "You're telling us there's an assassin loose in the palace, and he's one of our own?"

Zane rolls his eyes. "Yes, chancellor. That's what he's telling you.

A devious grin grows on General Kayne's face. "How fortunate that the princess wasn't harmed. Where was she last night? Perhaps staying with a friend?" He raises an eyebrow accusingly at Antai. The implications are obvious.

Grandpa leans forward in his throne. "Where the princess is or isn't staying is none of your business, general." His voice is low and threatening. "I would advise you to mind the bounds of your authority."

"Of course, your highness. My apologies."

I study General Kaynes' face. It's far from regretful. A small smirk still lingers on his lips. He's manipulative, sure, but it's hard to imagine him abusing his sons. I hope Tick is wrong about him.

After a short silence, Chancellor Gwenevere breaks the tension. "Do we even know if the intruder meant the princess any harm? Perhaps it was a scare tactic. Or an offended maid who wanted revenge. It could have been anything. We have no reason to believe this was an assassin."

General Kaynes laughs through his nose. "I don't know about you, chancellor, but none of my maids carry around daggers."

Grandpa uses his cane to sit up on his throne. "Unfortunately, the dead guard isn't the only evidence of intended harm to the princess. Roselyn's handmaiden, Nevela, was taken by the attackers. She was likely mistaken as the princess. Whoever is responsible managed to remove her from the palace grounds without alerting the guards. This was a carefully executed and well-planned attack. This wasn't an angry maid. We're dealing with a serious threat here."

"This couldn't be the equalists, could it?" Chancellor Quine asks. "Pickers aren't capable of this."

Zane lets out a short laugh. "Of course they're capable. They have guard uniforms and amulets. They have the means and the motive. And it won't stop with the princess. The attacks will continue until they get what they want."

Chancellor Gwenevere eyes turn to slivers. "If they can run free in the palace, how do we know the amulets are safe? Shouldn't that be our first concern?"

Grandpa shakes his head. "That is the least of our worries. The vault is sealed by an Adamic spell. There's only one key, and it's in my personal possession."

The council nods its approval. Gwenevere shrugs, unsatisfied.

Chancellor Bolo rests his hands on the bulge of his belly. His double chin wobbles as he speaks. "I mean no offense by this, but why kidnap the princess? If the equalists really thought they had the princess, why not just kill her?"

General Kaynes leans back in his chair. "Isn't it clear? They wish to use her as leverage. I imagine the king would trade a great deal to ensure his granddaughter's safety."

Antai watches me carefully, his copper eyes overflowing with worry. Grandpa adjusts his grip on his cane and purses his lips.

"I believe you're right," Grandpa agrees. "What's our next course of action?"

Chancellor Quine responds first. "Defend the palace at all costs. We need more royal guardsmen. Pull them from the ring if you have to."

General Katu shakes his head. "I must disagree. The ring is already unstable. This week, equalists looted the western market. We need every guard available if we hope to maintain order."

Thoughts flutter inside my brain. I can't get Diego's family out of my head. I know the council won't like it, but I have to try. I slowly raise my hand in the air and hold it there until Grandpa notices.

"Yes, Roselyn, you may speak."

I stand. "What if we tried a more diplomatic approach? After all, it was a compromise that ended the Blood-rebellion."

Chancellor Bolo grumbles to himself. "If we reward them every time they rebel, they'll never stop."

"Maybe they shouldn't." The words are out of my mouth before I can stop them. Everyone stares at me as if I just cursed God. Everyone except Zane. He rests his chin on his knuckles with hopeful anticipation. I take a deep breath.

"What I meant to say is that the laborers have a right to be unsatisfied. If we lived in their shoes, we would be unhappy too. But I have a possible solution. I propose that we allow them to elect a representative to join the council."

Chancellor Bolo snorts and shakes his head. Chancellor Gwenevere rolls her eyes.

"Hear me out," I beg. "If they had a representative, we could negotiate small compromises. It will be the representative's job to keep the equalists from rebelling, and the laborers will blame the representative if they don't see the change they expect. In the end, I think the riots will stop. I really do." I curtsy to the council and sit down.

"This is ludicrous," Gwenevere complains. "If we invite a laborer into the council, he'll run back to the equalists with all of our secrets. It's not a solution; it's self-sabotage."

"Perhaps," General Katu says. "Or perhaps they will see there is no simple solution to injustice. Perhaps it will curb their anger."

General Kaynes looks at Grandpa. "Shall we vote on it, your highness?"

Grandpa sits up straight and narrows his eyes. His tree bark skin wrinkles with indecision. Finally, he looks up at the council. "All in favor, please manifest."

Zane and Katu raise their hands. They're the only ones. Grandpa sits with his arms in his lap, looking straight ahead. My heart sinks until it's resting on the bottom of my stomach. Of all people, I expected him to back me up.

"Very well," Grandpa says. "For now, the council will remain as it is. Any other matters to go before the council?"

Chancellor Gwenevere pipes up. "Are we ever going to discuss what happened in Lycon? You spent weeks there. Please tell us you have answers."

Grandpa clears his throat. "Very well. As I mentioned in my report, there were no survivors. We found the sanctuary walls compromised. Large sections had been destroyed, which nullified the defensive spells. The deceased showed evidence of feeder bites. That's all we know."

"How does one destroy a sanctuary?" Chancellor Quine asks. "How do we know we're not next?"

Grandpa keeps his face emotionless. "The only thing powerful enough to destroy Adamic is another Adamic spell. I believe an adalit is leading the attacks on the sanctuaries. If we kill said Adalit, we keep Cavernum safe."

Chancellor Bolo rubs his hands over his hairless head. The underarms of his robes are dark with sweat. "What is he after? Why would an adalit destroy a sanctuary? And why now, after 18 years of silence?

Grandpa plays dumb. "I don't know, but we must be prepared for an attack."

"We need more men," General Kaynes claims. "We're spread too thin, both in the palace and on the wall. I suggest we pull the recruits into the field. Fifty more soldiers could make all the difference."

Zane shakes his head. His beard sways with each twist of his neck. "They're not even halfway done with training. They're not ready for combat."

General Kaynes scoffs. "If they're anything like my son, they'll do just fine."

Grandpa looks at Antai. "Commander Elsborne, you've spent the most time monitoring them. In your opinion, would they be ready for an early graduation?"

Antai stands. "To be completely honest, this year's recruits are extraordinary. They've received some of the highest scores I've ever seen. I think they'll be ready for the field soon. Keep in mind: their training will continue in the field as well."

"How soon can we get them in the field?" Grandpa asks.

Antai thinks a moment. "If you give Proticus a few more days to sum up the basics, I think they'll be ready. We can hold the final evaluation this Saturday and the graduation ceremony on Sunday."

Grandpa lifts his cane onto his lap. "Would anyone oppose such a motion?"

No one speaks.

"Excellent. All in favor, please manifest."

Around the room, hands lift in unison—all except for Zane.

"It's settled," Grandpa concludes.

My mind spins. I can't believe it. In one week, I'll be done with formal training. I'll be in the field, fighting feeders and enacting justice.

Zane slaps his palms onto the table. "Putting recruits on the wall isn't a solution. I was there when Hogrum fell. I know what we're up against. A single demon could slaughter them all. What we really need are more soul-anchors."

"I agree," General Katu says. "The enemy is growing stronger, and so must we."

Chancellor Gwenevere rolls her eyes and purses her thin lips. "Tell me you're not actually considering this? We already have enough guardians on the council."

General Kaynes furrows his brow as he thinks. "The equalists already suspect we're withholding amulets. If we suddenly bestow another soul-anchor, it will only confirm their suspicions. It may lead to more unrest."

Gwenevere smiles at General Kaynes. "For the first time, general, I must admit I agree with you. There were 18 years of peace between attacks. For all we know, it might be decades before the Adalit strikes again, if it happens at all. We don't even know if this Adalit exists. The equalists are our most pressing concern. Another guardian would only urge them to more violence."

Zane locks eyes with Gwenevere. His gaze is stone cold. "When the feeders come knocking on your door, chancellor, you're going to wish you had another guardian to protect you. I promise you that."

Katu grunts. "I agree with Zane. Whatever is out there, it destroys sanctuaries. We need all the help we can get."

"Perhaps a compromise," Grandpa suggests. "The council will remain as is; no soul-anchors will be bestowed. However, I'll distribute Adamic blades to the commanders. That way, we're prepared for anything the Adalit sends our way. All in favor?"

Hands rise around the room. It's unanimous.

Grandpa smiles. "Very well. Commander Elsborne will inform the recruits that they'll be graduating next week." Grandpa taps his cane on the floor. "Meeting adjourned."

As everyone exits the room, Grandpa motions for Antai and me to stay put. He lingers by his throne until the room is almost empty. "Zane, could you close the door on your way out?" he asks.

Zane complies and shuts the door with a gentle thud, leaving me alone with Grandpa and Antai. Grandpa spreads his arms, and I dive into them. I wrap my arms around him as he folds me inside the warmth of his cloak. I tuck my head into his shoulder and inhale the subtle scent of pine leaves.

"Is she really gone?" I ask.

Grandpa squeezes me tighter. "We'll get her back, Rose. I promise we'll get her back." His confidence puts my soul at ease. If anyone can save Nevela, he can.

Grandpa lets me go. "There are a few things we need to discuss. I won't be able to make it to our Adamic lesson tonight, so now is the best time. Frankly, I'm worried about your safety. The equalists are more dangerous than I thought. I want you back in the palace as soon as possible."

"But the palace isn't safe! Nevela is proof of that," I argue. "Aren't I safer where I'm at?"

"Maybe for now," Grandpa says. "But sooner or later, someone will find you. People are already getting suspicious. Someone will recognize you at the graduation ceremony if they haven't already." He stares into my eyes, and I see only his fatherly concern. "I can't protect you out there, but I can in the palace. I'm trying to mimic a locking spell from the vault. It's complicated, but I almost have it. By the end of the week, your chambers will be the safest place in the sanctuary."

I clench my fists. I've worked too hard for this. I can't give up now. Frustration starts to rise in my throat. My voice rises with it "What do you want me to do? Quit the guard?"

Grandpa grins. "No, I want you to win. If you rank first in the final evaluation, Commander Noyan will recruit you as a royal guard. You can move back into your chambers and continue your service in the palace. At the graduation ceremony, I'll reveal you as princess. What do you think?"

I don't know what to say. Everything is happening so much faster than I expected. I look at Antai, who beams back at me. His flawless cheeks are creased at the edge of his lips. His excitement makes me excited. By the end of the week, I'll be back in the palace. I'll be able to see Antai every night. I'll be home. The thought is too good to be true.

"I… I love it," I say. "It sounds perfect."

Grandpa stands. "Excellent. It's settled. I wish I had more time, but I really must be going. Antai will keep you informed if anything changes. I love you, Rose." He gives me one last hug and turns to leave.

"Wait," I beg. "What do I do with my soul-anchor? I can't compete with it, can I?" It wouldn't be fair. But then again, I've used it until now.

Grandpa smiles at me, amused by the question. "I trust you'll make the right decision."

"And what if I don't rank first? What happens then?"

Grandpa pauses. "You must. For the sake of Cavernum, you must."

Chapter 23

Matt

The trench is completely silent except for the occasional drip of water. I sit alone on the rocky beach and stare out over the lake. The Adamic light hardly penetrates its glassy surface.

I glance toward the stairwell. Strange. Zane is typically right on time. He said he would be here ten minutes ago, not that it really matters. I have nothing better to do. It's Sunday afternoon, and everyone is off with their families. Lynn is doing who knows what at the palace, and Diego is on another date with Velma.

Lynn. I can't stop thinking about her. There's so much I don't understand. She's friendly and sociable, but she hardly ever talks about herself. One second, she'll be chatting about her childhood, and the next, her jaw will go rigid. Conversation over. After a month, I still feel like I barely know who she is.

Has it really been a month? It's hard to believe. It's been four weeks since I've listened to music or taken a hot shower... four weeks since I've talked to Judy. I promised her I'd call. I need to find a way. I can't shake the feeling that I'm running out of time.

The thump of boots shakes me from my worries. "Sorry, I'm late," Zane calls out as he strides across the trench. "I had some council business to take care of." He's dressed more formal than usual: khakis with a black button-up shirt. He waits for me to climb to my feet and holds out an amplifier by the chain. "Have you been practicing like I showed you?"

"As much as I can." I slip my amulet around my neck and tuck it inside my shirt. The cold metal feels wet against my chest.

I look Zane in the eyes and let my mind roam deeper, searching for his thoughts somewhere beyond his eyes. My mind collides with what feels like a brick wall. I can't sense any emotions. No thoughts, just nothingness. I don't see a soul-anchor around his neck. He must be wearing it under his shirt.

"How's the energy shield coming?" Zane asks.

"Pretty good. We practiced it with Tick this week. I think I have it down."

Zane scratches his beard. "And the water dominion?"

"It's alright." I shrug. "I'm getting better at it." Water dominion was hard for me to pick up. The molecules are so shifty. They're hard to control. It wasn't until Zane let me enter his mind that I made any real progress. Now, it comes much easier.

Zane stares over the lake until a small grin forms above his beard. "How about some practice? Why don't you walk out onto the lake?"

"Wait. You mean like walk on the water?"

Zane nods. "No energy shields. No ice. Just you and the water. Make it support you like the ground does. It'll be good practice."

I look at the lake and back at Zane. I'm not so sure I can.

"Go on," he coaxes. "You can do it."

Determination fills my entire body. Zane may not be the most loving coach, but he believes in me. Except for Judy, I've never had someone care about me like he does. He's shown so much faith in me, and I want to prove him right.

I shuffle my feet to the edge of the rocky bank. There's a slight drop between the rock I'm standing on and the surface of the lake. I stare down into the black abyss beneath me. Just a foot from the water's edge, the shore gives way to deep water. If I make a mistake, I'll have no choice but to swim for it.

I reach my foot down until the sole of my shoe sends a ripple across the lake. I reach out with my mind until I can feel the water. It's constantly flowing and colliding. I command the molecules to condense under my foot, and the water obeys. I put a little weight on it, and the water pushes back.

"Let's go," Zane grumbles. "We don't have all day."

I take a deep breath and step off the bank. For a moment, my shoe dips under the surface. It disappears into the cloudy black void. Icy lake water pours into my shoes and rises up my shin. I close my eyes and command the water with all my might.

Rise!

Like a spring, the water lifts me back to the surface. I wave my arms as I struggle to keep my balance. The water shifts under my feet like a rolling log. Once again, I command with my mind, and the water grows more steady. I take another step, and this time, the water supports me. It feels like walking on a trampoline covered in thick mud.

Amazing! I'm walking on water. 5 steps. 10 steps. Each stride is easier than the last. Zane claps from the shore, filling the cavern with slow applause. I turn around and face him with triumph on my face. He's not smiling, but I know he's satisfied.

"You've improved," Zane says. "But what happens if you need to form an energy shield? Someday, you'll need to mount an offense and defense at the same time. You need to learn how to multitask."

Zane reaches down and scoops his hand into the lake. When it emerges, he's holding a softball-sized sphere of ice. He smiles at me without an ounce of remorse. "Defend yourself." Like a baseball pitcher, he steps into the throw and hurls the ice straight at me.

The ice ball arcs through the air. I only have a second to react. I reach with my mind and command an energy shield to form. With a crack, the ice collides with my shield mere inches from my chest. The ball shatters, sending ice shards into the lake.

Before I can let out a breath of relief, the water beneath me liquifies, and I slip through the surface of the lake. In an instant, ice-cold water engulfs me. I clench my teeth in an effort not to inhale water. I open my eyes, but all I see is a flurry of black bubbles. My jeans cling to my legs and threaten to drag me deeper into the darkness. My arms are slow and sluggish as I flail in the water. I can't be more than a few feet underwater, but no matter how hard I try, I can't find the surface. My head aches from the cold, and my lungs burn. In a desperate rage, I kick my feet and swing my arms.

Finally, my face breaks the surface, and I suck in a gasp of air. My muscles are shaky from the cold, but I manage to keep myself afloat. Once I catch my breath, and the panic subsided, I start the slow swim towards shore.

Zane watches from the bank with his forehead scrunched. I can't tell if he's worried for me or just disappointed. What was he thinking? What if I inhaled water? Would he have jumped in to save me if I drowned?

Anger dampens the cold and fuels my muscles. I grab hold of a boulder on the shore and pull myself out of the water.

Zane waits until I'm on my feet. "Hold still."

I do as he says. The air around me grows sauna hot, quickly putting a stop to my shivers. My anger disappears with them. Suddenly, I feel a slight tug on my hair and clothes. My skin trembles as the water droplets are whisked into the air. They evaporate into a small cloud of steam that drifts into the air above me.

Amazing! I press my hand against my jacket. It's completely dry. Not even a dampness remains. I look up at Zane. "Thanks."

He nods. "You did good."

"I failed. I almost drowned."

Zane sighs and sits down on a rock as he speaks. "Dual dominion is extremely hard to master. It takes most people years to learn. I didn't expect you to ace it on your first try."

I remain standing, my previous anger beginning to return. "Then, why do it?" I demand.

"The stakes are high in the guard, Matt. Fail in the field, and you're dead. Or worse, someone you love dies."

I remember what Lynn told me about Zane's family. I wonder if he somehow blames himself.

Zane looks at me with his lips pressed tight together. "You have a lot of potential. I just want you to remember what's at stake. Mastering dominion has to mean everything to you. You'll be going into the field soon, and you still have a lot to learn. I want you to remember that. Train like your life depends on it." He motions to the rock next to him. "Now, sit down. There are some things I need to tell you."

My heart starts to race. Ever since our first lesson, I've been waiting to ask more about my tattoos. Weeks ago, I asked Zane if I'm a demon. He made two things very clear. One: yes, I'm a demon. Two: I should never ask about it again. But I have more questions than ever, and my patience is running out.

Zane rubs his hands together. "I just got out of a meeting with the high council. They want to move your graduation to this weekend. Your final assessment will be Saturday."

"Oh." I try to hide my disappointment. "Is that good or bad?"

"For you... bad," Zane says bluntly. "You need more time to catch up to the high-born. Time you no longer have."

It makes sense. I've only had a month to learn what took them years. I've made a lot of progress, but I still can't compete with Lynn or Vyle.

"What's the final assessment like?" I ask.

"It's a dueling assessment. Everyone fights in two duels. Whoever ranks first goes to the palace as a royal guard." Zane hesitates for a moment. "The losers usually end up in the infirmary."

I don't like the idea at all. I don't stand a chance. If Vyle were allowed to unleash on me, I doubt I'd survive. He'd inflict as much pain as possible.

"Does everyone have to fight?" I ask.

311

Zane shakes his head. "You can choose to forfeit. You'll give up any chance of ranking first, but if you're going to lose anyway, it's better than the alternative. Most recruits choose to forfeit at least one of their fights."

It doesn't sound worth it to me. "What do I get if I win? More money?"

Zane nods. "You'll be an elite if you win. More money. More authority. More autonomy. You'll live in the comfort of the palace."

I think of Judy. She's the reason I'm here. She's the reason I joined the guard. I need to get my hands on my amulet. I need to find a way to heal her.

"If I win, do I get my own amulet back?" I ask.

"Sadly, no. Guards only get to use an amulet while on duty. You'll have to return it to the armory after every shift. Royal guards are no exception."

I point at Zane's chest. "But not you. You get your own, right?"

Zane grunts in a way I've learned means yes. He stares out over the lake as if he's speaking to someone else. "Guardians are different. Someday, if you become guardian, you'll get your soul-anchor back. As long as you work for the king, it will be yours to keep."

"And what if I decide to leave tomorrow? Would I get my soul-anchor back?"

"That would be up to the king," Zane says. "But no... probably not. The king can't let that much power go unchecked."

It feels weird to be referred to as powerful. I can't imagine the king worrying about me as a liability. Another idea pops into my head. "And what if I stole an amulet?" I wonder. It seems crazy, but I'm getting desperate.

Zane snorts a short laugh. When he sees I'm serious, he raises one of his bushy eyebrows. "I wouldn't recommend it. I doubt you'd get far. Remember: the punishment for stealing an amulet is death. And I would be the one hunting you down. I don't want to see you hung."

"Right," I say. "Nevermind then."

Zane thinks for a moment. His lips pull tighter. "You want an amulet for your mom, don't you?"

I nod. "I can save her. I know I can. I just need an amulet."

Zane opens his mouth and blows the air from his lungs. "It's not that easy, Matt. Healing is extremely difficult, especially on someone as sick as your mom. You can't just walk in and make her better. Healing has its limits. It usually takes two or three healers several hours just to heal a non-lethal wound. And that's with years of training."

"Then teach me!" I exclaim. "I can learn!"

Zane shakes his head. "I would, but I don't know how. Moving the elements is one thing, but healing is entirely different. It requires knowledge—very detailed knowledge. Biology and anatomy and chemistry. Knowledge I don't have. You'll have to find somebody else to teach you."

I open my mouth, but Zane holds up his hand. "Have you ever wondered why we don't use dominion to grow our crops?"

I'm stumped. It sounds like such an obvious solution to starvation, but the thought never occurred to me. No explanation comes to mind.

Zane continues. "It's the same reason healing is so difficult. Living things are complicated. You'd have to manipulate complex chemical reactions: cells and proteins and enzymes and DNA. A single mistake with DNA, and you could cause more harm than good." Zane tilts his head and stares me down. "One mistake, and you could cause cancer rather than cure it."

Zane sighs and looks up at the cavern ceiling. "Dominion isn't everything, Matt. Sure, we can walk on water and set the air ablaze. We can do incredible things. Sometimes, that makes us feel like gods... but we're not. We're just people. We can't always choose who lives and who dies."

Frustration builds in me like a volcano. I'm about to explode. "What's the point?" I demand. "Even if I learn to heal, it'll be too late. By the time I become a guardian, she'll be dead! Why am I even here?"

Zane sits quietly until I'm done ranting. He doesn't try to soothe me. He just gives the facts. "There are several Guardians who still haven't chosen apprentices, myself included. If you place first this week, you'll be the youngest lieutenant in the sanctuary. That would make you a pretty strong candidate. I thought you should know."

Ideas whir in my head. "I have an advantage with my mind reading, right? Do you think I could win?"

"It's possible," Zane sighs. "It's definitely possible." Somehow, his expressionless face gets even more serious. "Just promise me you'll be careful with your… gift. You can't go too far under any circumstances. If anyone finds out, they'll have you hung."

"About that…" I have so many questions. I don't know where to start. "My tattoo is the only thing that makes me a demon, right? So if we removed the tattoo, I would be norm—"

"Shhhh!" Zane hisses. He peers suspiciously towards the exit. "This is not the place, Matt."

"Then, where?" I demand. "And when? It's been weeks, and you haven't told me anything."

Zane groans. He rubs his jaw with his palm and looks at me with pity. "Soon… I promise." He stands up and dusts off his pants. "Now, as I was saying, I think you have a shot at placing first. I'll help you either way, but I need to know what you're gonna do. Fight or forfeit? Which one is it?"

"Ummm…" I'm not sure. I ask myself the questions.

Will I regret it if I try?... No. Even if I end up in the hospital, I can say I tried. Judy would want me to try.

Will I regret if I don't try?... yes! I'll regret it forever. If Judy dies when I could've saved her, I'll never forgive myself.

My mind is made up.

"Okay," I breathe. "How do I beat Vyle?"

Zane smiles. "Get up. I have something I want to teach you."

The stables are huge. Hundreds of horse heads peek out from their separate stalls. I spot donkeys and mules as well. Sunlight sweeps through the cracks in the wooden boards, and dust floats in the air. The constant buzzing of flies tickles my ear.

"Ugh!" Zander tucks his nose into the crook of his elbow. "It smells worse than the ring in here." For once, I agree with Zander. The place reeks of fresh manure. I try to breathe as little as possible, and only through my nose.

Tick leads us deeper into the stables. We walk slowly, stepping over horse droppings in the walkway. An amplifier swings underneath my shirt. It's Thursday, which means tomorrow is our last day of training—two days until the final assessment.

Diego looks at one of the horses and frowns. It's a large black horse with bulging dark eyes. Long pink scars stripe the horse's neck. It looks like a chunk is missing from the horse's shoulder. "Dude, this is sad. it's like a horse prison in here," Diego mumbles.

Velma goes on her tiptoes to see over the stall. "These poor things. They barely have room to lay down."

The stalls are only five feet across—just wide enough for the horse to turn around. Flies cling to the horse's face and clutter around his eyes. As I watch the horse, I start to feel something. A certain sadness. It's not like the sadness I'm used to. It's simpler. More innocent. Almost childlike. I feel an aching sense of confinement. A longing to play and run. I blink and look away, trying to shake the feeling from my head.

"Alright, kiddos, listen up. I have a few announcements," Tick calls. He stands looking perfectly groomed in the center of the straw strewn walkway. "First of all, this is our last dominion lesson, so I want your best effort."

"What about tomorrow?" Crasidla demands. "Don't we have a lesson tomorrow?"

Tick shakes his head. "Not this time. Tomorrow is your last day before the final evaluation. We'll have our classroom lesson like normal, but we won't have strength or dominion training. I want you all well rested for the final evaluation. You'll have the afternoon free to do as you wish." A few kids let out whoops of approval.

"And secondly, Saturday night will be your graduation party. The details are somewhat of a guard secret; you'll find out the night of. Be at the guard tower by sunset, and we'll take care of the rest. I promise you won't be disappointed."

Confusion flows through the crowd of recruits.

"The party's after curfew?" one boy asks. "Is that allowed?"

I hear Velma whisper to Diego. "Leave it to the guard to break their own rules."

Tick avoids the questions. He keeps his face neutral. "Again, the party is a guard secret. Not all of our traditions would be approved by the public. Even after the party, I expect you all to keep your mouth's shut."

"Yes, sir," we echo.

I understand the secrecy. If the laborers knew we were partying at night while they're getting flogged for breaking curfew, they wouldn't be too happy.

Tick smiles. "Good. Now, today's lesson is on animal dominion."

I hear a few recruits groan. One boy raises his hand. "When are we going to learn to shock people?

"I wish we had time," Tick says. "But because of your early graduation, we won't be able to cover everything. You'll have to learn electrical and metal dominion with your trainers. These skills are not urgent. On the contrary, many of you will be stationed on horseback next week. You must be able to control your animal."

When no one argues, Tick continues. "When you exercise dominion on an animal, you interact with a living soul. It's a very different experience than elemental dominion." Tick motions to a workhorse in the stall nearest him. "You'll be able to communicate with the horse, and the horse will communicate with you. You'll sense what the horse thinks and give it commands. Now, don't be alarmed if you find yourself controlling the horse from the inside. Eventually, you'll be able to control the animal directly, the same way you control your own body. It can be a bit... disorienting the first time."

"We possess the horse?" I think aloud.

Tick scrunches his dark eyebrows. "Your soul communicates directly with the horse's body, so I suppose it's like possession."

He turns his attention back to the horse. "Just like us, animals have dominion over their own bodies. They have their own thoughts and desires. If your command aligns with the horse's desires, dominion will be almost effortless. However, unlike the elements, animals can resist your dominion."

Vyle narrows his eyebrows. "But we can force them to do it, right? In the end, we have dominion. We're in control."

"That's correct," Tick admits. "With enough practice, you can make an animal do basically anything."

Vyle grins at the nearest horse. "Even kill itself?"

Tick grimaces and nods his head. "Yes, even kill itself." He turns toward one of the stables and reaches for the latch.

"Is this the same thing demons do?" I call out.

The stables grow silent. Even the horses seem to hush. I don't mind if people stare. I just want answers. If Zane won't give them to me, maybe Tick will.

Tick rubs his palms together and exhales hard. His jaw tightens, but he forces out the answer. "Yes, Matt. It is." He turns to face us. "What you're about to do to these horses, a demon could potentially do to you. That's what makes a demon so dangerous. In the end, they have dominion over us. Resisting is hopeless. The only option is to run."

Everyone is dead quiet. Diego gulps loudly, and Lynn holds a hand over her heart. I can see the fear in her eyes. *I'm one of them.* I think. *They're afraid of me.*

"Alright, let's get to work." Tick flips the latch on the nearest stall and the brown horse trots forward. "Do as I do. Start with simple commands." Tick reaches up and rests his palm on the horse's forehead. The horse whinnies and collapses to its knees. It lays down at Tick's feet like a dog expecting a treat.

"When you feel ready, climb on and go for a ride around the pasture." As soon as Tick swings his leg over the saddle, the horse climbs back to its feet, lifting him into the air. "Don't try to mount if you're not confident," Tick warns. "Every year, at least one recruit gets bucked."

When no one moves, Tick claps his hands. "Chop chop! We're losing daylight."

Everyone spreads out in the stable and picks a horse. I walk back to the black horse with the scars. I approach from the side where I'm sure he can see me. He snorts and paws at the dirt.

"Hey there, buddy. I'm Matt. I think we're going to be friends." I reach out my hand, and the horse dips his head forward, desperate for attention. I stroke his cheek softly. "Awww, you're friendly. What should I call you? Black Jack? Shadow? Midnight?"

"His name is Steve." The voice is masculine and mucusy. I turn and find a middle-aged white man watching me from the shadows of the stables. "I named him myself," the man brags. Half of his face sags when he talks as if he had a stroke. His pale eyes are bulging, and his patchy blond beard is disgustingly stringy. Worst of all, something that looks like mud is smeared on his overalls. The man adjusts his grip on a shovel and scoops more horse poop into a wheelbarrow.

"Is this your horse?" I ask.

The man cackles as if it's the silliest thing he's ever heard. "Hell no, it ain't. I just pick up the poop. I like to name all the horsies. I've known them all since they was born. We spend a lot of time together. Don't we, Betty?" He smiles at the horse closest to him, revealing a mouth of rotting chompers.

I look back at Steve. "Where'd he get the scars?" I ask.

"Poor feller. He fell in the canal when he was just a little thing. It took five men to drag him out. They pulled him out with ropes and scratched him up pretty good. He didn't walk for a week."

"Is he healthy now?"

"Oh, yes, sir. Strong as an ox."

I look into Steve's eyes and let my mind drift forward. This time, excitement courses through me. He knows I'm going to let him out. I collect my thoughts and command.

Lay down.

Steve takes a step back and folds himself flat onto the hay. I look over the gate and find him peering up at me expectantly.

"C'mon. Let's get you out of here." I unlatch the gate and swing it open. I shimmy next to Steve and swing my leg over the saddle. I slip my feet through the stirrups and grab hold of the pommel.

Stand.

Straw falls from his belly as Steve shakily climbs to his feet.

Forward.

Steve happily obeys. He trots out of his prison enclosure and towards the exit of the stables. I can feel his excitement growing as we approach the stable doors. Joy radiates from his back and forces a smile on my face.

Run!

As we exit the stables, Steve erupts into a furious gallop. I use my legs to absorb the thrust of each bound. I lean forward and let my thoughts mix deeper with Steve's.

It's a beautiful day. The afternoon sun bathes the flats in its pale yellow light. The air is fresh and crisp. A spacious pasture surrounds the stables with clumps of green grass and yellow daisies. His joy is my joy. I can sense his legs churning beneath me. I can feel his childlike excitement.

Faster!

Steve tears through the grass at an astonishing pace. I can sense his fatigue, but he pushes forward anyway. I use my knees like a spring and let my body roll with each gallop. Suddenly, Steve starts to veer to the left. I instantly see why. Up ahead, an irrigation ditch bars our path. It's ten feet across at most. It should be easily jumpable, but Steve is terrified. He tries desperately to change directions. His terror courses through my body.

Forward! I command. *You can do this!*

I grit my teeth and let my mind envelop Steve like a calming blanket. Steve submits and angles back toward the canal. I can sense his hesitation, but I urge him forward. We're almost there now. Just a little closer!

Jump!

Instead of leap, Steve plunges his hoofs into the grass and locks his legs. My inner thighs dig into the saddle, my momentum almost pulling me off his back. We come to an abrupt stop just feet from the canal's edge.

I'm stunned. He disobeyed me. I wasn't in control, after all.

I think of what Zane said during our last lesson: the stakes are high. I have to train as if my life depends on it. I let my imagination run wild. What if we were being chased by feeders? We'd both be dead right now. Failure isn't an option. I look at Steve with newfound determination. I can feel his fear, but I won't take no for an answer.

Forward!

Steve whinnies and stomps his feet in frustration. He doesn't budge.

Forward! I shout it in my head.

Steve takes a short step forward and two steps back. He tries to turn away from the canal, but I don't let him. I let my mind sink further into his head. Deeper and deeper, I push my thoughts. When I open my eyes, I'm no longer sitting on Steve's back; I'm looking out of his eyes.

The feeling is unnerving. His body feels foreign and familiar at the same time. When I look down, Steve's eyes respond instead of my own. This time, I'm in control. I force one of his legs forward. I feel his muscles flex, and his hoofs connect with the soft earth. One step at a time, I move us closer to the canal. We're close enough now to see over the edge. A foot of muddy water flows in the bottom. Steve is terrified. His panic echoes inside my head, but I ignore it. I let my determination override his thoughts.

I take another step. Then, another. His hoof is just inches from the canal. One more step, and I could send us both toppling over the edge. I lift his foot and suspend it over the water below. Triumph fills my chest. I did it! I won. I conquered the beast.

A new feeling surfaces inside my head: betrayal. Steve is no longer afraid of the trench. He's afraid of me. I feel his hatred towards the man on his back.

What am I doing? I retract my mind, and Steve scurries away from the canal. I can still sense his emotions: distrust and confusion. I betrayed him. I hurt him.

"I'm sorry, boy." I rub his back as he calms down. *I'm sorry. I won't do it again. I promise.* I think back to all the animals I used to hunt. Guilt fills my chest like wet cement. If I knew then what I know now—if I knew how much they feel, I would've never pulled the trigger.

"Wow, you're a natural." Lynn's voice snaps me from my thoughts. She trots up alongside me on a majestic white stallion. When she sees my solemn gaze, she scrunches her nose. "Everything alright?"

"Everything's fine. I was just thinking."

"What about?" Lynn says. "If you don't mind me asking?"

I sigh. "I was just thinking about before. Just a few months ago, I used to hunt these animals. I've killed so many. I never knew they were so…"

"Intelligent?" Lynn asks.

I look down at Steve. "So human."

Lynn flashes a solemn smile at her horse. "They're pretty incredible, aren't they?" She presses her face against the horse's neck and strokes his mane. I try not to feel jealous of the stallion.

"Have you been riding a lot?" I ask.

Lynn gives the horse a quick peck. "All the time. Growing up, the princess let me go riding whenever I wanted." For a moment, she goes quiet and smiles to herself.

"What?" I ask.

"The first time I rode a horse, I was six. It was the first time I'd ever seen the flats up close. My grandpa took me out here and put me on the back of a pony. All I could do was hold on as the pony walked me around. I couldn't believe how big everything was. I remember telling my grandpa it was the best day of my life." She smiles longingly. "It's weird to think how much has changed."

I get what she means. When I was little, I thought this was all fantasy. If only Judy could see me now. "What would you say the best day of your life is now?" I ask.

Lynn bites her lip and stares down at the grass. After a moment, a slender grin sneaks onto her face. Her lips pull tight as she tries to conceal a sheepish smile.

"What?" I ask

Her cheeks flush red beneath her almond skin. It's subtle but undeniable. She ducks her face to hide it. "Nothing. Nothing." She sits up tall and beams a bright, pure smile. The kind of smile that makes you forget the bad in the world. She thinks a moment longer.

"If I had to choose one, I would say the first time I performed with the royal orchestra. I practiced for months. My grandpa and my two best friends were there watching. They gave us a standing ovation. It was nice to be a part of something so beautiful. You know?"

I can't say I do, but I nod anyway. "Do you ever regret choosing the guard?"

"No," Lynn replies firmly. "With the guard, I can still play music. At least in some small way, I get both."

"Maybe you can play for me sometime?" I hope.

"Yeah, I'd like that." She tilts her head towards me. "What about you? What was your favorite day in the beyond?"

"Hmm, I don't know." I have to think way back before the cancer. "Do you guys have Christmas here?" I ask.

"Christmas?"

"No!" I gasp. "Don't tell me you don't have Christmas!" I should've known better. A place where old ladies are flogged in the street could never know the Christmas spirit. "Okay. What's the biggest holiday in Cavernum?" I ask

"Probably Fall Festival," Lynn decides.

"Well, Christmas is our fall festival. This will sound a little crazy, but we convince little kids that a big, fat man flies around the world and delivers presents to every house.

Lynn stifles a laugh. "You're kidding."

"I'm serious. But that's only a part of it. There's a bunch of other fun traditions. Mostly we just spend time with family and give gifts. Growing up, we never had a lot of money. My mom was a teacher, and she didn't get paid a lot. We couldn't afford the toys my friends had. Anyway, when I was 12, all my friends had skateboards and I would watch them ride around the street."

"Skateboards?" Lynn scrunches her nose and gives me a blank stare.

"A skateboard is a piece of wood with wheels. You stand on it and—"

"Oh!" Lynn exclaims. "You mean a pine roller."

"Okay. Yeah, a pine roller. Anyway, for Christmas that year, my mom surprised me with a pine roller. A really nice one. I spent that whole day practicing tricks in the street while my mom just sat on the curb for hours and cheered me on. She was probably so bored, but she made me think I was some kind of prodigy. It sounds stupid, but I thought it was the best day ever."

"No. It doesn't sound stupid," Lynn insists. "It sounds perfect." She leans back in the saddle and gazes longingly over the flats. "It sounds perfect." She whispers to herself. I wonder if she's thinking about her own mother—about all the fall festivals she missed out on.

Horse hooves clop behind us. I turn and find Velma in the saddle. She rides a small, tan pony and wears a worried scowl.

"Velma, what's up?" I call out.

"It's Diego. He's been quiet all day, and now he won't talk to me. Something's wrong." She looks at me with wide, pleading eyes. "Will you talk to him? He might open up to you."

I look around. "Where is he?"

Velma points toward the barn. Diego is slumped on the back of a mule. He sits lifeless on the saddle as the mule grazes on the long pasture grass.

"What's wrong with him?" I ask.

Velma rolls her eyes. "Don't you listen? That's the problem. He won't tell me. He won't say anything."

"Alright. I'll talk with him," I agree. Whatever it is, I bet I can find out. Lynn gives me an encouraging smile as I coax Steve toward the barn.

Diego doesn't even look up as I approach. I tug on the reigns until Steve trots to a stop. "Hey man, are you okay?"

Diego lifts his head just enough to look at me, then it drops back into his lap. He doesn't say anything. His eyes aren't red, so I assume he hasn't been crying. If he's feeling sad or angry, he doesn't show it. He only stares at his lap. In his hands, he clutches his mother's gold cross.

I try to keep my tone light. "You have Velma pretty worried. She wanted me to see if you're okay."

"I'm fine," Diego mumbles. His mule takes a few steps toward a fresh clump of grass.

I don't want to bug him, but I don't want to leave him like this either. "Can I sit with you for a bit?"

Diego shrugs his shoulders. We sit in silence as the other recruits gallop around the stables. After a few moments, Steve joins in the grazing.

I urge Steve forward and position him directly next to Diego's mule. If I reach out my arm, I can touch his mule's backside. I need to be as close as possible if I'm going to read his mind.

I close my eyes and let my mind drift towards Diego. His emotions wash over me like waves. First is a sense of uncertainty and dread. Then, hopelessness and loneliness. A feeling that no one understands. I don't dare go any deeper. If I do, I'm afraid Diego will sense my presence. But I want to know more. I let myself float in his emotions until a thought forms in my head.

What if she doesn't come? What if she never comes?

Of course! How could I forget? I heard Tick mention it to Diego in the beyond. Tomorrow morning, the convoy arrives in Cavernum. Diego's mom might be on it.

"Diego, is this about tomorrow? Do you want to talk about it?"

Diego shakes his head.

I let myself drift through his emotions a moment longer. Then, I slowly leak my own thoughts into the mix. *She'll be there. It'll work out. You can talk about it.* I try to combat Diego's anxiety with a sense of calmness. Like an I.V., my positivity slowly drips until it fills his veins. It takes a while, but his hands slowly loosen on the reins.

Diego lifts his head and his eyes meet mine. "I'm freaking out, dude. I don't know what to do. It's all I can think about." He looks down at the cross. "I should be excited, but I'm not. I might see my mom tomorrow, but I don't want tomorrow to come. I don't want to know the truth, you know? Right now, I can believe she's still alive, but if she's not there tomorrow, I'll have to accept it. I'll have to accept that she's gone."

"She could still be out there," I remind him. "Even if she's not there tomorrow, she could still be alive."

Diego grits his teeth. "You don't know my mom. She's smart. If she survived, she would find a way to Cavernum. I know she would. She'd probably already be here. If she's not here tomorrow, it's because she's not coming."

I don't want to argue, especially not about this. "I can't say I know exactly what you're going through, but I think I have an idea," I say. "When Judy was first diagnosed with breast cancer, it was already stage four. They only gave her six months to live. Every day, I was afraid to see her because I was afraid she would be worse than the day before. I didn't eat. I hardly slept. When 6 months rolled around, I thought she would die at any moment. But she didn't. Over time, things got better. It's been over two years, and she's still alive. I'm not trying to say everything's fine, cause it's not. I just want to say it gets better. There's still hope."

Diego doesn't say anything. I can't tell if he's thinking about what I said or lost in some other thought.

I change the subject. "How does your family feel about it?"

Diego looks up at me. This time, there's a glimmer of guilt in his eyes. "They don't know yet. I haven't told anybody. I don't want them to get their hopes up for nothing. They already have enough to worry about."

I don't know what he means, so I let him continue.

Diego looks down at his mule. "Mary is getting sicker. A lot sicker. She's been throwing up for almost a week. Diarrhea too. My dad thinks she needs antibiotics, but they cost a fortune. Even with my guard money, we don't have enough. We're trying to save up." He sighs and leans on the pommel. "They've already accepted that my mom is gone. If she's not there tomorrow, it's like she dies all over again. They can't handle that, especially not Mary."

"Diego, if you guys need the money I cou—"

Diego gives me a sharp look. "No. Don't worry about it." He blows out air through his puffed lips. "We'll figure something out. Tick has been showing me some tricks." He shrugs. "Who knows, maybe I'll rank first and get promoted."

"You think you have a shot?" I don't mean to sound doubtful, but even with my demon abilities, my chances are slim. Diego would need a miracle.

He sighs. "I don't know. Probably not." I watch as hopelessness consumes his demeanor once again. "But what choice do I have?"

"You could let us help. I'm sure Lynn and Velma wouldn't min—"

"No!" Diego shakes his head. "My dad wouldn't want that. Besides, Velma's family has their own problems. I don't want to put this on them."

I wonder what he means, but I don't ask. "Are you going to wait for the convoy tomorrow?"

"Yeah."

326

"Alone?"

"Yeah."

"I can go with you if you want," I offer. "So you have someone to talk to while you wait."

Diego nods. "Okay. That'd be cool." He lifts his head and smiles. "Thanks, dude."

"Do you think Tick will mind us being gone?"

Diego shakes his head. "I already asked him yesterday. He said it's okay."

"When should we leave?" I ask.

"I'll wake you up in the morning," Diego says. "I probably won't sleep anyway. We leave at dawn."

Chapter 24

Matt

A cool morning breeze sweeps across the flats. It's not cold, but Diego shoves his hands deeper in his pockets. He's wearing a gray hoodie over his training uniform. He shifts his weight and exhales unnecessarily loud, never taking his eyes off the archway.

The sun is already a foot in the sky. The convoy should've arrived an hour ago. We stand a stone's throw away from the outer wall, gazing hopelessly through the archway at the beyond. The empty road is spotted with puddles from last night's rain. Behind us, workers already till the fields in the distance.

Diego shifts his weight and crosses his arms across his chest. The longer we wait, the more restless he becomes. I don't have to read his mind to know he's freaking out.

"Do you think something happened?" Diego asks. "Did we get the wrong day?"

"I bet they're just late. They'll come," I assure him.

Diego's brow knits tighter together. "They better." he sighs. He looks up from the wall. "You don't have to stay if you don't want to. If you hurry, you might make breakfast."

By now, everyone is probably done eating. Pretty soon, the cafeteria will close. But I can't leave Diego here. No one should have to face this alone. I shake my head. "I'm fine. I'll stay a little longer."

Diego turns back to the wall and holds his hand over his eyes to shield the sun. He peers through the archway into the dimly lit forest. Another few seconds tick by. Diego drops his arms with frustration. "Dude, I can't take it. Where the freak are they?" He sits down next to me on the side of the road. "Ask me something. I need a distraction."

"Okay. If you burped in a bag, how much space would it take up?"

Diego half laughs, half cringes. "What the freak? That's disgusting." Then, he starts to think.

It's good to see him smile, even for a fleeting moment. "Don't answer that. I don't want to know," I say. "For real this time: what do you miss most about the real world?"

Diego doesn't hesitate. "The noise. I miss the noise."

I suppress a laugh. "The noise? Seriously?"

"Yeah, dude. In LA, there's always noise. Cars, music, babies crying, cats fighting, you name it. There's always something in the streets to listen to. But here, it's so quiet at night. It's hard to sleep."

I nod. "I miss refrigerators. I would give anything for a bowl of cereal and milk right now. Cinnamon Toast Crunch or maybe Fruity Pebbles."

Diego cracks a smile. "I miss ice-cream… and milkshakes." His smile slowly droops. "There was an ice cream shop down the street from my house. My mom used to take me and Mary every Friday after school. We would just eat and talk about our day. Even if I got into fights at school, she would take us. She never missed a week. No one else's mom ever did that. Not in my neighborhood, anyway. She was the best." He lets out another loud sigh. "I miss her."

Sand crunches behind us to the rhythm of footsteps. They're soft, quiet footsteps. I turn and find Velma walking down the road. She's almost to us.

Diego jumps to his feet. "Velma... What are you doing here?"

She wraps her arms around him and buries her black bangs in his neck. "You don't have to say anything. Tick told me what happened. I just want to be here for you."

"It's already been an hour—"

"She'll come." Velma cuts him off, talking over his shoulder. "Any minute, they'll come."

They hug for a long time as I stand alone on the road. Eventually, they transition to a seated hug. Velma closes her eyes and rests her head on his shoulder. They don't talk. They just sit. Her presence is all Diego needs. He rests his head on top of hers and closes his eyes.

I should let them be alone. I start backing away. "Hey, Diego, I'm going to go grab some breakfast. I'll wait for you back at the guard tower." Diego acknowledges with a wave of his hand.

I turn and head towards the city. I only take five steps before I hear it: the deep grinding of a semi-truck engine. I spin around and peer through the archway. Sure enough, a white semi-truck is visible at the end of the road. And another one behind that.

Diego is on his feet, teeth and hands clenched. Velma has her arm around his waist. She watches his expression with a nervousness of her own.

Brakes squeal as the trucks slow to a crawl. When they approach the wall, their engines fall silent. The trucks coast through the archway single-file and slowly roll past us. Diego sprints after the truck like a dog after the mailman. I jog after him.

As soon as the nearest truck stops, the rear door slides up into the ceiling. A guardsman immediately jumps out and begins helping down the refugees. From my view on the ground, I can't see very deep into the truck. The faces appear just before they descend. Diego stares with wide eyes.

The guard helps down a middle-aged white woman. Then, a family descends. A tall black man with long bushy hair climbs out. A skinny Vietnamese man hops down next and accepts a toddler from his wife. Two children climb down after them. With each person, my heart beats faster. With each refugee, the odds look worse and worse. *What are the odds she's the last one off the truck?*

After helping one last woman, the guardsman abandons the truck and begins giving instructions to the refugees.

"Excuse me?" Velma calls out to the guardsman. "Are there any refugees on the other trucks?"

The man shakes his head. "Just supplies." He resumes his instructions to the refugees. I wait for another head to appear between the rows of seats, but no one comes. I can't believe it. *She didn't make it!*

Diego is still staring at the truck. He waits like a statue for his mother to appear. Velma is speechless as well. Then, something scapes on the metal floor of the truck. I turn just as a head appears. It's a man. He utters a swear word and lugs a giant suitcase after him. He gives us a weird look before following the others to the front of the truck.

Diego climbs into the back of the truck and peers inside. He hops back down, wearing a mask of defeat. With the back of his wrist, he wipes angrily at the tears in his eyes. "C'mon. Let's go."

Velma tries to give him a hug, but Diego shrugs her off.

"Hey!" I say. "She could still be out there. Don't give up so easily."

Diego stops in his tracks and looks between Velma and I. "She's gone, okay. I have to accept it." Something in him changes, and his eyes are a bubbling tide pool. "We never even had a funeral." The tears roll down his cheeks. "I never got to say goodbye."

"Where are we going?" Diego asks.

Velma leads us off the main road into an alley. "Just c'mon. We're almost there." The alley deposits us on a larger road. I can hear the sound of laughter and boisterous conversation.

"Here we are!" Velma exclaims. She stops in front of a stone building with swinging double doors. Two large windows give me a view of the inside. The building is dimly lit with a long wooden bar down the middle and several small tables scattered throughout. Two large barrels rest on top of the bar. An old wooden sign hangs by a chain above the doors. It reads: BOB'S BREW.

"You brought me to a bar?" Diego doesn't try to hide his disappointment.

"Not just any bar," Velma insists. "Bob's Brew! It's a guardsman bar!"

I look through the window, and sure enough, the three men at the nearest table are in uniform.

"Excuse me." A man mumbles as he walks around us and into the bar. He isn't wearing a uniform, but his bulky biceps are all the evidence I need.

"Besides…" Velma points to a small flier in the corner of the window. In bold black ink, it reads: **New Customers Drink Free!**

"Fine, you convinced me," Diego says. His previous hesitation is gone.

"Me too," Lynn chimes to my surprise.

"Count me in," Klinton says.

Velma pushes through the double doors, and we follow her inside. A large, jolly man greets us from behind the bar. Saying he has a beer belly would be an understatement. He's the first obese person I've seen in Cavernum. He looks like an oversized Santa with dirty blonde facial hair.

"Welcome, little friends! Come to try the amber nectar, have you?" He gives us a homely smile and leans on the bar for support. I have a feeling he's already had a few beers himself.

"It's our first time here," Velma says. "New customers drink free, right?"

"Only if you promise to come back!" Santa bursts into laughter, spewing spit like a spray can.

"We'll both take a beer." Velma says, pointing between herself and Diego.

"Coming right up!" Santa grabs a mug and holds it under the tap of a large barrel. A frothy orange liquid fills the mugs to the brim. Santa slaps each glass down on the counter and points at Lynn. "And for you, pretty lady?"

Lynn thinks for a moment. "Do you have a lemon, ginger beer?"

"Pfft." Santa rears back as if it's the worst thing he's ever heard. He slaps his hand against the barrel. "Listen up, missy. The only beer here is my special brew. So what'll it be?"

Lynn frowns. Her bottom lip tucks slightly under her upper lip. "Are you Bob?"

"Sure am. The one and only."

"Just the beer, I guess," Lynn sighs.

"And you?" Bob asks, pointing at Klinton.

"Same as them."

And now the moment I've dreaded. Bob looks at me expectantly.

"I'll just have a water," I say the phrase quickly, like ripping off a bandaid.

Bob blinks and takes a step back. "You have the opportunity to drink the Lord's sweet brew at no cost of your own, and you choose to drink nature's piss. That vile liquid—"

"Just give him the water!" Velma says.

Bob puffs out his chest like a startled hen. "Fine. It's your funeral." He pumps a metal crank, and a stream of water trickles from a rusty spigot. He fills a mug and hands it to me across the bar.

Velma picks a small rectangular table near the back of the bar. I sit next to Lynn and across from Diego and Velma. Klinton takes a seat on the edge. As soon as we're seated, Diego is gulping his beer. "Hmmm, not bad."

I study my glass of water. Large flakes of something white float circles around the glass. Even worse, the water has a faint green tint.

Lynn is eyeing my water too. "Hey, Matt, I wouldn't drink the water here. Ring water is a little…" She lets the sentence hang in the air.

"You can say it," Velma says. "It's dirty. It's unclean. I won't take offense. That's why we drink so much beer. The alcohol kills the germs."

I push the mug into the center of the table. I'm not that thirsty anyways. "What about the water we drink at the guard tower?"

Velma rolls her eyes. "Oh, I can promise you it's clean. Heaven forbid one of their precious guards fall ill."

I glance at Diego, wondering how he's feeling about all this. He stares at the table and takes another gulp of the beer.

"Why don't you drink beer?" Klinton asks me. "Do you not like the taste?"

I shrug. "I'm not sure. I've never tried it."

"What?" Velma cries. "Not even once?"

Lynn and Klinton look equally shocked.

"In America, you have to be 21. It's the law."

"What a stupid law," Velma mumbles.

I want to argue with her but decide it's not worth it. Cavernum obviously isn't concerned with the health of the public.

Lynn watches me with a curious look in her eye. "If it's not the taste, then what is it?"

I sigh. I might as well tell them. "My dad—or not really my dad—he was Judy's husband. He died before she adopted me. Anyway, he was an alcoholic. One night he got drunk and tried to drive home. He slid off a bridge and drowned."

"Matt, I'm so sorry," Lynn starts.

I wave it off. "I never knew him. But it crushed my mom. She made me promise to never drink, and I don't plan to."

"I can respect that," Velma says, taking a swig of her beer.

Lynn nods her agreement. She stares at her glass in thought. She's barely touched it.

"What does it taste like anyway?" I ask.

Diego swirls the beer in his mug. It's almost empty. "Every beer is a little different. The first time it tastes nasty. It's bitter and kinda sour. Almost like puke. But eventually, you get used to it. This one's actually pretty good."

Klinton pipes up. "It's kinda sweet like molasses. It's hard to describe if you've never tried it." He takes a sip from his mug. "I can't believe we graduate on Sunday. It's kinda sad. We'll all be going our separate ways."

It is sad. I can't remember the last time I had friends like these. The notion of leaving them hurts more than I thought it would.

"We could end up working together, right?" I think aloud. "How often does that happen?"

"Hardly ever," Lynn says. "It's rare for a zone to have two openings. We might be in the same district, but we won't see each other very often."

"I better get a good trainer," Velma says. "I'll lose it if he's some sexist old fart."

Klinton wears an excited smile. "My brother is going to be a trainer for the communications bunker. He'll get paired with a dry-blood, so there's a good chance I'll be with him."

"That would be wild," I say. "When will we find out who our trainers are?" I look to Lynn as the expert on the subject.

"We'll know everything by tomorrow." Her expression is flat and factual. "They'll announce it directly after the final evaluation."

It's hard to imagine. In a week, I'll be working in my new career. It doesn't feel real, as if I'm living a stranger's life. I always imagined I'd have years of college and medical school to complete. Instead, I'm about to graduate from a magical police force and work as a guard for some deranged king. It sounds ludicrous.

"I'm going to miss you guys," Klinton admits. "Promise me we'll still hang out on our days off."

"We better. You guys are all I have," I say.

Velma and Diego echo my response. Lynn says nothing. She just stares at her glass.

Velma notices it too. "Hey! There's no need to get all sappy yet. We still have tomorrow night. It's supposed to be the party of a life-time."

Tomorrow night is the graduation party. I've heard people raving about it all day, but I don't get what all the hype is about? There's no technology in the sanctuary. A party without music is like a cheeseless quesadilla.

"What's so special about this party, anyways?" Diego grumbles. "What is there to do here after dark?"

"What do you mean, there's plenty of fun things to do," I insist. "We could play hide and seek… or we could tell scary stories around the campfire."

Velma catches on. "Maybe we'll have a poetry reading or make a massage train?"

"On a serious note," I say "I bet it's in the trench. It's the only place with enough light."

Klinton's eyes light up with excitement. "Maybe they'll heat the lake, and we can go swimming. That would be pretty cool."

A smile twitches at the corner of Velma's lips. "Maybe they'll bring in a caged feeder, and we'll take turns poking it with a stick." The image forces smiles around the table. Except for Diego. His face remains uncomfortably grim.

"Hey, Klinton," I say. "Your brother is in the guard. Did he ever say anything about the party?"

"He never mentioned it. He's not the type to tell a secret."

Lynn looks around and then leans in as if she's about to share a juicy rumor. "If you really want to know, the party is in the beyond," she states matter-of-factly.

Everyone stares at Lynn as if she said the party was on the moon. Velma laughs. "You're kidding, right?"

Lynn looks a little offended. "No, I'm serious. We ride the convoy trucks into the forest, and they play music from the beyond. They bring a bunch of palace wine too."

"Palace wine?" Diego frowns. "Who pays for that?"

"We do," Lynn says. "The entrance fee is 200 bars a person. They subtract it from our next pay."

Diego wrinkles his face in disgust. "What a ripoff. If I wanted a crappy DJ, I'd go back to LA."

Klinton doesn't look very excited either. "Who told you all that?"

Lynn tenses defensively. "I know a few officers from the palace. They told me about it."

My thoughts turn back to that night at the power plant—at Hogrum. The feeder with the tattoos. The lightning. The pain. I don't want to relive it. "Won't the music attract feeders?" I ask. "Isn't that dangerous?"

"There'll be guards there too," Lynn assures me. "A feeder would be stupid to try anything."

"I don't know," Diego shrugs. "That's what they thought about Lycon."

"I'm with Diego," I admit.

"Really?" Velma gripes, her voice soaked with frustration. "We're guards for God's sake." Velma picks up her glass and then sets it down again. "This is why they don't tell us about the party. They know we'll all chicken out if they do."

"I'll go," Klinton says. "If I'm going to work in the bunker, I might as well get used to the beyond."

Velma looks hopefully at Lynn. "You're coming too, right?"

Lynn scrunches her nose in thought. She looks up at me. "Is the music worth it? I've heard they have sounds you can't make with an instrument."

I smile. "That would be Dubstep. There's definitely no instrument like it. I would love to see your face when you first hear it."

"Why? Is it that good?" Lynn asks.

I tilt my head from side to side. "Mhhh. I wouldn't really use the word good. More like unique. Imagine putting an orchestra through a blender."

They give me blank stares. I always forget they don't have electronics.

Diego sighs. "A blender is like a high-powered meat grinder."

"An orchestra through a meat grinder?" Velma questions. "Is that supposed to make sense?"

"It will when you hear it," I say.

"Is Dubstep the most popular music?" Lynn asks.

I fail to hold back a laugh. "Not exactly. There's such a variety, it's hard to say which is most popular. There's hip-hop, pop, reggae, indie, rock, rap... the list goes on and on."

Diego cracks a quick smile. "You're going to love rap."

With each genre, Lynn's smile blossoms even bigger. It grows from a bud to a rose at full bloom. "Alright, you convinced me. I'll go," She finally decides.

Klinton looks to me expectantly. "What about you, Matt?"

It's a no brainer. The party is outside the wall. I can finally call Judy on my phone. Feeders or not, I'd be a fool to say no.

"I'm in."

Diego folds his arms across his chest. "You guys go without me."

Velma stares at Diego with wide, pleading eyes. "C'mon Diego. You'll be the only one missing out."

He lifts his empty mug and peers inside before setting it back down. "I'm just not feeling it." After what happened to his mom, no one can blame him. He's been through a lot. But I know it's more than that. He doesn't want to pay the entrance fee. He's staying home so his sister can get her antibiotics.

"Need a refill?" A voice booms from behind me. It's Bob. He holds a pitcher of beer in his hand.

"Yes, sir." Diego starts to lift his mug but stops when he meets Velma's judging gaze. Her eyes seem to say. 'Careful, we have evaluations tomorrow.'

He holds up a finger. "Last one. I promise." Velma says nothing, which Diego takes as permission. He lifts his mug, and Bob fills it to the brim.

Lynn sits quietly, staring off into the corner of the bar. I follow her eyes and find a dusty brown sheet covering some kind of furniture.

The shape looks familiar. I motion towards the dusty cloth. "Hey Bob, is that a piano over there?"

"Sure is. That little music maker cost my pop a fortune." Bob waddles over to the corner and rips the sheet off the piano. Dust bunnies are launched airborne like confetti. The piano itself is a simple brown color with pale yellow keys. It looks old but undamaged. "You know how to play?" Bob asks.

I point at Lynn. "No, but she does."

Lynn eyes the piano how a starved dog eyes a smoked ham. "Would you mind if I play a song?"

"Be my guest," Bob bellows. "No one's played it since Pop died last year. He tried to teach me, but I never got the hang of it. My heart was always in the brew."

Lynn takes a timid seat on the piano bench. It creaks surprisingly loud for such a small weight. She tiptoes her fingers down the keys testing each one. "What should I play?"

"Play your favorite," I suggest.

Lynn faces the piano and bows her head. Her hair falls down around her face, but Lynn doesn't mind. She lifts her middle finger and lets it drift gently down on the keys. She plays the same key over and over, setting a tempo for herself. Then, she layers on a series of chords while maintaining the same steady beat with her middle finger. The music is both sad and peaceful. It's nothing fancy, but the melody is captivating. My mind follows along with the tune, trying to predict the next note.

The bar is silent. Everyone watches the girl at the piano. Passersby congregate outside the door to listen. Suddenly, Lynn adds a third layer to the music. In between chords, her fingers flutter over the keys like a hummingbird. Her body, a wind chime in a storm, sways with the music. I'm mesmerized, as much by her as I am by the music. Her fingers fall effortlessly over the notes without error. My thoughts slow, and all I hear is the melody. It soaks into my mind, filling the cracks with a sense of calm.

Then, ever so slowly, the layers fall away, and the chords stop. Lynn is left tapping that same key slower and slower. Finally, she holds it down until the ringing stops.

Amazing! I clap as the rest of the bar stomps their feet. Lynn's face turns red. She does a quick curtsy and returns to her seat.

"Bravo!" A voice calls from the doorway. Tick steps into the bar with two other men. "If it isn't my favorite students. Do you mind if I join you for a minute?" he asks.

"Please." Lynn motions to the empty chair on the end.

Tick turns to his buddies. "Save me a seat, I'll be right over." Tick sits down and takes one look at Diego's empty mug. He grows still. The very fact that Diego is here is evidence that his mom isn't. "I'm sorry," Tick mumbles. "I hoped it would be different."

Diego doesn't look him in the eye. "Thanks," he breathes quietly.

Tick frowns. "Well, I just want to wish you all luck tomorrow. I want you to know I'll be rooting for you five. I'm going to miss you guys after graduation."

"Will you be training again next year?" Lynn asks.

"Actually, no. I've been hired to work in the palace as a guard for the royal family."

Lynn snorts as she sips from her mug. Unlike the stew incident, she manages not to inhale the beer. "You'll have to tell the princess hello for me."

"I will," Tick says. "If one of you ranks first, we might see a lot of each other. Anyway, I should get back to my friends. There'll be plenty of time for talking at the graduation party tomorrow night." He pauses. "You're all coming, I assume?"

We grow quiet. "Is it really in the beyond?" Velma blurts.

Tick's eyes widen to the size of silver coins. He glances around the bar and leans in closer. "Who told you that?" He doesn't seem upset, just surprised.

Diego takes that as a 'yes' to Velma's questions. "Is it safe?"

Tick exhales and rests his elbows on the table. "Listen, we're going to have 30 guards there for security. I'll be there too. I promise I won't let anything happen to you guys. Also, the party will be by the bunker. They'll be keeping watch, and if anything does happen, we'll be a short run from the wall. It won't be any more dangerous than our field trip was. I promise."

No one speaks. Our concerns have been met.

Tick stands up straight. He sets his eyes on Diego. "If you guys come, I'll teach you more self-dominion. You can change your eye color, hair color, skin pigment, bigger muscles…" His lips curl in a wily smile. "Anything you want." He stands before we can respond and starts toward his friends. "Don't drink too much. I'll see you tomorrow."

Velma faces Diego, a hopeful grin on her face. "You're coming, right? There's no way you'll pass that up."

Diego doesn't meet her eye. He holds his now empty glass in his hand.

"Please, Diego," Velma begs. "It won't be the same without you."

"I'm not going," Diego mutters. "I'm sorry. Please, let it go."

Bob's voice cuts through tension. "Last call for brew! We're closing in 5, but you can bet your britches there'll be more brew tomorrow."

"Let's go," Velma grumbles. "We have a big day tomorrow."

Tomorrow, I fight for my spot in the palace.

Tomorrow, I fight for Judy.

Chapter 25

Rose

"Antai! Where are you taking me?" I demand.

He leads me by the hand directly through the cornfield. I duck my head and trudge through the leaves behind him. There's no moon out tonight, and I can hardly see where I'm stepping. A leaf slaps me in the face. Another pokes my eye.

"Antai?"

Antai doesn't look up from the ground. I can see the hint of a smile on the corner of his lips. "It's not a surprise if I tell you everything. But if it makes you feel better, we're almost there." He seems to know exactly where he's going. I swear he's leading us into the tallest section of corn. I try to follow close behind to avoid getting slapped again by the leaves. After a few seconds, he turns around excitedly. "Alright, close your eyes."

I oblige, and Antai scurries away, his footsteps crunching over dead corn leaves. "You better not leave me," I call out.

"Leave you for who?" Antai laughs.

"You know what I mean."

I hear him rusting around and then the strike of a match, the glow of which turns my eyelids from black to red. After several seconds, I hear him approach me once again. He takes my hand. "Okay, you can open them."

I open my eyes and suck in a breath. "Antai!" I'm standing at a small clearing in the cornfield. It's barely wide enough to fit a blanket laid out for the two of us. Three small candles provide just enough light to see a picnic basket and some small pillows.

"I figured it's time we have a real date," Antai grins. "No one should be able to see the candlelight through the corn. We finally have some privacy."

"Oh, thank you, thank you!" I jump and wrap my legs around Antai's waist. He catches me with ease and supports me with his hands under my thighs. The candlelight only amplifies his features. I run my hands through his dark hair and interlock my fingers behind his head. Next thing I know, his lips are on mine. He pulls me even closer and takes my bottom lip between his teeth.

My heart races, and I can't seem to catch my breath. I lift my chin, and his lips fall instinctively on my neck, sending shivers of pleasure down my spine. His lips, soft and warm, crawl down the nape of my neck and over my collarbone. My heart races faster, the lower he goes. His abs tense under my thighs, awaking a hunger deep within me. I pull him tight until our bodies are indiscernible.

Finally, Antai comes up for air. His eyes lock with mine. Two brown gems filled with longing and desire. His heavy breathing tells me he didn't pull away out of boredom. He doesn't want us doing something we'll regret. He's always the responsible one.

"Wow," he laughs.

"Wow," I agree. My face stretches unusually wide under my smile, but I can't make it stop. I know I'm blushing uncontrollably.

Antai sets me down, flustered and enthralled, next to the blanket and reaches for the picnic basket. "I hope you don't mind, I brought a midnight snack. I figured it's been a while since you've had a proper dessert."

He hands me a plate with a generous serving of chocolate cake. I can see several layers of chocolate and cream and a red drizzle on top—maybe raspberry or strawberry. "It's cheesecake," Antai says. "The chefs made it this morning."

"Seriously, Antai, this is too much! You're too good to me."

Antai knows he's outdone himself. He only smiles and hands me a fork. "For you, my queen."

I take a bite. "Mhhhhh!" It's a delicate cheesecake with a crumb base, a layer of fudge, raspberry syrup, and flakes of something nutty—probably almonds. It's perfection! I take another bite. "Mhhhhh."

Antai laughs.

"What?"

"Oh, nothing." He grins. "I'm just glad to know you're enjoying it." He takes a bite of his own cake and exaggerates a loud moan. "Mhhhh."

I blush. "It's been awhile, alright. I forgot how good this stuff is."

"No need to be embarrassed," Antai says. "I just wish you enjoyed kissing me that much." He takes a seat on the blanket.

"If you tasted like this I definitely would." He smiles to tell me he knows I'm joking. I take a seat on the blanket, and Antai sits next to me so that our hips are touching. We eat slowly, enjoying the sounds of crickets and the rustle of leaves.

Despite the serenity, my mind is in chaos. I don't want to ruin the mood, but I ask anyway. "Any news about Nevela?"

Antai shakes his head. "Nothing yet. There hasn't been much equalist activity lately. We tried another search of the tunnels, but we haven't found anything yet. I'm sorry, Rose."

I expected as much, but it hurts to hear aloud.

Antai tries to get my mind off it. "How do you feel about tomorrow? Nervous?"

"I don't know. I'm just excited for this whole thing to be over."

"Think about it, Rose. After tomorrow you'll be back in your room in that ridiculously huge bed of yours. I'll be able to see you every night. You won't have to keep anything a secret, and the world will know how badass you are."

"But am I badass?" I doubt.

Antai smiles the most assuring smile. "Trust me. You have the baddest of asses."

I let myself giggle. "Okay, but that's only if I win. What if I don't?" That thought has been haunting me all day.

"I highly doubt that's going to happen," Antai starts. "But if you don't rank first, there are several openings in my quadrant. I could make sure you're stationed close to me. It wouldn't be the end of the world."

The thought makes me feel a little better. "Maybe someday we'll be guardians together?" I say. "That would be cool."

Antai sits up and narrows his eyebrows at me. "Did I just hear the sole heir to the Cavernic throne say cool?"

I laugh. "I guess you did."

Antai makes a tsssk noise and shakes his head in mock disapproval. "Those lowlife recruits are really rubbing off on you. Next thing I know you'll be drinking beer straight from the keg."

"Maybe I will," I say.

Antai leans back and tucks his hand behind his head. "That would be cool. You and I on the council. Think of all the good we could do. All we need is a tragic accident to befall Chancellor Gwenevere." He flashes me another smile that makes my heart flutter.

We lay there in silence for a while, staring up at the stars. Now that I have the candlelight, I can see him much better. He's not wearing his typical uniform. Just black combat pants and a black tee. He doesn't have his gun with him, but something else is strapped to his waist.

"An Adamic blade!" I say. "How long have you had it?"

Antai shrugs. "About a week. The king didn't waste any time. He opened up the vault, and each commander picked out his own."

"Can I see it?"

Antai removes it from the sheathe. Pinching the flat of the blade, he extends the handle toward me. It's heavier than I expected. The silver blade is 1 ½ feet long with a golden handle.

"It suits you," I say. *Simple and deadly.* I give the blade a gentle swing. "Antai Elsborne, slayer of demons."

"Hardly," Antai scoffs. I know what he's thinking. He doesn't have a soul-anchor. His mind is ripe for the taking.

His face darkens as I hand back the blade. "The king is really worried, Rose. He's been locked in his study all week. I've never seen him like this."

I frown. "Any news about The Lost Library?"

"The king has been prying Titan for more information, but he hasn't had any luck. He's preparing for the worst." Antai pauses for a moment. "Are you planning on going to the graduation party?"

"I don't know yet," I lie. "Why?"

"I don't think you should go," Antai says. When he sees my glare, he holds up his hands. "Look. I'm not going to tell you what to do. I made that mistake once already. But at least listen to my reasoning. Your chambers have already been broken into twice. They're obviously after you. If anyone knows that you'll be there, it would be the perfect opportunity to strike. Not to mention it's outside the wall. The feeder threat is worse than ever. Sure, they'll be guards there, but what if there's a demon? What if they have Adamic armor?"

"If you're so worried, why don't you come? You have a blade now."

Antai shakes his head. "That's Commander Chyve's jurisdiction. I can't just invite myself. I'm not supposed to leave my quadrant."

"Then lend your blade to Tick. He can keep us safe."

Antai grumbles to himself. "I'm just saying you should think about it. I really don't think it's safe, Rose. You may be a guardsman now, but you're still the princess. Your life matters to more than just me." He lays back and stares at the stars.

"I know, I'll give it lots of thought, you have my word." I set down my plate and cuddle next to Antai. I'm glad it didn't turn into a full-blown fight, but I can't shake the feeling that he's right. Last time Antai warned me, I didn't listen. As a result, I fell from the palace wall as flames devoured my flesh. I could've died.

I hope this time is different.

Velma weaves another strand of my hair into the growing braid. "You really can't braid your own hair?" She asks. "How did you get ready in the morning?"

She sits on the edge of my bed, and I sit at her knees on the floor. "I suppose I never needed to. The other maids would always help me," I say. It's not a complete lie this time.

Tick shouts from the hallway outside our door. "Everyone upstairs and get an amulet! We're leaving in 10 minutes!" Following his announcement is the thunderous roar of footsteps as recruits race for the stairwell. I hear Velma exhale behind me.

"Nervous?" I ask.

"I don't know how I feel," she breathes. "As long as I don't have to fight you, I'll be happy. In fact, there are a few people I'd love to take a crack at."

I have a feeling I know who. Crasilda has given her a hard time since the first day of training.

"That should do it." Velma tucks the end of my braid into a hair tie and lets it fall against my neck. It's not very fancy—a typical three strand braid—but it will keep my hair out of my eyes.

"Thanks, Velma. I owe you."

"Don't sweat it." Velma climbs to her feet and holds the door open for me. "Let's go. We're gonna be late."

"You go ahead," I say. "I have to take care of something first."

Velma raises her eyebrows at me. When I don't explain, she shrugs. "Okay, see you at the armory." The door closes behind her, and I'm alone in the room.

I reach my hand into my bra and remove my soul-anchor. I cup it in my hands and admire its beauty. The symbols are perfectly crafted. I wonder how long it took my dad to make it. Would he be proud of me now? Would he want me to compete without it? My gut tells me he would, but I wish I could hear him say it.

I slip my soul-anchor through the split seam of my mattress. I cut the hole with a dagger last night. It's the safest place I could think of. This way, even if someone rummages through my things, they won't find the amulet by mistake. Now, I'm like everybody else. If I win today, it'll be by merit and merit alone.

Satisfied, I walk over to my dresser and pull open the second drawer. All I need now is my mouth guard. The door behind me creaks open slowly. Someone steps into the room and gently closes the door with a click. The footsteps are soft and gentle. Velma must have forgotten something.

"Just grabbing one last thing," I call out.

I grab my mouthguard and turn around. My heart drops. Vyle stands next to my bed, a silver amplifier draped from his neck. "Hello, Lynn."

Before I have time to react, the door creaks open again. This time, Zander and Croyd step inside. Each of them displays an amplifier of their own. Panic rises within me. It's three against one. There's nowhere for me to run. My soul-anchor is hidden in the bed right next to Vyle. Without it, I'm defenseless. I put on a smile and hope my instincts are wrong. "Hello, boys. Can I help you?"

"Enough of the games," Vyle barks. "I know you've been cheating. Where did you get it?" He takes a step closer.

"Get what?"

"Don't play dumb. The soul-anchor. Did you steal it from the palace? Do you work for the equalists? You had to get it from somewhere?"

Vyle watches me with a smug smile. It's the kind of look you give a little kid when you've caught them in their lies. I can't believe it. He actually thinks I'm a criminal. He thinks I'm the bad guy. His hand stays on his amulet the entire time. He's afraid. He brought his pack of dogs because he doesn't think he can take me on his own.

"Give us the anchor, and we won't hurt you." Vyle offers so generously.

It takes all my effort not to glance toward my mattress. I run through my options, which aren't many. Even if I could grab hold of Vyle's amulet, I can't fight off all three of them at once. Right now, playing dumb may be my only option. "Whatever problem you have with me, take it up with Tick. Now, if you'll excuse me..."

I take a step towards the door. For a second, it looks like he's going to let me leave. Then, Vyle turns to Zander and Croyd. "Hold her down." They both reach for their amulets.

The air in front of me stiffens. A scream, shrill and desperate, escapes me as I'm thrust backward into the wall. My skull cracks against the stone, and specks of light dance in the air around me. If it weren't for the pressure pinning me against the wall, I would collapse to the floor. The pressure grows, squeezing my arms and legs against the stone wall. I can't lift my head. I can't even wiggle my fingers. It feels as though I'm being buried alive by invisible soil.

Hysteria clouds any inkling of judgment I have left. I scream at the top of my lungs. "Tiiick! Maaatt! Hel—"

Vyle raises his hand, and a lump of invisible pressure lodges itself inside my mouth. I try to scream, but the only sound I make is an unintelligible gargle. I'm being gagged by dominion.

Vyle sneers. "No one is coming to save you, Lynn. You'll have to save yourself. Go ahead. Use that amulet of yours."

The lump in my throat dissolves once again, leaving me free to speak. I let my hysteria aid my act. "Please, let me go! I swear on the holy prophets, I don't know what you're talking about!"

Vyle's murderous grin grows larger. "I figured you'd say that." He's glad I'm playing dumb. He wants an excuse to hurt me. "Maybe this will change your mind."

He raises his hand once again and closes his eyes. At first, I don't feel anything. When I try to draw in a breath, the air resists me. It's like trying to inhale water... or stone. My diaphragm contracts, but my lungs won't expand. Just when I think it can't get worse, the air is suctioned from my lungs. It whistles as it leaves my constricted throat. Then, everything is silent. Oddly silent. Terror drills into my chest.

I'm in a vacuum! I'm suffocating!

Almost immediately, my lungs begin to burn. In a matter of moments, it turns from uncomfortable to excruciating. I try to breathe with every fiber of my being, but my lungs remain empty. My chest heaves in vain. My lungs cramp with pain. Without my amulet, I'm as good as dead.

Vyle never takes his eyes off me. I can't find an ounce of sympathy in his pale, dead eyes.

He's going to kill me!

Vyle lowers his hand, and air rushes back into my lungs. Never has a breath of air tasted so sweet. Vyle takes a step closer, his confidence rising with my suffering. "C'mon, Lynn. I know you have it in you. Reach for your amulet. Give me the beating I deserve."

"I don't know what you're talking about." I gasp between breaths. "I don't have an amulet. I swear to God." I look towards the door. If only Matt would walk in... or Antai or Grandpa. Anyone!

"Fine. You asked for it." Vyle lifts his hand once again.

The world falls silent as the air around my head is sucked away. I try to hold my breath this time, but the pressure is too strong. It sucks the air right out of my mouth. Once again, my lungs seize and cramp. It's the most pain I've ever experienced. Even more than my burning arm. I desperately want to scream, but I can't. Nothing comes out of my open mouth. All my muscles tense. The only thing I hear is my heart pounding. I'm sure it'll burst at any moment. Darkness crawls at the edge of my vision until it consumes everything. My body goes numb. I feel like I'm floating.

I'm dying! I'm actually dying!

Finally, the air rushes back around me, and I suck it in as fast as I can. When my vision clears, I find myself on the floor. Zander and Croyd no longer hold me against the wall. They watch me with soft eyes and sympathetic faces. I try to sit up, but my body is weak. Instead, I curl into a ball, gasping like a dying fish.

Vyle stares at me with bloodlust in his eyes. His face is red with effort. He doesn't try to hide his frustration. "Next time, I won't stop. Do you hear me! I won't stop this time. This is your last chance to give me the soul-anchor."

He isn't doing this because he thinks it's right. He's doing it for himself. Exposing me as a cheater is his best shot at ranking first. He'll do anything to win.

"Go to hell!" I gasp. My head is cloudy, and it's all I can think to say. *But what if he does kill me? He's definitely capable. Maybe I should tell him after all.*

"Fine!" Vyle seethes. He grabs me by the shirt and tosses me against the wall like a rag doll. "Hold her up," he barks at his minions.

Croyd looks unsure. His forehead is wrinkled with worry. "But—"

"Just do it!" Vyle demands. "Now!"

They hesitantly obey, and once again, I'm pinned against the wall. Vyle raises his hand. "You brought this on yourself."

"Stop!" Croyd bursts. "You'll kill her. I don't think she has it."

Vyle whips his head towards Croyd and Zander, who each take a step back. "Fine." He walks up to me until his nose is inches from my face. "If you won't give it to me, I'll find it myself."

He puts his hands on my hips and lifts my shirt. His hands slither inside like a serpent seeking warmth. They slither their way up my waist, feeling for any sign of an amulet. I shake and kick against the invisible hands pinning me, but it's no use. I'm helpless. I'm powerless. Everywhere his fingers touch, I want to scratch off. I want to wiggle out of my skin and disappear. I hate him. I want him to die.

The smile he gives me makes my skin crawl. "Where did you hide it?" His fingers tiptoe up my rib cage, closer and closer to my chest. He's enjoying this. He wants to search me... to feel me. His hands are almost there now, tracing along the edge of my bra... sliding inside.

He won't stop! I realize. He'll search my whole body until he finds it—which he never will. I can't let this happen! I won't allow it!

"I'm the princess," I croak. The words are hardly a whisper, but Vyle hears. He retracts his hands as if burned by a hot pan. He steps back and stares into my eyes. I watch as recognition flickers over his face. He knows it's true. His jaw drops open as he realizes what he's done. He assaulted the princess—a crime punishable by death.

Vyle staggers back. He's speechless. He's horrified.

"What is it?" Zander asks. "Vyle, what's wrong? What'd she say?"

Without a word, Vyle turns and charges out of the room. Croyd and Zander give me one last confused look and follow him out the door, leaving me alone in my room. For several moments, I can't move. Finally, when they don't come back, I collapse to the floor. I don't resist as the tears begin to flow. I only sob for a few seconds. I can't let myself wallow in self-pity. Not today of all days.

C'mon, Rose! Get up! You're a princess! You don't have time to cry! You have to be strong. Make your parents proud!

With a whimper, I push myself to my feet and pick up my mouth guard from off the floor. I let my anger wash away the pain. With a deep breath, I push open the door and start for the armory. Within the hour, I'll be facing Vyle in a duel. I'll get my chance for revenge in the arena.

As I walk, my thoughts play on repeat in my head: *I'll kill him for what he did. I'll kill him for it.*

Chapter 26

Rose

"Are you sure you're okay?" Velma whispers. She sees me clutching my amplifier under my uniform. I know she's trying to be a good friend, but I really don't want to talk about it.

"I'm fine." I give her the best fake smile I can muster. I doubt it's very convincing, but she stops pestering me.

"We're almost there," Tick announces.

We march through the core in a double-file line. The royal plaza is just up ahead, but it's not our destination. We're going underneath —into the tunnels.

Tick stops and faces us. "Alright, kiddos. Watch your step." The street up ahead drops into a large staircase that descends underground. The staircase is wide enough to host a large crowd. It's the entrance to the royal arena. I've seen it many times before, but I've never gone inside until now. I scurry down the steps and into the mouth of the tunnel. At the base of the stairwell, the tunnel is barred by a large iron gate. Normally, the gate is locked, but today it's propped wide open. A guard stands at the entrance and nods to Tick.

We follow Tick through the gate, and the guard shuts it behind us with a click of the lock. *No turning back now.* The tunnel is lit by small torches secured to the wall. They must have been recently lit because they only burn for a few hours.

No one speaks as we march down the tunnel. We're all preoccupied with what's to come: violence and survival, victory or defeat.

Already, I can see the light at the end of the tunnel. The closer we get, the more nervous I become. This is where my future will be decided. If I want to go home, I have to win.

The tunnel opens, and I find myself gaping at the majesty of the arena. We're standing at the top of the audience section high above the arena pit. The entire arena is brightly illuminated by Adamic symbols. They glow like spotlights from the cavern ceiling.

Immediately, we descend the steps towards the arena. The audience section is merely a series of steps carved out of the grey, granite stone. Like a giant funnel, each row forms a circle around the arena center. Way down at the bottom of the cavern is the dueling pit. It's tiny compared to the rest of the cavern, a diameter of no more than 50 feet.

The audience is empty except for the very first row. There, a crowd of guard officials waits for us above the dueling pit. Antai is down there somewhere. Already, I feel a little calmer.

"Wow," Crasilda marvels. "This place makes the trench look like a wine cellar."

Tick turns back to face us, gesturing to either side like a tour guide. "There's over 100 rows of seating with a max capacity of 25,000. Back in the day, this place used to fit the entire sanctuary."

As we descend, I can see the arena with more clarity. The dueling pit is set deep into the granite floor. It's composed of a circular stone platform surrounded almost completely by water. Rocks, both large and small, are scattered across the platform. From this distance, they look like crumbs on a messy table.

The only ways into the dueling pit are two separate stairwells on opposite sides of the arena. A thin walkway stretches over the water, connecting each stairwell to the dueling platform. The surface of the water, filthy and opaque, falls a foot short of the platform surface. If someone were to fall in, they could easily climb back out.

Tick points to the dueling pit. "For safety reasons, the dueling pit is set much lower than the audience. The walls are ten feet tall."

"How deep is the water?" a recruit asks.

Tick furrows his thick eyebrows. "I'm not really sure. Definitely too deep to stand in."

As we approach the bottom row of seats, I find my grandpa seated among the guard officials. Antai is to his left, and General Kaynes, dressed in his usual silver robe, is seated to his right. Two dozen lieutenants line the row behind them.

Tick stops us on the third row and bows to Grandpa. The rest of us follow his example.

"Be seated," Grandpa commands.

The man seated directly behind Grandpa stands up. He has a petite nose and a thick mustache. It's Commander Noyan.

"Hello, everyone, and welcome to the final evaluation," he calmly announces. "I'm Commander Noyan, head of the royal guard. Throughout your training, you've each been assessed and ranked according to your various skills. Some of you may be quick with a pistol." Commander Noyan gives an obvious nod at Klinton. "Others might be fast on their feet." He nods at a lanky core-born whose name I still don't know.

"But you know what...?" He rears his head back and shouts. "None of that matters in the palace!" He smiles when he sees our confused faces.

"Speed is great for chasing a thief, but it won't do you any good when your enemy has an amulet. A pistol won't do you much good either. For a threat like that, you need dominion. That's why, today, we will be testing your mastery of dominion in a very practical sense.

Now, here's how today will work: each of you has been assigned two opponents of similar aptitude. You will duel twice and be ranked according to your performance. Just to be clear, your performance will be compared against all other duels. Just because you win both of your duels, it doesn't mean you'll rank higher than someone who only wins one. Their opponents may be more skilled than yours. Is that clear?

"Yes, sir!" we echo.

"Good. After the duels, I will have first choice at which of you will become a royal guard. The other officials will then have the option to fill their openings as they see fit. Even if you don't place first, it's in your favor to do your best. Some positions are more likely to be promoted than others. Any questions?"

Klinton raises his hand. "If we fall in the water, are we disqualified?"

"Let me ask you this," Commander Noyan says. "If an assassin falls in one of the royal fountains, is he disqualified?"

"No, sir," Klinton squeaks.

"Damn straight! Water may be one of his best weapons. The duel isn't over until your enemy is dead or subdued."

"What are the rules?" Velma asks.

"There's only one rule," Noyan bellows. "Stay in the arena. Other than that, anything goes. For your safety, we have referees around the arena who will intervene if your life is in danger. But be warned, you will get hurt. In case of any life-threatening injuries, we have medics and healers standing by." On cue, several girls in white skirts smile and wave. I count five of them.

Commander Noyan takes his seat behind Grandpa. "Let the dueling begin."

Tick stands up with a clipboard in hand. "When you hear your name, go straight into the arena: Langdon and Wekley!" I breathe a sigh of relief. The boys descend opposing staircases and face each other in the center of the arena. To my surprise, Antai follows them down. He must've volunteered himself as a referee. That way, when I duel Vyle, he can be there to make sure nothing happens to me.

"Begin!" Tick shouts.

I watch from the third row as Langdon unleashed a blast of fire that coats the other boy's torso. He immediately screams and falls to the floor. In seconds the match is over. Antai extinguishes the flames, but the damage is already done. Both of the boy's arms are charred and peeling.

The arena is silent. I can hear the boy whimper as Antai helps him up the stairs and into a healer's arms. The other boy returns quietly to his seat. I glance down at my arm. There's no scarring, but I remember the pain. My heart goes out to Wekley.

"Gregor and Klinton."

Klinton doesn't stand up. His odds are grim. Gregor has weak dominion, but Klinton is bloodless. He can't use dominion at all.

"I forfeit," Klinton shouts. I don't blame him after what I just witnessed. Fighting would have been foolish.

Tick jots it down and calls two more names. Already, I'm feeling nervous. Maybe an amplifier isn't enough. I'm not good enough to beat Vyle on my own. I don't want to end up like Wekley. Or worse.

I watch every fight closely, hoping to pick up on techniques. Some recruits play defense, waiting until their opponents overexert themselves. Others attack quickly, hoping to overwhelm their enemy. The most common outcome is forfeit. Match after match ends before it begins.

Except for Klinton, none of my friends have been chosen. It appears they're saving the best for last.

"Diego and Zander!" Tick calls.

"You've got this," Velma assures Diego. "Remember what Tick taught you."

"Kick his ass!" Matt adds. I can't help but smile.

Diego shimmies past the other spectators and descends the staircase into the arena. He squares up with Zander in the center of the platform and closes his eyes.

Then, I see it. Something glitters in Diego's hand. Except he's not holding anything. It's his actual hand that glitters. It's coated in a shiny, metallic substance. I watch as the metal seeps slowly up his arm. When the metal creeps above his elbow, it stops. Zander sees it too. His smug smile disappears.

"Begin!"

Diego holds up his metal fists and takes a step at Zander, who counters by spraying a wave of fire. Diego backpedals to avoid getting burned. His arms may be metal, but his head and body aren't fireproof. Diego charges again, but a wave of fire drives him back. Every time Diego makes a move to advance, Zander responds with a blast of fire. He's desperate to keep Diego at a distance. One punch from his metal fist could shatter Zander's skull.

"He's playing with you!" Croyd yells. "Use the rocks."

Zander bolts for the closest boulder. It's a knee tall, spherical chunk of granite. With the help of dominion, he picks it up in his arms and heaves it at Diego.

Diego sidesteps, evading the boulder by a hair's width. The boulder crashes into the ground behind him, sending tremors through the stadium. The largest boulders must weigh hundreds of pounds. If one were to hit Diego, it would all be over.

With a sweep of his hand, Zander sends rock shards hurtling at Diego, one after the other. They each clank off of Diego's metallics hands as he swats them away like pesky birds. In a single motion, Zander grabs hold of a massive slab of granite and, roaring like a caveman, does a spinning toss. This time, Diego holds his ground. He raises his hands, and the air shimmers. The granite slab crashes against his shield and falls at his feet with a thud.

Diego bends over and picks up the rock with both hands. Except for a few chips, the slab is mostly intact. It's three feet wide, roundish, and only an inch or two thick. Diego holds it like a shield in front of him and advances on Zander. Only his metal fingers, curled around the edge of the slab, are exposed.

Zander launches another rock, but it flies slower this time and ricochets harmlessly off Diego's shield. Zander is fatigued, and it shows. As Diego approaches, Zander blasts him with fire. The flames splash harmlessly against the stone shield. Each wave of fire is smaller than the last. Zander is now huffing and puffing. He's drenched in sweat and stumbles like a drunkard. Diego continues to advance, forcing Zander to the edge of the area. His back is mere feet from the water's edge.

Finally, Diego throws the granite slab at Zander, who raises a shield at the last second. The stone collides with the air only inches from Zander's face. Diego charges, pounding his iron fists against the shield. Diego swings his whole body with each punch, sending ripple after ripple. After a dozen blows, the shield gives, and Diego jabs at Zander's face. Zander barely has time to lift his arms in defense. Diego's fist collides with his forearm with an audible crack. Zander cries out and clutches his battered limb. Diego swings again.

This time Zander extends his hand. He screams as he throws his energy into one last desperate attack. A single flash of blue light crackles between them. Diego shudders and crumples to the floor. He lifts his head and tries to sit up, but Zander is quicker. He lifts his foot and stomps down on Diego's face.

I force myself to watch as the back of Diego's head slams into the floor. Blood streams from his flattened nose. It's bent to one side. Diego moans but doesn't move. Zander lifts his foot and stomps again.

"Enough!" Tick shouts. I can hear the disappointment in his voice. Zander cradles his arm and retreats back up the steps. With the help of a guard, Diego climbs woozily to his feet and ascends the staircase.

A medic waits for him at the top of the stairs. He inspects Diego's face for several seconds before placing both thumbs on either side of his disfigured nose. Diego squeals as the medic forces his nose to one side, setting the bones. It's swollen and bleeding, but otherwise, he has no major injuries. As soon as the medic leaves, Matt and Velma swarm him.

"Dude, where did you learn to go metal?" Matt exclaims. "You destroyed him."

"It doesn't matter," Diego sighs. "I didn't win."

"Hey," Velma interjects. "It's not just about winning. It's about showing them what you can do. You did awesome!"

"I guess," Diego mumbles.

Velma wraps her arms around him and walks him back to his seat. She whispers something in his ear, and a glimmer of a smile twitches in his face.

Tick calls two more names, and the boys hesitantly enter the arena. The match comes to a swift end as a recruit is pommeled by a boulder. Tick looks back at his list.

"Crasilda and Velma."

"Yesss!" Velma smiles and jumps to her feet. "Wish me luck." She gives Diego a quick kiss on the cheek before jogging down the steps. As soon as they're both in the arena, Tick gives the signal.

"Begin!"

Velma moves first. She backpedals to the side of the platform, keeping her eyes on Crasilda the entire time. She's only a step from the water's edge.

Crasilda still hasn't moved. She only widens her stance. The air shimmers around her hands, forming two small energy shields the size of dinner plates. As she lifts her hands to her chest, the shields move with them. It's a smart move on her part. Smaller shields conserve energy.

"Congratulations!" Crasilda speaks loud so that everyone can hear. "I heard about the baby."

The baby?

Velma's jaw drops open.

I glance at Diego. He glares down at Crasilda, his face contorted with rage.

"How old is your sister?" Crasilda asks. "16? Much too young for motherhood."

Velma raises her hand, and suddenly, an icicle shard floats up out of the water. It's a foot long with a needle-sharp point. With a flick of her wrist, Velma sends it flying at Crasilda.

Crasilda moves her hand to intercept the icicle. It shatters against her shield, scattering ice across the arena floor. Velma launches two more icicles, each deflected by Crasilda's shield.

"My dad was assigned to her trial," Crasilda taunts. "He spared her the lashings, but she's not fit to be a mother. He decided the baby would be better off as a royal servant."

Velma shakes with rage. She closes her eyes. This time, five icicles rise out of the water in unison. With a grunt, she swings both arms and launches all five at once.

Crasilda changes tactics. Her shields disappear, and she closes her eyes. When the shards are a few feet from piercing her, they dissolve back into formless globs of water. The remaining droplets, no more than a summer sprinkle, rain down on Crasilda with no effect.

Crasilda wipes the water out of her eyes and laughs. "Don't worry. She'll get a better education than you ever did. And who knows, maybe she'll get assigned to my family. We'll raise her as one of our own."

Velma's rage escapes as a scream. She throws two more icicles in quick succession. Both are easily deflected.

"I'ma kill her," Diego seethes. "I'ma kill that bitch."

Velma lifts her arms, and a giant mass of water rises out of the moat behind her. She shapes the water into a liquid wall the size of my mattress, positioning it between herself and Crasilda. The base of the wall adheres to the ground, but the rest floats vertically in the air. Velma moves the liquid forward, slowly advancing on Crasilda.

Crasilda unleashes on the wall, blasting fire with both hands. "When I'm done with you, you're going to wish you chose the fields." Each fireball causes the water to emit a puff of steam, but the mass of water is hardly diminished.

Crasilda narrows her eyes. She extends her hand, sending an energy wave into the watery wall. The water wobbles like a spring, absorbing the impact. A small portion of water is tossed from the wall, but Velma continues to advance. She's forcing Crasilda closer and closer to the edge of the platform.

Crasilda starts to panic. The air ripples as she launches another energy wave into the liquid barrier, this one stronger than the last. Water is thrown from the upper portion of the wall, greatly reducing its size. Crasilda sends another energy wave, which breaks Velma's focus. The liquid shield sloshes to the floor, quickly spreading thin across the arena. Crasilda takes advantage of the moment and charges.

Velma doesn't even try to recover her shield. Instead, she kneels and presses her hand to the floor. A sharp crackle fills the air. In a blink, the water on the arena floor freezes, creating a thin layer of ice.

As soon as Crasilda's foot meets the ice, it slips out from under her. She lands on her back and, carried by her own moment, drifts helplessly across the ice. Immediately, Velma sends an energy wave at Crasilda, sending her careening toward the moat. With a splash, she slides off the platform and into the surrounding water.

Velma isn't finished yet. She rushes to the edge of the moat, takes a deep breath, and closes her eyes. Before Crasilda can surface, the top layer of water solidifies into ice. I hold my breath as I watch. I can see Crasilda's outline under the ice. For several seconds, nothing happens. I start to wonder if she's lost her amulet in the water. Then, a faint red light appears beneath the ice. A small circle of ice begins to melt. I expect Velma to freeze it back, but she lets it liquify. As soon as the ice is gone, Crasilda's head bursts out of the water, and she sucks in a breath.

THUNK!

An icicle shard lodges itself deep into Crasilda's shoulder. Another shard hovers an inch in front of her nose. Crasilda looks down at her shoulder in disbelief as wisps of blood dissolve into the water. She doesn't scream or yell; she only gapes with an open mouth.

"Enough!" Commander Noyan bellows. "I want two healers fixing that shoulder now!"

Velma crouches next to the moat. "You're lucky I didn't go for your face." Then, she struts out of the arena as the guards lift Crasilda from the water.

Diego greets her at the top of the steps with a hug. The other recruits rush to congratulate her. After seeing a display like that, I'm grateful Velma chose the guard and not the equalists. I wouldn't want to be on the receiving end of her anger. I'm about to join the celebration when I hear my name.

"Lynn and Vyle!"

Already my heart is pounding. I have to fight him again. The man who almost killed me. I have to do it all again in front of everybody. I make eye contact with Grandpa, and he gives me a simple smile. The kind that says 'you can do this.' I look to Antai. As soon as our eyes meet, he winks. It's all I need.

I muster a brave face and start the long walk down to the arena. Each step feels like an eternity. *You can do this, Rose! Velma got her revenge, and so can you! Make him pay for what he did.*

I stride into the center of the arena and place my hand on my amulet. There's only one problem: Vyle isn't here. He's not on the staircase either. I search the audience and find him standing by his friends.

He takes a deep breath. "I forfeit."

Forfeit? I'd expect a lot of things from Vyle, but never a forfeit.

A series of murmurs cascade through the audience. One of the voices is his father's. His face is red, and he doesn't look pleased. "What are you doing?" General Kaynes hisses. "Get down there and fight!"

Vyle doesn't budge. He takes another deep breath. "I won't. I forfeit."

General Kaynes stands up in a rage. He storms over to Vyle, who stands pale as a ghost. "I'd like a word with you in private." He grabs his son by the wrist and drags him several rows away from the nearest spectators. A long, awkward silence ensues as Vyle whispers in his father's ear. Everyone watches in silence as they try to guess what he could possibly be saying. But I know. He's telling his father what happened—about how he tortured the princess.

General Kaynes stands up straight and gives me a long stare. His rage is replaced with uncertainty. "Very well, my son forfeits. Let's proceed."

Grandpa watches me with quiet concern. He knows something is amiss. I'll tell him all about it as soon as I can. Vyle won't get away with this. I'll make sure he's punished—if not by me, then by the law.

Tick looks down at his list. He doesn't read the names right away. He's considering something. Finally, he lifts his head. "Vyle and Matt."

This time Vyle doesn't hesitate. He's already descending the stairs to the arena. Matt stands and starts to leave.

"Be careful," I say.

Matt smiles. "I'll try." Then, he hurries down the steps and into the arena. He's oddly confident—almost excited. Vyle is already waiting for him. He stands with his hands raised in front of him. His lips curl in a murderous grin.

Tick waits until Matt is settled. "Begin!"

As soon as the words are out of his mouth, the stage goes black. I struggle to comprehend what I'm seeing—or what I'm not seeing. I'm staring at the same spot as before, but there's no image to focus on. I can see the rest of the stadium in perfect acuity, but when I look at the center of the arena, I see nothing at all. It's as if a black mist has descended on the center of the stage.

"What's happening?" Diego gasps.

"It's light dominion!" I'm both perplexed and amazed. Matt is preventing the light from leaving the stage. And because the light can't reach my eyes, all I see is black. It's impressive, but I don't know how it'll help Matt. Vyle may be blind, but Matt is too.

The guard officials are equally impressed. They lean forward over the railing as they whisper to each other. Antai watches the darkness with fascination. I hear noises coming from the black void of the stage: the sizzle of heat and the crackle of electricity. I flinch as a cloud of fire erupts from the void. I can see the flames, but I still can't see who made them.

The black void expands and pulsates as if it's a living breathing thing. Every few seconds, I catch a brief glimpse of movement from within. If Matt's making the void, he seems to be struggling.

"Where are you?" Vyle thunders from somewhere inside the darkness. "Show yourself, you coward!" Another fireball erupts from the darkness. Vyle is attacking blindly in all directions. Then, as quickly as it began, the black mist vanishes, and my eyes adjust to the scene.

Impossible!

Matt is standing behind Vyle with his hand extended towards Vyle's neck. Before Vyle can react, Matt's fingers make contact with his skin, and the crackle of electricity splits the silence. Instantly, Vyle goes rigid, collapsing to the floor. He lets out a guttural cry as his body seizes uncontrollably. Matt grits his teeth, keeping his hand pressed tight against Vyle's neck. The crackling continues.

"Enough!" General Kayne's bellows. His nostrils flare as he struggles to hide his rage. "That's enough."

Matt steps away with a victorious smirk as Vyle gasps on the floor. He did it. I can't believe he did it. Matt defeated Vyle in a matter of seconds. He rushes up the stairs with a huge grin on his face.

"Dude, you won!" Diego says between grins. He's already in a better mood. "How does it feel?"

"Like Christmas morning," Matt says between breaths. The light dominion took its toll on him. He leans with his hands on his knees.

"Congrats!" I add, but the words feel hollow. I'm glad Matt wasn't hurt, but with a performance like that, he'll be a contender for ranking first. I'll have to put on a show in my next match if I want to win.

"Thanks," Matt says. "He was smart to forfeit against you. He didn't stand a chance."

I force a smile. "I like to think it's true, but I guess we'll never know for sure." But it's not true. Vyle did stand a chance. Without my soul-anchor, he might've actually beat me.

Matt looks away. "Well, I better get some rest before the next match."

He wanders to an empty row and lays down. I don't blame him for wanting to be alone. Chances are one of us will be his next opponent. He'll need all the rest he can get.

The second round of duels ends quickly. Klinton fights another dry-blood and manages to pummel him into submission. Diego fights a core-born and pins him to the floor with an energy shield, earning himself a quick victory. Velma's opponent forfeits before the match even begins. I become more nervous with each name that's called. There are only a few recruits left who haven't fought a second time. Two more names are called. Then, two more.

"Alright everyone, this will be our last match," Tick announces. He looks down at his clipboard; then, he calls my name.

"Lynn and Matt!"

Chapter 27

Matt

One down, one to go.

I lay on my back, my arms shielding my eyes from the glowing symbols looming above me. My body aches from my duel with Vyle. With each minute that passes, I hope my strength will return, but the sand in my bones only settles deeper.

I still can't believe Zane's plan worked. The light dominion was completely his idea. Even in the black void, I could sense Vyle's every move. It gave me the advantage I so desperately needed. One little shock and I won. It was all over in seconds.

It's not over yet.

In my weakened state, I still have to face one more opponent. I sit up, leaning against the step behind me. Resting isn't helping, so I might as well watch. The current duel finishes as one recruit slams the other with a boulder. Vyle was ranked above me, so judging by the trend of today's duels, my next opponent should be ranked below me. I thought it would maybe be Diego or Velma, but I've heard each of their names called twice. Zander and Croyd as well.

What will it be like if I win? Will I meet the princess? Will I find friends in the palace? Will I heal Judy? Only one thing matters right now: victory.

"Alright, everyone, this will be our last match. Lynn and Matt!"

I bolt upright, my heart sinking in my chest. *Please, not her. Anyone but her.* Her mind is a locked chest, her thoughts an unseen treasure I can't seem to reach. Over the last month, I've tried and failed countless times. Without my gift, I have no advantage. No way to fill the gap between her experience and my own.

I'm doomed.

By the time I'm on my feet, she's already descending the stairs into the arena. I take a deep breath. What would Judy say?

Her voice echoes in my head. *You can do this, Matt. There's always a chance. If you don't believe it, then you've already lost.*

I descend the steps slowly, trying to buy myself more time to think. Even if I could read her mind, light dominion wouldn't work. She's seen my trick, and something tells me she'll know how to counter it. Her defenses are too strong for any normal attack. If only I could separate her from her amulet, but it's tucked within her shirt the same as mine. No ideas come to mind.

I have to think of something different. Something new...

I stop a few feet from Lynn and form a fighting stance. She gives me a half-hearted smile—a rueful smile. I find myself clinging to that smile, the slender curl of her lips. Her delicate nose and the smooth roll of her cheeks. It's hard to fight something so beautiful. It's hard to harm someone you wish to hold.

I meet her gaze, and her hazel eyes harden. Instead of the tender empathy I'm used to, all I see is fierce determination. Her eyes, bronze like a deadly blade, seem to speak to me. They whisper reluctance, desperation, and a touch of regret. For a second, I feel her hesitation, but it's quickly replaced by an undaunting resolve for victory.

It's not to the death, Rose. Just injure him and end it quick. He's just a distraction.

368

The thoughts echo in my head as if spoken in the wind. Not my thoughts, but hers. My mouth falls open, and I forget what's about to happen.

"Begin!"

Energy wave!

The thought is in my head before I have time to react. The air in front of me ripples, slamming me with the force of a speeding bus. I'm thrown off my feet, and the crowd cheers as the floor blurs beneath me. When my back connects with the ground, I somersault to a stop with the grace of a drunken sloth. I'm missing the skin on my elbows, but I'm otherwise unscathed. I'm barely on my feet before Lynn is crashing down on me.

Fire!

Her thoughts echo in my head. This time, I'm ready. As the air ignites before me, I direct the flames around me with my mind. All I can see is an infernal red. All I can feel is the heat against my skin.

The fire isn't meant to harm, only distract. As the flames block my view, Lynn sends another energy wave humming towards my feet. I sense it coming. I jump and feel a whoosh of air pass beneath me. I feel her astonishment even before her eyes widen. The attack was almost undetectable, yet I dodged it with ease.

Throughout it all, I keep my eyes locked with Lynn's. Her emotions waft toward me like a scent on the wind. Someway, somehow, I can read her mind. Whatever barrier existed before, it's no longer there.

I have a chance.

I take advantage of Lynn's hesitation and command heat into the air. The flames swirl from my fingers and curl around Lynn's energy shield. They lick at her like a log in a bonfire. With her shield wrapped around her like a cloak, she presses forward through the flames. Eight feet away, five feet away.

Already, fatigue saturates my bones. My flames falter, and I have no choice but to retreat. I backpedal as Lynn, with each step she takes, launches an energy wave point-blank. I manage to form a shield just in time. Each wave reverberates against my shield with a twang.

I'm beyond exhausted. I can't maintain my shield any longer. It dissolves with a ripple. Lynn wastes no time, electricity crackles on her fingers and she lunges. The crowd cheers.

I barely manage to twist away from her hand and send one last stream of fire. She easily deflects the flames with her mind. She knows I'm done for. Any second, I'll reach the limit of my soul and collapse. But I don't give up. I throw every last ounce of energy I have into stoking the flames. If I'm going to lose, I might as well go out with a bang.

That's it! I can't believe I didn't think of it sooner. If I can do light dominion, why not sound dominion. I know basic physics. Sound is just vibrations in the air. I can do this. I relinquish the flames and fix my eyes on the air just above Lynn's right shoulder. I only have a second before Lynn's next attack finishes me. I close my eyes and command with all my soul.

Bang!

A gunshot splits the silence accompanied by Lynn's shrill cry. Her body teeters to one side, and grasping at her ear, she falls to her knees. Her hand comes away, a faint smudge of blood visible on her index finger. I ruptured her eardrum. It actually worked.

Sadly, I'm not doing much better. I strained myself. My vision swims, and my ears ring. My head has a drilling pain down the center, but I can't stop now. Lynn is kneeling at my feet. One shock, and I can end this. I stretch out my hand. *For Judy!*

Lynn's head snaps up, and her eyes meet mine. In that brief instance, I sense her pain, like a distant ache that stretches from her ear to mine. I sense her desire to win and her unfailing determination. She needs this. She needs this more than anything. *Cavernum depends on it.* But then, all her thoughts are replaced by a single command.

Liquify!

I sense it coming, but I can't do anything to stop it. Before I can move, the ground beneath my feet dissolves like quicksand. In an instant, my legs disappear into the floor and then my waist. The stone arena, molding around my face and mouth, swallows me whole. The world falls silent. I try to claw my way out of the earthy sludge, but the liquid stone hardens back into its solid state. My body is pressed and squeezed on all sides by the weight of the rock. It's molded around my ears, between my fingers, and up my nose. The sensation is physically painful and psychologically torturous.

I can't move! I can't breathe! I want to scream, but I can't so much as open my mouth. *Help! Someone, help me!*

Suddenly, the stone around me softens, and a hand grabs hold of my shoulder. It drags me out of the ground as liquid rock spews off me like freshly poured concrete. Once I'm free, the chant of the crowd overwhelms me. They're ecstatic. Even Klinton and Velma are chanting Lynn's name. She stands a few feet away, beaming at the crowd like a practiced performer. I almost expect her to bow. Then, it dawns on me.

It's over. She won. Lynn will be going to the palace. What little hope I had of saving Judy is now gone. *I failed her.*

"You alright?" Commander Elsborne gives me a hand and helps me to my feet.

"I'm fine. Thanks for saving me."

"No problem," he mutters, but his eyes are no longer on me. He watches Lynn with pride and desire in his eyes. It's not a look of lust like most guards give her, but one of adoration. One of his eyes flutters shut in a subtle wink.

Confused, I look to Lynn. She smiles back at him with that same infatuated gaze. She looks at him in a way I've never seen her look at anyone. I let my mind drift deeper, and then I feel it.

Affection. Admiration. Respect.

Love.

I awake to the sound of Diego's voice. "Hey, Matt. Wake up, dude. You're going to miss the party. Everyone's downstairs."

I grunt and roll over. "What time is it?"

"It's already dark. You gotta get down there. The trucks are gonna leave soon."

I must've slept the entire afternoon. I roll out of bed and slip on my shoes. I'm still dressed in my training uniform. After losing to Lynn, I came straight to my dorm and fell asleep. It was the best decision I could have made. My mind-shattering headache is now only a dull ache. My shaky muscles are mostly rejuvenated.

I pull out my duffle bag from under my bed and fish around for my cell phone. It was fully charged when I arrived, but part of me worries it'll be dead when I try to turn it on. I find it and slip it into my pocket. It feels strange and nostalgic at the same time.

"You sure you're not coming?" I ask.

Diego nods. "I'm fine. Just keep an eye on Velma for me. I don't want some 30-year-old guard hitting on her."

"Trust me. You don't have to worry about that. If there's anyone who can deter unwanted attention, it's Velma."

"Please," Diego says. "I'll feel better knowing you're watching out for her. I mean, there's bad dudes out there like Vyle and his brother."

"Don't worry. I'll keep an eye on her."

Diego smiles. "Good. Now, go have fun. And I want you home by midnight. I don't want to be up all night worrying about you." He smiles. It's good to see a glimpse of old Diego. I hope he sticks around.

I smile. "Bye, Dad, love you."

Diego's grin grows bigger. "Love you more."

We both laugh, and I hurry out the door and down the stairs. By the time I'm outside, the recruits are climbing into the back of the three semi-trucks. I climb into the last one. I'm relieved to find only a few people inside. I'm not ready to face Lynn. Not after today. Her thoughts cling to my mind like bugs in a spider web. *He's just a distraction.* What does that even mean?

It's obvious she has feelings for the commander. She probably fell for him while folding his laundry or something—the classic maid mistress. Not that it matters. It's not like we were going to fall in love and get married or anything. I don't know why I even care so much. I should be happy for her like a good friend.

And then there's the fact that she called herself Rose? How am I supposed to make sense of that? She told me her mother loved flowers. Was Rose some kind of nickname?

A handful of guards file in and close the rear sliding door. Immediately, the truck lurches into motion. I settle into my seat and listen to the recruits chatting in front of me.

"I heard the graduating healers are invited. My brother says they're the hottest girls in Cavernum."

"Did you know their training takes a whole year? Can you imagine? And they only accept 10 recruits at a time."

"My brother dated a healer once," a third recruit adds. "He said she could do this healing massage that was to die for."

I think of the girl who healed me in the palace. Kendra was her name. Her gentle hands. Her compassionate smile. It's no wonder they have a reputation for being beautiful. She was at the evaluations today too, but I never got the chance to talk to her. I hope she didn't see me get sucked into the ground.

The truck shakes as the terrain suddenly changes. There are no windows, but I know we pulled off the road and onto the path that leads to the meadow. That's where Lynn said it would be. The truck takes a sharp turn and stops. We're here. The back of the truck slides up, and everyone pours out. I hop down and round the back of the truck.

Not bad. The three trucks are parked on opposite ends of the meadow with their headlights facing the center. Recruits already huddle in small groups throughout the clearing. As I walk towards the center, the music starts playing from all sides. All three truck stereos, I realize, are synchronized and play a techno song with a deep base.

People already sip beers and wine they got from the back of one of the trucks. If I didn't know any better, I'd guess I'm at a high school party.

Within minutes, the meadow turns into a dance floor as recruits experimentally shake their hips to the newfound music. Judging by the size of the crowd, it looks like everyone's here—everyone except Diego. I also count at least 20 on-duty guardsmen and 10 healers.

I spot Velma and Lynn across the field. Velma watches the party with a bored expression while Lynn stands with her eyes shut and bounces her knees to the music. Her face glows with childlike delight. I smile. At least she's enjoying herself. I turn and start towards a group of healer girls. Maybe I can find Kendra.

"Hey, Matt! Over here!" Klinton's voice calls out. I turn and find him returning to Lynn and Velma with drinks in his hands. For a second, I want to wave them off.

Judy would be ashamed of me. I already know exactly what she'd say. I can hear her voice in my head. *For goodness sakes, Matthew. Go congratulate the girl. I didn't raise you to be a sore loser, especially not when it comes to love. What did you expect? The man's a commander.*

The thought brings a smile to my face. I swallow my pride and force myself to join them. I don't see the commander, which makes me a little more at ease. I lock eyes with Lynn. "Congratulations on today. You really deserve it." I try to keep the disappointment from my voice.

Lynn gives me a sympathetic smile. "Thanks. I'm sorry about the whole—" She motions to her feet. "—ground sinking thing."

"I'm sorry about your ear. How is it, by the way?"

Lynn touches her ear. "It's good as new. The healers fixed it up in the palace."

The palace, of course. That will be her new home now that she's a royal guard. I nod, and an awkward silence ensues.

"I forgot to tell you," Lynn says. "District 15, the one you're assigned to, it's in Commander Elsborne's quadrant."

Of course it is. Lucky me.

"He says that two of the captains will be retiring in the next few years, so you'll have a good chance of being promoted. He was really impressed with your duels."

I'm about to reply as politely as I can when Klinton waves his hand wildly through the air. "Kowen, over here!"

A guard smiles and makes his way over to us. He's dressed in uniform with a pistol strapped to his belt. Unlike the other guards, he's not wearing an amulet.

Klinton motions to the man. "Everyone, this is my brother, Kowen. He's going to be my trainer."

Kowen says hello and shakes all of our hands. When he gets to Lynn, he lingers. "Congratulations on your win today. You'll have to tell me what palace life is like." It's strange to think that starting tomorrow, Lynn will be Kowen's superior. He already speaks to her as such.

"Thank you. You'll have to tell me what life outside the wall is like."

"Oh, it's nothing special, I assure you." He turns back to his brother. "Hey Klinton, I want to introduce you to some of the guys." With that, they take off, and it's just the three of us left.

The song changes to a remix of some pop song I don't recognize. Lynn's eyes grow unnaturally wide as she listens. "I don't know if I love it or hate it," She laughs.

"Well don't just stand there," Velma tells me. "Aren't you going to teach us how they dance in the beyond?"

I'm about to make a joke about grinding, but Diego's not here to get it. I sigh. "At most of the parties I've been to, people just jump and shake their butts. That's all you need to know."

Lynn looks disappointed. "Seriously?"

"Give us an example," Velma demands.

My face gets hot, but I force myself to do it. I get low and roll my body to the music. I probably look like an idiot, but they only laugh, which restores my confidence. "Seriously. Just do what comes naturally. It's easy. No steps required."

More and more recruits flock to the dance floor. I stretch out my hand to each of them. "C'mon, let's go dance." I guide them into the crowd. A small circle has formed on the dance floor where one guard breakdances in the grass. Everyone cheers. The circle closes in, and we dance like a bunch of middle schoolers at our first dance—nervous and excited and teeming with hormones.

For a while, I forget that Judy's dying. I forget that Lynn loves another guy and that Diego's sister is ill. I forget it all as we dance under the stars. I try to keep from staring at Lynn, but she's picked up the rhythm incredibly fast. She shimmies her hips to the floor and rolls her body back up.

She loves someone else. You need to get over her. But my eyes don't listen. She flips her chocolate hair and swings her hips. It's mesmerizing. Once again, I find myself staring. When I look up, I find Lynn's caramel eyes staring back. She's watching me, not in an offended way, but in the same way I was watching her: with intrigue, with desire.

I need to get away. "I'm going to go get a drink," I lie. I push my way out of the crowd and head for a toppled log at the edge of the meadow. I take a seat and rest my elbows on my knees. My phone digs into my thigh, reminding me of Judy. It's time, but the more I think of it, the sicker I feel. How will I be able to explain to her why I haven't called? And even worse, what if she doesn't answer? Once I call, I'll have to face the truth, whether for better or worse. I don't think I can handle it if she doesn't answer. I need her reassurance right now. I need her wisdom and her love.

I need her to be alive.

"Do you mind if I sit here?" The voice is familiar. It's a soft voice, yet clear enough to be heard over the sound of the music.

I look up and find two emeralds of eyes smiling back at me. Her blonde hair isn't as long as last time. It's curled and bounces on top of her shoulders. "It's Matt, right?"

I nod vigorously, looking like a deer in the headlights. I search for the right thing to say, but my mind is cluttered by her beautiful face.

She studies me, her green eyes overflowing with friendliness and compassion. I don't need an amulet to sense her goodness.

"You probably don't remember me, but I healed you in the healer's loft. My na—"

"Kendra." I stammer. "How could I forget? You had to deal with my neck infection, and I asked you a million questions."

She flashes her brilliant white teeth and relaxes at the sound of her name. "Trust me, it was a pleasure." She looks out over the meadow to where a group of girls is watching us and giggling.

"Are those your friends?" I ask.

"More like coworkers. We don't always get along. My real friends are in the field."

I hesitate. "Are... are you ring-born?"

"Core-born," she corrects. "My best friends and I competed for healing together, but I was the only one accepted."

"Is it true they only accept 10?"

Kendra nods. "It's the smallest guild in the sanctuary."

"You must be really something to get accepted," I think aloud.

Kendra plays it off. "I bet you could've made it too. You know, I was disappointed when you didn't show up for The Dividing. I was hoping you would choose healing."

"I wish." I give her a wry smile. "Do you know if they accept guild transfers?"

She cocks her head. "Is that a joke? Why switch now? You're second in your class. You'll be an elite in no time."

I shouldn't bother her with this, but the words tumble out before I can stop them. "Don't get me wrong, I'm grateful to be here, but sometimes I think guards are just overpaid bullies. I've yet to see them help anybody. If I was a healer, at least I'd be doing something good."

I expect her to correct me, to say that the guards do great things, but she doesn't. She puts her hand on the bark between us. "I thought the same thing before I was divided. I thought I'd be saving sick children and healing the injured. I thought I would be doing something worthwhile, but instead, I heal officers of their ear infections so they can go out and whip kids half to death. And while children die of disease, I spend my days healing the chancellor of her acne." Kendra takes a deep breath, and when she realizes she's been ranting, she blushes. "I'm sorry. It's just… it's not easy being a healer either."

As sad as it is, I can't stop the smile forming on my lips. *Velma would love this girl.*

"What?" Kendra asks defensively.

"Oh, nothing. It's just nice to know there are others who think like that. I have some friends who would love to meet you."

Kendra narrows her eyes at me and gives me a thin-lipped smile. "Well, if they're anything like you, I'd love to meet them too."

My heart beats faster, and my face grows hot. I want to say something clever back, but my mind turns to Diego's sister instead. A sliver of hope embeds itself in my heart. "Do they let you heal who-ever you want?"

Kendra shakes her head. "They only let us heal in the palace, or on special assignment. And when we're off-duty, they take away our amulets. We have no say in the matter."

Damn it. They somehow find a way to destroy all hope. "I'm sorry. That sounds rough."

Kendra shrugs. "Yeah, well, that's life. At least for now, anyway."

"Kendra!" Two healer girls call her name and wave her towards the dance floor.

Kendra stands. "Want to come dance with us?"

Yes! Yes, I do! The conversation's just begun and already she's leaving. "I would. I really would, but I have to take care of something first. Maybe I'll find you after."

"Please do. Well, it was nice talking to you, Matt. If you ever want to talk, just get shot or something."

I laugh. "Okay, maybe I will. And if you ever want to talk, just steal something, and I'll be there."

"Bye, Matt." Kendra disappears into the crowd, and I turn to the forest. It's eerie at night. The shadows here seem deeper and darker than those in Colorado, but I don't have a choice.

No guard tries to stop me as I wander into the darkness. They probably assume I'm going to take a pee. I try not to jump as two bodies appear behind a pine tree. One of the guards pins a healer girl against the tree trunk with his body. She holds his face as they kiss with mouths unethically wide. I turn the other way and wander a little farther. When I'm convinced I'm alone, and the music is only a dull thud in the distance, I pull out my phone. I hold down the power button and pray.

Please work. Please work.

A white light suddenly consumes the screen. *Thank you, God.* I type in my password and check the battery: 42%. It could be worse. I open my favorites and click on the only name: Mom. The phone rings and rings and rings.

Judy's voice comes on, a voicemail from years ago. Her voice is clear and cancer-free. "This is Judy MacArther. Please leave a message."

My heart beats faster. It's an hour later in Colorado. Maybe she's just asleep. Please just be asleep. I call again.

Ring… ring…. ring… I hear a soft click as the line connects.

"Matt? Matt, is that you?"

Chapter 28

Rose

The music is everything I dreamed it would be. The bass is the heartbeat of the night, pulsating through the air and throbbing in my chest. It's almost impossible to distinguish all the sounds I'm hearing, but notes combine into something edging on addicting. It's so utterly unique from the music I'm used to. The vocals speak to my mind, but the beat calls to my body, urging me to move.

My soul-anchor jostles in my bra as I sway with the crowd. Despite its bulky weight, it feels good to have it back. After what happened with Vyle, I'll never take it off again.

Matt dances just a few feet beside me. It's evident he's familiar with the music. His arms bend and pop to the rhythm of the vocals, whereas his hips move slower, in perfect harmony with the bass. When the music stalls, he freezes, and then he whips his body as the bass drops again. He's a puppet, obeying with precision the commands of his music master. His wavy hair sways with the loll of his head. His chiseled jaw is taut—his eyes, two icebergs surrounded by a sea of sand-colored skin. I know I shouldn't be staring, but I let my eyes linger. After tonight, we'll be a world apart. The palace wall may as well be an ocean between us. If I see Matt again, it may not be for years. He's been a welcomed distraction this past month, but tomorrow he'll be nothing more than a memory. *It's better this way.*

Matt's eyes meet mine, and his dancing falters. I hate how much I like the way he looks at me. I don't turn away. I let his eyes search mine, and my skin is suddenly warmer. *Don't overthink it, Rose. He'll be gone after tonight.*

Matt turns away first. "I'm going to get a drink." I watch as he pushes through the crowd. He doesn't turn towards the alcohol truck, but rather towards the forest. I don't question it. Perhaps, he needs to use the little guard's room.

Velma stops dancing. "Want to get another drink?"

I gladly oblige. The dance floor reeks of unbathed masculinity, and I'm beginning to get sweaty myself. I follow her to the back of the alcohol truck, where a dark-skinned guard with a white apron is taking requests. His eyes fall on me.

"Champagne, please," I say.

The man pours the bubbling liquid into a tin cup. It's not as fancy as palace crystal, but it'll do. He hands me the drink. "Celebrating something?"

Velma puts her arm around me. "This girl, I'll have you know, is going to be a royal guard tomorrow."

The guard's eyes widen ever so slightly. "Congratulations, miss. That's quite an accomplishment for a woman."

Velma rolls her eyes. "You mean that's quite an accomplishment, period."

The man bats his eyes, confused. "Excuse me?"

"Just forget it." Velma snatches a bottle of beer and storms away. I follow at her heels, bewildered by her outburst. She picks a spot away from the lights and out of earshot of any guards. She plops down on the ground, and I sit down next to her. The grass is cold and damp with midnight dew. It feels nice against my sweaty skin. Velma takes a deep breath and sighs. "I can't wait to see the look on his stupid face when you become a guardian someday."

"Or you," I say.

Velma shrugs. "Maybe. I just wish they'd see us as equals for once. I'm sick of being treated like I'm disabled for being a woman."

"Deep down, they know we're equals," I assure her. "Even if they don't like to admit it."

Velma rolls her eyes. "I don't know how it is in the palace, but the men in the ring definitely don't know it. They're convinced that they're God's gift to the planet, and women are destined to be their happy helpers. My sister got married last year. When she tried selling blankets for extra money, do you know what her husband told her? He said a woman doesn't belong on the street; she belongs in the kitchen or in the bedroom." My disgust must be evident because Velma softens her tone. "We're nothing more than a pretty face and a pair of boobs to them."

People can't really believe that? It's almost unfathomable. I've never heard anything sexist in the palace, but then again, who would dare say something like that in front of the princess? Perhaps my status is a shield from reality. *Perhaps Cavernum isn't what I thought it was.*

"They're not all like him," I remind her. I had to tell her the same thing about high-borns just a month ago. "Just think of Matt and Diego and Tick." *And Antai and Grandpa.*

"Yeah, well, Diego's special. Matt and Tick too. But most of the men I know are all the same. When I told my dad I wanted to be a guardsman, he told me I was delusional, that I should marry one instead. He said Cavernum's safer in the hands of men. Can you believe that? My own father wanted me to fail. And the sad thing is, part of me believed him."

I remember what Diego's grandmother once said at lunch. *Men simply make better soldiers.* Just a few years ago, I would've believed it too. But now I know better. "Times are changing, Velma. When you tell your daughters how you became guardian, they won't doubt that they can do anything—be anything they want to be."

Velma nods. Her expression softens for a moment only to crease with anger lines. "Do you want to know how my sister got pregnant?" She continues without waiting for a response. "Six months ago, she got raped by our uncle. Our own God damn uncle! She was the best of us: pure and kind and innocent. And that… that demon of a man took it all away. Now, even if she survives childbirth, the baby will grow up to be a servant." Her voice isn't terribly loud, but her tone is screaming with indignation. Her wild eyes stare into the night. Her open mouth quivers, hungry for justice. "And the worst part is, my uncle didn't get a single lashing. Not one." She waves a finger angrily in the air. "If she were a high-born, he would've been hanged, but instead, he goes free. How's that for equality? How's that for changing times?"

I'm horrified. I want to think it's a lie, but in my heart, I know it's true. I've heard of women getting blamed for a man's misconduct. But getting away with rape? It's unforgivable.

"I'm so sorry, Velma. I can't imagine…"

Velma sighs again, trying to release her anger through her breath. Once composed, she speaks quietly. "For months, I imagined how I'd kill him. I had this whole plan. I'd join the guard and wait until I graduated training. Then, I'd say I caught him out past curfew and whip him till his heart stopped beating." She sighs again. "But killing him won't fix anything. Nothing I can do to him can fix what he did to Wendy."

"Things will get better. I know they will." But the words sound hollow leaving my lips.

I'll make them better. I'll talk to Grandpa. I'll reopen her case. I'll do something. I have to do something.

Velma shakes her head. "Who's going to make it better? You and me?" Her outrage isn't directed at me, but I feel attacked just the same. "Even as guards, we have no power. There's nothing we can do."

But I'm not just a guardsman; I'm the princess. I have all the power to make change. Tomorrow at graduation, Grandpa will reveal my royal identity, and I'll return to the palace. What will Velma think of me then? Will I prove her wrong? Will I prove her right?

I know I should let it go, but I feel the need to convince her that things are getting better. Cavernum is changing for the better.

"What about Chancellor Gwenevere?" I ask. "She's the first woman on the high council. And Commander Kirsten Hunt, the first female commander. 100 years ago, The Dividing didn't even exist. Things are getting better, Velma. Even if we can't see it yet, change is coming."

She faces me, her eyes glistening with grief. "I can't wait another 100 years, Lynn. I need change now. Wendy needs it now." She puts her palms on the grass behind her and tilts her head back to gaze at the stars, trying to find an answer amongst the constellations. A sliver of a moon hovers above the treeline. I let my mind wander through the starlight, distracting myself with its beauty.

"You remind me of my mom," Velma says softly.

"What?"

"What you said, the way you said it. It reminds me of my mom."

I raise an eyebrow, and she explains. "When I was in primary school, believe it or not, I was terrified of the dark. Like deathly afraid. I used to cry at night and beg my mom not to blow out the candle. I dreaded the sunset more than anything. More than going hungry or the winter frost.

At the time, we lived in a tiny apartment on the top floor. My sisters and I shared the same bed. It was right next to the window, so we had a perfect view of the sky. There were no torches on our street, and everything was pitch-black. When my mom would blow out the candle, the only thing I could see was the moon. Some nights, my mom would lie with us until I fell asleep. When I would cry, she would always tell me the same story to calm me down."

I feel the sting of loss. What stories would my mother have told me when I was a scared child? Would she have lain with me at night until I fell asleep?

"What was the story?" I ask.

I expect Velma to resist, but instead, she begins narrating without hesitation. "When God first made Adam and Eve, he made them on a bright and beautiful morning. They awoke together, and hand in hand, they explored their new world. They were amazed. Never before in their lives had they seen the light. They found beautiful forests and crystal-clear rivers. They found vibrant flowers of every color and animals of every species. And they were truly happy.

But, as the day went on, the sun started to sink lower and lower in the sky, until finally, it disappeared behind the mountain. Adam and Eve were terrified. Never in their lives had they seen night. They made a fire to escape the darkness, but eventually, their fire burned out. They huddled together in the dark and cried, afraid the sun would never return. They worried they would have to live the rest of their lives in darkness.

But God didn't want his creations to be afraid. When he saw them suffering, he had an idea. He put the moon in the sky as a promise that the sun would rise again. Adam and Eve saw the moon and knew the darkness was only temporary. Even though they couldn't see it, the sun was making its way around the world and would soon rise the next morning. Still today, the moon shines as a promise that, even if we can't see it, the sun is coming. Good things are on their way." Velma sighs and keeps staring at the heavens.

"It's a beautiful story," I say. "I've never heard it before."

Velma shrugs. "My mom would never admit it, but I'm pretty sure she made it up. For years, it got me through the night. I would stare at the moon and remind myself that God didn't want me to be scared—that good things were coming. But, I'm not so sure I believe it anymore. I'm just so angry at him, Lynn. I'm just so mad all the time."

"At your uncle?"

"At God! At whatever psycho made this messed up world. Why did he go through all the effort to create us only to abandon us? If he really wants us to be happy, why did he let Wendy get raped? Hell, why are we trapped in this damn sanctuary, while feeders roam free to do whatever the hell they want? Why?"

I wish I knew. I've wondered those same questions. The more I think about it, the more absurd it seems. *Why God? Why is Nevela in the hands of the equalists? Why are my parents dead? What purpose does all this suffering serve?* I don't say anything. I have nothing to say. I wish grandpa were here. He'd have an answer.

Velma breaks the silence. "I want to believe the story. I want to believe that good things are coming, but I just don't anymore. I'm afraid if I do, I'll spend my whole life waiting and waiting, and it'll never come. I'm afraid my daughters will spend their whole lives waiting for the same things I am."

"That's not going to happen." The certainty in my voice surprises me. I think of that little girl whose father was hanged before her eyes. I think of the old woman who was whipped in the flats. I think of Vyle and how he tortured me in the guard tower. Of Wendy and her abuser. Cavernum is not the city I once thought it was. Cavernum needs to change.

I stare up at the sky just as the moon disappears behind a cloud. "Change is coming, Velma. I know it is. Any day now, the sun will rise on Cavernum, and we'll be a part of it. We might not be able to see it now, but we will soon."

Velma looks over at me as if seeing me for the first time. She smiles. "Thanks, Lynn. Thanks for just listening. It means a lot."

Before I can respond, soft, stealthy footsteps approach from the direction of the party. I expect to see Matt, but instead, my eyes fall on Vyle. He approaches cautiously and stops a safe distance away. He holds his hands behind his back, standing almost courteously.

"What do you want?" Velma snaps, channeling her rage from our previous conversation.

Vyle smiles his usual pretentious smile, as if we're fools to think he'd ever wish us harm. "I just came to congratulate Lynn on her victory." His voice hangs on my name. "Also, I want to say I'm sorry for how I treated you both and I hope we can start over. If there's anything I can do for you, let me know."

"What's the catch?" Velma barks. "What's in it for you?"

"Quite the contrary, I want to be of service to you." He narrows his eyes at me. "I imagine you'll need all the allies you can get in the coming days. I want you to know that I'm here to serve." With that, he turns and slinks back the way he came.

I'm stunned. His words sounded somewhat genuine, but I know it's an act. He's only doing this because he knows who I am.

"What a kiss ass." Velma sneers. "He tries to kill Diego and the moment you're promoted, he's here offering to wipe your butt. It's pathetic."

"I know." I don't want to waste any more time thinking about Vyle. I can deal with him once I resume my role as princess. Before the party, I told Grandpa everything that happened. He is going to hold a disciplinary hearing, and Vyle will finally get what he deserves.

"I'm going to get another drink." I climb to my feet and hurry to the alcohol truck. I know Antai wouldn't approve. I can hear his admonition in my head. *C'mon, Rose. Think this through. You need a clear head out here. Vyle knows your secret. He told General Kaynes and heaven knows who else. Any one of these guards could be an equalist. You need to be watchful, not wasted. Don't do anything you'll regret.*

But I don't care. This is my last night as Lynn. Tomorrow, I have to accept all the responsibilities that come with royalty, and I'm not ready for that. I take another tin cup full of champagne, and we wander back to the dance floor, sipping all the way. The champagne is bubbly and sweet. It tickles my tongue and rises up my nose. I finish the cup and leave it on a table. The bubbles rise to my head and threaten to lift me off the ground. But I'm still in control. I don't regret anything.

Velma and I find Tick on the outskirts of the dance floor, encircled by googly-eyed recruits. He's dressed in his usual uniform with his amulet tucked into his collar. A small dagger hangs in a sheathe from his belt. It's not just any dagger, it's Antai's Adamic dagger. He must've lent it to Tick after all. I'm touched.

One recruit in particular, a boy named Anton, stands directly in front of Tick. He clutches an amplifier in hand as Tick coaches him.

"It's really not that hard. Focus your soul into every strand of hair, all of them collectively. Then, command the pigment to change colors. It's that simple."

Anton, closes his eyes and I watch as the pigment slowly fades from his jet black hair. By the time he opens his eyes, his hair is an ugly, ashy white. He looks like he's aged 20 years. "Did it work?"

Tick covers his mouth and snorts. "Ummm, not quite, but it's nothing you can't fix. Oh, and you forgot your eyebrows. Why don't you try it again."

Anton closes his eyes, but nothing happens. A few of his friends snicker. His eyes flutter open? "How about now?"

"Still the same," Tick says.

The boy tries again and again, but his hair remains snow white. "It'll come with time." Tick assures him. Anton bitterly hands back the amulet, and Tick holds it up. "Alright, who's next?"

No one volunteers. They don't want to end up like old man Anton. Finally, Velma steps forward. "I'll do it."

Tick's face lights up when he sees us. "Ahhh, my favorite graduates! Just the people I wanted to see." He holds out the amulet to Velma. "Let me give you your options. You can change eye color, hair color, whiten teeth, you can permanently paint your fingernails if you like. You c—"

"Can I get a tattoo?"

Tick pulls his lips back, revealing his bleached teeth. He sucks in through a clenched jaw. "You can, but I wouldn't recommend it. You'd have to do the art yourself. They usually come out sloppy."

"Please, the design is simple. Just tell me what I need to do."

Tick shrugs. "Alright, but you can't say I didn't warn you." He reaches into his pocket and pulls out a pen. "I brought this just in case. Draw out the design first. It'll help you visualize it. Then, command the pigment to form underneath the ink. It has to be deep in the skin if you want it to last."

Velma grins and snatches the pen. She turns over her left arm and presses the tip against her wrist. She drags the pen in a series of waving arcs. Then, she proceeds to scribble in her drawing. She lifts the pen and smiles at the image. It's elegantly simple in the moonlight.

"Any special significance?" Tick asks.

"Not really," Velma lies, but I know the truth. *Change is coming. The sun will rise again.*

Velma stares at the crescent moon and touches her hand to her amulet. Suddenly, one of the headlights of the closest truck fizzles out with a slight pop. The light on the dance floor dims, but only slightly. The music continues, as does the dancing.

How odd.

Pop. Pop. Pop. More headlights go out as their bulbs explode. The plastic casings of the high-beams remain intact, but the bulbs themselves spontaneously shatter.

Dominion. I'm sure of it, but who, and why? Tick whips his head around wildly, searching in the dark for any intruders. He reaches for Antai's Adamic blade, and his skin glazes over with metal. Around the meadow, guardsmen unholster their pistols and point them into the darkness. My stomach drops.

We're under attack.

Tick shoves Velma and me toward the center of the meadow. "Stay in the crowd. I'll be back." Then, he's gone, his voice getting smaller as he commands. "Hold the perimeter. Shoot on sight!"

Pop. Pop. Pop. The last of the lights go out, casting us into total darkness. Colors float before me as my eyes struggle to adjust. In the moonlight, all I see is the outline of the bodies around me. Then, all hell breaks loose.

Like ravenous wolves, they emerge from the tree line. Their forms are nothing but shadows, moving unnaturally quick through the grass. I count three, or maybe four. It's impossible to tell in the darkness. But

I know we're surrounded. We're corralled in the center of the meadow, like sheep waiting for the slaughter. There's no escaping.

The feeders have arrived.

Chapter 29

Rose

BANG! BANG! BANG!

The guards open fire as frantic screams pierce my ears. Recruits run every which way. Most press into the center of the meadow. Others run for the road; they don't get far. Their screams are evidence.

Do something, Rose, you have an amulet. You can help. But I don't know how. Everything is chaos. Sounds of death prick my ears. People are pushing and shoving, running in all directions. A guard shouts for help somewhere behind me, then he screams. The type of blood-curdling scream one makes as his soul is torn from his body.

The roar of gunshots is almost constant. I hear the crackle of electricity. The hiss of flames illuminates the night. A snapshot of the chaos lingers in my mind like a photograph. More screams. Another fireball erupts to my left. I turn and spot the silhouette of a guard in its center. As the fire recedes, he falls to the floor and rolls, desperately trying to extinguish the flames that consume him. I want to run, but I don't know where. Death is everywhere. Feeders are everywhere.

KABOOM!!!

An explosion shakes the earth. The alcohol truck disappears inside a rising ball of flame. The mushroom cloud rises high into the sky, leaving a trail of black smoke.

I can see! The burning wreckage of the truck illuminates the meadow in a ghastly orange hue. My surroundings flicker in the light of the flames. Then, I see it. It's the only thing walking amid the chaos. It wears a black robe with a hood pulled over his face. It strolls through the meadow, only 20 feet away, as recruits scramble to escape. A healer girl turns and bolts, but her feet lock up, and she falls flat on her face. Suddenly, an unseen force drags her through the grass by the ankles. She claws helplessly at the dirt as she's dragged ever closer to the feeder.

"Help! Heeeelp!!!"

Fear clouds my mind, and I'm frozen. I watch as the girl is lifted into the air, dangling upside down before the feeder. She's a mouse, helplessly squirming before a hungry boa. Quick as a cobra, the feeder clamps down on her neck.

1 second. 2 seconds. 3 seconds.

Before I can blink, it's over. The girl stops squirming, and the feeder comes up for air. Her lifeless, limp body drops to the floor. The feeder wipes its mouth and looks around for its next victim. Its eyes find mine. At that moment, the wreckage illuminates its disturbingly human face. Its skin, gaunt and colorless, is pulled tight across its skull. Its lips and nose are nothing out of the ordinary, but its eyes are crazed and demonic. They reflect the flames like a direct portal to hell. They're devoid of sympathy and reason and all human emotion. They're empty of everything except one uncontrollable desire.

Feed.

The creature steps toward me. I shake myself from the spell and press my hand to my chest. This is what I've trained for. *I'm ready.*

I strike first, unleashing an energy wave at its chest. The wave collides with the feeder's shield, inches from its face. I send a surge of fire, but it warps around the shield, leaving the creature untouched. In the firelight, the creature smiles a blood-chilling grin. It's teeth are thin and needle sharp. Then, it attacks.

The air around me comes to life. A force grabs my ankles with the dexterity of human fingers. Invisible hands latch onto me from all sides. Two invisible entities pin my arms to my side, and another grabs my throat. Before I know it, I'm getting dragged toward the feeder just like the healer girl.

I push back against the force with my mind, but I can only take on one entity at a time. I claw at my throat, but there's nothing there, just pure force acting on my skin. The feeder is like nothing I've ever encountered before. It has the precision and control of several life-times.

15 feet. 10 feet. I glide on my back across the dew oiled grass. I only have seconds to save my life. If fire didn't work, maybe ice will. I focus my mind on the air around his body.

Freez—

The thought is forming in my mind when a force appears inside my shirt and lifts my amulet off my chest. In an instant, my connection to the elements is severed. The unseen hand pulls the soul anchor from my bra and yanks it off my head. I watch as my only weapon floats through the air and into the feeder's hand. *I'm defenseless. I'm doomed.*

BANG!

The feeder's head shudders, and the force on my body disappears. The feeder collapses face first in the grass, blood oozing from the bullet wound in the back of its head. Vyle stands over the dead feeder with a pistol in hand. A wisp of smoke trails from the barrel like a genie's lamp. In his other hand, the chain of an amplifier coils around his fingers. His hands are bloody, probably from snatching the amulet off a dead guard.

Vyle saved me. Why would Vyle save me?

"Get up, princess," he barks. "We need to move."

That's why. He didn't save Lynn, or even Rose. He saved the princess. That's the only identity he cares about. When I don't respond, Vyle groans. He peels my amulet out of the dead feeder's hand and tosses it to me. "Put it on. Let's go."

Looping the amulet over my head and into my shirt, I scramble to my feet. The road is on the opposite end of the meadow. We have to cross the chaos if we want to get back to the sanctuary. Vyle leads the way, and I follow. To our left, a guard is battling a feeder and losing, but Vyle pays him no heed. Most of the guards are dead. Most of the feeders too. We weave through the cowering crowd as quickly as possible and traverse the body strewn dance floor without a problem. Vyle stops at the edge of the meadow, his eyes wide with fear.

Two feeders emerge from the trees, then another. They don't try to attack, but stand as sentinels, guarding the dirt road. It's the only way back to Cavernum. They want to keep us here, far away from the wall.

A metal hand clasps over my shoulder. "Get behind me. When I say run, you run." I open my mouth to argue, but Tick silences me. "Stand down, princess!"

Princess? He knew? He knew the entire time? *Of course he knew, Rose.* Grandpa would never leave me unsupervised and unprotected. Tick was my babysitter all along.

Tick presses the Adamic dagger flat against his forearm, the blade indistinguishable from his titanium skin. His metallic body reflects amber in the firelight as he takes off across the meadow. For a human candlestick, he's surprisingly light on his feet. He charges the nearest feeder with frightening speed and power.

An energy shield ripples in front of the feeder. If the feeder sees the knife, it must not know the blade is Adamic. Tick slices effortlessly through the shield and plunges the blade into the feeder's gut. The creature lets out a screech as Tick drives the blade upward, lifting the feeder's toes from the ground. Its inhuman cry falls silent.

The next feeder is more cautious. As Tick charges, it douses Tick's torso in a continuous torrent of fire. His guard jacket disintegrates beneath the heat. His newly exposed muscles ripple, and his silver skin glows molten orange. Tick cries out in pain but doesn't slow down. He runs through the flames and lashes out with a swipe of his blade. The feeder reels back as blood spews from a gash in its throat. Before the feeder can bleed out, Tick thrusts the knife into the feeder's chest and finishes the job.

The third feeder attacks from behind, catching Tick by surprise. In the darkness, I don't see the air ripple, but I see as Tick is thrown ten feet through the air. He slams into a tree trunk at the edge of the meadow with enough force to splinter the wood. The blade disappears into the grass at his feet. His back, still red-hot from the feeder's flames, singes the bark like a branding iron.

Please be okay! Please be okay! A blow like that could easily kill a man. I clutch my amulet and take a step to help, but Tick is already back on his feet. He scoops up the knife with a grunt and trudges towards the feeder. The creature raises its hand. This time Tick is ready. His energy shield is battered by boulders and chunks of earth, but it holds. Tick breaks into a run. I hear the crack of thunder as a flash of lightning strikes Tick's body. The grass at his feet bursts into flame, but Tick hardly falters. Then, the feeder turns and runs.

So they do feel fear.

Tick whips his arms, and the dagger flies. Whether guided by dominion or not, it finds its mark, embedding itself in the feeders back. The creature drops like a stone. Tick retrieves the blade and stabs him once more for good measure.

I can't believe my eyes. All three feeders lay dead in the meadow. Tick killed them single-handedly. I've never seen anything like it.

Suddenly, a fourth figure emerges from the black beyond the trees. It doesn't wear a cloak like the others. It's arms are twig thin, and it's eyes sunken deep into its face. The feeder walks slowly toward Tick, undaunted by it's dead brothers strewn before it. Tick adjusts his grip on the blade so that the tip is pointing toward the ground. Then, he charges.

The feeder does nothing. It only waits, unsettlingly still. Almost lifeless. When Tick is a dozen feet from the creature, he stops in his tracks. His shoulders go rigid, and his knees lock. For a few short seconds, nothing happens.

What is he doing? Why would he stop? But the answer is obvious. Tick wouldn't have stopped.

Tick is possessed!

In shaky movements, Tick's arm slowly lifts the Adamic blade and places the tip against his own chest. I watch in horror as the knife sinks deep into his flesh, cutting through his armor as easily as a wedding cake. With each inch, Tick seizes and chokes. He feels everything as the knife slides between his ribs. Blotches of his metal skin turn from silver to tan and back to silver again. His head jerks, and his legs quiver, but his arm is perfectly steady as it drives the knife deeper. When the silver blade fully disappears within his skin, Tick falls still. His head slumps, and his body crumples to the grass. He doesn't get up.

Tick is dead.

I want to cry! I want to scream, but I don't have time. I have a demon to kill. I'm the only one with a soul-anchor. I'm the only one immune. I grab my amulet and run at the feeder as fast as I can.

"Lynn, no!" Velma cries, but I don't stop. As soon as I'm next to Ticks body, I plant my feet just as he did. I'm now within range of the demon's mind. I force myself to look it in the eyes. I see it searching for my mind to inhabit. Only it won't find it. This is my chance. I reach down and wrestle the blade from Tick's chest. When I turn back to the demon, I find its eyes glistened over and devoid of life. Its body is completely inanimate. I look down at Tick a moment before his eyes flicker open.

No! Please no!

I stare in disbelief as Tick climbs to his feet. At first, his movements are shaky and uncoordinated, but then he stands tall and steady. His eyes settle on me a moment before he lunges.

I swipe with the knife and catch him in the arm. The blade cuts deep, but Tick doesn't so much as flinch. He swings again, and I barely form a shield in time. I scramble back. Tick raises his arm, and a flash of lightning splits the night. It explodes against my shield and throws me onto my back. Before I can recover, Tick is standing over me, his fist swinging for my face.

I close my eyes and await death. The air whooshes above me as the familiar sound of an energy wave reverberates in my ears. I open my eyes to see Tick thrown across the meadow. Vyle stands to my left with his arm outstretched, the amulet still coiled around his fingers. He saved me. For the second time tonight, Vyle saved me.

I only have seconds before Tick returns. "Shoot the demon!" I scream. Vyle aims his pistol at the comatose demon and fires. To my dismay, the air ripples, and the bullet deflects into the night. The demon smiles as Tick's body thumps to the ground, once again a lifeless corpse. The demon returned to his body.

Vyle advances on the demon.

"No!" I scream. He'll possess Vyle just as he did Tick. "Stay back! Get away!" I beg. This is my fight. I tighten my grip on the dagger and charge. I stretch my mind into the air between myself and the demon.

Fire!

A constant flow of yellow flames erupts between us. The flames diverge harmlessly around the demon, but I'm not the least bit disappointed. It's only meant to be a distraction. As the feeder defends the flames from the front, he leaves his back unprotected.

Pull!

The energy wave strikes the demon square in the back and thrusts him toward me. His shield moves with him, but I hold the dagger extended in both arms. It slices through the barrier and embeds itself in the demon's chest. I release the dagger as the demon staggers back. It grabs the hilt and starts to tug it from its own chest. I won't allow it. I command an energy wave, only this time, I picture it flat, paper-thin, and razor-sharp.

Slice!

I send the wave pulsing towards the demon's neck. Just as I'd hoped, the energy wave passes through its flesh with hardly any resistance. The demon slumps to its knees as its head topples off.

At last, the demon is dead.

Vyle's voice calls out from behind me, amplified by his amulet. "Everyone, run! Get to the sanctuary!"

Suddenly recruits are rushing past me on their way to the road. Velma appears at my side. She leans over the demon's body and wrestles the knife from its chest. "C'mon, Lynn. We need to move." She takes my hand and pulls me toward the road.

I pull back. "What about Matt?"

"He's probably ahead of us. He'll be fine."

I let her lead me toward the trees. It only takes a few seconds to reach the gravel road. From here, it's just a short sprint. A quarter-mile at most. We're almost there!

Up ahead, the recruits part around an object in the road. When I get closer, I see why. A feeder lies flat on its back in the gravel. Its body is sprawled perpendicular to the road. Its head faces toward me, and its eyes are wide and unblinking.

It's dead.

Unlike the others, I don't bother to run around the feeder's body. As the corpse approaches, I lengthen my stride and leap. Just as my foot leaves the ground, the feeder bursts to life. His hand snatches my ankle out of the air, and pain jolts through my leg as I'm yanked to the ground.

Bzzzz.

Electricity cuts through me a razor blade. It severs all my muscles until my bones hang limp. I fall to the ground, and the feeder loosens its grip. He thinks he's won.

Adrenaline courses through me. Time seems to slow. I can't move my body, but my mind is unhindered. I focus on the point in space between our bodies.

Push!

The air ripples between us, and our bodies launch apart. I tumble helplessly in the gravel. Stars. Ground. Stars. Ground.

In the time it takes to lift my head, the feeder has already climbed to his feet. Before he can retaliate, I focus on the air around him and scream in my head for as long as I can!

Buuurn!

The air around him ignites in a spiraling vortex of pure heat. I squint my eyes in the brightness, but all I see is yellow-white light. The heat singes my skin, but I don't relent. When I'm convinced he's dead, I release my hold on the elements, allowing the flames to shrink back to oblivion.

Impossible!

The feeder stands before me, wholly untouched by the flames. His clothes are nothing but smoldering ashes, yet not an inch of skin is singed. Then, I see it. His skin is covered with black tattoos—tattoos I know well.

"Adamic armor," I breathe.

Velma hears me and springs to action. She charges the feeder, clearing the gap between us in less than a second. She raises the blade above her head and leaps!

The air ripples.

Velma gurgles as her throat is snatched mid-air. Her momentum swings her legs forward, but her head remains pinned to the same point in space. Her feet dangle a few inches off the ground. She swings the knife with her arm, but it falls short of the feeder's face. Velma kicks her feet and claws at her neck. She's completely silent as she chokes. Not a whisper of air escapes her mouth. I struggle to my feet and press my hand to my chest. But I'm already too late.

SNAP!

Velma's legs fall limp as the bones in her neck collapse. She sways for a split second before her body drops to the floor!

"Noooooo!" I'm screaming before I can stop myself. I need to help her. Somehow, I need to save her. I pray she's still alive. It's just a broken neck. Healers can fix paralysis. I've seen them do it.

The feeder picks up the blade and stalks toward me, stepping over Velma's body like trash in the ring. A devilish rage consumes me. I want to kill that creature. I want to torture him and kill him slowly. I want nothing more than to watch the life drain from his eyes. But right now, fighting is futile. I focus on the ground at his feet.

Liquify.

The road is less dense than granite, and it swallows him faster than expected. As soon as his head dips below the surface, I'm ready with the next command.

Solidify.

The ground crackles as it hardens back together. Then, everything is silent. For a second, I think I've won, but the ground starts to bubble. Steam sprays from the road like a geyser. A hand bursts from the earth. Then another. The feeder crawls out of the ground as molten soil slowly oozes off him. He takes one look at me and charges.

I put up a shield, but he cuts through. I heave a chunk of earth, knocking him off his feet. Then, I run for my life. I'm wobbly, but I manage to stay on my feet. I focus on my muscles, using dominion to lengthen my stride.

I make it 30 yards before my feet are swept out from under me. I land with arms outstretched and slide to a stop in the gravel. I roll on my back, but the feeder already stands over me. He raises the dagger.

Then, he swings it down.

Chapter 30

Matt

"Matthew? Matt, is that you?" Judy's voice sounds good. Definitely not healthy, but not dead either. It's the best sound I've heard in a long time.

"I'm here, mom. It's me."

"Oh, my. For a second, I thought I was dreaming. How are you, dear? Is everything okay?"

"I'm great. Everything's great. I don't even know where to start. How are you? How's the cancer?" I hold my breath.

"I'm alright. The doctors decided there's not much else they can do for me. They sent me home to hospice care last week."

I expected as much, but the news still stings. I feel like I just got kicked in the stomach.

"Tell me about Australia, Matt. I want to hear everything." I convert her question to one I can actually answer: *Tell me about Cavernum, Matt.*

"It's different than I expected. But the people here are really nice. I've already made some good friends." I feel like I'm telling her about my first day of school.

"Oh, yay, Matt. I'm so glad to hear it. Tell me about them."

"Well, my best friend is Diego. I met him on the bus our first day. He's a really good guy. He grew up in LA. He's been going through some tough stuff with his family, so he gets me better than the guys back home. We bond over shared trauma."

I hear Judy chuckle on the other line. "And how's school going?"

"Good. Really good, actually. We had final exams today."

"Already?"

"Yeah. It's an accelerated course. I finished second in the class of 50, so I'm pretty happy about that."

Judy laughs a pleased chuckle. "Oh, that doesn't surprise me at all. You always had a knack for schoolwork. Even when you were little, you never once asked me for help with homework. Not that I could've helped you anyway." Her loud breathing crackles in the phone. "And what about your research? Are you already working on that?"

I translate it. *And what about healing me? Are you already working on that?*

I try to sound positive. "I've started helping in the lab, but we're not having a lot of success. If we do find a cure, it'll take years." *Maybe a lifetime.*

"Are you happy, Matt?" Judy asks.

The question takes me by surprise. I think of the night I've just had with my friends. Of Lynn and Diego and Velma and Klinton.

"Yeah, I'm happy." *More than I've been in a long time.*

"Then you're successful, Matt." Judy declares matter-of-factly. "Happiness is the greatest measure of success. It's the goal that unites us as human beings. Everything else in life is just fluff. Many of the people the world calls successful are so busy they forget to enjoy life. If you're happy today, then you're more successful than most. Remember that, Matthew."

"But what about you?" I ask. "Happiness won't save you; you need a cure."

There's a brief silence. For a second, I worry I've lost connection. Then, her voice projects loud and stern. "Matthew James MacArthur, you listen here. I'm an old woman whose son is living his dream. If I die, I'll die the happiest bag of bones who ever lived. It's not your job to cure me; you hear me? You didn't give me cancer, and it's not your job to cure it. I don't want you worrying about that when you could be out enjoying yourself with your friends."

"Okay."

"Good." Judy sighs, and her tone reverts back to her playful self. "So... is there a girl?"

I smile at the phone. For once, I don't mind the question. "Kind of," I admit. "There's a girl, but she's already taken. She has feelings for another guy."

For a moment, Judy doesn't speak. "What's her name? Can you tell me about her?"

"Her name's Lynn." I pause, trying to keep it general to avoid lies. "She's the smartest in our class. She's actually the one who placed first in exams. She's a musician, but she gave it up to come here. She's also really nice. I don't know, there's just something about her."

"So... Is she married?" Judy asks.

"What? No, of course not."

"Then, she's fair game," Judy declares. The sarcasm is gone from her voice. "If you really like her, chase her. Girls love to be chased. They crave it. Deep down, they want to feel wanted. They want to feel irreplaceable. It shows them you know what you want and you're willing to fight for it."

"I don't know," I say. "Can't it come off as creepy?"

"Only if you're ugly." Judy laughs. "If you're ugly, it's creepy, but you're not ugly, Matt. You have nothing to worry about. Did I ever tell you I was engaged when Dave came back from Vietnam?"

I laugh at the thought of Judy in a love triangle. "You've never told me that."

"I was engaged to marry Henry Coleman. But when Dave got back from Vietnam, he never once let me forget how he felt. He made it hard on me. He made me choose. And in the end, I chose him. You see, Matt, women will avoid choosing at all costs. You have to make them choose. If it doesn't work out, then you'll never have to wonder about what could've been. And if it does work out, you'll be so glad you did."

But he's a commander. I don't stand a chance. "I'll think about it," I agree. Deep down, I know she's right.

Suddenly, I hear a hawk screech. I look up to see the silhouette of a bird blotting out the stars. *That's weird? Why would a messenger hawk be flying so late at night?*

Then, I hear the scream. In the distance, the music cuts out. It's immediately replaced with gunshots. I cover the microphone, hoping Judy can't hear the commotion. My instincts tell me I shouldn't speak. Whatever's out there will hear me. But I can't hang up on Judy. I can't leave her wondering if I'm okay for another month.

"Mom, I'm going to need to call you back."

She must hear the panic in my words. Her voice is that of a protective mother. "Matt, Is everything alright?"

KA-BOOM!

An explosion shakes the air and the ground quivers. Judy definitely heard that. I turn to the direction of the meadow and see a smoke cloud above the trees. It's illuminated by the orange glow of firelight.

"Mom, there was just a big car accident outside my apartment. I'm going to go see if they're alright. I'll call you again soon."

"Go, honey. I'll be here."

"I love you." I hang up the phone and shove it into my pocket. I know I should run the other way, but something calls me toward the meadow, or rather, someone. I have to make sure Lynn's okay. I have to make sure they're all okay. They would do the same for me. I crouch and tiptoe through the grass, periodically pausing to assess my surroundings. Every scream I hear begs me to turn around, to hide under a log and wait till morning, but I keep moving. A twig snaps to my left. I dive behind the closest tree and hold my breath. If a feeder finds me here unarmed, I'll be dead in seconds. The footsteps come closer and closer. They're almost to me now.

Then, I hear a sniffle and a whimper. I step out from the tree and a healer girl cowers with her arms in front of her face. She scrambles back and trips on a rock, landing on her butt.

"It's okay, I'm a guardsman. I'm here to help."

The girl covers her mouth, tears flowing relentlessly down her cheek. I take her by the hand and lift her to her feet.

"Can you tell me what happened?"

"F-F-Feeders. I r-ran. I ran."

A bright flash illuminates the forest behind me. Immediately, thunder rumbles through the air. I look around. I don't see any movement. No imminent danger. The lightning came from the meadow. Following me would only put her more at risk.

"Wait here, and I'll come back for you. Don't go anywhere. Okay?"

The girl nods and sits down behind a tree. The downpour of gunshots has slowed to a dripping faucet. I turn toward the meadow and fall into a jog. When I approach the tree line, I slow to a creep. At the edge of the meadow, the engine of a semi-truck crackles and pops in the flames. The metal is charred black, and the cabin windows are blown out. The truck, I realize, was the source of the explosion. My fib wasn't as far off as I thought.

On the far side of the meadow, I see the recruits gathered together. Above the sound of the sizzling truck, I hear Vyle's voice. "Everybody, get to the sanctuary!"

Like a well-planned prison break, the recruits flee from the meadow. In a matter of seconds, it's nearly deserted. A lone guardsman leans over his injured comrade in the grass. Another boy sits on his heels and cries. Dead bodies litter the meadow, but I don't see any feeders. If they were here moments ago, they left in a hurry.

I break into a sprint across the meadow, scanning the bodies as I run. *Please don't be Lynn. Please don't be Lynn.* Something shiny catches my eye.

No! Not him!

My stomach twists as I lean over Tick's body. His face is only half silver, like some kind of metal masquerade. His shirt is burned off, but his skin is unharmed except for the bloody wound in his chest. His gray eyes watch me with the disinterest of the dead. I press my finger to his eyelids, dragging them closed. Only one eyelid shuts. His metal eyelid doesn't budge.

I'm sorry.

There's nothing I can do for him now. I snatch his amulet and break the chain to get it off him. Then, I sprint. If I hurry, I might be able to catch up with the group. I tear through the forest and onto the gravel road. I see the stampede up ahead, but they're far. I dig my feet into the gravel and swing my arms as fast as I can. When I look up, the mass of recruits isn't any closer. I won't catch up.

Then, I see her. A girl is running at me full speed. Judging by her height, it's either Lynn or Crasilda. Something chases after her as slabs of lava fall from its shoulders.

A feeder!

I grip my amulet tighter in my fist and pump my arms. She's not far now. Less than 100 feet. She stumbles and slides in the gravel. The feeder closes on her. *Please be Crasilda!*

50 feet. I pump my arms harder. Now, I see the feeders face. Adamic tattoos blanket his skin. *He's invincible.*

The girl throws up a shield, but the feeder cuts through it with a knife—an Adamic knife. *He's unstoppable.*

A slab of earth throws the feeder back, but it only delays the inevitable. I should turn around and run. I can't help her. He'll kill me too.

20 ft.

The feeder stands over her now. My eyes fall to the girl. Her slender frame. Her luscious hair.

Lynn!

The feeder lifts the dagger and swings.

I throw my whole soul at the feeder. I dive into his mind and submerge myself into the black cesspool of his thoughts. They flood my ears and rush into my head. They pour down my throat and choke me. Images flash in my mind. My teeth on a girl's neck. Children running—running from me. Then, I feel the power. It's an energy I've never felt before. Neither heat nor electricity, but something else entirely. It pushes against my skin as if there's too much of me packed inside. The pressure is almost unbearable, but it feels amazing.

I open my eyes and see Lynn's face staring back. Her neck is craned to get away, and her eyes are wide with terror. It's me she fears—or rather, the feeder I've possessed.

Knock her out. Take the girl.

My arm starts to swing the dagger, the base of the handle aimed at her temple.

Stop!

My muscles flex, fighting against themselves. The knife quivers in my hand. I feel him fighting against me. Trying to swing. Trying to hurt her. Lynn still hasn't moved. Her eyes flicker between my body and the feeder in utter bewilderment. She scrambles to her feet and positions herself behind my body.

Demon!

His eyes shift, and now I'm staring at my own body. He knows what I am. My expression is blank, my breathing oddly shallow. At first glance, my body looks half-asleep.

An unfamiliar rage fills me with the urge to kill, to rip my body in half, to feed off its corpse. The power inside me begs to escape. I know as soon as I command, the elements will obey. His eyes move to my neck. I see his thoughts in my mind: an immense pressure crushing my throat.

Squee-

Stop!

I exert my mind, fighting back against the feeder. His body is locked in a struggle between our souls. I focus on the knife. If I can just drop the knife, Lynn can kill him with it. I feel my grip loosen. The knife teeters in my hand. Then, his desire to kill overwhelms me. For a second, I forget what I'm fighting for. All I want is to kill that person before me.

Shlunk.

I scream as the knife enters my back, not the knife I'm holding, but a different one entirely. It enters between my shoulders and exits below my collarbone. I feel it separating tissue and slicing nerves. I've never felt such pain, like a coal poker melting through my flesh. An endless agony consumes me. *MAKE IT STOP!!!* I close my eyes and retract my mind.

"Ahhh!" I gasp in my body as the pain fades from my soul. I stare into the eyes of the feeder before me. His head slumps. He's already dead.

A man stands behind the feeder. He's about my height with blonde, curly hair. His nose is tall and wide. He's much too old to be a recruit, at least 40, and he's not wearing a guard uniform either. So who is he?

Mystery man dislodges the knife, and the dead feeder tips like a domino. I grab my amulet, but he doesn't move to hurt me. Instead, he sheaths his own Adamic blade. The feeder was his only target.

Mystery man studies me with sudden curiosity. He gives me a strange look. It's a slender smile with a hint of comradery, as if we share a mutual secret. Then, without a word, he slinks into the woods and meshes with the shadows.

I fall to my knees and press my palms to my temples. Foreign memories still clutter my mind. I can taste the blood in my mouth. I can feel them squirm as I feed. The euphoria lingers under my skin. I crave more.

"Matt, are you okay?" It's Lynn. She looks at me with a mixture of worry and suspicion.

"Yeah, I'm fine. I just need a second."

But Lynn is no longer listening. She's running down the road. She stops next to a body and kneels down beside it. Her voice is half whisper, half sob.

"Velma?"

She's lying in the road with a stillness only the dead can muster. Except for the odd angle of her head, she looks unharmed. For all I know, she could be sleeping. I touch my amulet and let my mind drift toward her. I search with my soul, but there's nothing to find. Her body is empty of thought and emotion. Her soul is gone.

She's dead.

Rose feels for a pulse, and I can't bring myself to stop her. A single memory lingers in my mind: Velma coming at me with a knife, she jumps, and I grab her throat with ease. Then, I squeeze. It only takes a second for her neck to snap. The memory is accompanied by a rush of satisfaction.

I killed her. I remember it.

No! It's only a feeder memory, not my own. I know it wasn't me, but I can't shake the guilt. I want to cry, but my other emotions won't let me. My mind is still flooded with feeder thoughts.

Footsteps approach. This time, lots of them. I struggle to my feet as a small army of guards runs toward us. The man leading them has a silvery robe that looks like it belongs on a fashion runway. I recognize him from yesterday; it's Vyle's father. He spots Lynn, and his face blushes with relief. He runs to us as the rest of the soldiers march toward the meadow. Never once does he notice Velma.

"Are you okay? Are you hurt?"

Lynn shakes her head. A moment later, Commander Elsborne bursts from the ranks and sweeps her into a hug. "Oh, God, Rose. Thank God you're okay." She clings to him, her hand on the nape of his neck. She rises on her toes and arches her back to get closer to him. She opens her mouth to speak, but he cuts her off. "Not here. Wait until we're in the palace."

He starts to lead her away, but she yanks back. "I'm not leaving her." Her voice is anguished and defiant.

The commander holds her by the shoulders and speaks to her in a soft, soothing voice. "You can't do anything for her, Rose. I'm sorry, but we need to get you back to the palace. She would want you to be safe, wouldn't she? If that were you, would you want her out here or safe in the walls?"

Lynn lingers a moment longer before nodding her head. Just like that, they usher her away, and I'm left standing in the road.

"Hey!" I stop a soldier as he passes. "There's a girl hiding in the woods about 100 feet north of the burning truck. She's waiting for someone to get her."

The guardsman pats me on the shoulder. "I'll take care of it. Just get yourself back in the sanctuary. You've done enough."

I turn toward the wall and freeze. Diego is running down the road. He's wearing pajamas and boots, and his hair is a ruffled mess. He sees Velma at the same moment I see him.

He runs to her and falls to his knees, shaking her by the shoulders. "Velma, wake up. Velma, please get up." His hand trembles as he feels for a pulse. Panic settles into his voice. "No! Velma, stay with me! You're okay. You're okay." The tears are already flowing as he starts CPR. Every few compressions, a tear drips onto her shirt.

"Someone, help me!" he screams. "I need a healer! Please! Please help her!"

No one stops to help him. They all know it's too late. The other soldiers watch him, grateful it wasn't someone they knew, grateful their lives aren't changed forever.

I feel the sting of loss, but it's a drop in the ocean compared to what Diego must feel. His best friend is gone. Never again will he hold her hand or hear her laugh; never again will he kiss her lips. All their secrets, all their jokes are nothing but memories. Whatever life they could've had is gone forever.

Diego's stops CPR and collapses on her chest. His fingers tighten on her shirt, folding cloth between his fingers. "Noooo! Velma you can't die. Please don't die. I need you. Please come back! Please!" His cries cut me to the core. In a way, he is the real tragedy. Velma suffered

410

for a moment, but Diego will relive this moment forever. I want to get away, but I can't bring myself to leave. Then, his eyes find me.

"You!" His voice is completely foreign, a wail of rage and grief. "This is your fault! You said you'd watch her! You said you'd make sure nothing happened. And now she's dead! You let her die!"

I take a step closer. I want to explain what happened. I want to mourn with him. But Diego doesn't want any of that. "Get away! Just get away!"

I'm stunned. I gape at him as the seconds tick by. Before I can think of what to say, someone grabs my arm. Zane's voice rumbles in my ear. "Come with me." He starts to walk, but I resist.

"You're making it worse," Zane hisses. "He's lost the girl he loves. He needs to mourn. Trust me, I've been there. I know how he feels right now. Your presence will only make it worse."

I comply, falling into pace with Zane. "Where are we going?" I eventually ask.

"To talk. It's time you got some answers."

After the chaos of the night, the trench feels eerily silent. I take a seat on the rocky shore next to Zane. Still, all I can think about is Diego. I left him with Velma's body, to carry her back all by himself. To bear the burden of her death alone. *I'm a terrible friend. I'm a terrible person.*

"Matt, I need you to tell me everything that happened. Start with when the feeders arrived."

I motion towards the exit. "Aren't you worried about someone hearing?"

"I'll use sound dominion. No one will hear us."

You couldn't have just done that last time? I keep my complaints to myself. I tell him everything: about calling Judy, about finding Tick's body, about possessing the feeder, about the memories. Zane says nothing until I finish with finding Velma.

"The feeder you possessed. You said he wasn't trying to kill Lynn. He wanted to take her?"

I nod my head.

"Do you know why?"

"That's all I got from him," I admit. "I don't know why."

Zane scratches his beard. "This feeder, was it the same one that attacked you in Hogrum?"

I don't think so. This one was smaller. And in his mind, it didn't feel like he recognized me. It wasn't him."

Zane nods. I can tell something heavy weighs on his mind. He avoids my eyes. "To answer your question from last time, yes. If you remove your tattoo, you'll no longer be a demon."

"I want it gone," I say. "I want these memories out of my head forever." Even still, I'm filled with someone else's rage. I can still feel the power pressing at my skin. The urge to feed. It's a part of me now. I can't escape it.

Zane sighs. "I figured you'd say that. In the end, it's your choice, but I want you to think of the good. Tonight, you saved Lynn's life when no one else could. I know you've had to sacrifice for that, but your abilities can be a weapon for good."

I don't know what to say. He's right, of course. Lynn is worth all this. I would've done the same thing a hundred times if I had to.

"I know it's hard," Zane says. "That friend I told you about, his name was Kildron. The first time he possessed a feeder, he didn't talk to me for days. I found out later, he wanted to kill himself. The feeder's thoughts drove him mad."

"Did he ever get better?" I ask.

"It took some time, but he did."

"How?" I demand, my voice desperate.

"By doing the opposite. There was this girl he loved, Jenevrah. She was a saint. He fought the bad with the good in her. She let him read her mind, and they shared the burden together. It wasn't easy, but he got through it."

Who's my Jenevrah? Is it Lynn? Or maybe Kendra? Or someone else entirely. For now, I don't have one. I'll have to fight this alone.

Zane looks down at me. "You can read my mind if you want. It might help."

It sounds weird, but I agree. He removes his soul-anchor, and I let my mind collide with his. I feel his sadness and his guilt. I feel his anguish at watching me suffer. His abhorrence of death clashes with the feeder's thirst for blood. His goodness dispels the feeder's love of suffering. Above it all, I feel his assurance that I'll get through this. He believes in me.

For the first time since the feeder, I feel better. I feel human.

Zane's breath comes louder. I see his arms tense. Whatever relief I'm feeling, Zane is experiencing the opposite. Slowly his shoulders relax, and he looks at me. "Better?"

"Yes, thank you."

Zane grunts his acknowledgment. "Any questions for me? Now's the time to ask."

Now that my mind is free to think, the questions clutter my head. "Why tattoo a baby? Why not wait until I'm older so I can choose for myself?"

"To protect you," Zane says. "A demon has absolute dominion over man, but so do other demons. Two demons are on level ground."

"Why would a demon want to possess a baby?"

"It's not uncommon for a demon to use someone's child as leverage. If your parents interacted with other demons, you'd be in constant danger growing up. The easiest way to protect you from possession is to make you a demon yourself."

"But what about my amulet? Wouldn't that have protected me too?"

Zane shrugs. "Soul-anchors are a powerful protection, but they can always be removed. You're much safer as a demon."

It makes sense. Maybe my parents weren't crazy after all. My mind returns to tonight. The man who saved me, the curly-haired feeder-killer. Who was he? If he was hunting feeders? Why run from the guard? Why not seek refuge in the sanctuary?

"Are feeders ever good?" The question seems absurd, but I ask it anyway.

Zane grumbles. "Feeding isn't like possession, Matt. A demon can be a good person if they use their gift for good. But feeders are evil. They consume a human soul. It's more than murder. It's the single greatest sin a person can commit. Do you hear me?"

"I wasn't suggesting it can be justified. I just mean... does anyone ever recover?"

Zane's eyes pierce me like daggers. I've struck a nerve. "Listen carefully, Matt. Feeding isn't some drug addiction. You can't just muscle your way through feeder withdrawals and hope you don't relapse. The effects are permanent. It shatters your soul. Corrupts your mind. It fills you with a power stronger than any drug. It eliminates pain and lets you live for centuries." His voice is almost shouting now. "Do you think after all that, a feeder can go back to the aches and pains of everyday life? I'll tell you they can't. And they'll kill again and again to keep it that way."

Zane takes a deep breath and rests his hands on his knees. "I'm sorry. It's just... I've lost some good friends to it, and no, none of them have ever recovered."

He looks at me, his anger once again locked deep behind his eyes. "You must promise me, Matt. No matter what happens, no matter how desperate you become, you won't ever resort to feeding."

"I promise." I can't help but feel that this isn't entirely about me. I swallow and look up at Zane. "Your friend, Kildron—the one who helped you learn dominion—did he become a feeder?"

Zane nods his head once, the grief still fresh in his eyes. "Sadly, yes. I'm afraid he did."

Chapter 31

Rose

My candle is almost burned to the base. Last I checked, it was three o'clock in the morning. I lay in my bed with my sheets twirled tight around me. The silk near my face is darkened with tear stains.

My door cracks open with a slow creak. Antai's face appears in the slit. When he sees that my eyes are open, he slips inside and shuts the door behind him. "Still can't sleep?"

"Every time I close my eyes, I'm back in the meadow." I wipe my eyes, but my fingers come back dry. I ran out of tears a long time ago. I've been lying awake in my bed for over two hours. I must look like a mess. My eyes are swollen, and my hair is a rat's nest. "How bad is it?"

He sits on the edge of my bed and takes my hand under the covers. Already I know the number must be high. "12 guards, 9 recruits, and 4 healers. There are still 2 people missing."

25 dead! One of those numbers was Tick. He died trying to clear a path for me to escape. Another was Velma. She died trying to protect me from the armored feeder. How many others died because of me. If I hadn't been there, none of this would've happened. *It's my fault she's gone.* Frustration wells within me until I can't contain it any longer.

I turn my face into my pillow, and my shoulders shake. Antai doesn't say anything. He strokes my hair, letting the strands drag through his open fingers. I let my mind focus solely on the sensation. I look up at his eyes and find them watering. I've never seen Antai cry, not once. For a brief moment, I forget my own pain. "What's wrong?"

Antai clears his throat. Even with glistening eyes, he remains in control of his voice. "Byron was on duty tonight. They found his body in the meadow."

No! Before Antai was an officer, he trained a cadet, Byron, for a full year. Byron was like a brother to Antai—his best friend besides myself.

"It's my fault," I say. "This is all my fault. They were only there for me. If I had just—"

Antai's face grows stern. He takes my cheek in his hand and silences me with his eyes. "You don't get to think like that. You couldn't have avoided this. None of us could've known this would've happened. Okay? The feeders did this and no one else."

"But I should've known. I could've anticipated. If I had chosen the orchestra, they would've taken me instead of Nevela, and everyone would still be alive. It would've been better that way."

"Don't say that." Antai's voice turns sour. "Don't ever say that again. Not in front of me." He takes a deep breath and wrestles back his emotions. "I need you right now, Rose." He squeezes my hand so tight it almost hurts. "It sounds terrible, but I would trade all their lives for yours in a heartbeat. Because I need you—not just as Rose, but as Queen Malik. I need a queen I can trust. Cavernum needs a queen it can trust. If you die, we have no future."

But I don't want to be queen. I don't want any of this. I would happily trade it for a simple life in the ring. But then I remember Wendy. How could I possibly say I envy her position?

I think of Velma: her fragile body, broken on the road. I think of her tattoo—the one she never finished. *Change is coming!* I can make that change. I can make a difference. I have to. I have to make her death worth something.

There's a knock on the door. Octavian enters. He gives a quick nod to Antai before addressing me. "Princess, the high council has summoned you. Please report immediately."

Antai holds my hand the whole way there, helping me up the stairs when I'm shaky on my feet. I wish he could come in and sit with me, but the council was specific that no commanders are welcome. They're worried that there's a spy in the palace.

The guards push open the doors, and I step inside. I stand before the map of the city and face the council. Grandpa gives me a supportive smile. "Welcome, Rose. The hour is late, so we'll try to keep this brief. We just have a few questions about your statement." Grandpa holds up a piece of paper on which I've written everything that happened. "Kaynes, do you care to begin?"

"Of course, your highness. Roselyn, you mentioned in your report that the feeder was lying on the ground, letting the others run past him. Is there any chance he was injured or unconscious, and that's why he let the others run past him?"

I try to make my voice as confident as I can. "No, his eyes were open, and he was watching for me. He had Adamic armor, so he couldn't have been injured."

"Are we really going to believe this?" Chancellor Quine questions. "The feeders in league with the equalists, trying to kill the princess. Isn't it a bit absurd?"

Zane glares at Quine with unblinking eyes. "What's absurd is denying the facts before your face. Most of the bodies were left untouched. If the feeders weren't there to feed, and they weren't there to steal amulets, what other explanation could there be?"

"This is preposterous," Chancellor Bolo bellows. "Are you suggesting that someone close to the princess collaborated with a demon? That they leaked information about the princess's whereabouts?"

Zane shrugs. "How else would they have known?"

"There's one problem," Chancellor Quine argues. "How would they've known what the princess looks like? None of the feeders have laid eyes on her before."

Zane looks around the room. "As you all know, I was exposed to demons in Hogrum. One of their abilities is to steal and transfer memories, even memories of faces. It's possible that a demon was able to steal a memory of the princess from someone who knew her, and then shared it with the other feeders."

"How many people knew the princess would be there?" Gwenevere asks. "They're all potential suspects."

Eyes turn on Grandpa, who sighs. "As far as I'm aware, these are the men who knew: General Zane, General Kaynes, his son Vyle, Proticus, Commander Elsborne, and myself." A few eyebrows twitch at Vyle's name.

General Katu looks troubled. "Who would've had a motive to do it? How could they possibly benefit from this?"

"General Kaynes did!" I say. I can't prove anything yet, but it's the only thing that makes sense. "His son, Vyle, assaulted me the morning of evaluations. If Vyle is convicted, he'll get expelled from the guard. Eliminating me protects his son. What more motivation do you need?"

General Kaynes gives me a warning glance. "Do you really think I would risk my son's life to protect him from a faulty charge? Do you really think I'm that foolish? And wasn't it my own son who saved you from the feeders?"

The council members consider this for a moment. They seem satisfied by his defense. General Kaynes gives me a victorious smile. "Besides, I think we're all forgetting a certain someone with inside information. Tell me, princess, did you ever tell your servant girl that you were entering the guard?"

Nevela! "Yes, I told her but..." *It couldn't have been her. Could it?*

General Kaynes relishes his victory with his pompous chin held high. "Here we all are, accusing each other of treason, while the servant girl has likely spilled everything to the equalists. Heavens knows a girl like that couldn't withstand a torture interrogation."

I curl my hands into fists and press them into my thighs. It's the only thing stopping me from striking the table.

Chancellor Bolo rubs his bald chin. "But she wouldn't have known about the graduation party. It was changed after she was kidnapped."

Kaynes rolls his eyes. "Yes, but the entire guard knew about it. If she revealed that the princess was a recruit, any guardsman could've told them where she'd be tonight. The entire guard is a suspect. They may not even know they betrayed the princess."

No, Nevela didn't tell them. The very night that General Kaynes discovers my identity, there's an ambush. That can't be a coincidence.

"And what about the boy?" Gwynevere says. "The feeders didn't kill him. How do we make sense of that?"

General Kaynes looks to me. "You said they stood there as if they knew each other. Is that correct?"

"Well, yes, but—"

General Kaynes doesn't let me finish. "Perhaps he's working with them? Perhaps he's the one who disclosed the party's location?"

Zane leans forward in his seat, his voice edging on anger. "If you're going to fabricate stories, at least make them plausible. Where would the boy have spoken with a feeder? Since he arrived in Cavernum, he never left the walls unsupervised. And assuming he did work with the feeder, why would he try to protect the princess? It doesn't add up."

Grandpa taps his cane on the floor. "Enough! We're wasting our time with speculation. It's late. Let's finish this meeting, and we can adjourn tomorrow if we need to." He turns to me. "Rose, meet me in my study. I'll be there in a minute."

"Right now?" *But it's almost four o'clock in the morning.*

Grandpa furrows his eyebrows. His voice is a low hiss. "Go!" The message is clear: *don't ask questions.*

I bow and exit the room. The guards shut the door behind me. I have a terrible feeling about this. What could be so urgent that it can't wait until morning?

Whatever it is, it can't be good.

Grandpa's study is more cluttered than usual. Open books are spread over the table, replacing every inch of wood with written word. Pillars of stacked books encircle grandpa's reading chair in the corner. The bookshelves bordering the room are unacceptably bare, like a child underdressed for winter. Several sheets of gold foil sail atop the sea of books. It's not an irregular sight; Grandpa is always practicing Adamic and mastering new spells. I take a step closer and study the foil. Every sheet has the same symbols.

My heart stops as I read the symbols. *Dominion over mankind by the power of the devil.* It's the demon spell. Why would Grandpa be writing that spell? It's witchcraft. It's devil worship. It doesn't make sense.

I step away from the table and turn my attention to Grandpa's reading chair. Two books rest page down on the cushion. Grandpa most likely set them there as he got up to leave. One is King Titan's journal. The second book I don't recognize. I pick it up, being sure not to lose Grandpa's place. The pages are yellow and wrinkled, easily several hundred years old. Each page is divided into two passages. The top is a language I don't recognize—perhaps Hebrew or something ancient. Below is a commentary written in English.

I begin reading at the top of the left page:

The abilities of a demon aren't limited to short term possession. There are several instances in Genekiah's writings where demons are recorded to possess a body for days, sometimes weeks. During the event, the demon's body remains in a comatose state and vulnerable to attack. To protect themselves, demons hide themselves in coffins and bury themselves in the earth.

Demons have also been known to possess the bodies of the dead. These demons are often referred to as skin-walkers. They use these disposable bodies to do their bidding while keeping their true identity hidden. In this way, demons can be very manipulative and deceitful. Demons often make their enemies their closest friends by day, only to work their evil deeds by night. They—

The door opens, and I jump. Grandpa shuffles inside. He eyes the book in my hand. "An interesting read. I borrowed it from Lycon before the attack," he says casually.

I motion to the Adamic foil. "What is all this? Tell me it's not what I think it is."

Grandpa doesn't even look over. "I can't, because it is." He shuffles to a drawer and rummages through it. He removes a leather bag and quickly fills it with books from the bookshelf.

"You said no more secrets."

"It's not a secret, Rose. Now just isn't the time. I'll explain everything when I get back. I have nothing to hide from you."

"What do you mean? When you get back from what?"

"I'm leaving for Beskum tonight."

"What?" I hardly believe what I'm hearing. Beskum is a sanctuary in Africa. Its libraries are ancient and extensive, only second to those of Hogrum.

"I graduate tomorrow, Grandpa! You're supposed to announce who I am. You can't leave now!" *Last time you left, I almost died.*

"I'm sorry, Rose, but this really can't wait. I received word an hour ago that the queen has been possessed. They want me to attempt an exorcism. Zane will have to be the one to disclose your identity. He's already agreed. He'll keep you safe. I wouldn't leave if it wasn't absolutely necessary. I'm worried demons have infiltrated Beskum." He sighs. "The last time that happened..."

I remember the letter from my father. He said the demons had infiltrated Hogrum's high council. "You think the Adalit will strike there next?"

"I do, and I might be able to stop it." His eyes are soft and full of regret. "I wouldn't go if it wasn't absolutely necessary."

"If Beskum is in danger, then you will be too!" My breath is coming faster, and fear clouds my thoughts. "What if they invade?" So much could go wrong. I need Grandpa here. I need him by my side tomorrow.

Grandpa says nothing as he leans on his cane. He looks at me with his usual fatherly smile, as if he knows things I don't yet understand. "Have I ever taught you about relics?"

I should be mad he's ignored my questions, but now I'm curious. "What's a relic?"

"First, let's establish what's not a relic. Amplifiers, soul-anchors, Adamic armor, Adamic blades, all of their spells are common knowledge among adalits. If necessary, I can replicate these items anytime. Correct?"

I nod my head, confused where this is leading.

"Relics are everything else Adamic we don't understand. They're ancient artifacts that date back to the days of the prophets. They're rare, but the spells are powerful and diverse. No two relics are alike."

"Like what?" I ask.

"The possibilities are endless." He thinks for a moment. "Before Hogrum was destroyed, they had a relic that could alter your appearance. They also had a mirror relic to instantly transport between Cavernum and Hogrum."

Teleportation! My jaw drops open. "What happened to it?"

"My father worried it would be too powerful in the wrong hands. He destroyed our half of the mirror long before Hogrum fell, and thank goodness for that. Imagine what could've happened if he didn't"

I imagine feeders running rampant through Cavernum. The thought makes my skin crawl. "Do you have any relics?"

Grandpa smiles. That's the question he's been waiting for. He lifts his crown off his head and holds it in both hands. "This crown has been in our family line ever since the founders of Cavernum crowned the first king." He sets it on the table where I can see the interior and points to the inside rim. Carved into the gold are half a dozen Adamic symbols.

"It's a relic," I gasp.

Grandpa nods. "The spell is beyond my understanding, but its function is simple enough. It creates a permanent energy shield to defend me from harm. As long as I wear it, I'm untouchable. The only attack it can't defend is an Adamic blade."

I gawk at the crown. It's amazing. It's the equivalent of full-body Adamic armor. Now, I understand why Grandpa has been hesitant to disperse Adamic blades. It's the one weapon that can kill him. To do so puts himself at risk.

"Are there any others?" I ask.

Grandpa opens his mouth and pauses. He's trying to decide whether or not to share something.

I shake my hands in the air. "Come on. Just show me."

Grandpa smiles and walks to the back of his study. He opens a drawer and takes out a tiny chest—no bigger than a loaf of bread. It's wooden with metal bindings. Instead of a lock, a small metal panel is carved with Adamic symbols. He sets the chest on top of the shelf. "This relic has been in our family for generations. My father called it an inheritance box. It can only be moved or opened by someone with royal blood."

"What's inside?"

At my question, Grandpa picks up his bag and resumes packing. "I'm afraid that's a question for another day."

"But—"

"It's late, Rose. One question will lead to another. Another time, please." He takes my hand in his spongy palm. "I'm so proud of you, Rose. I wish I could be there tomorrow; I really do."

"It's okay. They need you more."

Grandpa gives me one last proud smile and kisses me on the forehead. "I love you, Rose. Now, go get some sleep. You have a big day tomorrow. I'll be back as soon as I can."

"Night, Grandpa, Love you."

He watches me go and closes the door to his study. I walk in a daze down the hall, trying to make sense of the night. The more I think, the more unsettled I become.

I think of the box and its secret inhabitants. I think of the book on his chair and the gold foil. Only one thing is sure.

Grandpa is keeping secrets from me. Grandpa is learning the demon curse!

Chapter 32

Matt

The royal plaza is teeming with life. I walk along the perimeter to avoid the crowd, careful not to bump strangers with the gun strapped to my hip. I'm still not used to the extra girth. An amplifier swings from my neck, a symbol of my newly appointed power. My brand new uniform is both formal and jet black, the appropriate apparel for a funeral. But this funeral is unlike any I've ever seen.

The cremation altar marks the center of the plaza. It's nothing but an enormous heap of logs the size of a helicopter landing pad. All 20 bodies are laid to rest atop the wood. They're hidden from view by an ornate white cloth. It dips and swoops over the forms of the dead. I wonder which lump is Velma. My eyes fall on the smallest mound, and I force myself to turn away.

I make my way slowly toward the stage. Royal guards form a human barrier around it. They don't bat an eye as I slip between them and up the steps. I walk between rows of wooden chairs. The stage is crammed with them, each chair with a name tag of its own. Most of them are already filled with traumatized recruits. I find my name on a chair at the back of the stage. **Klinton** is written on the chair to my right. The chair to my left reads: **Diego**.

Tick. He was the one who organized the seats for graduation. He wanted us to sit together. The thought makes everything that much more bitter. He was a good man. A good friend too. Even to Vyle, he was merciful and kind. And now he's dead.

The seat to the left of Diego's is empty. There's no name tag, but I know who it was for.

Velma. I haven't spoken to Diego since it happened and I'm not looking forward to it. Facing him is like confronting Velma's death all over again. I'm terrified that he'll never forgive me, that our friendship is another casualty of the attack.

Anger ignites inside me like an ember and slowly spreads until my mind is aflame. Why did Velma have to die? After all she did to escape the ring? Why did Tick have to die? Why couldn't it have been Vyle or Zander? Why couldn't they have died instead?

I search for Lynn and find her sitting next to Zane at the front of the stage. *What is she doing up there?* Before I can give it much thought, Diego climbs onto the stage. He takes a seat next to me and crosses his arms over his chest. He stares straight ahead. I shift uncomfortably in my seat as the tension rises. What can I possibly say to make things right? *I'm sorry I didn't watch out for her like I promised. I'm sorry I did nothing to save her.*

"I'm sorry." Diego's words catch me by surprise. He uncrosses his arms and looks down at his lap. "I'm sorry for what I said last night. I didn't mean it. I was only mad at myself. I needed someone to blame. I'm sorry." His hands ball into fists and then relax. "I should've been there, and I wasn't." He looks up at me, his dirt-colored eyes are muddy with past tears. "Thank you."

I'm both stunned and relieved. "For what?"

"Zane told me you killed the feeder. I want to thank you for it. I feel better knowing that monster is dead."

Technically, I didn't kill it, but I don't correct Diego. If it saves our friendship, I'll let him believe it's true. "I'm sorry I couldn't do it sooner. Maybe she'd still be here if I did." Diego winces but doesn't deny it.

He stares off into the crowd, and I follow his gaze. For such a small graduation, I wouldn't expect so many people. The crowd is easily as big as it was for the execution a few weeks back.

"I'm surprised there are so many people." I try to lighten the mood.

Diego furrows his brow. "My dad says he's heard rumors in the field. They say the equalists are planning an assassination."

"An assassination? For who?"

"The princess," Diego says it like it's the only logical answer.

I look around. I don't see a princess. I don't even see the king. "Is she here?"

Diego looks around too. "I don't see her. Maybe she found out and stayed away?"

"Or maybe the rumors were just rumors?" I suggest.

Diego shrugs. "My dad doesn't think so. He wouldn't even let my family come watch the funeral. He thinks it's too dangerous." If it's true, it would certainly explain the crowd. They haven't come for the funeral. They're here to witness an assassination.

We wait in relative silence for the ceremony to begin. At some point, Klinton takes his seat to my right. Just when I start to get restless, Zane steps to the front of the stage.

"Good morning." His grizzly voice projects smoothly over the plaza. "We're here today to celebrate those who fight for our freedom. We're here to recognize those who are willing to pay the ultimate price so that we can live in peace. Too often, these men and women are victimized and painted as the enemy, but they sacrifice their lives fighting in your defense. How many of you would be willing to do the same? How many of you would lay down your life in defense of a total stranger? Not many of you would. Yet, these soldiers have done just that."

He directs his gaze to the cremation altar. "Their deaths weren't in vain. They weren't unnecessary. They weren't a result of misfortune or bad luck. They were a sacrifice, a sacrifice for the welfare of a nation.

Cavernum lives because guards are willing to die. We owe them our lives. We owe them everything we have. May we hold their names sacred for as long as we live."

An elegant speech for such a barbarian. I smile at the thought of Zane stooped over a desk writing a speech. Sometimes I underestimate the lumberjack.

Zane steps down, and an old man in a white robe steps forward. I wish Lynn were here to tell me who he is. If I had to guess, he looks like some kind of priest. He raises his shriveled hands high above his head. "Blessed be the name of God, for even in death, we live." The old priest clasps his knobby hands together and bows his head for several seconds. "Death, from a mortal perspective, is a terrible tragedy. But from a godly perspective, it is beautiful and crucial. Our souls are set free by death. Free to pass into the great beyond. Free to transcend into a state of peace and tranquility.

Death only hurts the living. We lose the presence of a loved one. However, our loved ones enter the presence of he who loves all. While we mourn our losses, the dead rejoice with the hosts of heaven. And now, as their bodies return to dust, let us remember that their souls return to God."

Once again, he raises his hands above his head. "Please recite with me the prayer of the dead." The crowd speaks in recitation.

"We ask thee, God, this holy day.
To bless the souls for whom we pray
And guide them safely back to thee
That from all pain, they may be free
And reunite with family
To live forever happily
For all time, eternity."

Two guardsmen use dominion to light the edges of the altar. I watch the flames consume the wood and everything inside it. Is the pastor right? Will I see Judy in the next life? Will I meet my parents?

Will I see Tick and Velma again? It's comforting to believe, but I'm not entirely convinced.

The crowd is silent as the fire burns. The wood pops and crackles. Embers float like snowflakes on the wind. Offstage, the royal orchestra plays a depressing piece of classical music. The smoke taints the air with burning flesh. I feel sick, not just from the smell, but from the idea of inhaling little pieces of my friends.

"Get your hands off me. Help! I'm being framed! Help!" A girl's voice pierces the silence. In the front row of the crowd, two guards wrestle a girl to the ground—one average-sized and the other a virtual giant. When she resists, the giant guard smacks her in the head with the stock of his rifle. The smaller guard kneels on her back. "You're under arrest for possession of an amulet."

The girl submits as the guard slaps handcuffs on her wrists. Even pinned to the floor, I can tell she's tall for a girl. Muscular too. She looks young, maybe a few years older than me. Her pixie cut is dirty blonde and barely covers her ears. Already, blood stains her hair and trickles down her cheek. The guards, without an ounce of sympathy, hoist her to her feet and drag her out of the crowd.

Diego goes rigid next to me. His eyes are wide, and his mouth makes a perfect O. "That's him." Diego whispers in my ear. His breathing is short and forceful. "That's him!"

He isn't looking at the girl, he's watching the smaller guard who's carrying her. The man's skin is an olive tone, and his jet black hair curls into a bush on his head. His oval face is bordered by a neatly trimmed beard and mustache.

"Who?

"That's the guy who killed my mom."

"What?" I want to refute it, but after everything that's happened, I refrain. "Are you sure?"

"That's the guy," Diego insists. "Look at the scar on his eyebrow."

I squint. Sure enough, a scar slants above his right eye, leaving a bald patch in the center of his eyebrow. *Could it be?* It must be a coincidence.

"Diego, there's no way. A feeder can't enter the walls. It can't be him." *Unless he's not a feeder.*

"I'm positive. That's the guy. You think I'd forget his face?" Diego takes a look around before scooting to the edge of his seat. "I'm going to follow him." He's out of his mind, but I can't let Diego leave alone. He'll get himself locked up or worse...

I watch as the guards drag the girl alongside the stage and towards the palace gate. For a brief moment, they're within range of my mind. I push my soul towards Scarface. An overwhelming sense of paranoia envelops me. Guilt and fear soak deep into the seams of my mind. Whatever he's about to do, he's afraid of getting caught.

Could it be true?

Diego lowers himself off the stage and follows the guards toward the palace gate. I leap down and run after him in a low crouch. No one tries to stop us.

At the gate, Scar is already talking to the palace guards. They take one look at the blond girl and wave all three of them through.

I grab Diego's shoulder. "Diego, stop. This is crazy. They're in the palace. We're too late."

Diego shakes his head. "No, I'm not letting him get away again. I'll tell the guards everything if I have to."

What will he say? *That guard is actually a feeder who killed my mom in Los Angeles.* "They won't believe you, Diego." But what if he's right? What if the girl really is being framed? We have to do something.

I step in front of Diego and approach the palace gate as confidently as I can. "Let me handle this. Don't say a word."

The royal guard holds up a hand. He's not big or strong, but he's a royal guard. What he lacks in size, he must make up in intelligence. His eyes dance between us, analyzing every ounce of our appearance. I can already tell this won't be easy.

"State your name and business."

"I'm Matthew MacArthur, and this is Diego Ortega. And do we really need all this formality? I mean, two guys like us, you know why we're here."

I flash a harmless smile, look him in the eyes, and press my mind into his as delicately as I can. His thoughts nudge against my mind just enough to discern.

Judging by your disrespect, I'd guess a disciplinary hearing. God, I hate cadets.

The royal guard sighs. "Tell me your business, or I'll cite you for negating your superior. How does that sound, Mr. MacArthur?"

I fake an offended face. "Hey, I don't want any more trouble. I've already got enough as it is. We have disciplinary hearings today."

"With what judge?"

"Judge Lumb."

The guard's hand drifts towards his gun. *He's not taking cases today. It's his daughter's graduation.*

"Oh, you know what," I laugh. "That was last time. This time it's with…" I snap my fingers. "Oh, it's on the tip of my tongue. He's the short one."

Judge Zelzar?

"Judge Zelzar!" I blurt. "That's his name. This is the second time I've been cited for drinking on the job."

The guard nods. His shoulders relax, and his hand drifts away from his holster. "What time is your hearing?"

I give him a quizzical look. "You strike me as a pretty smart guy. I'll give you 10 bars if you can guess it right."

There aren't any hearings until after the funeral service. The earliest it could be is 2:30. "Just answer the question."

I smile. "Your loss. The hearing isn't until 2:30. We just wanted to get here a little early."

The guard nods. "Well good luck on your case. Judge Zelzar is known to be pretty strict."

"Thanks, sir. I appreciate it. Oh, and just out of curiosity, what did the girl do? Where were they taking her?"

She was caught with an amulet. She'll go to the pit for questioning. "Mind your own business, cadet. Now, get a move on."

We don't look back as we hurry through the archway and into the palace. Diego looks up at me and smiles. "When the freak did you learn to lie like that? I thought we were dead."

I shrug. "A new talent, I guess."

The path to the central building is long and ornate. We speed walk as fast as we can without looking suspicious. We round a long pool of koi fish, and Scar comes into view. The pixie cut girl is complying now. She walks between them with her head held high. When they reach the palace entrance, Scar whispers a few words and the guards step aside. I start to panic.

"Are the disciplinary hearings in the main tower?" I worry.

Diego shrugs. "I hope so, dude. I really hope so."

We climb the steps and stop in front of the guards. I fake a bored demeanor. "Matthew MacArthur and Diego Ortega, reporting for disciplinary hearings."

The guard looks me over up and down, then Diego. He rests his hand on his belt. "Down the hall, then, take a right. The court is at the end of the hall. You can leave your weapons with the guards at the court entrance. They aren't allowed inside."

"Excellent. Thank you, sir."

We hurry down the hall. As soon as we're out of earshot, I breathe a sigh of relief. "Did you see where they went?"

Diego takes the lead, guiding me down a hallway on the left. "This way. They can't be far."

We walk down a grandiose hallway until we reach a staircase made for an elephant. It only has one option: up. The pit, however, is down in the dungeons. Wherever Scar is taking that girl, it isn't the pit.

The palace is quiet as we climb the steps. It leads us to another massive hallway. Just when I think we're lost, I see the blood. It pools on the marble floor, emanating from a lifeless guard. A single black dot marks where the bullet entered his forehead. I never even heard a gunshot.

By the time I look up, Diego is halfway down the hallway. I hurry to catch up. We've barely turned the corner when two maids emerge from one of the side rooms. They walk towards us, arms glued to their sides, eyes twitching nervously. When we get close, they duck their heads and scurry on their way. As soon as they're out of sight, we break into a jog.

We don't go far before we find the next body. Blood still runs from an incision in the guard's throat, painting his white uniform red. There's no sign of a murder weapon. Whoever did it can't be far.

Ding! Ding! Ding! Ding! Ding!

The sound of church bells reverberates through the palace. Down the hallway, I hear the shouting.

They found the first body. They're sounding the alarm.

I don't even want to imagine what'll happen if the royal guards catch us here. I'm certain they'll blame us for the murders. We'll be hung by the end of the week.

Diego and I share a panicked glance before rushing down the next hallway. This one is decorated with elaborate suits of armor. Like medieval mannequins, they model swords and shields and hollow-eyed helmets. I clutch my amulet tight in my fist as I tiptoe down the hallway.

A painting on the wall catches my eye; it's a portrait of a woman. She's beautiful. Her hazel eyes pop from the canvas. Her lips are full and her nose is as delicate as a flower. My eyes cling to her features. It's her. It doesn't make sense, but it's her.

Lynn?

Diego stops too. "Is that who I think it is?"

I nod. But I don't understand it. Her face is on the wall with King Dralton. Why would a servant be on the wall? *Unless she isn't a servant!*

That would explain why she was in the garden that night. Why she knows so much about dominion. Why I couldn't read her mind. Why her past is such a secret. Why the commander is obsessed with her. *Rose*—that was what she called herself. It all makes sense now.

Lynn isn't a servant. Lynn is the princess.

"C'mon." Diego takes off down the hallway. "We don't have time." But I can't get Lynn out of my head. *The assassination. What if she's in danger?*

I take off after Diego as the shouting gets louder. They've found the other body. They're close now. Any seconds the guards will be upon us.

Bratatatata!

The roar of distant gunfire pierces the stone walls. It's impossible to tell where it's coming from—somewhere beyond the palace wall. The shouting of guards recedes down the hallway, drawn away by the new threat. For now, we're alone. But at what cost?

Please be alive, Lynn.

Diego stops in front of me, and I nearly run into him. We're at a dead end. The door in front of us is different from any I've seen. The door frame is made of gold, and the door shines like polished silver. There's no door handle, only a keyhole in the center of the door. The end of a skeleton key protrudes from the keyhole. Adamic symbols are carved all over the door's surface.

The palace vault!

As I get closer, I see the door is cracked open an inch. Voices echo from the inside. I press my ear to the crack, and Diego does the same below my shoulder. It's a man's voice, deeper than any voice I've ever heard.

"It won't take long for us to load the amulets. Why don't you go check the carriage and make sure it's ready to go."

Scar's voice mumbles something in reply, but I don't wait long enough to hear it. I scramble away from the vault and into the nearest door. It looks like a bedroom of some kind. As soon as Diego is inside, I press the door closed and hold the handle twisted so that it doesn't make a noise. Footsteps get louder and then quiet again.

"What do we do?" I gasp. "They're robbing the vault?"

"Hell if I care. Let 'em take it all. I'm going after him." Diego pulls the door open and charges down the hall after Scar. I glance back at the vault and groan. I have no choice. I can't let Diego face him by himself. I turn and sprint after him.

Scar is almost to the staircase when Diego catches up with him. "Hey, remember me?"

Scar flinches and whips around. His gun is raised in a second, and he aims the silenced muzzle at Diego's face. He squeezes his eyes shut and pulls the trigger.

TINK!

The bullet deflects off Diego's face and into the wall. He wears the metal like a silver mask. It spreads over his ears and down the back of his neck. Scar moves the gun to Diego's chest and fires twice more.

TINK! TINK!

Amazing! Diego hardly flinches as the bullets bounce off his chest. His entire body is now completely encased in metallic armor.

"Go ahead! Try to kill me!" Diego's voice reverberates like tin foil. "Kill me like you did my mom!" He rushes like a bull, head down and recklessly enraged.

Scar raises his hand, and the suits of armor come to life, moving to block the hallway. They don't walk like people but shift mechanically through the air. One swings an axe, and Diego catches the axe head in his hardened palm. He flings the first suit of armor into the second. They crash into the wall, clattering to the floor in a jumbled heap.

Diego keeps running, but two more suits intercept him. One suit swings a sword, which Diego deflects with his forearm. The other swings a spiked metal ball at the end of a long chain. Diego catches the ball out of the air, but the chain slithers up his arm like a snake. It coils around his waist and binds his arms to his side. The chain tightens.

Diego sucks in a breath and strains against the chain. With a snap, one of the links breaks, and Diego tosses the chain against the wall. Two more suits of armor catch up with him. This time, they disassemble in the air. The chest plate slaps against his chest, crinkling as it tightens around him. A helmet slips over Diego's head, and shin guards clap onto his legs. Before I know it, the entire suit of armor has assembled around him. It pulls Diego to the ground and spreads his limbs apart. He struggles against the armor, but he can't get up. It's my turn to intervene. I grab my amulet.

Darkness!

The hallway goes black. I reach with my mind and search for Scar in the abyss. I find him as he turns to run the other way. A memory comes to mind: the way the feeder choked Velma, the way he held her in the air with nothing but force. It's familiar to me, like an old habit.

Squeeze!

Sunlight floods the hallway as I lift Scar into the air by his neck. Rather than struggle, he turns his metal minions against me. A suit of armor swings a broadsword at my face. I barely keep my head as I duck beneath it. It swings the sword again, and I arch back. The very tip of the blade cuts through my uniform and pricks my shoulder. Panic starts to fill me. I can't hold him and defend myself. I can't multitask.

The sword swings again, this time at my waist. I release my hold on Scar's throat and focus on the space between the sword and I.

Shield!

The air ripples as the blade rebounds away from me. A split-second later, metal clanks behind me. I turn around, but I'm too late. A steel shield slams directly into my chest. I'm thrown onto my back, and stars swim before my eyes.

Just when I think it can't get worse, my amulet lurches in my grasp. I cling to it as it drags me across the floor. My sweaty fingers start to slide, then slip completely. My amulet skitters across the marble floor, landing on the other side of the hallway. I'm helpless. The broadsword hovers above my head. I wait for the blade to end my life, but it doesn't. Scar hesitates.

He doesn't want to kill.

Diego wrestles free of the armor and tackles Scar at the waist. Landing on top of him, his fists fly in a silver blur. Blow after blow connects with Scar's face. Any one of these punches could be fatal.

"Diego! Stop!" I snap him from his rage. Scar's face is a mangled mess. His features are indiscernible beneath the smeared blood. His

436

breath becomes shallow and labored. Diego grabs hold of Scar's amulet and breaks the chain with a yank. Climbing to his feet, Diego lifts Scar with one arm and slams him against the wall. He holds scar's head directly in front of his own.

"Look at my face!" Diego demands. "Do you remember me? Do you remember who I am?"

Scar groans and winces as he opens his eyes. He stares blankly at Diego's face, saying nothing.

"How about now?" Diego leans in even closer. The metal recedes to the edge of his hairline, revealing his brown skin.

Scar gasps. His pained eyes double in size. "You? You're the boy…"

Diego grabs him by the hair and throws his head back against the stone. His head jostles as Diego shakes him. "I'm the boy whose life you ruined. I'm gonna make you pay for what you did. You're gonna suffer like she did."

Scar doesn't try to resist. His voice is pained and pathetic. "I never wanted to… I didn't want t—"

Diego silences him with a punch to the gut. "Shut up! You don't get to make excuses. There's no forgiveness for what you did! There's no mercy for someone like you."

I retrieve my amulet and come up behind Diego, letting my mind drift toward Scar. His eyes are a shattered window into his tortured soul. I feel nothing but self-loathing and regret. He wants to die. He wants everything he's ever done to be erased. He's not a bloodthirsty killer, but a deprived and damaged man.

Scar swallows. The muscles in his face twitch before he spills his conscious to Diego. "I swear. I didn't want to do it. I didn't have a choice. He would've killed me. It would've been my family instead. I had to protect them."

"Liar!" Diego punches the stone next to Scar's head. Shards crumble from the wall as Scar squeezes his eyes shut and shivers.

"I'm sorry. I'm sorry. I didn't want to do it," Scar sobs. "I didn't want to do any of it."

Diego's fist trembles in the air. He wants a reason to hate this man. He wants to believe this man is responsible. That by killing him, his mom is avenged. That killing him would be a service to the world. But instead, he finds a broken man begging for forgiveness.

Diego curls his fingers tight and cocks his fist behind his ear. "You killed her and you alone. And now you deserve to die."

Scar shakes his head. "Wait! I've done terrible things, yes. But I didn't kill her." He looks Diego in the eyes.

"Your mom is still alive."

Chapter 33

Rose

Antai holds my hand as I watch the fire burn. I don't know what to think, what to feel. I'm an old rag, wrung dry of all emotions. The only thing left is anger.

What are you going to do about it, Rose? Velma died for you. How will you make things right? I look down at my arm. A black sun overlaid by a crescent moon is tattooed on my wrist.

I gave it to myself this morning. I need to remember what I've decided. I need to remember what I fight for. *Change is coming. You can be that change, Rose.*

But what if I can't? What if I only make things worse? Antai must see my uncertainty. He gives my hand a gentle squeeze before whispering in my ear. "I'm with you, Rose, no matter what."

I squeeze his hand back. If all else fails, I know Antai will stand by me. Even now, I wear his Adamic armor under my uniform. He wouldn't let me leave the palace without it.

Once the fire has reduced to ashes, Zane resumes position at the front of the stage. He turns his back to the audience. "Guards, on your feet, raise your right hand."

I stand with the others and lift my hand to the square. Zane sucks in a breath. "Repeat after me: I pledge allegiance to Cavernum." We echo his words for the audience to hear. "I pledge both body and soul to the defense of this great nation. To serve the common man. To use the power bestowed upon me in the name of God, at all times and in all places."

Throughout the pledge, several protesters scream insults. —"You only serve yourself!"—"Pledge allegiance to my ass!"—

Zane turns and faces the audience. "Cavernum, I present to you this year's graduating class." The audience both cheers and boos. My heart beats faster. It's almost time. For the second time in my life, I have to address my people.

Zane's voice booms over the noise of the crowd. "Now, as tradition demands, the class leader will address the graduating class." He twists his neck and smiles at me. "Before she takes the floor, allow me to introduce her. Her comrades may know her as Lynn, but that's not her real name. For her safety, she was divided under a false identity. She competed among her peers and rose victorious."

I shift in my seat and rub my sweaty palms on my pants. My classmates whisper behind my back.

"She's proven herself an accomplished soldier, not only in training but in combat as well. When the feeders attacked last night. She risked her life to defend her fellow soldiers. She is courageous, strong, and loyal. She's everything a guardsman should be… and a future queen."

The crowd gasps. Zane turns and gestures at me with his open palm. "I present to you, Princess Roselyn Malik, heir to the Cavernic throne."

Antai gives my hand one last squeeze before I climb to my feet. I step to the edge of the stage and take a deep breath. I had a speech prepared, but all that changed last night. Right now, I speak from the heart.

"A little over a month ago, I spoke to you in this very spot. I suggested a simple policy change that I hoped would improve your quality of life. My suggestion was simple: more supplies from the beyond. I honestly thought it could make a difference, but now, I see how foolish I was.

Joining the guard was the best decision I ever made. It helped me see the truth about Cavernum. The laws are corrupt. The leaders are corrupt. The Dividing is corrupt. Cavernum is corrupt. But it doesn't need to stay that way. Together, we can change things. Together, we can make things right."

The audience, wide-eyed and wide-mouthed, stares at me in disbelief. Their surprise fills me with satisfaction. *I refuse to be the princess you think I am.*

"I joined the guard, thinking I was someone special. I thought I was gifted. I thought I was brilliant. But in reality, I was blind. I had everything handed to me on a silver platter. I did nothing to earn what was given to me. I was blind to the inequality around me. I was sh—"

Ding! Ding! Ding! Ding! Ding!

The bell in the north watchtower rings out over the plaza. Five fast tolls. I know what it means.

Palace intruder; requesting backup!

Antai and Zane are already on their feet. Antai motions for me to stay before climbing off the stage. I take a deep breath. They can take care of it. I'm needed here. I need to finish this. "—I was sheltered and I was wrong."

I turn around and face my classmates. "This month, I've had the pleasure of getting to know all of you. You give me hope for Cavernum's future. You have great power and great potential, but all of you must make a choice. You must choose whether you will use that power to serve yourself, or whether you will use it to serve the people. I pray you will choose the latter. Together, we can bring change to Cavernum. Together, we can make things right."

I turn back to the audience. "Today, I pledge my allegiance to you, citizens of Cavernum. I pledge to give my life in your service. I know many of you have hated me in the past, but today, my loyalties have turned. Today, I have joined you in the fight. I am your ally. I will not riot and kill as you do, but I will do everything I can on your behalf. Even if I become an enemy of the palace, even if my friends combine against me, even if the high council plots my downfall, I will fight for you. I will die for you!"

I take a deep breath. *This is for you, Velma.* I shout at the top of my lungs.

"Give me equality, or give me death!"

For a moment, the audience falters. It must sound fake, staged, insincere. If I were them, I would be skeptical too. But then, they roar as one body. They stomp their feet and scream. At first, the slogan is nothing but a mumble beneath the roar, but then it grows louder and louder.

—"Give me equality or give me death! Give me equality or give me death!"—

I gaze across the crowd, basking in the glory. This is what I've always dreamed of. I'm giving the people hope. I'm fighting for something I believe in. And the people are responding. Some jump up and down. Most stomp their feet and wave their arms in an overjoyed frenzy. No one throws bottles. No one rebels. They don't have to anymore. They're not desperate. For once, they have hope.

One man catches my eye in the very front of the crowd. He stands unmoving in the churning sea of bodies. His unblinking eyes stare directly at me from within his hood. I stare back. He wears a tattered, dirty coat—the coat of a laborer—yet his body is far from famished. His shoulders are broad and muscular. He stands with the confidence of an elite, chin up and shoulders back. He's close enough I can see the green in his eyes. They're dark green, almost like algae. There's stubble on his boxy chin. His face is perfectly calm, perfectly focused.

Something silver flashes between the churning bodies. He points a polished silver pistol at my chest. Terror takes hold of my soul. All I can think about is the hollow eye of the pistol staring me down. I reach for my amulet, but I'm too slow. The woman next to the assassin screams just before he pulls the trigger.

BANG! BANG!

Two bullets punch me in the ribs, shoving me backward. I try to keep my balance, but I hit the floor hard. Antai's armor has done an impeccable job of dispersing the impact. Except for tender ribs, I'm unharmed.

"Princess down! Open fire!" an unfamiliar voice commands the guard. Chaos fills the courtyard as gunshots rain down on the crowd. They come from the rooftops. The guards are shooting at the assassin. A boy cries out. A woman crumples next to him.

What are they thinking? Why are they still shooting? Don't they know that they're hitting civilians?

Bratatatata! The patter of gunfire doesn't stop. I shudder as everything clicks. *The missing uniforms! Of course!* The shooters aren't guardsmen, they're equalists in disguise. This isn't an assass-ination, it's a massacre. And the 'guard' is responsible. They staged the scene: a laborer kills the princess, so the 'guard' massacres the crowd in retaliation. It's unthinkable. It's unforgivable. It would be enough to incite a rebellion—start a war.

I have to stop it!

It only takes a second to regain my breath. I stumble to my feet and scan for the assassin. A circle of bodies marks where I last saw him, but I don't spot him among the dead. He must have escaped in the fleeing crowd.

Everyone scatters in different directions—some towards the palace, some towards the ring. Everyone wants cover, but the courtyard offers nothing but flat stone. The gunfire continues on the rooftops; more civilians fall under the downpour. Before I have time to assess my options, a hand is tugging me away from the stage. It's gentle but firm.

"Antai?" *He came back for me!* His fingers intertwine with mine as a spherical shield ripples around us. "Hurry, we need to get away from the wall. There are too many guards."

I look up to see half a dozen guards—or equalists disguised as guards—firing down on the crowd. I hate them. I want to go back and kill them, but Antai pulls me away. "Stay with me and keep your head down. We're moving into the crowd."

Together, we leap from the stage. My knees bend, and my free hand slaps the pavement to slow my fall. Then, we're running with the flow of the crowd. Everyone pushes and shoves to ensure their own survival. No one seems to notice the princess in their midst.

I take another glance at the wall when I stumble over something large and bulky. It's a body. Only Antai's grip keeps me from joining it beneath the crowd. The equalists did this. They're killing innocent civilians. *What if I chose the wrong side? What if oppression is the only way to maintain order?* I swallow down my nausea and keep running.

The plaza exits into a street up ahead. The crowd slows as it funnels into the narrow roadway, making it a perfect target for the equalists. I hear a scream, then another. A dozen yards ahead of me, laborers fall to the rhythm of gunfire. I follow my ears to the source of the slaughter. Above the road, a bridge connects the adjacent rooftops at the mouth of the plaza. Two guardsmen lean over the stone railing and pepper the crowd with single shot-fire. It's obvious they don't want to kill everyone, just enough to start a war.

"Antai, look!" I point to the bridge. The equalists see us at the same moment Antai sees them. They redirect their guns and pull the trigger.

The clear energy bubble ripples as a bullet ricochets into the boy next to me. He drops with a scream, blood bubbling from a wound in his calf.

"Nooo!" I lunge for him and push back the crowd with an energy shield of my own. They flow around us like a river around a stone. The boy looks at me, eyes wide with fear. He whimpers as he tries to crawl away. He's no older than 12, but he's old enough to recognize me as the enemy.

"Damn it." Antai takes one look at the boy, and his shield disappears. He won't risk any more ricocheting bullets. In response, the equalists open fire. A dozen bullets, rather than tear us to shreds, slow to a halt in the air. They hover weightless before my face; then, they catapult back the way they came. A curtain of lead collides with the bridge, spraying stone dust and blood into the air. The equalists shudder as the bullets rip through them. They collapse out of sight behind the parapet.

Burn in Hell!

I turn back to the boy sprawled before me. He's no longer trying to escape but stares teary-eyed at his bloody leg.

I get down on my knees and scoot closer. "Hey there, don't be afraid. I'm not going to hurt you; I'm here to help. My name's Rose. What's your name?" The boy calms at the sound of my voice. He opens his mouth twice before managing a squeak.

"Thomas."

Antai is already unlatching his belt as he approaches. I know what he's thinking. I take the boy by the hand. "Okay, Thomas. I need you to be brave. We're going to tie a belt around your leg to stop the bleeding. Hold my hand and squeeze if it hurts, okay?"

He nods his head and takes my hand. He's already squeezing before Antai begins. When the belt tightens down, he screams.

"Thomas? Thomas?" A man forces his way against the flow of the crowd and into the plaza. "Thomas? Can you hear me?"

"Dad!" The boy shouts and scrunches his face in pain. Antai scoops the boy into his arms and starts toward the man. The father's face pales at the sight of the blood. "Thomas! My God! What happened?"

Antai passes the boy into his father's arms. "He took a bullet to the leg. The belt should stop the bleeding, but he needs a medic, or he'll die."

He'll die anyway. I think. A medic isn't enough. The bullet won't kill him, but the infection will. The father is a laborer and won't be able to afford antibiotics. The boy won't survive.

The man nods grimly. "Thank you." He turns to me. "Thank you, princess, I won't forget this. God bless you." Then, he disappears into the crowd. Once again, my soul swells with satisfaction. I feel like I'm fighting for the right people. My parents would be proud; I know they would.

"Come on." Antai leads me further and further away from the plaza. We turn down an alley and connect back to another main road. Every 20 seconds, Antai looks over his shoulder.

I follow his gaze, but I don't see anything out of the ordinary. "Antai, what's wrong?"

"Someone's following us. I think it's an equalist." He picks up the pace and leads us down another small alley. He seems unusually nervous about such a simple threat. Compared to Antai, the equalists are nothing more than angry amateurs.

"Why are we running?" I manage between strides. "We need to fight. We need to go back!"

"No, we need to get to the palace," Antai says. "Didn't you hear the bells?"

"Then, why are we running away from it?"

He flashes me an arrogant smile. "Just trust me. I have a plan."

Finally, we turn onto a street I recognize. We sprint down North Gate Boulevard and pass in front of the central sanitation building. Antai stops in front of a small building next door. He tries the handle, but it's locked. It only takes him a second to unlock it with dominion. The door clicks before swinging open. I step into the room and choke on the worst smell imaginable. The air is saturated with feces. I can almost taste it.

It takes a moment for my other senses to catch up, but my eyes quickly adjust to the dim light. The room is empty except for a circular hatch in the floor. Judging by the hellish smell, there's only one place it could lead.

"The sewer? This is your big plan?"

Antai smiles. "What gave it away? The smell?"

I'm not in the mood for jokes. "Antai, this is a terrible plan."

Antai clutches his heart and fakes a sad face. "Ouch, Rose. Hurtful."

"I'm serious. What if we run into more equalists? What if we get lost?"

When I don't crack a smile, he grows serious. "Honestly, Rose, we'll be fine. I've been mapping these tunnels all month, and I haven't seen a single equalist. What I did find, I'll have you know, is a tunnel that leads straight to the pit. 90% sure I can get us there by memory." He watches me wrestle with the notion before adding, "You'll barely get your feet wet."

"And the other 10%?" I ask.

Antai shrugs. "We build a home in the sewer and raise sewer babies."

I try not to laugh. *People are dying, Rose. You're wasting time.* "Fine. Let's do it."

Antai unscrews the hatch and lifts it open. After you, m'lady." A smell, more potent than the last, wafts up at us. Just like the communications bunker, iron rungs lead down into the darkness. *Do it for Velma! Do it for Cavernum!*

I tuck my chin to my chest and use my shirt as a filter. Still, the putrid air infects my lungs. I take a deep breath and lower my feet into the darkness. The rungs are cold and slimy to the touch. When my feet finally touch the floor, they splash.

Light!

A soft yellow glow reflects off the muck around my feet. Small chunks are visible in the gooey liquid. I'm standing up to my ankles in sewage.

"Ewww! Antai! You sa—"

"Shhh!" He stands perfectly still at the top of the ladder. I can see the underside of his chin as he peers towards the door. I don't know what he sees, but I can tell by the way he stands it means danger.

Antai bursts to life. He doesn't bother with the ladder. Instead, he slaps his hands to his side and jumps into the tunnel. I turn my face a fraction of a second before the sewage splashes my cheek.

"Run!" Antai grabs my arm and once again, we're sloshing through the tunnel for our lives. "Put out your light. He won't be able to track us in the dark." I do as he says and we're plunged into darkness.

Splash!

Someone drops down into the tunnel behind us. I spin around, but the figure has already moved into the shadows. I hear the sloshing of his steps as he trudges toward us. My heart races.

The ground goes dry around my feet as Antai collects the liquid into one giant mass. Without delay, he sends the tidal wave of sewage flooding down the tunnel behind us. But Antai doesn't stop there. I hear the crackle of ice forming by my ear, followed by the shatter of icicles down the tunnel.

A fecesicle! I'm both impressed as appalled. The slightest cut and the equalist will contract a deadly infection. Antai launches another volley of fecesicles, followed by a short silence. The enemy doesn't retaliate, which must mean he's dead. I hope he drowned in sewage. I hope he suffered.

Antai grabs my hand and pulls me through the tunnels. We turn right, then left, then left again. A few yards after the turn, Antai leads me up a step and onto dry ground. As we slow to a walk, Antai whispers in my ear. "We're through the worst of it. It's not far from here."

"Can I make a light?" I ask.

"It's too risky. If he survived, he'll see it."

The floor starts to tilt downward, which makes sense considering the pit is deep underground. We walk deeper and deeper into the earth. The smell of sewage lingers from our clothes. I feel claustrophobia pressing in on me.

"The tunnels flooded up ahead. But don't worry, it's only a short swim. It'll wash off most of the sewage."

Sure enough, we only take a few more steps before my shoes splash in the icy water. I wade into the water, scrubbing my arms and face. I never thought I'd be so grateful for an icy bath in pitch-darkness. We wade across the water and dry ourselves with dominion on the other side. We walk a short ways before Antai grabs my arm in the dark. "Quiet," he breathes in my ear.

We wait in silence, then wait some more. I strain to hear something other than my own heartbeat. I'm about to blow him off when I hear it. The quiet splashing of someone wading through water.

The equalist! He survived after all. He's still following us. But why? Why hasn't he attacked? It doesn't make sense? Whatever the reason, I don't want to wait around to find out. Antai grabs my arm, and we run through the tunnels. "We're almost there," he pants.

He stops suddenly and tugs me to the floor. Once I'm on my knees, I see it. A faint trickle of light leaks through a small hole in the side of the tunnel. It's barely wide enough for a person to crawl through. Antai shimmies through first, then me. I stand up and find myself at the back of a prison cell. The walls are stone, and the door is made of iron bars. Adamic symbols mark the walls like cave paintings. Normally, these walls are inescapable. The pit is an Adamic prison. It can hold the most deadly of feeders. Whoever made this hole in the wall would've needed an Adamic blade at the very least.

Antai wastes no time, he turns around and grabs his amulet. "Stay back." The sound of an avalanche engulfs me. The tunnel we just crawled out of collapses with a thunderous roar. The knee-high hole in the wall is immediately plugged with rocky debris. It's a miracle the entire dungeon didn't collapse with it.

Antai dusts his hands proudly. "That should hold him."

But I can't stop staring at the hole. "You knew there was a tunnel into the palace, and you left it? What if the equalists used it to break in?"

Antai shrugs. "I thought it would be useful. And I was right!"

I roll my eyes, but I doubt he sees it in the dimness of the dungeon. It was reckless and stupid. Antai has never been one for protocol, but he should've known better.

"Come on!" Antai pushes on the iron door, the ungreased hinge squealing as it swings open. He grabs a torch from the wall, and we run past cell after cell. Most are empty, but some prisoners press their faces to the bars as we run past. Their eyes glow like cats in the torchlight. After climbing a flight of stone steps, the stairway opens up to another hallway of cells. We climb two more flights of stairs before arriving at the main floor. At last, we're in the palace.

"Now what?" I ask.

Antai points to the ceiling. "We need to get to King Dralton's study."

"What? Why?"

"Just trust me. I'll explain when we get there," Antai insists.

I don't question it. If there's anything I've learned in my life, it's that I can trust Antai. He'll never lead me astray. We hurry up the stairs as fast as we can. Antai says nothing as we pass the first body. The guard lies dead in a pool of his blood. When we pass the second body, he gives me a look as if to say 'what happened here?' We tiptoe down the hallway and push open the door to Grandpa's study. I breathe a sigh of relief. It's empty.

"Okay, Antai. Tell me what's going on."

Antai goes straight for one of the drawers at the back of the study and rummages around. "Here it is." He pulls out a device that looks like an oversized pair of metal goggles. Rather than flat lenses, two spherical crystal balls are set into the frames. A thick metal band creates a loop about the size of my head. Engraved into the metal loop are unfamiliar Adamic symbols.

"A relic?"

Antai nods. "It'll let you communicate with King Dralton. He always has the other pair with him. He needs to talk to you.

"About what?"

"He'll have to tell you himself." Antai holds out the goggles, and I put them on. They're heavy and uncomfortable on my ears. I stare into the foggy crystal orbs and wait.

Nothing happens. Finally, I look to Antai. "It's not doing anything."

He points to my chest. "You'll have to take off your amulet. Soul-anchors interfere with the connection."

It makes sense. If a soul-anchor can prevent possession, why couldn't it stop a relic from communicating halfway across the world? Yet still, I hesitate. The last time I took off my amulet, I was nearly choked to death. I don't want to be vulnerable. I don't want to take it off.

Antai waits patiently. He knows what I must be thinking. He doesn't try to rush me. I untuck my amulet from my uniform and hold it in my hand. *If anyone can keep me safe, it's Antai. As long as I'm with him, I'm safe.*

I hand my amulet to Antai. Then, I put back on the goggles. Nothing happens. I wait a few seconds longer. Still, nothing happens. Antai starts to laugh. Then, he holds up my amulet and laughs louder. I've never heard him laugh like this in my life. It's more of a maniacal cackle.

As the laughter comes to an end, I take two steps back. "Antai?"

He grins as he grips my soul-anchor in his hand. "Oh, I expected better, Rose. You make things too easy."

Antai reaches under his chin and peels the skin away from his face, or at least it appears that way at first. As soon as his skin separates from his face, the illusion disappears. The skin transforms into an ovular metal mask with two crude eyeholes. Adamic symbols stretch across the forehead of the mask.

A relic!

The man holding the mask no longer resembles Antai. I've only seen him once, but I recognize him immediately. The algae green eyes. The boxy chin. The blonde stubble.

I'm staring into the eyes of my assassin.

Chapter 34

Matt

Diego blinks. His hands go slack, and he takes a step back. "What did you say?"

"I didn't kill her. She's still alive."

Diego's face goes blank, like a computer rebooting. His jaw hangs open, quivering with the start of unspoken words. I can see the gears churning in his head. I expect him to ease up. I expect to see relief, but instead his hand tightens on Scar's uniform. "Liar!" Diego shakes him like a misbehaved child. "You're stalling. You're trying to buy your friends time. Tell me the truth! Admit you killed her."

Scar gapes at Diego in innocent confusion. "I'm not stalling. Please, believe me. I didn't kill her. He needed her al—"

I wince as Diego slugs him in the stomach. "Stop lying! Just stop it!"

But I know it's not a lie. I sense regret in his words, but no deception. *She's actually alive.*

"Diego!" I snap. "I think he's telling the truth."

His hand slowly releases Scar's uniform. Diego takes a step back, and his eyes meet mine. I let his emotions engulf me. I want to understand.

Anger consumes me like a deadly poison. I want Scar to tremble in fear. I want him to suffer like Diego did. I want revenge. But even stronger than the anger is the fear: fear that Diego's mom is alive. More specifically, fear that Diego will lose her all over again. Fear that he'll have to relive her death in all its agony. Finally, underneath it all, I feel the hope. Diego clings to it. His mother is alive. He might see her again. He wants it more than anything.

As Diego turns back to Scar, I feel his bloodlust slowly dissipate. The man is no longer a source of revenge, but a source of answers. Diego narrows his eyes. "You said he wanted her alive, right?"

Scar nods his head.

"Who's he?" Diego demands.

"They call him the Demon Master, but he calls himself the Holy One.

Demon Master? Holy One? The two names couldn't be more contradictory.

"This Demon Master, what does he want with my mom?"

Scar shakes his head wildly. "I can't say. I made an oath."

"Well, break it," Diego threatens. "Or I'll break you."

Scar responds quieter than normal. "You don't understand. He can punish me in ways you can't imagine. He'll hurt my family. He'll make me do it myself."

Shivers run down my spine. I find myself feeling sorry for the man. He's nothing more than a victim. If Judy was ever in danger, I'd do almost anything to keep her safe.

"He'll never know," Diego begs. "Please, just tell me."

"Believe me; he'll know," Scar says. "He knows everything. He can see into your soul. If I tell you anything, he'll find out. He'll make them suffer. I can't risk it. I'm so sorry."

A switch flips in Diego. He grabs Scar by the neck and slams his skull into the stone. His fingers press into his throat. "Tell me, or I'll kill you. That's your choice."

Scar grimaces under Diego's iron grasp. "Do it! Please, do it! You'll be doing me a favor. I can't do this anymore. They'll be safer if I'm dead."

Diego pulls his hand away and steps back. Scar has nothing to lose. There's no way to get him to talk. But maybe he doesn't have to.

I grab my amulet and let our minds intertwine. "If she's alive, where is she? Just tell us that?"

Scar shakes his head. "I'm sorry. I can't say."

She's with the Holy One.

"We just need a location," I say.

"Even if I told you, it wouldn't do you any good." *You'll never save her. She's as good as dead.*

Frustration boils within me. "Just tell us this: what does he need her for? Why does he need her alive?"

He grimaces. "I should've never said anything. I'm sorry." *It's worse than death. You're better off not knowing.*

Scar looks Diego straight in the eyes. "I'm sorry for what I've done. I would do anything to fix it, but I can't. All I can do is stop it from happening again. I should've done this a long time ago."

Without warning, Scar grabs hold of Diego's amulet. I hear metal clank down the hall. Diego tears the amulet free from Scar's grasp and stumbles back a moment before the spear impales Scar in the side of the ribs. The protruding spear shaft angles toward the floor. I draw a straight line in my head and decide the tip must be somewhere near his heart. Scar gasps before sliding down the wall onto his butt.

"No!" Diego tends to him like he would a loved one. He cradles his head and applies pressure around the spear shaft. "Where's my mom? Please! Where's my mom? I need to know."

Whether the man is trying to speak or simply breathe, I can't tell. He gags and coughs as blood pools in his open mouth. His throat gurgles like a clogged drain. Then, he falls silent.

"Where's my mom! Please. Please." Diego's voice cracks.

"He's dead." I don't mean to be blunt, but I don't know what else to say. "I'm sorry, Diego."

Diego lays down Scar's head and hovers over his body. He doesn't say anything, he just stares.

"Diego, I'm sorry, but we need to go. They're still robbing the vault."

Still, he says nothing. In a few short moments, hope was dangled before his face and snatched away. The only man with answers died in his arms. He needs time to mourn. *I'll have to do it myself.*

"Wait here, Diego. I'll be back." I try to devise a plan as I run through the halls. I need backup. It's the obvious solution. The guards may not have believed me about Diego's mom, but I can convince them the vault is being raided. I'm about to call out for a guard when I hear the voices

"What about Torvik? He never came back." A deep voice asks—the voice of a giant. It comes from around the bend.

A girl responds, her voice familiar. "If he's not with the wagon, we leave him. We can't jeopardize the mission."

I stand frozen in the hallway. It's the vault thieves. Who else could it be? If I run now, they might not see me. I can escape, but so will they. I have to decide now: fight or flee?

I take a deep breath and grab my amulet.

Chapter 35

Rose

My assassin grins at me as he slides the deadbolt across the door. When the study is securely locked, he loops my amulet over his head and tucks it into his uniform for safekeeping.

"Oh, Rose. It's so good to finally talk face to face. I'm sorry for all the deception. It was the only way to get you here alone." He has a beautiful Australian accent from the beyond, which makes everything he says that much more repulsive.

Goosebumps rise on the back of my neck. When I was in the tunnel, I was running with my assassin. I held his hand. It seemed so real. He talked like Antai, moved like him, used dominion like him.

How could it be? I saw him shoot me in the plaza. Then, I remember. *The bells! Of course!* Antai left for the palace a minute before I was shot. After shooting me, my assassin put on the mask. Then, all he had to do was find me onstage. The entire time, I assumed Antai came back for me. My heart sinks. *I honestly thought he came back for me.*

My assassin smiles casually as if we're meeting for tea. "Forgive me, I'm being rude. Allow me to introduce myself. My name's Jack."

I take a step back. "How do you know me?"

"Oh Rose, I've known you for quite some time. We're actually closer than you think."

Quite some time? "What are you talking about? I've never seen you before."

"Oh, please. Isn't it obvious?" When I say nothing. He rolls his eyes. "Here, let me give you a hint." He lifts the mask to his face. When the metal touches his cheeks, it morphs into a feminine face. The skin is fair and pale. Long blonde hair falls around slender shoulders. The girl standing before me is barely five feet tall. I gasp.

Nevela blinks and smiles at me. "Oh, Rosey. I missed you so much!" Her giddy voice sings at me.

"Y-you're Nevela?" I stammer. The thought chills my blood. The implications are too much to comprehend.

Nevela laughs. "Oh, God, no. I couldn't keep this up for 15 years. Besides, the mask can only mimic real people. The Nevela you know still exists." He beams with self-pride. "But you have to admit, I make a pretty good replacement. It's been nearly a year, and you haven't suspected a thing."

A year! "But... that's impossible. She was only kidnapped a week ago."

Nevela laughs as if it's the silliest thing she's ever heard. "Oh, Rose. Nothing is impossible with a morph mask." She taps on her cheek. "It happened last Remembrance Day. You and the king were parading through the city while I led her into the tunnels." She laughs again. "The funny thing is, I was wearing this. She thought it was you the whole time."

"No! You're lying to me." *It can't be true! It can't be!* "You stole the mask from Lycon. You kidnapped her last week."

Nevela—or should I say, Jack—reaches up and peels off the mask. The illusion falls away, and Jack is once again standing before me. "No, Rose. Last week I got bored and left the palace. With you in the guard, there was no reason to stay. Unfortunately, a guard tried to stop me." He looks down at the mask in his hand. "And this handy little relic originates from Hogrum. The Holy One has more resources than you could imagine."

The Holy One? Hogrum? Unanswered questions dance through my head. When I say nothing, Jack pouts his lips. "I wouldn't lie to you, Rose. Not after all we've been through together. Every day, I've made your bed and folded your laundry. I've painted your toes and brushed your hair. When you got the flu last winter, I held back your hair while you vomited. I was there for every concert, cheering you on. When you confessed your love for Antai, I stayed up with you all night to give you advice. For months, I carried your love letters back and forth." His smile is genuine, but it makes my skin crawl. "We have history, Rose. There's no escaping it."

I feel sick. My head swims. It's hard to fathom: for the last year, every memory of Nevela was really him. Every time Nevela did my hair, it was him stroking my neck. It was him helping me into dresses and watching me bathe.

Jack sees my horror. "Oh, don't give me that look. I never laid a hand on you. The Holy One forbade it. Besides, your friend is in good hands."

"What have you done with her?" I demand.

Jack gives me a taunting smirk. "Nothing. She's joined our cause. A wonderful seamstress, that girl. In fact, she helped patch up these uniforms. All the women adore her. Now that I think of it, I'd say she's happier than she ever was as your slave."

That can't be true. He's lying. She would never join the equalists.

"W-why do it?" I choke out the words. "Why not just kill me a year ago?"

Jack sneers. "I never wanted to kill you. If I wanted you dead, I would've aimed for your head."

Duh, Rose! He knew I had the Adamic armor. He helped me put it on for the Remembrance Day parade. He never wanted me to die.

"Then, why?" I beg.

"The Holy One is interested in you. He needed someone to be his eyes and ears in the palace. I kept an eye on you while he was preparing, getting stronger. But now he's ready, and it's time to move forward. Lycon is just the beginning."

Is he suggesting what I think he is? The Holy One is the Adalit. He must be.

I can't fight, but I can keep him talking for as long as possible. My only hope is for someone to come and save me. "And this Holy One, why is he so interested in me?"

"Do you really not know?" He points toward the chest on top of the shelf—the inheritance box. "He needs what's inside. And you're going to get it for me."

I shake my head. "I'd rather die than help you. Your people killed women and children. They shot them in cold blood. How can you be okay with that?"

Jack's eyes narrow, and he purses his lips. "The Holy One never does anything that can't be undone. You don't yet understand. He'll explain everything when you meet him."

Meet him? The thought chills my blood. I'll do anything to avoid that. My eyes turn to the inheritance box. "What's inside? Why does he need it?"

Jack grins victoriously. "What? Your Grandpa never told you? How sad; the king keeping secrets from his little granddaughter. Aren't you curious what's inside? Don't you want to know what he's been hiding?"

The truth is, I do. I'm beyond curious. But I'll never admit it. "Go to hell!"

"I figured you'd say that. Fortunately for you, the Holy One values your life. But it would be a shame if something happened to a certain servant girl I know."

"Don't touch her!" I scream.

Jack presses the mask to his face, and Nevela is once again standing before me. "Help me, Rose. It hurts. Please, make them stop!" Her voice is so real. I picture her in chains, scared for her life. If they're willing to shoot children, I don't want to imagine what they would do to Nevela.

"Fine. I'll do it. But only if you let her go."

Jack considers it. "Do you promise to come quietly?"

I don't have a choice. If I don't comply, he'll find a way to force me. At least this way, Nevela will go free. "Yes. I'll come quietly if you let her go. I promise."

"Good. Now, open it."

I pick up the box from off the bookshelf and carry it to the table. The box is hollow and oddly light. I give it a quick shake, but nothing moves inside. It feels empty.

I glance up at Jack who's watching the box with starved eyes. He steps closer and leans over the box. "Do it. Open it."

I put my hands on the lid, and the wood grows warm at my touch. I take a deep breath and lift the lid. The box is empty except for a tiny sliver of white in the corner. It's a small slip of paper folded in half. I take the slip in my fingers and unfold it. Small, neat print is written on the paper.

Faza Le Bekanzah.

As soon as I read the paper, I know I've made a mistake. It's an Adamic phrase, or rather, the way to pronounce it. It's only a small step in becoming adalingual, but even a minor phrase can be dangerous. It could be a weapon, or perhaps a killing curse. If I had my amulet, I would burn the paper, but I don't. Before I can rip it to shreds, Jack snatches it from my fingertips.

His eyes scour the paper, relishing every syllable. Then, in a puff of smoke, the paper combusts. "Thank you, Rose. The Holy One will be most pleased."

I take a deep breath and focus on his chest. *Please be a killing curse.* I speak the words as clearly as I can. "Faza Le Bekanzah!"

I wait… Nothing happens.

"Tssk tssk tssk. Already, you break your promise. I like you, Rose. I really do. But Nevela will have to pay for that. That was the deal. One more attempt like that, and she might not survive. Do you understand?" I nod my head, and his mouth parts into a devious grin. "Good. Now stay still."

He presses the mask to my face. The inside of the metal feels wet and sticky. I struggle as it molds around my nose and seals my lips shut. I can't breathe. I hold my breath and try not to panic. Jack touches his amulet with one hand and keeps the other on the mask. He's using dominion, speaking to the mask. Just when I'm about to rip off the mask for air, the metal oozes into my mouth, and my lips part. I suck in a breath.

A rush of shivers flows down my spine and along my extremities. My skin quivers like gelatin, and my bones feel like water. My uniform grows tighter and tighter around my arms. I look at Jack, but something is off about him. He's shorter. Or maybe I'm taller. I reach up to my face, and the spines of stubble prick my fingers. A startled voice grumbles in response. It's the voice of a man.

Jack cackles at my horrified expression. "You'll get used to it. Come. We don't want to miss our ride. Walk at my side and say nothing, or Nevela dies."

He unlatches the door and leads me into the hallway. The palace is still empty. The one time in my life I need a guard, they're nowhere to be found. We descend the staircase to the ground floor and march toward the central tower. Up ahead, I can see the red carpet of the grand entrance.

Already, my mind is a jumbled mess. What else does the Holy One want with me? Will I ever see Grandpa again? Will I ever see Antai again? Even if someone sees me, they'll never know who I am.

It's over, Rose. They won.

Just when I'm about to relinquish myself to despair, a man stumbles into the hallway covered in dirt and dust. His hair is a matted mess, and his uniform is more brown than black.

Antai! A flash flood of understanding pours down on me. It wasn't an equalist chasing us in the streets and following us in the tunnel. It was Antai. He didn't retaliate because he risked hitting me in the dark. My heart swells. *He came back for me!*

Antai is frantic. His desperate eyes scan the hallway and fall upon us. "You two, stop!"

Jack fakes a puzzled look. "Yes, commander. We were just doing as you asked."

Now, Antai is the puzzled one. He scrunches his eyebrows. "What?"

"We just saw you with the princess. You asked us to evacuate."

Antai's face comes alive. He grabs his amulet. "How long ago? Where was I heading?"

Jack motions toward the way we came. "Just a moment ago, outside the king's chambers. I don't under—"

But Antai is gone, running down the hallway. I have to think fast. In a moment, he'll be gone. Do I risk Nevela's life in exchange for my own? Can I help her better as a prisoner or a princess? What would Grandpa do?

I'm sorry, Nevela.

I peel the mask from my face and throw it to the ground. Instantly, a wave of vibration washes over me. I scream at the top of my lungs. "Antaiiii-!" Jack clasps his hand over my mouth, but he's too late.

Antai freezes in his tracks. He spins around and forms a shield an instant before Jack fires two shots. The bullets glance to the side, shattering a vase and chipping the wall. Antai lifts his hand and closes his eyes. Out of nowhere, Jack's gun is torn from his grip and slides across the floor.

Jack's smile slowly returns, not the least bit concerned about his gun. He wraps his arm around my neck and uses me as a human shield. He extends his other arm and a brilliant beam of red energy collides with Antai's force field. Where the laser meets the shield, small beams diverge in all directions, bathing the hallway in red light. The hum of energy tickles my ear. The floor sizzles and a tapestry bursts into flame. I've never seen dominion like this before. I start to panic.

Please be okay! Please be okay!

Then, as fast as it began, the laser beam disappears. Antai stands defiant amid a circle of charred stone. For the thousandth time in my life, I'm amazed by his abilities.

Antai raises his hand to attack, but Jack speaks first. "All right, you win. If you spare my life, I'll surrender." Jack releases his hold on my neck and lifts both hands in the air.

"Take off your amulet," Antai commands.

Jack reaches into his shirt and removes a gold amulet. He drops it at his feet. The moment I see it, I know I'm in danger.

The amulet is my own.

Before I can run into Antai's arms, a strange feeling envelops me. Dark thoughts crawl into my mind. I imagine Antai lying dead in the hallway. I can almost see the blood gushing from his chest. A strange satisfaction fills me.

What's happening? These aren't my thoughts! I can feel someone else breathing inside my head. They slither deeper inside me and make a nest in my soul.

"Rose, get behind me!" I hear Antai speak, but when I try to run, nothing happens. Antai glares suspiciously at Jack. He trains his gun on my assassin's face, ready to fire at the slightest movement.

I try to look to Antai for help, but my facial expressions disobey. I can't even control where my eyes look. Suddenly, my foot takes a step forward. Then, the other. I throw all my thoughts into stopping my legs, but they move on their own accord. I can't control my body.

Jack isn't just an equalist. Jack is a demon.

I'm possessed!

My body stops halfway between Jack and Antai when I feel myself crouch. With horror, I watch my hand pick up Jack's pistol from off the floor. My eyes settle on Antai, who keeps his focus trained on Jack. I want to scream at him. *He's not the one you have to worry about, it's me! You have to stop me!*

My body scrambles to Antai and hides behind him as if seeking protection. I'm now out of Antai's sight.

"Get on the floor and put your hands behind your back!" Antai shouts at Jack.

Me, Antai! Look at me!

Antai shakes his gun. "I said get on the ground!"

I raise my arm and look down the iron sights. The pistol aims at the center of Antai's back, directly at his heart—his fragile, beautiful, unprotected heart. I'm wearing his armor. It saved my life today, and now it will cost Antai his.

NOOO!!! In one last-ditch effort, I fight my arm with every ounce of willpower I possess. My finger doesn't hesitate.

BANG!

The gunshot erupts in my ear. Antai stumbles two steps forward before he collapses. He clutches his chest and rolls onto his back. His eyes, full of hurt and betrayal, meet mine. The look alone is enough to shatter my heart. *I didn't mean to, Antai! I didn't mean to!* Pain fills my soul to the brim. Sorrow threatens to collapse the pillars of my mind. Not even possession can stop the tears from rolling down my cheeks.

Antai tries to talk, but he chokes on his own blood. For now, he's still breathing. He's still alive. If I act fast, I might be able to save him. I must've missed his heart by a thread. The healers can still save him.

If I wanted you dead, I would've aimed for your head. The words echo in my mind.

My arm aims the gun at the center of Antai's forehead, and my finger pulls the trigger. His head whips back as the bullet passes clean through. Then, he lays still. There's no saving him now. I killed him. I really killed him.

Antai is dead.

Chapter 36

Matt

I hold my amulet in hand and stare down the hallway from where the voices originated. *You can do this. Zane trained you for this.*

Two figures round the corner, each holding a handle of a massive wooden chest. One is the tall guard I saw with Scar. He's much taller than I initially realized, around 7 feet. He's a bonafide giant. His pecks are watermelons, and his thighs are tree trunks. The other figure is the pixie cut girl. She's no longer wearing her cuffs.

She's not a prisoner; she's one of them!

For a second, neither of them move. They're surprised to see me. They drop the chest in unison, something metal rattling inside. Goliath reaches for his gun with his stubby fingers.

Squeeze.

I lift him into the air by the throat. His massive body puts enormous strain on his neck. He kicks his legs and wheezes. I know what I should do: I should break his neck. But I can't bring myself to do it. I can't kill him.

SCREEEECH!

A terrible noise erupts in my ears. It sounds like nails on a chalkboard, only louder than a jet engine. I've never heard anything so excruciating in my life. I lose my focus and clasp my hands over my ears, but it doesn't stop the pain. The noise is drilling a hole into my eardrums. I'm pretty sure I'm screaming, but all I hear is that terrible screeching. Pixie Cut Girl smiles at me from across the room. She's winning, and she knows it.

The noise makes it impossible to think. It fragments my thoughts and fills my mind with chaos. I stand with my hands over my ears, completely vulnerable to attack. I need a shield. I need something. In a last-ditch effort, I grab my amulet and scream at the air around me.

Silence!

The screeching stops along with every other noise. I watch in silence as Goliath raises his arm at me. I don't wait around to see what happens.

Darkness.

I'm already moving as darkness floods the hallway. I sense Goliath crouching in the same place I last saw him. It's almost too easy. I'm about to douse him in fire when a hand grabs onto my arm. My body goes rigid as electricity courses through me. My muscles clench and cramp. Light floods the hallway as my thoughts are replaced with pain. The first thing I see is Pixie Cut's face. She stands beside me with her hand on my forearm.

How? How did she see me?

She releases my arm, and I fall to the floor. I land on my back, my head cracking against the marble. Pixie Cut removes a knife from her belt. It's not Adamic or anything fancy, just a thin steel blade. She holds it in her hand and steps over me. My muscles are useless; I can't run. Even if I fight with dominion, I can't defeat them both. I only have one option left.

I close my eyes and throw my soul into her mind. I brace myself for the bloodlust and hunger, but it doesn't come. Her mind is nothing like the feeder's. Her emotions are subtle and suppressed. She's completely in control. Her hatred and rage are stifled by loss, love, and hope. She wants to make the world a better place. She hopes for redemption. Her mind is inviting, almost pleasant. I push deeper.

Memories wash over me. They move too fast to make sense of them. There's a boy. His arms are around me, and he's kissing my neck. Then, the image changes, and he's lying on his back. The flames slowly consume his corpse as tears run down my cheek.

I open my eyes and see myself lying at my feet on the floor. My body looks as if it's asleep—almost peaceful. *It worked. I possessed her.*

Her arm extends until the knife hovers above my heart. This time, I can think clearly. It's much easier to distinguish her thoughts from my own.

Kill him quickly and finish the mission. There's no anger associated with her desire. It's strictly business. Her arm swings down.

NO! I direct every bit of will power I possess into her arm. Just before the blade pierces my chest, I wrench her arm to the side. The knife strikes the tile a few inches from my stomach. I open her hand, and the knife clatters to the floor.

I may not be able to fight them both, but I can make them fight each other. I make her face Goliath, who gawks at her in disbelief. I focus on the air around his head. The memory is still fresh. The frequency of the sound wave. The amplitude. I can recreate it. I've done it hundreds of times.

Screech!

Goliath covers his ears with his hands. His head thrashes from side to side as he tries in vain to relieve the pain. I feel sorry for him, but I don't let up.

No!

Her soul collides with mine. I try to resist, but the momentum is already moving in her favor. She drives me out of her body like a battering ram. I open my eyes and find myself lying on the floor. I'm back in my own body, but I'm not alone. I can still feel her soul pressing down on me.

I'm possessed! She's a demon too!

Before I know what's happening, I unloop my amulet from around my neck and throw it to Goliath. Then, my hand reaches for the knife on the ground. My fingers wrap around the handle, lifting the blade above my leg.

No! I fight with my whole soul. We're both demons; we're supposed to be on equal ground. For a second, I manage to retract my arm, but it's a losing battle. She has more experience, more expertise. She wrestles my mind away and regains control.

"This is for trying to possess me." My mouth moves, speaking her words. With a thrust, she drives the blade into my thigh. I scream, but the sound never leaves my head. I know Pixie Cut can feel it too. My face winces in response to her pain.

"And this is so you don't give us any more trouble." She twists the blade, opening a wide gash in my quadricep. The blood immediately begins to flow. And then, her mind disappears, and my body is once again my own. I try to stand, but the pain is too much. I collapse back to the floor.

Pixie Cut bends over and grabs the chest handle. "Come on. Let's get out of here."

"What about the guard?" Goliath grumbles. I realize he's talking about me. Pixie Cut must be in charge. She's the one who makes the decisions.

"Leave him. We need to go."

Goliath's hand drifts toward his gun. "Iris, he's a liability. We can't leave him."

"We're not killing him. He's one of us. He'll join us eventually."

Goliath snorts out his nose to emphasize his disagreement. "As you wish." He picks up the other handle. He has to stoop to keep the chest level with Iris. Together, they lug the chest down the hall and around the corner.

I don't move until they're out of sight. I'm lucky to be alive, but there's nothing I can do now. I'm wounded and without an amulet. I need to act fast. I unlatch my belt and wrap it around the wound. I take a deep breath and cinch it tight. I'm glad no one's here to hear my moans and groans. I press on the belt with my palm and try to think of a plan. *Carriage!* They mentioned something about a carriage. As far as I know, there's only one exit large enough for a carriage: the palace gate. But I'll never get there in time. The best thing I can do for myself is get to the healing loft before I pass out.

Of course! The answer is so obvious. Right next to the healing loft is the tower garden. It has a clear view of the palace courtyard. If I can get up there, I might just be able to stop them.

I try to stand, but the searing pain saps my strength. The slightest movement of my leg racks my body with spasms and rips the air from my lungs. But I can't waste any time. I scoot myself against the wall and push myself up with one leg. Then, I hop. When I pass the dead guard, I barely manage to pick up his rifle. Like a crutch, I point the muzzle toward the floor and lean on the stock. Blood is now pooling in my boot, but I can't stop.

BANG. From somewhere down the hall, a gunshot echoes. BANG. Another gunshot.

I pause at the mouth of the staircase and listen. Everything is quiet, but I still get the sense that someone needs my help. A part of me wants to move towards the gunshots—to be the hero—but I have to be realistic. I can't walk. I don't have an amulet. One task at a time: stop the thieves.

I sling the gun over my shoulder and take the handrail in both hands. With a grunt, I pull myself up the first step. Then, the second. Then, the third. Each one feels like it's own type of torture. My head is woozy, and my strength is failing.

I can't do this. I'm not going to make it.

Footsteps echo behind me. My stomach drops, and my body tenses. I squeeze my eyes shut, preparing for the worst.

"Matt?" Diego gasps. "What the freak happened to your leg? Are you okay?"

"Diego! Thank God. Help me get to the tower." He opens his mouth to ask questions, but I stop him. "Just trust me! I'll explain later. There's no time."

Diego takes one look at my leg and sizes me up. He tucks his amulet into his shirt and gives it a pat. "This might hurt a little. I'm gonna carry you like a baby?"

"What?"

Diego scoops his hand under my knees and uses the other to cradle my back. "Like a baby," he says. Then, he's running me up the stairs, amplifying his strength with his amulet. We fly up the flights, two stairs at a time. Before I know it, we're surrounded by flowers and vines.

"Carry me to the balcony. Set me down on the bench."

Diego deposits me on the bench overlooking the sanctuary. I have a clear view of the palace gate and the pathway leading up to it. Then, I see the plaza, and my heart drops into my stomach. Bodies litter the cobblestone floor like black and red ants. *Is Lynn among those bodies somewhere? Is she still alive?*

The carriage bursts into sight from underneath the terrace. It's pulled by a triad of horses running a straight course toward the gate. They're already moving fast. I only see one man at the reins. He's a new guy, much smaller than Goliath, smaller than Scar too. He whips the horses, spurring them faster and faster. The amulet chest is perched on the back of the carriage.

A few guards on the wall spot the carriage, but they do nothing to stop it. It looks like any other carriage of guardsmen. I have to act now. In a few moments, they'll be out of sight beyond the wall.

"Can you hit him?" Diego asks.

"No, but I can hit the horses." I rest the rifle on the stone guardrail for stability. Peering through the scope, I set the crosshairs in the center of the three horses. I only have to hit one of them. I take a deep breath and pull the trigger.

BANG!

The left horse is struck mid-back and instantly goes down. To my delight, it drags the other two horses with it. The wagon wheels catch on the cobblestone, and the whole carriage flips violently onto its side. The chest is dashed against the road and shatters to pieces. Amulets scatter across the ground like spilt glitter. As soon as the guards on the wall see the amulets, they burst into action. "Shoot to kill, don't let them get away."

Pixie cut girl—Iris is her name—crawls from the wreckage. She takes one look at the scattered amulets and runs. She moves too fast to shoot, sprinting towards an empty section of the wall. Goliath flees as well, a few steps behind her. But the driver stumbles towards the amulets. His head is bowed, scanning the floor for the proper weapon. He bends over to pick one up. I have the sights on the center of his back. For a split second, I hesitate. I've never shot a person before. I've never killed anyone. But I'm a guardsman now. If I ever want to become a guardian, I have to obey orders.

I squeeze the trigger.

The bullet barely catches the driver in the left hip. His leg buckles, and he falls on his side. He knows it's over. At this point, he doesn't try to fight or flee. He drops the amulet and raises his hands in surrender.

Diego squints over the balcony as the guards handcuff the man. "You got him!" he gasps in disbelief.

"I got him," I echo. I can't believe it worked. I turn as Iris and Goliath approach the wall. In a matter of seconds, they run up an invisible staircase leaving floating ripples with each stride. Then, they disappear over the wall and out of sight. They got away, but not with the amulets. Their plan failed. I should be happy, but all I feel is confusion.

He'll join us eventually. What did Iris mean by that? Is it because I'm a demon too? Or is there something more to it? The memory confuses me most of all. It lingers in my mind, a remnant of the girls' possession. She's standing in the trench in a training uniform. She holds an amulet in her hand as a grizzly voice instructs her. "You have to push deeper, Iris. You can't possess me from the outside. Now, try again."

"Okay," she says. She glances up and looks Zane straight in the eyes.

Chapter 37

Rose

I blink and blink again, but every time I open my eyes, he's still dead. A flood of emotions builds inside me, pressing on the back of my eyes. If I wasn't possessed, I'm certain I'd be on the floor.

I love you, Antai! I love you!

I never got to tell him. I wanted to wait until the right moment, but now he's gone. He was the one sure thing in my life, and he's gone. We were supposed to get married. I was supposed to be his queen. I never admitted it before, but I always assumed it would come true.

I want to scream. I want to cry. I want to die and never wake up. I don't want a future without Antai. I don't want to live without him. There's only one last thing I want to do before I die; I want to touch him. I want to kiss his cheek and tell him how I feel. I want to feel his skin one last time while it's still warm. I want to fall to the floor and hold him, but the devil inside me won't let me.

Please! I beg in my head. I know the demon can hear me. *Please just let me touch him!*

Only for a second, his mind replies. Suddenly, the darkness in my mind vanishes. As soon as it does, the sobs overtake me. My throat constricts, and the air comes in gasps. I fall to my knees next to Antai, running my fingers through his hair. I press my cheek to his and relish the last of its warmth as my tears wet both our cheeks.

"I love you, Antai. I never told you, but I love you. My heart belongs to you. Please, know that." I hug him tighter than ever before, knowing I may never hold him again. Any second, Jack is going to rip me away and drag me into the tunnels. I'll go willingly. At this point, I don't care what happens to me. If they kill me, maybe I'll see Antai again. Maybe it'll be best that way.

I hear someone approach from behind me. Their feet move in a slow sliding shuffle. Before I can turn around, a brittle, wheezing voice speaks.

"Havaknah Ra." The words are unfamiliar, but deep down inside me, some ancient part of my soul understands.

Burn!

A bloodcurdling scream erupts from Jack's mouth. I turn to find him writhing on the floor. There are no flames, but the smell of burnt flesh poisons the air. I want to look away, but I'm captivated by the scene. His skin bubbles and boils. He thrashes on the floor, smearing blood across the bleached marble. His hair completely disintegrates before the screaming stops. He lies motionless on the floor. Whether unconscious or dead, I can't tell, nor do I care.

The voice!

I look up and find Great-grandpa Titan standing in the hallway. He's barefoot, wearing nothing but a nightgown. What's left of his stringy hair sticks up in all directions. He shuffles past Jack and peers into my eyes. I see a spark of sanity inside them. He reaches his gnarled hand to my face and wipes away my tears. Then, he turns to Antai. "Step aside, my love."

I climb to my feet and take a step back. I hear joints popping as King Titan slowly lowers himself onto his knees. He takes one look at

Antai's wounds before resting both of his hands flat on Antai's head. Then, he speaks.

"Kuna Baraga Vishnata Mitka Almaknah..."

His voice is frail, but the words seem to sing through the air. They rise and fall melodically with every syllable. There are too many words to keep track of, but once again, my soul understands.

Heal the head and the heart! Restore both body and soul!

King Titan lifts his hands and steps back. *Impossible!* The blood still cakes Antai's head, but I can't find any evidence of the gunshot wound. There's not a single nick on his head.

Please, be alive. Please! I fall to his side and press my ear to Antai's chest.

Bum, bum. Bum, bum. His chest rises and falls with each breath. The tears flow, but this time, it's from joy. I've never been so happy in my life. *Antai's alive! My love is alive!*

"Thank you!" I gasp at King Titan. He stares at me blankly from a few feet away. He healed Antai with Adamic. He brought him back from the dead. It's unbelievable, but I can't deny it. I saw it with my own eyes.

King Titan didn't just find the Book of Life; King Titan is adalingual.

Chapter 38

Matt

I stand on the stage next to three other men. Each of them, like me, demonstrated bravery on the battlefield. We're to be awarded a medal of honor. But for some stupid reason, Diego isn't up here with me.

I have a hunch it's because of my leg. I'm only being awarded because I was injured. Being wounded makes my courage more palpable. It's visible proof of the danger I braved. After the thieves escaped, Commander Noyan interviewed us about the palace invasion and promptly released us from custody. I spent the night in the infirmary while Diego went home to his family.

I look out over the plaza. The cremation altar is much bigger than yesterday's. There are so many bodies, too many to count. Some are equalists, some guardsmen, but most are the innocent—fathers and mothers, brothers and sisters, children and the elderly. All are heaped together in one giant mass, waiting to be burned.

A few rows away from the stage, I find Diego watching me. His face is grim, his eyes shadowed with worry. I see his two brothers and

Isabela standing next to him, but Mary isn't there. I fear the worst. Last I heard, she was deteriorating, and they still can't afford antibiotics.

General Kaynes steps forward. He straightens his silvery robe and glares over the crowd. "Citizens of Cavernum, I am saddened to report to you the most heinous of crimes. Those among you who call themselves equalists have stolen the uniforms of our guard. Disguised as guardsmen, they fired upon you from the walls. They slaughtered their friends and neighbors in an attempt to incite rebellion."

Some laborers scream back. —"Liars!"—"It's a conspiracy! You're the killers"—

General Kaynes ignores them. "Furthermore, they committed grand treason in a failed attempt to murder the princess."

Lynn!

She sits onstage only a few feet away from me. Her hair is braided and coiled into a magnificent bun. Her dress wraps tight around her waist and hips only to flush out around her knees. It's a speckled light gray color, like ashes. I've never seen her dressed so elegantly, so beautifully. She looks like she could be on the cover of some fashion magazine. For the hundredth time, I find myself staring… wanting.

No! I can't let myself think that way. She's the princess. Everything I know about her is a lie. The girl I had feelings for might not even exist. She was just some fictional disguise for the princess to hide behind. Lynn doesn't exist; only Rose.

But what about when she protected Diego and I from Vyle? What about that night in the garden? What about our conversation in the pasture? That was real, wasn't it? Regardless, I force myself to look away.

General Kaynes continues. "Lastly, these criminals attempted to steal and disperse guard amulets to the public. If it weren't for the bravery of the guard and these heroic individuals…" He motions at the four of us onstage. "They may have succeeded. On behalf of Cavernum, I would like to award each of them the golden flame." As General Kaynes talks, Commander Noyan pins a medal to our uniforms one by one. It's a small gold circle with the imprint of an elongated flame.

"The flame is a source of light and guidance. Similarly, these men are a light and a standard for all to see and follow. They are shining examples of courage and honor." General Kaynes motions toward the cremation alter. "Unfortunately, we have lost many good men of leadership these last two days. We need new soldiers to step up and fill their shoes. The men before you have not only proven their abilities, but they have proven their loyalty to Cavernum. Therefore, I am proud to promote each of them to the rank of lieutenant."

Lieutenant? But lieutenants are platoon leaders. Lieutenants live in the palace as elites. Could it really be true? I look for Zane across the stage and find him smiling back at me. He gives me a nod of recognition.

"Thank you for your service. You may be seated."

I find Diego's face in the crowd. We make eye contact, and he gives me a thumbs up. But his smile soon fades, and his hand drops back to his side. Something's wrong, I know it. But now, I can help. As a lieutenant, I'll be able to afford things like antibiotics. I can finally help Mary. I might actually become a guardian someday.

I take a seat in the row behind Zane. He twists around and flashes a proud smile. "Congratulations," he whispers before facing forward.

"Thanks," I whisper back.

General Kaynes clears his throat and directs his gaze toward the gallows. "And now, it's time for the perpetrators to receive justice. These men were judged for the following crimes: theft, possession of firearms, possession of amulets, impersonation of the guard, murder of the first degree, and grand treason. They have been found guilty on all accounts and are condemned to death by hanging, to proceed immediately."

This time, I don't feel so bad. These men weren't just rioting, they blatantly killed innocent people. For once, I think I agree with the high council. These men deserve to die.

"According to the law, you will each be allowed one minute to give your final words." General Kaynes points a finger threateningly at the crowd. "Let these men stand as a reminder that justice cannot be avoided. The law is set, and those who defile it will pay for their crimes. There are only two options: obedience and life, or rebellion and death. The choice is yours."

A guard's voice rings out from the gallows. He stands next to the executioner and reads from a piece of paper. "The condemned will be hanged as their names are read... Patrick Lamar."

The first man climbs the gallows and faces the crowd. He waves an arm at the cremation altar. "Look at the bodies before you. Laborers and elite will be burned together. By the end of today, they'll be reduced to a single pile of ashes, completely indiscernible from one another. Equal."

His voice grows louder and louder. "Why, when we are united in death, are we divided in life? We are all made by the same God, but one of us is dressed in silk robes while the other is flayed with a leather whip. One of us slaves in the fields while the other grows fat on the fruits of their labor. We use the dominion God gave us to oppress our own kind. God would be ashamed of Cavernum! God would be ashamed of all of you!

But let me warn you. God has called a prophet to restore order. The Holy One is coming to free his people. He will feed the hungry and heal the lame. He will protect the humble. And the wicked who oppose him will be destroyed. Already, he has prophesied your downfall. Repent now or be slain. Your blood will run in the streets. You can't escape his power. You can't escape!"

The guards are quick to hook the noose under his chin. The floor swings from under his feet, and his neck snaps. People cheer, but I watch silently. I thought the Holy One was evil, but this man thinks he's some kind of savior. To feed the hungry and heal the lame? Could it be true?

Already, the guards drag the next prisoner up the steps, not because he won't comply, but because he can't walk. The white bandages that wrap around his hip are soaked in blood. It's the man I shot, the carriage driver. His shoulders sag, and his head hangs slack, his chin almost touching his chest. This is the first time I've gotten a good look at him. They stand him on his feet, and he lifts his head. My heart stops.

"Enrique Ortega!"

"Nooooo!" Diego is already shoving through the crowd, running full speed for the gallows. A guard moves to stop him, but Diego swings first. His fist cracks against the guard's jaw, and the man drops to the floor. Diego dives on him, thrusting his hand into the guard's shirt. After fishing around for a second, his skin flashes silver.

"Stand down, soldier!" a guard shouts from the gallows. "That's an order!"

Diego ignores him. He charges forward, and the crowd rushes to get out of his way. Another guard moves to stop him, but the electricity crackles uselessly against Diego's skin. He shoves the guard aside and breaks free of the masses. He's just a stone's throw away from the gallows.

Zane climbs to his feet and closes his eyes. Diego's stride instantly grows slower. His shoulders slump, and his feet drag on the stone. With every step, he grunts to lift his feet. It's as if his legs weigh a thousand pounds. He takes one last step before collapsing to his hands and knees.

Gravity dominion! I realize.

Finally, Diego's muscles give out, and he lays plastered to the ground. He strains against his own weight but fails to lift his head from the floor.

"It's okay, Diego." Enrique speaks softly from the gallows. If I wasn't seated on the stage, I wouldn't be able to hear him. "It's okay. Don't fight them. Don't fight."

Dread weighs down my lungs and catches in my throat. He can't die. Enrique was a good man. He treated me like a son, gave me a home. He has a family who loves him. He's a good man. They can't kill him.

This is all my fault.

Diego finally gives up and lies flat on his stomach. The metal slowly fades from his skin. He opens his hand, and an amulet clatters to the floor. The guards handcuff him and hoist him to his feet.

Enrique swallows hard. "Diego, Javier, Jorge, Isabela, I need you all to listen to me." His voice is weak, but his words are strong and full of purpose, not the hopeless ramblings of a dying man. "All I wanted was to give you a better life. That's all I ever wanted. I thought I could do it on my own." His words catch in his mouth. "But now, Mary is sick and…" He swallows hard. "I realized I can't do it. I can't give you the life you deserve. But the Holy One can."

Isabela is already sobbing with her hands over her mouth. Diego still gapes in shock.

"I never meant for people to die. I didn't want to hurt anybody… but every battle has casualties. Every war requires sacrifice. It's the only way to bring about change. I believe in this cause. I believe in the Holy One. He's coming, and he'll make everything right. God has finally heard our prayers."

Enrique teeters and grabs onto a guard for support. "If I could go back, I'd do it all over again. My only regret is that I lose my time with each of you. I wish I had a hundred years to tell you all the things I want to tell you." He speaks fast, knowing his time is short. "Javier, Jorge, take care of your grandma and take care of Mary. Give them the love I would.

Isabela, you're going to make a beautiful bride someday. I wish I could see you in that dress. I wish I could be there to give you away. Find a good boy who treats you well. Accept nothing less."

Finally, he turns to Diego. "Diego, you're going to be the bread-winner now. I need you to take care of them. Don't resist the Holy One. Don't fight him. You can't win. Join him while you still can. He'll save Mary. He'll save us all."

They loop the noose over his neck, and the floor drops away. I squeeze my eyes shut. When I open them, Enrique is dead. It's all over in the blink of an eye. An entire lifetime ended in the time it takes to snap your fingers.

I stare at his body, rocking like a tire swing in the breeze. First, Diego lost his mother. Then, Velma. And now, I've hung his father before his eyes.

This is my fault.

"You murderers! You killed him!" Diego screams it at the stage. "You're no princess; you're a killer. How could you let this happen?" I spot Lynn, wide-eyed and dumbstruck. She looks as sick as I feel. Something tells me she had no say in this.

The guards drag Diego out of the crowd and towards the palace. As he passes the stage, his eyes meet mine. His look shakes me to the core. I see murder in the depths of his eyes. He blames me. He hates me. Why wouldn't he? I shot his father.

My heart beats faster. I lean forward in my seat until my mouth is by Zane's ear. "What's going to happen to him?" I demand. "Where are they taking him?"

Zane sits stone still and says nothing.

"Tell me! Are they arresting him?"

"No," Zane hisses. He takes a deep breath and lets out a long sigh. "He's being expelled from the guard."

"What? No! They can't!"

"He publicly opposed a hanging to save his equalist father. He can't go unpunished. Trust me, Matt. It's better this way." But I don't trust him. I don't trust Cavernum. Maybe Enrique was right. Maybe the Holy One is the good guy after all.

He'll join us soon enough. Did she know I would feel like this? Did Iris sense it in my soul when she possessed me? I sensed goodness in her too. She's not evil. She's not the enemy. But should I join her? There's only one way to find out for sure.

I need to find her.

Chapter 39

Rose

I sit on the edge of Antai's bed and watch him sleep. His skin has its usual glow. His chest rises and falls like the ocean tide. His muscled arms rest calmly at his side. Everything appears normal, except he hasn't awoken, and it's been three days.

Except for the funeral, I haven't left his side. The maids bring me my food here. I eat next to him. I sleep next to him. I talk to him. I hold his hand. I cry. But mostly, I wait.

I take Antai's hand in mine and sigh. "I wish you'd wake up already. I don't know what to do. Grandpa's still not back yet, and I'm getting worried. The city is still a mess. I don't know what's right anymore, Antai. I want to help the people, but I can't support the equalists. Not after what they did. I need your help. I need you to wake up."

I look at his lips, so full and smooth. "I miss you, Antai. There's so much I need to tell you about. Please wake up."

"He will soon." Grandpa's voice startles me, and I spin around. I never heard the door open.

"Grandpa!" I leap from Antai's bed and wrap my arms around his hollow frame. "I thought you were dead. What took you so long?"

Grandpa squeezes me back. "The demon in Beskum was stronger than I predicted. Our original exorcism didn't work. In the end, the queen killed herself." He pulls back and holds my shoulders. "I'm sorry I wasn't here for you. I should've never left. But I will tell you, my travels weren't in vain."

I step back. "What do you mean?"

"You'll see soon enough. But first, how are you? Zane told me everything. I'm sorry you had to go through that."

"I'm fine," I lie. I'm glad Grandpa's alive, but I'm still mad at him. "Before we go anywhere, I want answers. They almost robbed the palace vault, Grandpa. They had a spare key? How is that possible?"

Grandpa looks as puzzled as I feel. "The Adalit must've made it. It's the only possibility." Somehow, the answer makes me feel worse. In order to make a spare key, the Holy One would have to be familiar with the original, which Grandpa keeps with him at all times. *Unless Grandpa made the spare!*

I look up at Grandpa. "He made me open the inheritance box. There was a slip of paper inside. Was it Adamic?"

"That's correct," Grandpa says. "Do you have it memorized?"

I think back. "I think so. Why? Do you know what it does?"

"Unfortunately, no. It's been there for as long as I can remember. I can answer more of your questions later, I'm sure you must have a lot, but right now I need your help. Come." He shuffles out of the room, expecting me to follow.

"Where are we going?" I ask.

"The pit. I want to ask our newest guest a few questions."

The pit smells like its name. The caverns are dank, and the air tastes of mold. Antai always called it the 'sweaty pit.' The thought sends tremors of sorrow through my soul. *Please wake up!*

I descend another flight of stairs behind Grandpa, careful not to slip on the slick stone. Every floor contains its own row of prison cells. If necessary, the pit could hold hundreds.

At the end of the hall, Grandpa leads me into the interrogation room. I've seen it before, but never in use. There's nothing in the room except for two stone seats. They stand in the center of the room, facing each other. Iron shackles protruded like claws from the armrests. The only other feature in the room is a cold, old lantern hanging on the wall.

"Bring in the prisoner," Grandpa commands.

Two royal guards drag Jack into the room. The chains of his shackles clank with each step. The noise sounds like chatter in a busy room. The guards remove the chains and strap Jack into the far seat. They lock his wrists and ankles into the clamps and hand the key to Grandpa. Before exiting the room, they hang a fresh lantern on the wall. It casts eerie shadows in the room. Only Grandpa, Jack, and I remain. I try not to stare.

How can one word do so much damage?

Jack's skin is blood red, and blisters contour his face. Most of his hair is gone, including his eyebrows. The air wheezes through his scarred stump of a nose. I can't imagine what someone could do with the entire Adamic language.

Only Jack's eyes look the same; they're an island of algae in a bloodshot sea of red. His tattered shirt hangs low, revealing a black Adamic tattoo between his shoulder blades—the mark of a demon.

Grandpa takes off his crown and holds it out to me. "Put this on. It'll keep you safe."

I take his crown and put it on my head. It's much too big, but it stays on. "Safe from what?" Without an amulet, Jack can't possess anyone. I'm hardly in any danger.

Grandpa takes off his soul anchor and replaces it with an amplifier. He holds up the soul-anchor until I take it. Then, he slips on a new amulet. I recognize the symbols instantly: the demon curse.

"Safe from myself," he sighs. "If he somehow gains control of my body, I need to know you'll be safe. Don't let me out until you're sure it's me."

Grandpa hands me the key and slowly lowers his shaky body into the remaining seat. He sits facing Jack and rests his wrists in the open cuffs.

"You're going to... possess him?"

"It's the only way to get answers, Rose. I've been studying the symbol all year, but I haven't been able to create a functioning amulet until yesterday. It'll give us answers, but no one can know about this. Do you understand, Rose?"

I nod. If the high council knew, they would impeach Grandpa at best. At worst, they would try to execute him.

"Whenever you're ready," Grandpa says.

I take a deep breath. I align the two halves of the cuffs and lock them with the skeleton key. Not even grandpa can escape from these. Both the key and the cuffs are engraved with Adamic. *It's just a precaution,* I remind myself. I lock his ankles next. Grandpa smiles at me and nods. He's ready.

I retreat into the corner and wait. I grip the key in one hand and Grandpa's soul-anchor in the others. My heartbeat is all I hear, rapid and scared. Grandpa breaks the silence first with his aged, syrupy voice. "Who are you, Jack? How'd you get into Cavernum?"

Jack doesn't speak. He sits motionless upon his shackled throne. Grandpa stares at him for a while before he speaks again. The majority of the interrogation is happening inside their minds. The questions are only to direct Jack's thoughts.

"What do you know about the Holy One? What's his real name?"

Jack doesn't respond. He shifts in his chair, suddenly less relaxed. My knuckles turn white around the key. I can't take it. The silence is unnerving. I'm just waiting for something to go wrong.

Grandpa speaks calmly and softly. "What does the Holy One want with Rose? What does he want with Cavernum?"

Jack suddenly tugs against the cuffs. He scrunches his face and thrashes in his seat.

"Why do you serve him?" Grandpa presses. "What did he promise you in return?"

Jack arches his back and screams. "Get out of my head!!!" His wrists bleed from the cuffs as he squirms.

"He promised to bring back your daughter from the dead," Grandpa says flatly. "But at what cost? What would Kaitlyn think of what you've become? Of the people you've killed?" Jack thrashes like a caged animal.

Grandpa's playing mind games, literally getting inside Jack's head. His voice remains calm and steady. His eyes are closed now. "Who else works with the Holy One? How many of you are there?" Jack thrashes more. Blood runs down the side of the armrests.

"Who gave you the tattoos, Jack? Who is the Holy One?"

Jack opened his eyes in a final fit of rage. He writhes against the cuffs, lifting his body into the air. His voice is desperate. His accent does nothing to beautify his vicious voice. "No! You won't win. You can't stop him. He'll kill you. He'll save us all." Jack turns and looks directly at me. "And he will get you back!"

Grandpa is eerily calm. His voice is almost a whisper as if he's half-asleep. "Who? Who are you talking about?"

Jack swings his head against the back of the throne with a sickening thud. Then again, and again. I'm unable to look away. My heart beats faster and faster in my ears.

Smack! Smack! Smack!

He's trying to kill himself!

His head swings again only to stop an inch from the stone. The muscles in Jack's neck bulge with strain. Jack opens his mouth to speak. It's his voice, but the Australian accent is suddenly gone. Rather than deranged, the tone is calm and steady. "Who gave you the tattoos, Jack? Who do you follow?"

487

Chills race down my back. Grandpa speaks through Jack's body as his own body lies perfectly still, nothing but an empty shell. Both men are squeezed inside the same body. Several seconds pass without any words spoken. Jack's body sits rigid, muscles flexing in unison. Every few seconds, he twitches and seizes. No sign of either man surfaces.

Finally, after what seems an eternity, Grandpa gasps a breath in his own body. Jack slumps in his chair, defeated. It's over.

"Grandpa?"

Grandpa raises his head. "It's okay, Rose, I'm okay."

Before I can ask him any questions, Jack bursts to life. "Don't trust him, Rose. Your Grandpa's keeping secrets from you. Big secrets! He knows what the phrase does. He's using you. Don't trust him. He kno—"

Jack's protests suddenly fall silent. Spit flies from his lips as Grandpa mutes his screams with sound dominion.

"Rose, don't listen to anything he says," Grandpa insists. "He's a demon. He impersonated Nevela for a year. He tried to kill Antai. He can't be trusted." He looks at me with those caring eyes, full of patience and understanding. "Take as much time as you need. Ask me anything you like."

I don't need more time. Jack even admitted it. He called him Grandpa. That's all the proof I need. Even if he is keeping secrets, I have no choice. Antai is still comatose. I have no one else besides Grandpa. I unlock his cuffs and help him stand. He pulls me into a fierce hug, and relief washes away my worries. I squeeze him tight.

He takes me by the arm and pulls me towards the door. I'm eager to leave too. As soon as the iron door shuts, I look up at him for answers. "Did it work?"

Grandpa swallows hard. "It worked."

"And?"

Grandpa's eyes are wide and uncertain. Never in my life have I seen fear in those eyes. Never until today.

"I was wrong, Rose. I thought Beskum was next, but I was wrong. I should've seen the signs. It's so obvious."

"Grandpa? What do you mean?"

"The demons in Beskum were only a distraction. Cavernum was the target all along. Jack saw him in the caverns. He's underneath the city, Rose. He's preparing to attack."

My breath catches in my throat, and my blood runs cold. I already know the answer, but I ask anyway. "Who is? Who's underneath the city?"

Grandpa holds me by the shoulders unusually tight. For a second, he hesitates, but he can't hide this from me.

"The Holy One. He's already here."

End of Book 1

Dear Reader,

I can't thank you enough for taking a chance on my novel. Like seriously, out of all the books you could have read, I still can't believe you chose this little stack of pages. If you liked it, please leave a review online. In fact, don't stop there. Tell your friends. Tell your mom's dog. Let the world know that my novel doesn't suck. As for book two, I'll try not to keep you waiting too long. A cliff-hanger ending is cruel enough as it is.

Hopelessly seeking your approval,
Devin

Devin Downing grew up in Temecula, California, spending his childhood reading books on the beach and bashing bones at the skatepark. Today, Devin lives in Provo, Utah with his drop-dead gorgeous wife, Melissa. Apart from crafting complex stories, he enjoys hiking, ice-hockey, and writing about himself in the third person (yep, it's me! Hi, guys!). Devin is currently studying neuroscience at Brigham Young University because he wants his friends to think he's smart.

Learn more about Devin at **devindowning.com**

Printed in Great Britain
by Amazon